THE MASK

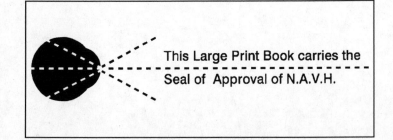

This Large Print Book carries the
Seal of Approval of N.A.V.H.

A VANESSA MICHAEL MUNROE NOVEL

THE MASK

TAYLOR STEVENS

THORNDIKE PRESS
A part of Gale, Cengage Learning

GALE
CENGAGE Learning·

Farmington Hills, Mich • San Francisco • New York • Waterville, Maine
Meriden, Conn • Mason, Ohio • Chicago

GALE
CENGAGE Learning

Thorndike Press® Large Print Thriller.
The text of this Large Print edition is unabridged.
Other aspects of the book may vary from the original edition.
Set in 16 pt. Plantin.

LIBRARY OF CONGRESS CATALOGING-IN-PUBLICATION DATA

Stevens, Taylor.
   The mask / Taylor Stevens.
      pages cm. — (A Vanessa Michael Munroe novel) (Thorndike Press large print thriller)
      ISBN 978-1-4104-8598-4 (hardback) — ISBN 1-4104-8598-6 (hardcover)
      I. Title.
   PS3619.T4924M37 2015b
   813'.6—dc23   2015035693

Published in 2016 by arrangement with Crown Publishers, an imprint of the Crown Publishing Group, a division of Penguin Random House LLC

Printed in Mexico
1 2 3 4 5 6 7 20 19 18 17 16

for Anne, Christine, and Sarah
knowing you has made my life
infinitely richer

Day 7

The attack, when it came, opened the floodgates of rage. Sound compressed. Time slowed to a water drip plonking into a puddle, echoing a musical note off concrete walls and floors; tires whooshing against the drizzle on the street outside as a car passed the parking garage exit; laughter pealing from the playground down the block. And footsteps, three sets of footsteps, moving in cautiously behind her back.

Vanessa Michael Munroe waited beside the motorcycle, one knee to the pavement, focused on the reflection in the bike's red fairing. Behind her head, shadows against the evening's light dropped hints of metal pipes protruding from raised hands, elongating and stretching as they drew nearer.

She counted heartbeats and felt the rhythm.

The muscles in her legs tensed and the chemical surge of adrenaline and anger

7

loosed its addictive calm.

The metal bars came down hard into the empty space where she'd been a half-heartbeat before: metal against concrete ringing loud in the enclosed space, symphonic in the thunder of war.

She came up swinging, helmet chin-guard in hand, all her weight, her full momentum thrown into that backward strike. The man on the right ducked too slowly, moved too late.

The swing smashed helmet into head.

He stumbled. Munroe grabbed the pipe and tore it from his hand. She whipped up and downward, to the back of his knees. He hit the ground and became a barrier between her and the two other men. Boot to his shoulder, she shoved him prostrate and then boosted over him, swinging hard.

The attackers swung, too, and hit for hit she countered, connecting the pipe with their bodies in solid beats because speed was her ally and speed was her friend, in and out and around, until they separated, becoming not one target but two. They were cautious now, angry and, perhaps for the first time, fully aware of the strength of their enemy.

Movement from behind told her that the man on the concrete had pushed to his knees. Munroe rotated back, struck hard, and he collapsed.

She faced the other two again, predicting move against move, guarding the rate of her breathing, conserving strength for a battle that had only begun.

The men shifted, foot to foot, and tensed for the attack and parry. They gripped their weapons, fingers rising and falling along the pipes in slow motion like spiders' legs along the ground.

She waited for them to come at her again.

Instead, they exchanged glances: nervous with the uncertainty of foot soldiers marching to someone else's beat in an evening that had gone off script.

The pounding inside her chest groaned in understanding.

The drive for release, for pain, pushed her at them.

She pointed the metal bar at one, marking territory, intended pocket for the eight ball, then strode toward him in misdirection and distraction.

He took several steps in retreat.

A shadow moved in her peripheral vision: his partner flanking and closing in. Munroe pivoted, swung, and connected the metal bar to his shoulder: small pain, a half second of diversion. He retaliated and opened himself up like a fool. She dodged and dropped, then drove the metal bar across his shin: crippling pain, unbearable pain, she knew.

In the beat between his shock and agony, she wrenched the bar from his hand and with two pipes to his none struck his rib cage. He doubled over. She knocked him flat and rotated toward his companion, who, in those same seconds, had backed away another few steps.

She feinted toward him. His eyes darted from her to his partners, and then he turned and ran. The crippled one dragged himself backward, out of immediate reach. He put up a hand, shielding his face in a show of defeat, and Munroe stood in place, rocklike and solid, eyes tracking him, breathing past the urges that drove her to strike again, to move in for the kill and finish what he'd started.

He grimaced and struggled up. Never turning his back to her, arms wrapped protectively around his torso, he hobbled toward the garage opening and then, moving around the corner, he was gone.

The condensation dripped another *plonk* into the puddle, another musical note echoed along concrete walls; another set of tires whooshed against the pavement beyond the garage exit; laughter in the distance morphed into the squeals of multiple children; and, with long, slow breaths, the violence of the moment ebbed and faded.

Munroe hefted the pipes and checked her hands, and then her clothes and boots. No blood. That was progress. She walked toward the unconscious man and stood over him, then put a boot to his torso and shoved the body over so that his face turned upward.

He was in his very early twenties, maybe five foot seven, all bone and sinew and stylish hair. She stared out toward the daylight where the other two had gone. Boys like this, full of bravado and without a lot of skill, had no business coming after her. They were a piece of the puzzle that didn't fit. She couldn't guess who had sent them, and that raised questions she hadn't begun to ask. This wasn't the beginning.

Sometimes it was impossible to start at the beginning.

When the story was complicated and the origin far back in a seemingly mundane pattern of daily life, the only way to make sense of it was to go back to before the beginning, to before the first hint of trouble.

Munroe wiped down the pipes for prints.

In the echo of the garage, footsteps shuffled and clothing rustled: movements small and cautious.

Munroe knelt and placed the pipes beside the body and, without turning, said, "You can come out now."

Day −63   8:00 P.M.

The opaque doors of Kansai International's immigration hall opened to a wall of bodies and a polite crush of expectant faces: the international arrival's rite of passage. Munroe scanned the crowd and, dragging the small carry-on around the metal rails, continued into the thick of the waiting throng.

Airport lights in the night sky winked through large plate-glass windows, marking another city and another time zone — this one a long, long stretch from the puddle jumps she'd made out of Djibouti, on the horn of Africa where the mouth of the Red Sea kissed the Gulf of Aden, then through the Middle East, and into Europe.

Frankfurt, Germany, to Osaka, Japan: sixteen hours in transit and now the traveling, the running, was finally over. Munroe shoved the backpack's slipping strap up her shoulder and turned a slow circle, searching, seeking.

For more than ten years, through untold airports and arrival destinations, strangers had peered beyond her with the same hopeful expressions, ever eager to spot a glimpse through closing doors of loved ones still on the other side. Across five continents she'd come and gone, ghostlike and invisible, while others welcomed family home, but this time — this time — a home waited to welcome her.

Not the country, or the city, or the land, or things built upon it, no. If there could ever be such a thing as *home* for a person like her, Miles Bradford was that home, and her gaze passed over the crowd again, seeking him out.

She spotted him finally: a splash of white skin and red-tinged blond hair leaning against a window, his face toward his phone, framed by parking lights and tower lights and shadows. She paused, drinking in memories that laughed and babbled like a brook over pebbles of pain, then maneuvered forward through legs and shoulders, suitcases and luggage carts, and the melee of joy that inevitably accompanied reunions.

She was halfway to him when he glanced up. His eyes connected with hers and the volume of the arrivals area shushed into white noise.

He stood motionless for a full second, two, three, phone paused in its descent to his pocket, grinning as if he'd just unwrapped a much-longed-for Christmas gift. She continued in his direction and he strode toward her, and when he reached her, he scooped her up, spun her in a circle, and drowned her smile with a kiss. She laughed as he set her down and didn't resist when he lifted the backpack off her shoulder and took the carry-on's handle.

"Good flight?" he said.

She nodded, unwilling to speak lest she break the spells of touch and feel and smell that whispered against her senses. She breathed him in to make a permanent memory and breathed out the dirt and grime and lies and death that had brought her to him.

Bradford dropped the bags and wrapped his arms around her again. He held her for a long, long while, just as he'd held her in Dallas the night she'd walked away, when he'd known she was leaving and had spared her the agony of saying good-bye. He kissed her again, hoisted the backpack, grabbed the carry-on, then took her hand and said, "Let's get out of here."

She followed him to the elevator, fingers

interlinked with his, and he glanced at her once, twice, matching her grin each time he did. He hadn't changed much — a few gray hairs added to his temples, deeper wrinkles in the creases of his smile, and maybe more muscle mass beneath his shirt, though it was hard to tell. He looked good. Smelled good. And in a mockery of their eight-year age difference, she'd aged five years in their year apart — still bore the remnants of conflict that had prematurely ended a maritime security company at the hands of Somali pirates — hadn't yet fully healed from the assault in Mombasa that had nearly killed her.

A four-day layover in Frankfurt had allowed a respite of hotel luxury; given her time to scrub away the worst of the weather wear, the dust, and the salt spray, and the effects of wide open spaces; and made it possible to trade sun-bleached clothes worn threadbare over the last year for new pieces, better suited to less demanding environments.

She'd come to Japan for him, because he'd asked her to. Because she'd known happiness with him, and loved him, and running from that terror had only brought more pain and death instead of the nothingness she'd sought.

They left the terminal for warm air, thick with the promise of coming rain. Bradford rolled the suitcase between endless rows of cars and finally stopped behind an off-white Daihatsu Mira so small it could have fit in the bed of his truck back in Dallas.

Munroe looked at him and then the car.

"Don't laugh," he said. "This is the country of itty-bitty things."

She took a step back and, in an exaggerated motion, turned her head left and then right, where up and down the rows on either side were a vast number of vehicles much larger than the Mira.

Smiling, Bradford shook his head and opened the hatchback. He stuffed the bags into the tiny storage compartment and slammed the door to make sure it shut. "You think it's funny now," he said, "you'll be grateful later."

"It suits you," she said.

"Trust me, I asked for something bigger."

"No, really, it's very cute."

He nudged her left, toward the passenger side. He said, "Just keep stroking that masculine ego."

Munroe sat and buckled, and when Bradford was behind the wheel with his seat pushed back as far as it would go, she stared at him.

"What?" he said.

"Cute," she said, and then she laughed.

He smiled, tucking a strand of hair behind her ear, kissed her lips, and then, palm cradling the back of her neck, rested his forehead against hers.

She breathed him in.

The parking garage, the bridge to the city, and the bright green neon on a giant Ferris wheel became a backdrop, and the last year a waning history, and it was as if no time apart had ever passed between them. This was contentment and peace. This was home.

That part never changed, in spite of everything else that would.

Day –62   5:30 A.M.

Tiny tugs against the sheets jolted Munroe from sleep, into instinct and terror, fight or flight. Memory rushed in close behind, replacing the past, the dreams, the pain, with where she was and why.

Bradford, beside her, rolled onto his back.

The floor fan shushed in oscillation. The window air-conditioning groaned in a low rumble. She drew in the cool dark of the room's cocoon to quiet her racing heart. Her body clock, still dragging its way out of Djibouti time, told her that it was barely early morning local time. She didn't know when they'd finally drifted off — late — and she might have grabbed a couple hours of rest, but she was awake now and that was that. Sleep was a cruel master and a fragile friend.

Bradford's breathing pattern said he was awake, too.

Like her, he slept little and slept light, but,

unlike her, his restlessness was the by-product of years in active combat, not trauma, and he didn't jerk awake, prepared to kill the person lying beside him.

Munroe breathed deeply, and with a soft, slow exhale the urge to flee and strike receded completely.

This was easy now, compared to how things had once been.

The years, as they faded, brought fewer triggers to yank her back into the brutality of adolescence and the equatorial rain forest and the man who'd beat her with fists and kicks and throws until she'd grown strong enough, fast enough, to fend him off; the man who'd put a blade in her hand and used her body as his carving board until the knife became her own way to salvation.

She was seventeen when she killed him, sneaking after him in the falling dusk, with the wind of the coming storm covering the sound of pursuit. She'd shot him in the back with a tranquilizer gun and stood over him as his eyes rolled up. Had straddled him in the driving rain and slit his throat.

The missionary's daughter, made to walk through the valley of the shadow of death, had come out the other side an apex predator.

She'd left his body to rot and buried the

20

fear instead.

Time had tempered the rage and violence. A little.

Bradford's fingers stroked her hairline and traced down her jaw.

The touch came without warning and set her pulse racing again, a rush that would have, in another time and place, thrust her into savagery.

He knew this as well as she did.

Eyes closed, she said, "That's a very dangerous game you play, Mr. Bradford."

He leaned in, lips brushing against her cheek and toward her ear. "I'm not afraid of you," he whispered.

The words reached down to her spine and she relaxed into him, felt the soft burn of his touch, measured his weight and movement, and when he continued down to nuzzle against her neck, she found leverage in his body. She pulled his arm out beneath him, flipped him, and straddled him.

He smiled and said, "Yes, please."

He was stronger, and taller than her five foot ten by an inch or so. He was former Special Forces, now high-stakes private security — a kinder, gentler term for mercenary — better trained, and had likely killed more people than she had. But he would never be faster. Speed was the skill that kept her alive, speed that had been sliced into her psyche one savage cut at a time.

She would need a few more nights sleeping beside him, a few more evenings of calm contentment, before the animal brain began to purr and stretch and the claws retracted. She brushed a finger along his nose and kissed his lips. "You should still be careful," she said, then stepped off the bed for the bathroom.

Bradford caught her hand and tugged her back. He studied her. Streetlight and moonlight filtered in through the wide glass window. She knew his thoughts, just as he knew hers: a year could be an eternity when filled with death and the threat of losing what meant most.

He pulled her closer.

"You'll be late for work," she said.

"They won't miss me."

"Let me go with you," she said.

He squeezed her hand, swung his feet to the floor. "There'll be plenty of time for that later," he said. He wrapped his arms behind her and drew her to him.

If she'd trusted him less, if she'd remained guarded around him the way she was in all other aspects of life, she would have sensed what she would only discover in hindsight. Instead she leaned down and kissed him, and he rolled her to the bed, and they both knew that in spite of their best efforts there was no way he wouldn't be late.

Bradford dressed and, knowing that Munroe watched, his teasing smile turned two minutes into five in a reverse Chippendale segue from pants to shirt to string tie. When he pulled the boots off a shelf, Munroe sat up and said, "No way. You can't be serious."

He held the brown ostrich leather out for inspection and dropped into the accent, thickening the honeyed drawl that only ever surfaced when he spent enough time back home around his family. "I hail from Texas," he said. "There are expectations, and no sense bringing disappointment."

Tone dry, she said, "You're missing the hat."

Bradford reached into the armoire, pulled out a cattleman, slipped it onto his head, tipped the rim, and said, "Ma'am."

Munroe rolled her eyes and scooted toward him.

In the years she'd known him, his uniform, depending on the occasion, had been jeans and a T-shirt, or camo and tactical gear, and his headgear, when he wore it, was a baseball cap or helmet. Out at his house, where land was plentiful and not all roads were

23

paved, he sometimes wore shit kickers and a hat as mud- and grease-stained as his jeans, but he'd never worn anything like this. Hell, she could count on one hand the people she'd met in Texas who'd dressed like *this* for any reason other than a night out on the town.

"Need to work on your authenticity," she said.

Bradford grinned, scooped laundry off the floor, and tossed it into a bin beside the cupboard. "No one's complained about my performance."

"If they knew better, they would," she said. "Hey, I brought you something." Munroe snagged her backpack from the foot of the bed, dragged it toward her, and rummaged through too much traveling crap to get to the bottom, then pulled out a box and handed it to him.

Bradford kissed her forehead, her mouth, and then took the box. "Now?" he said.

Munroe smiled. Nodded. She leaned back to watch as he tore at the ribbon and opened the lid, then chuckled when he laughed, a deep throaty laugh that made her heart hurt.

"You could hardly call *this* authentic," he said.

"It's atrocious," she said. "Found it in a

boutique window, as far away from Texas as you could hope to get. Made me think of you in its own weird way. Had to have it."

He pulled the belt out of the box: brown-red crocodile leather and gaudy aluminum buckle that half filled his oversize hand in an interesting imitation of western wear. "Nice," he said. "You see atrocity and you think of me."

"Was made for you," she said, and jutted her chin toward him instead of pointing, "given your new taste in clothes."

If she'd known then how prophetic those words would be, and what pain would come of such a harmless gift, she would never have bought the belt, never have given it to him, would have torn the leather from his hands. Instead, she giggled as he pulled off the old and slipped her gift through the loops.

"I love that you were thinking of me," he said. He leaned down to kiss her again. "You're crazy," he said. "Crazy but perfect."

Smiling made her cheeks hurt. "Go," she said, but she was reluctant to let go of his collar and he made no effort to pull away.

She shoved him playfully.

Bradford grabbed a phone off a stack of papers on the floor and tossed it to her. "My numbers are already in," he said. "Charger's in the kitchen. So are the instructions if you need them. I'll call you when I'm on my way home — maybe seven or eight."

She walked with him to the front and stood there in his T-shirt long after the door had shut, because he hadn't really gone. The cues reached out to her automatically, silences and lack of vibration on the floor, on the door: subtleties that most people would absorb without thinking if they were accustomed to listening for them, but most people weren't.

The door opened again and Bradford stuck his head inside.

"I missed you," he said, and he closed the door before she could reply. To the empty space she whispered, *I've missed you, too.*

Bradford's shoebox of an apartment was on
the fourth floor of a ten-story block building just southeast of Osaka's center, where
the streets were narrow even for his little
Mira, and telephone and electrical wires
hung overhead like strung spaghetti, and
adjacent structures abutted tightly against
each other all around.

They'd parked in an underground garage
and taken the elevator to a covered breeze-
way of clean brick tile and doors that
seemed impossibly close together. His
apartment opened to a sunken entryway, a
genkan, where they left outside footwear,
then stepped up to clean wood floors in a
tight hallway, where two bedrooms stood
across from the one toilet, in its own little
closet, the larger sink room doubling as a
laundry room, and the *ofuro* for bathing.

Capping the hallway, like the top of a *T,*
was the kitchen-dining-living room, and

there, at the start of the workday bustle, Munroe rolled open the balcony door, stepped out onto the narrow concrete strip, and leaned over the rail, scanning the density of cars and buildings, and glancing over signs and shops, for a first glimpse at how she might fill her daytime hours.

Bradford had been in Japan for a month, his car, apartment, and phone all part of the compensation package on a security contract that danced around the edges of what he did for a living — no guns, no bullets, no personal threats or people to protect, though that had made sense in a strange sort of way when he'd first explained it — while she'd arrived on a whim, with a tourist visa, a carry-on suitcase, and nothing to do.

After more than a decade spent working off-radar, a life spent scheming and adapting to find for some what others preferred to keep hidden, her mind ever plotting multiple moves in advance, she was now, quite suddenly, without purpose.

The absence, like a cloak ripped away, left nakedness in its stead.

In the bathroom-size kitchen Munroe dragged her fingers along Formica countertops so low they barely reached her hips. She nudged through cupboards and then the fridge, finding items that approximated what she would have found on Bradford's shelves in Dallas, albeit in much smaller sizes. Morning sunlight said food, but her stomach was still on Frankfurt time.

She plugged in the phone to charge, pulled out a liter of milk, found coffee, brewed a cup, and then sat at the two-person table. In the emptiness she stared out the window while the minutes ticked by and small sounds rose from the street to mingle with the electrical hum of the air-conditioner and appliances. She blew at the rim of her mug and sighed.

If this was what retirement felt like, retirement was a bitch.

She left the apartment on foot, carrying the phone, spare keys, and enough money to get her through the day.

She kept to the street edges, walking on gutter covers because there were no side-walks, peering down intersections with round traffic mirrors that stood in for stop signs and traffic lights. She branched off in new directions at whim while cars squeezed by on streets for two-way traffic that only had space for one. She passed umpteen bicycles and an overabundance of conve-nience stores — *konbini* — while snippets of conversation lifted on the air and the jumble of unfamiliar words hit her brain like jumpers to a dead battery, and discomfort, familiar and unavoidable, oozed down her spine into the pit of her stomach.

Soon enough she would find rhythm in the language, prosody to key the aural lock. Like a fish to a hook, her brain would latch on and the patterns would reel her in. Fluency would come whether she wanted it to or not.

This was her gift, her poisonous gift, a cursed blessing that had been with her since her earliest memories: the same ability that had guided her as a teenage interpreter into the arms of gunrunners, the same juju that had bisected her path with the path of the mercenary who, in teaching her to hate, would make her what she was.

Juju. Magic. Destiny.

A few weeks to grow comfortable, then another month — never more than two — for the strange wiring in her head to fully do its thing.

The need for food beckoned and an A-frame chalkboard on the ground level invited her to something like a café — *kissaten* — one floor up, with enough seating for ten, though she was the only customer. The menu was an interesting take on continental fare. She ate slowly, ears attuned to the television on the near wall with its pitch dipping and climbing between shows and commercials that could only have been produced under the influence of acid.

The discomfort inside her head charged on.

Munroe ate, then left the café to wander again. She took turns at random, stopping to compare the quantity and quality of vending machines more ubiquitous than parking spots; discovered the dichotomy of quiet temples, shrines, and *hokora* tucked in amid busy city streets; stepped into every shop and restaurant that drew her interest, touching and tasting and breathing and learning, until the evening came and she followed the trail of bread crumbs through Osaka's crowded footprint, home.

Bradford leaned in to kiss her as he did each morning, and Munroe opened her eyes when his lips caressed her cheek. Early light from the encroaching sun crept beneath the shades.

"Good morning, beautiful," he said. "I love you, go back to sleep."

His smile made her heart hurt with happy.

She stretched and rolled over as if he'd never disturbed her, as if she really would manage to fade back into oblivion after he tiptoed out: the same game they played each morning because pretending that they were normal somehow made it true.

Sleep, though still elusive, had become longer and deeper.

For her. For him.

Munroe followed Bradford's footsteps into the hall. In a few minutes he'd return to dress and she'd ask him if she could come with him, ask him to give her work, the same as she did every morning. He'd kiss her again and tell her not today, and she'd pretend that she didn't care.

In so short a time they'd found a routine, as if they'd always been. Being near him, even in spite of the separation that accompanied his long work hours, brought peace and contentment. That was enough.

Bradford's shadow filled the doorway and she reached a hand for him. He held her fingers and she let go reluctantly, all part of the morning ritual. But this time he leaned back down and, his face inches from her ear, said, "Come with me to work today?"

"Drop you off, keep the car?"

"Nyet," he said. "Come with me, keep me company."

Munroe bolted upright, knocking her head into his chin. She rubbed her forehead. "Ow," she said, then, "Really?"

"Yeah," he said, his face lit, "really."

Munroe scrambled to his side of the bed. "Girl clothes or boy clothes?" she said.

Bradford pushed hangers aside in the narrow armoire and then pulled off the only modest dress she owned and tossed it at her. "Girl clothes," he said. "Very, very girl clothes."

Munroe stuck out her tongue.

"Hey." He leaned down and, cupping his

33

hands around her face, kissed her lips, then pulled away and said, "Be quick, woman, don't make me late."

She smacked him with the dress.

Laughing, he ducked and she darted around him for the sink room and *ofuro* and locked him out.

He knocked and said, "Come on, Mike, let me in."

"Busy," she said, singsong and teasing. "Go make breakfast."

The commute was a forty-minute stop-start along a route that would have taken thirty without the traffic, and maybe fifteen without the traffic and the stoplights, to a facility on the eastern outskirts of Osaka's sprawl: two stories aboveground and two below. The building filled nearly half a block and, aside from the two-story glass entrance that sheared off and flattened one of the building's corners and the crisp neon signage that spelled out ALTEQ-BIO above the glass, it didn't even come close to imitating the high-tech image the company projected online and in brochures.

The parking lot, with its access arm beside a tiny guard box, wrapped from the street entrance around to the back and, although generous insofar as Japanese parking lots went, was but a fraction of what would have been needed if every employee drove to work. At seven-thirty in the morning the lot was already half filled.

They walked to the sheared-off corner, to doors that opened to a wide entry with a large stairwell at its center. Hallways branched off in multiple directions and the elevator to the lower level was off to one side.

Bradford stopped at the front desk and, under the watchful eye of two uniformed guards, signed Munroe in, then waited for a temporary badge while the *ding, ding* chimes of employees passing through the entry stiles filled the air.

The machines, like subway ticket controls, had arms that opened in response to the badges, and they lined the front from the rear of the guard desk to the opposite wall — enough to ensure that each visitor and employee had active clearance to enter the building, but nothing to keep a stolen badge from coming in with the wrong person: heavy security compared to other local facilities, but not much at all for a company serious enough to hire Bradford.

As if reading her thoughts, Bradford said, "Most everything up here is boring."

One of the uniforms handed Munroe a

badge and she draped the lanyard around her neck. Bradford nodded toward the elevator, where another guard desk stood behind a small queue of employees. "To get to the fun stuff, you've gotta go the extra round," he said, "and even my badge wouldn't get us through that."

Bradford led down linoleum-tiled halls.

With the exception of a few potted ferns at the front, the building's colors were limited to institutional white or varied shades of beige, making the interior even less impressive than the exterior.

Bradford's office was worse: a tiny space nearly filled by the one desk and two chairs that stood in for furniture. The window, which was hardly a window, opened out to the concrete of the building next door. Chairs and shoes — and possibly a table at one point — had scuffed up the paint, and the floor was industrial carpeting that had seen more tread and food and god-knew-what than its life span would have indicated.

Munroe said, "They must not like you very much."

"Nah, this is pretty standard. Money goes into research while everything else falls apart. Come, I'll show you the rest of the place."

He led back to the wide glass entry and

down another hall just as plain and bare as the one they'd been in. Doors on either side broke the monotony, as did the occasional turn or hallway branch, but nothing differentiated one from the next.

Employees streaming in through the front stiles arrived in greater numbers, heads down, seeing and yet not seeing as they wound their way to their workstations, but the overall people volume never rose. Rather, the facility hummed with the background noise of electronics and machines and the collective motions of hands and feet on many busy bodies.

In her head Munroe measured distance, a response to the slowly rising disquiet that set her on edge, as if she'd become a rat inside a maze with walls that might shift at any moment.

She'd done time within the corporate straitjacket, short as it had been, back when the trauma carried over from her adolescent years was still an unmarketable barrier toward earning a living rather than the skill set that had set her free, back when each attempt to hold down a normal job and maintain a permanent residence was a more miserable failure than the one before. But this wasn't that.

With perfect twenty-twenty hindsight,

when it was too late to really matter, she'd pin the discomfort down to the muted screams of instinct, that sixth sense of animal knowledge trying to tell her that her other senses were lying, that this was more than what it seemed.

Day –44   10:00 A.M.

Bradford stopped at a door with a card reader on the outside. He tapped his security badge against it.

The door clicked and Bradford pushed through into a room six times the size of his office. Monitor banks filled two walls, and the third was lined with desks and computer stations.

Two men stood when they entered, in their late twenties at the outside, both in street clothes as Bradford was, unlike the security guards at the front desk. They avoided direct eye contact while their strained expressions questioned Bradford for having broken protocol by bringing in an unauthorized person.

"Junior team members," Bradford said, and his words came with the unabashed, unconcerned quality of knowing he wasn't understood.

The young men kept rigid in Bradford's

presence, a cross between awe and awkward, and Munroe understood then why Bradford had chosen such a conspicuous uniform to wear to work each day: the boots and the starched jeans, the belt and the hat, weren't about fulfilling expectations so much as creating a persona, a legend. Problem was, a legend could be interpreted in multiple ways and a legend could be its own downfall.

Bradford asked for Tai Okada and the senior of the two answered in Japanese, which Bradford couldn't understand, and with sign language that indicated half an hour.

Bradford turned toward one wall of monitors, glanced at Munroe, and said, "What do you think?"

Behind her back, one of the desk jockeys said, *What's he doing here? Who's the woman?*

The other replied, *Nobody told me anything.*

Should we report this violation?

The big bosses hired him, they know more, better to let him do his job.

Munroe studied the jumpy black-and-white images tracking across the monitors — nothing spectacular, just standard CCTV fare. Bradford's question could have meant one out of a hundred things.

"Are you looking for something in particular?" she said.

Bradford's smile was impish. "Just wondering what your immediate impression might be. No filters."

"A lot of cameras," she said. "Not much for quality though. Probably for show — prevention — rather than discovery."

She looked askance at him and Bradford ignored her unspoken question. "There's more," he said.

More turned out to be another security room on the other side of the building, down another bland hallway, behind another nondescript door. They passed employees along the way, a few women who blushed and covered their mouths when Bradford said hello, and men who seemed to separate themselves between those who walked by as quickly as possible, eyes to the floor, as if by not acknowledging Bradford's presence he ceased to exist, and those who were overanxious to be his friend. In the wake of the final blushing, giggling woman, Munroe rolled her eyes.

"It's the clothes," Bradford said.

Munroe couldn't argue that the clothes had something to do with it.

Bradford tapped his card to another reader.

This room looked like any paper-pushing office in the basement of a federal building but for a wire rack of digital equipment in one corner and the enormous double monitors on each desk. Four walls, no windows, no art, just five cluttered desks littered with file folders and in-boxes and the stale air of too many bodies in too tight a space for too many days.

The man farthest from the door stood when they entered. He was as much foreign as he was Japanese, at least six feet tall with light amber eyes and wavy brown hair and, seeing Bradford, his expression darkened.

He stepped around his desk in their direction, eyes tracking up Munroe from shoes to head, and then, as if she was a trifling inconvenience, he turned to Bradford and said, "What do you need?" His accent spanned three continents and came to rest in Australia. His tone was from Antarctica.

"Thought Tai might be here," Bradford said, and then, in timing that amounted to a sigh of oh-well, he said, "Hey, Mac, this is Vanessa. Vanessa, Mac. Mac runs this department and he's damn good at his job."

Munroe offered her hand.

"Makoto Dillman," he said, and he shook

with more aggression than necessary. "Makoto or Dillman, never Mac."

"Got it," she said.

"And you are?"

"A visiting friend without transportation." Munroe tipped her head toward Bradford. "Had to twist his arm to be allowed to keep him company for the day."

"Right," Dillman said, and then turning to Bradford again as if Munroe didn't exist, "Not in here. You know that."

"My bad," Bradford said. "If you see Tai, send him my way."

Bradford reached for the door before Dillman could respond and Munroe could feel the stares as they stepped out. They started down the hallway, and if the compass in Munroe's head was correct, they headed back around toward the front. "What was that all about?" she said.

"That," he said, "was the Security Operations Center, the half of the security team that scares the bejesus out of the employees."

"I meant him. What was his problem?"

"That I was hired."

"You, you or just someone in general?"

"Started as someone in general," Bradford said. "I mean, the shame, right? What better way for your boss to announce to the entire

43

company that you're lousy at your job than to bring in some outside guy to do what you haven't? But now he has a problem with me personally."

"You've been poking the bear."

"Yeah," Bradford said, and he grinned.

"Bear's gonna bite you."

"Possibly."

"What's the deal with bifurcated security?"

"Think NSA in the SOC, as opposed to the feebs in front of the CCTV monitors on the other side of the building."

"Which half do you work for?"

"Sandwiched between, not welcome in either, dependent on both."

"Yuck."

"Tell me about it," he said. "I figured if I was going to tour you, it'd be poor form to skip the main attraction."

"Main attraction," she said, and smiled.

But Bradford had been right about that. Everything he'd shown her, she'd need again, and the question that would burn her in weeks to come was whether Bradford had already known at this stage, and if knowing was the real reason he'd brought her in.

Yelling seeped out from beneath a door and Munroe paused and stared in its direction. Bradford shook his head and she sighed and kept on walking. She didn't need to ask and Bradford didn't need to explain. This was just a louder version of what she'd already experienced from city streets to countryside among a rule-following population that feared shame above all else in a society that cultivated a fear of sticking out and making mistakes. Discovery came swift and sure for those rare few who stepped out of line, encouraging collective decision making at every level of public and private life so that only none, or all, could be blamed: a small step of progress from centuries past when citizens were expected to police one another and groups would be punished as a whole for the crimes of one.

Here, behind corporate walls, bosses badgered and bullied the junior staff — *sempai* — shooting down rock stars and star players before they were born, promoting for tenure rather than effort, and calling out and dissecting even minor blunders in group sessions, ensuring that being one with the hive was the only way to survive.

They found Tai Okada outside Bradford's office, leaning up against the wall, his face to a stack of papers, and jotting notes. His work attire, white shirt and dark tie, the same as every other man in the building,

45

somehow managed to appear slightly askew and sloppy, and his hair, just on the edge of needing a cut, dangled over thick-rimmed tortoise glasses.

He looked up when they approached, and seeing Munroe, he smiled.

Smiles from men in Japan were rare and his was the first she'd been offered within the facility. Munroe couldn't help but like him.

He bowed first, juggling pen and paper to shake her hand, and managing to affect the same sort of sloppiness in his actions as he did with his clothes. In English chipped and halting in the way of someone who had a lot of book knowledge but not much practice, he said, "Very nice to meet you."

Bradford opened the door. To Okada he said, "You could have used the desk. Let yourself in next time, okay?"

Okada nodded yes but the rest of his body said no.

To Munroe Bradford said, "Tai's my guy Friday. Runs interference between the departments, handles the language issues, explains the innuendo behind the corporate culture, and gets me what I need from the haters at the NSA and FBI." Inside the office, he paused. He looked at Munroe, then at the room, and glanced at the door. "You can wander if you want," he said, "or stay here. We've gotta go over some stuff. I'll surface for air for lunch — that okay?"

Munroe dragged the extra chair over to the corner and held up her phone. "I've got a book," she said. "Don't mind me."

Bradford's focus turned toward Okada and work, as if a switch had been thrown and she'd ceased to exist. So she sat and fought the urge to listen in, her mind still stuck on what Bradford had said about Okada's role. Information was only as good as its source, and if Okada was the funnel through which all of Bradford's information was sourced, then on this job Okada was Bradford's point of weakness.

Munroe shut down the thought.

Those were old patterns, old ways of thinking. This was Bradford's mission, not hers, and in spite of her requests to work along with him, he'd made it clear she wasn't welcome.

Bradford and Okada left the room and Munroe stared at the door. After all the times she and Bradford had worked together, had guarded each other's backs, kept each other alive, he now relied on someone else and had left her behind. It was new, this sensation of feeling useless, of feeling unneeded — unwanted.

Eyes to the screen, she tried to focus on the book but couldn't.

She pulled ear buds from her purse, tamped them into her ears, and cranked up the volume. Shut her eyes and drew a deep breath, moving backward into black and nothingness, but still the tingling burn persisted.

DAY –43   7:45 A.M.

Be extremely subtle, even to the point of
formlessness. Be extremely mysterious,
even to the point of soundlessness.
Thereby you can be the director of the
opponent's fate.

— MASTER SUN TZU

The light flashed green, the machine
chimed, the arm swung open, and Nonomi
Sato, in flat, comfortable, ugly shoes, walked
on toward the elevator bank, invisible in the
routine.

The soft *dings* rang on behind her, right
and left, layering over footsteps and hushed
conversation. This was the company's morning music, a melody of dread carried inside
every employee, dread that today might be
the day the corporate gestapo wanted another review.

Dread, harmonized with fear and suspicion.

49

Really, it was a beautiful song.

Sato stopped outside the guard station that led to the elevator. The prescreening procedure only allowed for one employee at a time.

Cameras watched, but she didn't worry about them. They were deterrents for conformists and rule followers, an obvious announcement that the eyes were always, always recording, keeping honorable people from violating their own sense of honor. For deceivers, the threat was in what couldn't be seen.

And even about those Sato didn't worry.

She belonged here.

She was five foot two, with shoulder-length hair pulled tight into a bun, and wearing a drab knee-length skirt and dress shirt; clothes indistinguishable from those of every other female in the building. For that matter, she was a woman, indistinguishable from any other woman in the building. But, unlike most of the others, her teeth were straight and white and her chest a full cup size bigger, courtesy of Thailand's best.

Sato handed the security man her badge and stood patiently, eyes lowered, as he matched the picture to her face, studying her intently.

He returned the badge, and when she

reached to take it, he didn't let go. Her eyes rose to meet his. He licked his lips. Folds of his chin pressed down into his collar and tiny beads of sweat dotted his hairline. Sato blushed, as was appropriate, and averted her gaze. The culture demanded such things.

The culture was suffocating.

Even nights tumbling in Bangkok's dirty alleys, or working a hustle in Manila's red-light district, would have been better than the claustrophobia and polite face-saving of Osaka's corporate halls. But business was business.

She would remain proper and demure for as long as it took. Would keep her thoughts concealed in the same way that conformity concealed her individuality. Mother would be so proud.

Sato pressed her palm to the scanner embedded in the desk.

The machine rolled and whirred and chimed the all-clear.

She bowed several inches while her face maintained a polite mask. The guard's hand brushed her thigh as she passed, his fingers racing in and up, claiming ownership for that brief second over what did not belong to him.

His boldness had grown, and with his boldness the violations had become more frequent. This, too, was part of the melody of dread and fear and suspicion. This was discordance, born from the ability to retaliate that emboldened those in positions of power to lord over the powerless.

Sato glanced at the guard's badge and caught the name again, confirmation of what she'd read the day before yesterday. *Haruto Itou,* his badge said. In spite of her mother's best attempts, kanji would always be a struggle and concealing this weakness was Sato's daily atonement.

Itou was in his twenties, perhaps, recently promoted and full of self-importance. His insolence was an annoyance Sato could endure for the sake of the job; his obsession and stalking was another matter.

He'd attempted to follow her home for the third time last night.

This was a problem.

Sato continued from the guard's post to the locker station around the corner. The door was already open, a workmate stuffing jacket and shoes into one of the many square cubbies that lined the room floor to ceiling.

Half of the lockers still had keys.

Sato chose an empty box and put her purse inside, performing for the hidden cameras and the audio recorders. She'd never searched for evidence of their existence — she wasn't a fool — she simply assumed they'd be there, of all places, where peasants, mistrusted by the feudal overlords, exchanged one garb for the next.

Sato traded her shoes for company-provided slip-ons, closed the locker, and clipped the key to the lanyard with her security badge. Aside from her clothes, no personal belongings were allowed beyond the elevator doors.

They'd check her more thoroughly coming out.

These were layers of precaution for which she could thank legions of industrial spies throughout the decades: Chinese hackers, American government, Israeli military, corporate spies, in any combination, mixed and matched and more because the world was one big pond in which hypocritical thieving scum controlled an ecosystem where the many, many little fish living near the surface snapped at flies, squabbling over scraps, playing in the sun, blissfully unaware of what went on in the murky depths.

Sato, too, was a bottom feeder, but not like the others.

The security protocols focused on preventing data transmission.

Thick walls without windows and self-circulating ventilation kept the lab free of contaminants and prevented listening devices and lasers from stealing data out of the air. Without cables leading to the lab computers, without wireless connections, there was no pathway for hackers to break in and steal.

If the security protocols worked as the company had designed them to work, the other players, with all of their intelligence, gadgets, and technology, were locked out of the game, but none of the precautions were designed with a woman like her in mind. As long as she worked here, nothing they did could stop her from taking what she wanted.

Sato returned to the elevator, where the line was now backed up with two people waiting for the body scan. At the building's front entrance, the cowboy walked in.

Sato kept her face toward the floor and observed him to the degree that she wasn't obvious. He stopped at the front desk and chatted with the guards for a minute, letting them practice their English on him and buying goodwill for cheap. He stayed in the open area longer than any other employee would dare, smiling and nodding like a simpleton while his eyes tracked over each person, taking in more than he let on.

That was easy when most everyone wrote

off his behavior as just more of the *gaijin* being a *gaijin,* even those who believed the rumors and gossip.

Sato moved forward one space in line.

The cowboy intrigued her. He was a hunter, keen enough to sniff out a trail. He'd proven that already, though he likely didn't know it yet.

As if he'd read her thoughts, the cowboy's head ticked up and he walked toward the elevator bank. Sato shifted her back to him slowly, a natural movement that wouldn't flash evasiveness and challenge the pack leader to chase.

The line moved forward. She stepped between the screening walls beside the elevator so some pervert in the security department could get a good snapshot of her body, and when she stepped out, she glanced up to find the cowboy watching her.

Sato blushed when she made eye contact and covered her mouth when she smiled so slightly, because the culture demanded this, too. She turned to the elevator and pressed her thumb to the biometric reader while the cowboy's eyes bored into her back. By the time she'd stepped inside and pressed her thumb to the interior reader, he was gone.

The doors closed and her hands and feet tingled.

For three years she'd toyed with her competition and teased the men in the security departments, but they were all like babies, easily taken and confounded by games of *inai inai ba*. But the cowboy, he was a man and a warrior, and the idea of facing off against a worthy combatant made her toes curl.

DAY −38   2:00 P.M.

The Kawasaki dealership, part showroom, part garage, was in a corrugated building off the inner loop, a wide thoroughfare just north and across the river from Osaka proper. Bradford pulled the Mira into the small frontage parking area next to a flat-nosed delivery truck and shut off the ignition.

Munroe squeezed his hand.

Lining the building's front window was an array of motorcycles, their aerodynamic curves and bright vivid colors a mocking laugh at the bleached concrete, harsh angles, discount stores, and factories that made up the area.

It had taken a while to find the place. That was a problem in a country whose address system only made sense to city planners and GPS: sets of numbers pinpointing block and building not geographically, but according to when each structure was built. There was irony in having left Africa for one of the world's most developed countries only to discover that directions by way of signage, restaurants, and landmarks were still a part of life.

Fingers interlaced, they walked toward the tight row of bikes in the way of treasure hunters who'd finally struck gold after so much searching.

Beyond the window other models filled the floor space, scooters and off-road bikes squished together and adorned with hand-written sale signs in reds and yellows like washing machines in a discount warehouse that just had to go, but these outside were the supersports, the big-girl machines; these were the *murdercycles*.

Munroe brushed her fingers across a headlamp and need tingled through her limbs the same way saliva flowed at the idea of vinegar. She knew the models by sight, could quote engine size, speed, torque, weight, trail, rake, and wheel base; knew how they handled, what she wanted, and why.

She continued the slow walk to the end of the line and stopped in front of a Ninja ZX 14-R: black-grilled, deep cherry-red, faster, angrier, and half the price of the Ducati he'd left behind in Dallas just over a year ago. And there she stayed, motionless, staring down at the machine, afraid to touch it, contemplating the freedom the bike represented and what it would mean to ride again.

Bradford put his arm around her shoulders and drew her tight to him. He kissed her temple and whispered, "Like getting back on after the horse has thrown you off."

Munroe nodded, unable to speak, but she didn't need to, because Bradford understood the present and the past in a way that defied the need for words.

She knelt beside the bike, one knee to the pavement, pressed a palm to the molded plastic, and let the memories wash through her. Bradford knelt beside her and placed a hand on her thigh, reassuring and fully present. Munroe rested her hand on top of his and wrapped her fingers between the empty spaces.

"You'll be okay," he said.

She leaned her head on his shoulder.

Nearly a month of concrete, grime, and population density had left her wanting to go where things were green and there was air, in a way that didn't require chaining her time to train and bus schedules or to Bradford's work hours the way borrowing his car did. Acquiring her own wheels was inevitable, but that didn't make one of the fastest production bikes around the default choice.

It had been a long time, too long, since she'd felt the roar, the self-induced terror, and the adrenaline rush that only a machine like this could give.

The last time she'd ridden she'd been tranquilized and kidnapped.

Then her world had burned down as, one by one, those she'd loved most had been tortured or killed as a way to control her.

Bradford tweaked her thigh and, keeping his hand in hers, Munroe stood. She stared down at the machine again, bright red, conspicuous and loud, everything opposite the nonstatement black on black that had always adorned her carnage on wheels.

Things were different now.

Different machine.

Different colors.

Different country.

Different circumstances.

Different life.

She wasn't superstitious in that way, but she'd be happy for the placebo effect all the same if that's what reverting to superstitions would bring her.

It wouldn't. But she couldn't have known that then.

DAY −26   7:20 A.M.

Those who win every battle are not really skillful. Those who render others' armies helpless without fighting are the best of all.

— MASTER SUN TZU

Nonomi Sato pulled into the lot, which was already half full. She found a spot, turned off the engine, set papers out on the passenger seat, and leaned over just slightly under the pretense of studying them.

Work didn't begin for another forty minutes, but her supervisors would have been in the lab since six at least, and she only had so much time before her absence would become an unspoken mark against her. Even so, there were priorities and greater priorities.

She waited for the cowboy.

He would arrive soon. He'd done well for a foreigner in embracing the hard hours

61

required by company loyalty — an American, no less, a rugged individualist from a land of individualists, adapting to a culture where self-identity came from belonging, and companies, as givers of self-value and worth, demanded work take precedence over everything else.

He'd done exceedingly well.

Maybe the cowboy, too, would suffer *karōshi*.

Death from overwork.

It simply wasn't possible for any person to work twelve or more hours, day after day, year after year, without rest on weekends or holidays.

Not without paying a physical price.

Sato paid the price, would continue to pay, but her duty had an expiration date. She would never be her mother, whose only value was as a diplomat's wife, the perfect companion in a white-glove world, the flawless hostess to dignitaries and the Thai and Malaysian elite. She'd never be her father, whose self-identity had been handed to him by the Japanese government and then abruptly taken away while he was still years from retirement, leaving him with nothing but a hole where self should have been, so he'd filled that hole with drink until the hole swallowed him completely.

Sato glanced through the window, turned a page, and continued the fake reading. At last, the cowboy arrived.

The motorcycle rumbled low and rolled behind the line of cars, the lead rider in black helmet, black jacket, and riding gloves, a perfect match to the red and black of the machine, and the cowboy an odd contrast with his boots and jeans in browns and blues.

Sato followed them in her rearview, then side-view, then the passenger's window as at the far end of the lot the bike drove into an empty parking space and up onto the sidewalk and looped back halfway toward the building front. Sato had seen the Ninja twice before and she'd found it odd then, and odd now, that the cowboy was the passenger. There'd been no reason to give the motorcycle much thought before, but things were different now.

The cowboy, hunter and trail sniffer, was good at his job. He saw what others didn't see, and whether he knew it yet or not, he'd entered her game, and that meant the motorcycle and its rider mattered; it meant everything about him mattered.

The driver straightened and shut off the engine.

The cowboy pulled off his helmet and

strapped it down to the sliver of passenger seat. He ran his fingers through his hair, shrugged out of a backpack, and retrieved his hat and several folders, then strapped the empty backpack down with the helmet.

The rider's visor flicked up and the two conversed, but the cowboy blocked Sato's line of sight and she couldn't see the face within the helmet.

A moment later, the visor was down and the rising whine of the engine carried back, and the motorcycle rolled along the sidewalk, down the pedestrian ramp, into the parking lot, through the gate, and was gone.

Sato gathered the papers and grabbed her purse. She stepped out and made it to the sidewalk before the cowboy reached her car, then walked slowly to allow him time to close the distance.

When he was directly behind her, she tripped.

The cowboy had good reaction time. He grabbed her arm before she'd completely tumbled and she cried out when he did, as much from fake surprise as fake pain. He pulled her back and she limped upright, blushing and apologizing.

The cowboy held her at arm's length and studied her face. "You all right?" he said.

Sato nodded.

That was the easiest way to remind him that she understood his language and an easy way to invite further conversation. She would allow him the illusion of pursuing her, and bedding her, and in so doing she would unburden his thoughts until she'd learned about him and uncovered secrets from his past, and then, piece by piece, she would neutralize the threat by destroying him.

But he didn't accept the invitation. She tried again.

"Thank you," she whispered, blushing at him once more. Then she smiled the killer smile that had for years, across cultures and borders, served as both rejection and invitation, virgin and whore, the smile that deprived men of the ability to reason.

The cowboy nodded, acknowledging her smile, and his gaze tracked down her legs, checking to see if she'd been hurt, but his eyes reflected no hint of awareness of her invitation. And then he let her go, and walked on.

Sato stared after him, following slowly, face flushed and hands shaking.

Rejection was a new experience and wholly unexpected.

Confusion tingled along her skin.

She hadn't pegged the cowboy as a closet

homosexual, although sometimes people were surprising in that way. Two riders on a motorcycle did raise that possibility, but no, this wasn't that. She'd watched him. He was a man's man. He appreciated women, even Asian women. Sato stared at the cowboy's back, measuring his broad-shouldered forward stride.

She'd underestimated him. Victory adapted form endlessly. She'd neglected that truth, relying on old tropes and easy habits *because* he was a man.

This was a failure to be rectified.

The elevator traveled down two levels and required Sato's thumb again before the doors let her out. They opened onto a small foyer, tiled and clinically white, with little black camera bubbles secured to the ceiling. The foyer then divided into two and Sato went left, into the women's changing area, which was a fraction the size of the room on the other side.

She keyed the combination for her cupboard and placed her lanyard inside. She exchanged her skirt and shirt for an approved set of thermals and pulled the pieces on, then closed the door and spun the lock.

She pumped the dispenser on the far wall to wash her hands and face with alcohol gel. No amount of moisturizer could make up for the drying damage of the alcohol and laboratory air; that was an unfortunate cost of doing business.

Sato left the locker room for the air curtain and the gowning room, where she pulled on one-time-use paper coveralls and swapped the slip-ons for rubber clogs followed by disposable shoe covers. Lastly, a hair cap swallowed the tight black bun and gave her head an angled alien look.

She faced a large steel door with a small glass window, stood to its right, and rested her chin on a pad for the iris scan. All this trouble to secure the lab, to keep the research and machines disconnected from the outside world.

All this trouble, and yet she was here.

Lab activity was already well under way when she stepped inside, printers running, techs feeding glass tubes through droppers. On the far wall was another door that led to the animals and the operating theater.

Mariko bowed slightly when Sato entered, a greeting between the lower lab's only two women that had become something of a ritual. Mariko nodded toward Akio Tanaka, and rolled her eyes.

He had ear buds in his ears, the volume up so loud that Sato could hear the music from a meter away, and he sat on a stool, hunched over a laptop with that glazed look that said he'd stayed working through the night.

Sato giggled and Mariko smiled. They'd talk later.

Here, sequestered away from the cameras, the listening devices, and the security men upstairs who analyzed every word and gesture, the mood was lighter and the jokes flowed freer. Sato continued on to her workstation. Dirty trays and slides awaited her, as did data sets and an hour's worth of the mundane that had stacked up in her absence — none of it that important.

She put a hand on Tanaka's shoulder so he'd know she was beside him.

He pointed to a three-inch stack of paper.

She'd sort through his handwritten notes and correlate them for input. As the assistant to the head researcher, she was privy to every trial, every test, success and failure alike, and down here, in the bowels of the facility, as close to the research as it was possible to get, where nothing violated the theft-prevention protocols that cut the lab off from the world, there was nothing to record her movement and habits, nothing to stop her from taking what she wanted.

Day –14   5:15 A.M.

Munroe woke to Bradford's rustling. The texture in the air, the fewer sounds reaching through the windows from the street, told her that he was up earlier than usual. He leaned over to kiss her, as he did every morning, but this time he stayed beside her, propped up on an elbow, tracing a finger around her belly button.

He whispered, "Come to work with me today?"

Munroe opened an eye and looked at him, beautiful in the shadows, muscled and half naked. They'd become like ships passing in the dark as the weeks dragged on and he left earlier, came home later, or sometimes not at all, leaving them to seek stolen moments and the occasional Sunday afternoon to collide in their own isolated ocean.

"I have to stay overnight," he said. "Take me in and spend the day with me?"

Munroe brought his hand to her lips, and

69

held it there longer than a kiss warranted. She didn't have to use words to say no because he wouldn't have asked the way he had if he hadn't already known her answer. He'd known it from the day he'd invited her into the office and made his very carefully crafted point, deliberately excluding her, fully aware that as the minute hands ticked their slow painful march around the clock, she'd hurt more than if he'd simply said *Maybe tomorrow* and had left her at home.

He'd gotten what he wanted: she'd never asked to be a part of his assignment again. She couldn't fault him for what he'd done. Life had a way of screwing things up for them, and work had a way of becoming life. From his point of view, keeping her away from his job was best for them both, might keep them together longer this time around.

Bradford shifted, sat up on the bed beside her. He pulled her hand back with his, putting it to his cheek. "If I said I'm sorry, would it matter?"

She leaned over and bit his thigh. He twitched and said, "Ow," but it came out more as a question than an exclamation.

She glanced up and smiled and said, "Sorry."

"Am I missing the analogy?"

"No," she said, and traced her finger around the indentation, "I just wanted to bite you." Then she rolled back and put her head on the pillow. "You've already apologized and I've accepted your apology. I've got no grudge."

"Then you'll come with me today?"

She sighed and turned toward the window: her version of *Maybe tomorrow.*

"It'll be different," he said. "You'll be with me all day and I'll give you something to do. Real work," he said, "not busywork." He held his little finger up in front of her face so she couldn't avoid it. "Pinkie promise."

She batted him away.

He was such a cheater.

"Okay," she whispered, and slid around him, off his side of the bed, and reached for the armoire. She pulled the one modest dress off its hanger, the same outfit she'd worn the first time, same outfit she'd have to wear again if Bradford ever offered another invitation. The lack of alternatives had come from the mistaken assumption that she could do as she'd always done in the past: travel light and source what she needed locally. Instead she'd discovered a robust fashion industry that had no concept of women her height and size, which turned online shopping with international shipping into her only option for women's clothes and shoes.

She hadn't bothered. Men's clothing worked fine, anyway.

"Hey," Bradford said. He tugged her hand and pulled her to him. He wrapped his arms around her thighs and rested his cheek on her stomach. "I know the way things turned out hasn't been easy for you — hasn't been easy on us — not what I imagined the workload would be when I signed on and definitely not what I described when I asked you to come."

She rested a hand on his head and ran her fingers through his hair. "I'm a big girl and I can deal with it," she said. She leaned down and kissed him, then left him for the *ofuro*.

Bradford held true to his promise and kept Munroe with him throughout the day. If Tai Okada questioned her involvement, he never let on, and in those first hours, the three of them poring over old documents, Munroe grasped what Bradford's role within the company had become.

Behind its run-down and dilapidated appearance, behind the show of cameras that didn't do much more than intimidate, was an invisible state-of-the-art network that monitored phone calls, protected data from cyber attacks, and analyzed employee connections and patterns based on the RFID chips embedded in the badges.

The strongest security features protected the underground labs, where the sensitive research and development took place. In addition to the multiple biometric stations that an employee had to pass through after the single point of entry, reinforced construction turned the lower levels into a bunker, making it impossible for technology to be stolen remotely through keystrokes or for monitor frequencies to be grabbed through the air. Nothing, data included, went in or came out that wasn't carried — and for that there were additional protocols.

The company's own personnel was the only route secrets might travel into competitors' hands, and although each employee had been heavily vetted, reviews were conducted regularly, and no thief or spy had been uncovered, the suspicion of theft persisted.

Bradford had been brought in to use his skills in the low-tech world of blood-and-guts security to seek out gaps that the high-tech guys might be missing. He was there for face-to-face interaction, to spot the combat enemy in peacetime the way he was trained to search out threat in war.

On the way to the break room, where most of the employees took lunch in one form or another, Munroe said, "You could have really used me on this assignment."

Bradford nodded. "Maybe I should have," he said, "but you know why I couldn't — still can't."

"Not can't, Miles, won't."

Bradford stopped and faced her, hurt in his eyes, pain in his posture. "It's the same thing," he said.

"I get that you're trying to keep me away from triggers," she said. "I get that our odds are better this way, but I've got nothing here, Miles. I'm going through the motions, trying to find friends, taking up hobbies, but come on, this is me we're talking about."

"A month or two and I'll be out of here," he said.

"You're missing the point. Another location isn't going to change anything, and as much as I love you, neither will spending more time together if I'm not working. Let me help you," she said. "Utilize my brain. Please?"

He searched her eyes, then took her hand and stared at their fingers, while inner debate marched across his face. Finally he said, "I just can't, Michael. Not the way things are right now. It's complicated. Let me finish this out, a few more months, that's all. Can you last that long — for me? For us?"

Munroe stood silent, arms crossed and motionless.

Bradford released her hand, cupped her chin, and lifted her face toward his. "I won't blame you if you feel you need to walk away again," he said, "if that's what you need to be all right. But I don't want you to leave, Michael, I really don't. Please stay until this is over and then we'll find a middle ground — something that works for both of us, I promise."

They stood there, face-to-face, at the end of the hall, communicating through the silence. She studied him, searched him, and then sighed, giving in because she knew that Bradford's reasons were drawn from a well of love and concern, and because, for the first time in her life, leaving was no longer possible.

Bradford stuck out his bottom lip, quivering with puppy-dog adorableness, and that forced her to smile. Then his focus ticked up and passed over her shoulder, and his eyes, like sharks cutting through water, began roaming, as was his way: always aware, always searching the surroundings.

He put his arm around her shoulders and said, "Let's grab food."

Munroe stole a glimpse toward the hall junction, searching for what had arrested his attention: two women with lunch bags in hand, walking side by side, their expressions contorting with the curves and lines of deep, earnest conversation.

The break room was a rectangle with half a long wall open instead of a door. One of the shorter walls was adorned with a sink and a counter, which was topped with microwave, toaster, and hot water pot, and its opposite was lined with vending machines that offered a universe of drink options, instant noodles, and instant hot junk food.

Bradford threaded between round tables and mostly filled folding chairs to the back of the room, while twenty or so faces did everything possible to avoid making eye contact.

Munroe whispered, "No one seems to like you much anymore."

"They're scared of me."

"Wasn't like that the last time I was here."

Bradford pulled out a seat and offered it to her. "I wasn't a hatchet man the last time you were here."

"Might not be fear," she said. "Might be

avoidance and embarrassment."

"Yeah?" he said.

She shrugged. She hadn't been in the facility long enough, hadn't seen enough, to know. She said, "Americans — Texans in particular — come with a lot of stereotypes beyond the clothes and the imagined horse and cattle ranches."

"Dumb country boy?" he said. "Wouldn't be the first time." And the way he said it implied that, if anything, he'd gone to lengths to cultivate that myth. "But I'm still a hatchet man."

Munroe scooted between chairs to the vending machines, cleaner and more modern than any other equipment she'd seen in the facility, exchanged coins for liquid nourishment, then returned to their table.

The two women who'd caught Bradford's attention in the hall walked in, broke their discussion long enough to take seats, then continued conversing in low, earnest tones as they set out their home-packed bento boxes of a dozen tiny portions and picked at their food, eating with dainty bites.

Bradford, steaming Styrofoam cup in hand, sat beside Munroe. His eyes ticked once in the direction of the women.

"What's up with them?" Munroe said.

"Trying to figure them out."

Munroe took a sip, stole a glance.

He removed the cup's paper lid and then raised the rim to his lips and blew against the steam. "Company executives seem pretty convinced that the theft is coming from China's direction, and they're the only two Chinese employees."

"That would be a bit obvious, wouldn't it?"

Eyes on the cup, he nodded. "Not to mention that neither of them have access to the lower levels, both have excellent work records, there's nothing out of order in terms of life habits or patterns, and they are both far too naïve and self-involved to be what I'm looking for. But at this point, I can't rule anything out."

Munroe glanced at him, then at the women. "Have you ruled out the possibility that, in spite of what you were told, you weren't actually hired to find a spy?"

"The thought's crossed my mind."

Munroe took another sip, let the conversation thread drop. Bradford jabbed wooden chopsticks into the cup and ate while employees came and went. The women rinsed out their lunch containers in the sink and packed them up and then they, too, were gone. As if there'd been no break in conversation, Bradford said, "What's your line of reasoning?"

Munroe capped the empty bottle and rolled it between her palms. "Just doesn't feel right," she said. "If it was me, and granted, not everyone thinks like I do, I'd hire a team on the sly. Seven or eight people who speak the language and can blend in — *not* foreign — and I'd stagger them in as new hires, maybe over a two- or three-month period. I'd set them loose in key areas of the company — would put at least two of them down in the lower levels — and have them do exactly what they claim you were hired for, but do it invisibly. Even without the belt, the hat, the costume, and the legend, as a foreigner you're incredibly conspicuous — you might as well wear a bell around your neck."

"Not too different from my own theory," Bradford said. He gathered the trash and walked it to the garbage. Sat again. "I figure someone's watching for something I don't know anything about," he continued, "that they're using my presence like a stick in the bush to flush game, a wedge to split the log, a straw man, a distraction."

"No idea who or what?" she said.

He shook his head. "I'll figure it out."

He was a mask but she read the obfuscations in him all the same. She smiled and let them go for the same reason she agreed to stay until he finished the assignment. In retrospect, it would be difficult to say if that had been a mistake.

He leaned back and brushed his thumb against her cheek. "I was hired to do a job and I'm going to get it done regardless of what the true motives might be."

"What's really going on down there in the lab?" she said. "I've read the brochures, perused the website, done a rough once-over on the company. None of what they advertise adds up to anything big enough to call in someone like you. What's worth so much that they guard it so carefully?"

"The Holy Grail of biofabricated engineering," he said.

"Humor me."

"Body-part replication through 3-D printing."

"Can't be that," she said. "Biofacturing has been going on for years."

"Sure, ears and noses, arteries, lots of variants of skin and soft tissue for transplants and pharmaceutical testing," he said, "even lab-grown muscle as a sustainable meat source, but most everyone is years, maybe decades, away from developing functional, transplantable organs."

Munroe raised her eyebrows and blew a

silent whistle. "They're close?"

"Dunno. I'm not allowed access to the lab or any of the research."

"What do you think?"

"Given how much they've invested in protecting whatever's going on down there, I'd say they believe they're way ahead of anyone else."

"No donor waiting list," she said. "Virtually zero chance of transplant rejection. Can you imagine the potential market if they're able to own and patent the process?"

"Assuming they figure it out," he said. "Just about every developed nation has companies and nonprofit teams working on the same type of research. Anyway, just because someone hits the finish line first doesn't mean they're a winner. There would still be years of clinical safety trials."

"If *anyone* gets to the finish line, we all win," Munroe said, "but still . . ."

Her sentence trailed off and her mind leapt sideways, scanning what she knew of the facility's security systems, searching for weaknesses, plotting out how she'd steal the data if she'd been the one hired to get at it.

Bradford raised an eyebrow and poked her arm playfully, but hard enough to say he knew what was up. "Don't forget whose team you're on," he said.

She grinned. "It's tempting," she said. "Why are they specifically looking at the Chinese?"

Bradford's gaze tracked over to the half-wall and the empty space where the women had passed through and where other employees continued to arrive and leave at irregular intervals. "I wish I knew," he said.

So did she. The question of Chinese involvement was one she'd come back to more than once over the coming weeks; the answer could have changed things if she'd had it at the beginning.

DAY –11   2:00 A.M.

The ability to gain victory by changing
and adapting according to the opponent
is called genius.

— MASTER SUN TZU

Nonomi Sato crept along the open hallway,
hugging the concrete railing, careful not to
cast shadows or leave traces of her presence.
She'd disconnected the security lighting,
but nothing could be done about the cloud-
covered moon or the bath of light pollution.

Sato turned the key, slow and quiet. The
lock gave and she depressed the handle,
nudging the door open one controlled
centimeter at a time.

Shoes in the *genkan* told the story of the
home's occupants and estimated their ages
and sizes: son, mother, father, grandmother.

This was almost too easy and that took
away the fun.

Sato stepped into the house, shoes still

on, clothes black, supple, and tight like a second skin, a nighttime skin, because night was when the carnivores came out to hunt.

Haruto Itou his badge had said, and she found him in his room, still awake and at his computer, with his back to the door. He never heard her enter. He was bigger and fatter; he would make a lot of noise if she fought him.

She crossed the tatami silently and whispered his name.

He startled, turned, and seeing her, put his back to the desk.

She put a finger to her lips and said, "Don't tell."

His mouth opened. With a seductive pout, she removed the pin from her bun and allowed the wig hair to tumble down in waves. Then she unzipped the upper layer of her body suit, exposed cleavage, and moved closer to him.

Itou offered a hint of a smile.

Sato bit her lip in sly promise. "You've looked for me," she said. Slow and sensual, she reached for his hand, brought it to her chest, and rubbed his fingers across a nipple. "You wanted to touch, and now I've come to you."

She stepped around and nudged her thigh between his legs, sidled up to his groin, and ran his hand down her belly, ever lower. "You want more?" she said. "You can have it all, just as you imagined."

He hardened against her thigh and his hands came alive on their own, groping with all the experience of a schoolboy.

She took his palms and pressed them together, nudged him back, and whispered, "We will need time. More than these few hours left of the night. We'll skip work tomorrow. Write to your department manager, tell him you're ill."

Itou hesitated and she pressed her mouth nearer his head, ran her tongue from the base of his ear, over his earlobe, and traced her fingers up his thigh. His breath caught.

"It's just one day," she said. "Or I could simply go home now and we can forget this embarrassing incident."

His mouth moved in a whisper, but no words formed, then he opened an e-mail. She teased him as he typed, struggling to keep up with the characters that rose on the screen. "Also, a note to your parents," she said, and she pointed toward the notebook on his desk. She wouldn't touch it, wouldn't touch anything inside this home unless she had to. With her hair tight beneath the wig and her body scrubbed clean before she'd dressed, she'd done everything possible to prevent leaving behind evidence that she'd been there.

He picked up the paper and found a pencil.

"There," she said, her fingers still tracing his inner thigh, her breath still heavy in his ear, "tell them you've gone for a while and not to worry about you, that there are things" — she paused and took his hand, pulling his thumb into her mouth, wetting his skin with her lips and tongue — "tell them there are things you must think about. That will keep them from bothering you and gives us time, yes?"

He put down the pencil and turned to face her, his face flushed, hands trying to get further inside her suit. She batted them away. "No, silly boy," she said. "Write the note so we can go and we can take our time and do things the proper way."

He scribbled, and she read over his shoulder, and when he had finished, she took his hand and guided him out of the room into the *genkan,* allowing him but a second to grab a pair of shoes before they slipped through the door.

Outside in the hall, she laughed a soft girlish giggle and ran, leading him along by the hand down the stairs and to the alley, where she'd parked the car.

The mountain road wound tight and narrow, a wall of rock on one side, a guardrail on the other, and enough pavement for a vehicle and a half. The drop over the edge and into the trees was a hundred feet at least.

Munroe gave the Ninja a little more speed.

The bike hugged the turn and her body moved with the machine, balanced and beautiful, and perfectly terrified. The heady rush crested in a wave, sweet and smooth, like morphine released through a handheld drip.

In the near distance, a delivery truck rounded a curve and the vehicle lurched its way toward collision. In pure slow-motion clarity, adrenaline surged, and the self-destructive forces that propelled her to gamble with her life rose from deep sleep.

Time spliced into nanosecond slivers. In her head she tossed life against a chemical high that soothed and shushed and pushed the world away.

The truck sounded its horn.

The engine on the Ninja whined; the urges cried for release.

Accelerate or brake, there was no third option.

The roulette wheel began to spin: probability colliding with possibility and churning out the odds of mortality. The road widened slightly. Munroe gauged distance and space, her foot shifted gears, and her hand nurtured the throttle, preparing to tear through the opening between truck and guardrail at the widest point.

Instead she decelerated, then braked, almost too hard to control the bike. The truck passed on her left, the wrong side of the road, the driver screaming obscenities through the window.

Munroe stopped and pulled off the helmet. Frustration rose to take the place of exhilaration and she sat silently for a long while, feet on the ground balancing the bike, head tipped up, listening to the sound of the forest that filled in for traffic as the adrenaline ebbed and the reality of the decision she'd almost made hit hard.

Shame replaced frustration.

She'd finally reclaimed the happiness

she'd had when she and Bradford were last together, before fate had sucked them into a vortex of loss, yet even that wasn't enough to protect her from herself.

The surprise wasn't that she'd been willing to throw everything away on a two-foot margin of error. It was that she'd stopped before the wheel of chance had finished spinning. She might not be so fortunate again.

She'd been in one place, without purpose, for too long.

The phone in her back pocket vibrated.

Munroe glanced at the sky, still far too bright for Bradford to be headed home. She answered his call, oozing sugar into her voice.

"Hey, stranger," she said. "What's going on?"

"Have dinner with me tonight?" Bradford said.

"Oooh," she said. "You're taking me out on a date?"

"That would depend on if you can find a way to pencil me in."

"I might be able to work that. Is it a fancy-clothes night?"

"Your fanciest."

"What's the special occasion?"

"Do we need one?"

"Now you're being tricky."

"Is that a yes?"

"It's a maybe."

"What if I beg?"

"I'll accept groveling."

"I'll be home at eight."

She smiled. "See you at eight." She stared at the clock on her phone. So far out of the city, she'd have to push to get to the apartment in time. This was fate tempting her.

Munroe shoved the phone into her pocket and pulled the helmet on. Bradford had said another month or two until he finished this contract, but that was wishful thinking. The job would drag on indefinitely, and she could only last so long within the constraints of societal control that accompanied safe predictability, ignore so many of the same stares and glares and fake friendly smiles, visit so many temples and shrines, spend so much time bathing in ancient culture, touch the limits of nuance in flower arranging and so many tea ceremonies, before she lost her goddamn mind.

Munroe checked behind her and eased back onto the road, giving the Ninja speed slowly, holding back against the addiction that called her to open up again and hurtle, bike screaming, into peace. If Bradford's goal was to keep her alive until his job was finished, something was going to have to give.

It would soon.

And she'd come to wish she'd not been so careless with that thought.

DAY 1   7:30 P.M.

Munroe knew, even before she parked, that
something was wrong. The hints and whispers, like blank spaces on a cluttered canvas,
were in the posture of those who headed
out of the facility's front doors, in the way
they clustered in groups while walking for
the train, in the furtive steps they took, rushing for their cars, as if they shared a common fear.

Munroe pulled the Ninja as close to the
corner as possible, and with the bike rumbling, she called Bradford to let him know
she'd arrived.

She got his voice mail and hung up without leaving a message.

He'd been late before; slow to answer
before.

Half the windows in the facility reflected
the dark of empty offices. Security lights in
the parking lot blinked on in the evening
light.

Munroe called again, got Bradford's voice mail again, hung up again.

On another night she would have attributed the lack of response to an extended meeting or to the insane work hours that kept him late into evenings and over weekends. But tonight her instincts rose and the texture between beats of silence hinted at more.

The clock on her phone now said eight o'clock.

He'd asked her to pick him up at seven-thirty.

Munroe sent a text and with each passing minute of nonresponse, the slow roil of fear and uncertainty stretched higher, from deep down in the pit of her stomach, where the churning always started before bad news arrived.

She slid off the bike and stared in the direction of the facility's doors. Called Bradford again. No answer again.

Anxiety filled her diaphragm in anaphylactic response to the allergen of experience: a life in which those few she grew close to, that she dared to love, were inevitably torn from her by death's wretched breath.

Munroe left her helmet beside the one bungee-corded to the passenger seat and, on autopilot, strode for the doors.

At the security desk she asked for Bradford.

Instead of phoning, as was typical, the uniformed guards told her to step aside and wait, then conversed in hushed tones.

The roiling thickened, suffocating in its prescient awareness that fate had come to snatch away the one she loved once more.

The guards came to an agreement. They made a call and then, with false reassurance, told her the wait would be but a moment longer.

Munroe heard the hurried, shuffling footsteps and knew from the beat that they didn't belong to Bradford. Tai Okada rounded the corner, his face a guise covering agony.

He didn't sign for her, didn't request a temporary badge.

He motioned to the front doors and said, "Please, let's go outside."

Fight or flight instinct collided with itself, because in the moment she could neither fight nor flee, and she followed silently, treading water with every lurch, drowning in each forward surge.

Okada stopped ten or more meters down, the building to his back at the midpoint between two windows where there'd be less chance of being overheard. He brushed hair out of his eyes. He fidgeted, his hands seeking each other, then releasing again.

Munroe stared at him.

"The police came for Miles today," he said. "They took him."

The words filtered from his mouth into Munroe's ears, and on hearing them she almost laughed with a heady rush that made her dizzy with hope.

Bradford was still alive.

"Why?" Munroe said.

"A woman has been killed in the building. They say Miles killed her."

Elation dissipated into a vortex of convolution and error.

Given the life that Bradford had led, he wasn't an innocent man.

War made murderers out of honest men — proclaiming guiltless by law what the conscience would later bear in shame — but there was innocence and then there was innocence, and if Bradford had targeted a kill, then the body would have disappeared and the evidence scattered and never found.

Munroe took a step into Okada's personal space, forcing him to look up at her, and like a five-year-old on constant replay, she said, "Why?"

"They found the body this morning," Okada said. He stepped to the side, out from under her glare. "She was killed this morning, early."

The answer was a nonanswer, information without connection, but the hair on Munroe's arms rose in recognition nonetheless. Bradford had received an early morning call and because of that she'd taken him in an hour ahead of his routine. "Tell me everything you know," she said.

Gaze focused on the sidewalk, Okada said, "I cannot." He twitched with the nervous right-left of a man expecting to be caught, questioned, and accused. Munroe measured the unspoken.

If Okada had known nothing, or he'd had nothing more to offer, he would have framed his statement differently. She took a step back and then walked away.

Munroe waited down the street in the dark, watching the facility entrance and the parking lot as the hours ticked on and Okada's few sentences played a taunting torment inside her head. She drained the battery on her phone searching for an idea of what she might be up against if a murder charge was now her enemy.

She was killed this morning, early. They say Miles killed her.

The police came for Miles today. They took him.

Unless Bradford's phone had been confiscated the moment he set foot inside the facility, whatever happened had happened early enough that he could have called to warn her of the shit storm headed their way.

He could have called and asked her for help in getting a lawyer.

He could have called to let her know that he wasn't fucking dead.

In the dark she waited, poison spreading, until nearly midnight when Okada left the building. He took his time beneath the lights, finding his keys, unlocking the car, sorting through papers with the dome light on, before turning the ignition and pulling out onto the road.

Munroe didn't bother with stealth when she followed. She wanted him to know she was there in the same way he'd allowed plenty of time to ensure that she'd seen him. He drove carefully, yielding fully at intersections, stopping for yellow lights, driving at just the speed limit on the two-lane thoroughfare that led out of the city, hemmed in on both sides by seemingly solid lines of apartments and businesses, restaurants, shopping centers, wooden houses, and the occasional rice paddy, glaring in its anomalous luxury of comparably wasted space.

Okada turned off the main road, traveling along curves and hills, until at last he pulled over into a tight slice of gravel beside a *takoyaki* shack, its telltale octopus-embossed red-paper lanterns hanging dark and foreboding from the eaves.

Munroe remained on the bike while he walked to the vending machines, lit brightly against the night, and purchased and retrieved a drink.

He continued beyond the shack for the seating area.

She slipped off the seat and, helmet in hand, followed.

The fragrance of starch and oil and spices still hung in the air, and ambient light from the vending machines kept the screened-in porch, like the shack and the lanterns, from plunging into total darkness. She found Okada on the far end of the bench that lined the nearest of two picnic tables, staring at the can of beer resting between his hands.

He didn't look up when she sat across from him.

"Do you come here often?" she said.

She spoke in Japanese, absorbed over the past two months, as she had when she'd worked with him in Bradford's office, because information would flow easier if Okada didn't have to sieve betrayed confidences through the filter of a language he didn't speak fluently.

Eyes on the beer, he said, "My wife has family nearby. We come with the children for dinner sometimes. It's a quiet place and you can watch the road."

As if to make his point, a set of headlights lit up the shack in passing and then silence swallowed them again.

Okada took a long swig of Asahi, set the

can back on the table, and reached for a pocket. He slid a thumb drive in Munroe's direction.

"Surveillance footage," he said. "The body was discovered just after seven. The police were there by seven-thirty. They arrested Miles at eight and took him right away. You can see for yourself and make your own conclusions."

She'd dropped him off at seven.

"Do you know where Miles is?" Munroe said.

"No."

"Where was he when they came for him?"

"In his office, sitting at his desk."

"Just waiting for them to take him?"

Okada glanced up with the oddest smile — curious, not happy — and she took that as a yes and ran the numbers, the timing.

"Did he know?" she said. "Was he aware of the body?"

Okada's odd smile shifted into a stare of bafflement.

"Assuming he wasn't the murderer," Munroe said. "Did he know?"

"When the victim was discovered, he was also called."

"You were with him?"

Okada nodded.

"Step by step," she said, "describe his reaction exactly as you remember."

Okada brought the can to his mouth, took a long swallow. Then, staring at his hands, thumbnails tracing lines in the can's sweat, he said, "The stairway door was blocked open, there were already others in the stairwell. We walked down together to reach them and when we rounded the midpoint we could see the victim below. Miles stopped and stared at the body, then continued slowly. He knelt beside her and studied her, but didn't write notes or take any pictures. Then he stood, looked at me, said he would be in his office, and walked up and out."

"That was it? Just like that?"

"Yes."

Munroe said, "Who accused him?"

Okada glanced at the drive on the table. "There is evidence," he said.

"Evidence or not, the police arrested him almost immediately. For it to have happened that quickly in a building of several hundred potential suspects, someone had to have pointed them to him."

"I don't know," he said.

"Does anyone know?"

"Maybe."

"Can you find out?"

"It would be very difficult."

102

She let that line of thinking drop. In his very Japanese way he'd just told her no.

Okada said, "Have you known Miles a long time?"

"I know him better than most people."

"He's good at what he does?"

"Very," she said, and left off the part about what it meant to work private security in war zone countries.

"Most people at work see him as incompetent," Okada said. "He wasn't welcome, and that made him enemies."

"He's not incompetent."

"An illusion," Okada said, "also fueled by gossip and rumor, because his presence shames us, highlighting our failed effort. I was with him almost every day. I saw how he worked. Smart and very professional in a non-Japanese way." Okada's face rose to meet hers and, for the first time that evening, he made deliberate eye contact. "Maybe too professional," he said.

Munroe read through the implications, hating the dance of avoidance and Okada's inability to simply say what he suspected.

"You are also professional," Okada said.

"That what Miles told you?"

Okada looked out into the dark, his lips pressed together in a barely audible hum. "You know my position before Miles came?

My responsibility?"

Munroe shook her head.

"On-site security," he said. "That's my department."

"Which half is that?"

"He had a nickname for me. He called me Feeb, you know what it means?"

Munroe nodded. "You were demoted because of him?"

"Promoted," Okada said. "I did assistant work, but not as an assistant, more as a guide through the language and culture. In exchange I learned from him about how we might improve our operations, hands-on, daily learning. We talked often. Mostly work, sometimes personal things, you could even say like friends. That changed after you spent the day at the office. He told me you were very helpful, but he became private after that. It's not my place to say. I assume he learned something and was afraid to speak of it."

Munroe studied the table. Beneath the pocked and cigarette-burned plastic cloth her fingers picked and pulled at her cuticles while threads of betrayal wound between fear and confusion, pushing her toward anger. She'd offered Bradford her help. Every single day, begging for something to do, and without fail he'd turned her away.

Yet he'd used her that day she'd come to his office and never allowed her to know it.

She shoved against the hurt, trying to force the emotion into silence, but it wouldn't stay; she sought detachment and couldn't find it; she turned her thoughts toward Okada's implications, toward the unanswered questions, but they rebelled, running back injured.

Munroe exhaled imaginary smoke and studied an invisible point above Okada's head, then picked up the thumb drive.

"Thank you for this," she said. "Why take the risk?"

Okada emptied the last of the Asahi and tossed the can into a nearby garbage can. Without looking at her, without answering, he stood and returned to his car.

DAY 2   2:00 A.M.

Time passed in the dark while the poison thickened, and when at last sitting and stillness became their own destructive force, Munroe returned to the bike and then to Bradford's apartment. She'd expected to face a crime scene but found the hallway empty. Eventually the police would come, they'd have to come, violating Bradford's home in a search for motive and corroborating evidence, but she'd be gone by then.

She unlocked the door to quiet orderliness and the familiar fragrance of Bradford's cologne lingering in the air, mixing the surreal into something only half-true. Munroe shut herself inside, closed her eyes, and leaned against the door. Then slammed the back of her head into the metal frame.

The pain was distraction, a break from the denial and disbelief that threatened to swallow her whole. She'd spent years running from the hope of happiness because in emptiness she had nothing to lose. She'd stayed away from Bradford to protect him, and now, having finally given in and tasted peace, here they were again, unable to escape the orbit of loss.

Munroe crossed the hall for the bedroom and paused in the doorway, mocked by the unmade bed, the clothes on the floor, the armoire doors still half open as Bradford had left them, in a rush to get to work after that early-morning call: fate's cruel laughter at what was, and what wasn't, and what had possibly never been.

She grabbed the laptop from beneath the pillow and took the computer to the living room. She inserted the thumb drive and found surveillance footage as Okada had promised. She watched through multiples of what were mostly chronologically ordered viewpoints of the same thirty-minute time frame, but only when the body was removed from the stairwell did she begin to understand.

The victim was one of the Chinese women that Bradford had pointed out over lunch. Tightened around her neck, presumably the weapon that had killed her, was a belt that Munroe would have recognized at any distance, no matter how grainy the footage. She paused the clip and leaned closer, staring at the black-and-white pixilated strip of leather and gaudy buckle. She traced her thumb against the image, replaying what Okada had said, correlating Bradford's actions with what showed on-screen.

Bradford had known he was trapped from the moment he saw the body. Even if he'd run, he never would have gotten off the island, and running would have only confirmed his guilt. So he'd waited for the police to come.

And never called.

Munroe stood and, fists clenched, strode to the bedroom.

She threw open the armoire doors and tore through Bradford's things.

He'd obviously not been wearing the belt when he was arrested, but it wasn't here either. God, he would never be that stupid.

She slammed the doors and returned to the couch, closed her eyes and rubbed her palms over them. She walked backward through the days, attempting to account for the last time she'd seen the belt — a couple of weeks, perhaps — hating that she'd never thought to question where it was.

She went through the footage again, searching for clues in what remained invisible. The murder itself had taken place off camera: a body left behind with only the smallest glimpse of the killer's hand. Nothing available in the moments before or the moments after, no lead-in angles from other cameras that would give a view of who this person was, and the only way for that to have happened was for the footage to have been tampered with.

There was a limited number of people who had access to the security systems, but Bradford was one of them and she would place money on it having been his clearance that had accessed the files.

Munroe closed the computer and leaned back against the couch. She tilted her head up and stared at the ceiling.

A body, missing footage, and a unique murder weapon: These were clearly drawn lines pointing to only one guilty party, an intentional narrative that left no room for doubt or mistake, evidence laid out so neatly that it was *too* convenient.

Surely anyone who'd worked in law enforcement for any length of time would find this suspicious. Wouldn't they?

Munroe sighed and dropped her head to her knees.

That type of thinking was a made-for-TV melodrama.

This was Japan, not the United States, but human nature was universal. Arrest and prosecution were never as much about guilt or innocence as they were about belief, bias, and the potential for winning the case. Easy answers and ready-made culprits made everyone in the justice food chain happy, so why should this be any different just because it was Bradford? He was a foreigner in a highly xenophobic nation — worse, an American, from the country of perceived stupid, violent people — and he was a trained killer who'd taken life many times.

Munroe searched for calm, the reptile beneath the surface, the indifference that severed emotion from fact and allowed her to plot through morass and confusion, but the animal brain was sleeping. She swore and kicked the coffee table and set the laptop and the fruit bowl rattling.

This was not who she was or who she was meant to be.

Emotion was weakness. She'd known this. Lived by this. And yet had so stupidly allowed herself to fall, believing in the fantasy that in giving herself over to what terrified her, she might find peace.

Instead she'd grown soft and useless. Cut her own legs out from beneath her.

She stood and walked to the kitchen, ripped the notepad off the fridge, yanked the pen off its accompanying string, and as a way to force clarity, began to sketch. There were three certainties: an innocent man; a dead woman; and an emerging technology that the company was trying to protect.

If the woman's murder had *only* been intended as the ultimate silencing tool, or a theft prevention device, or a subterfuge for some other nefarious plan, it would have been far simpler and cleaner for the killer to dispatch her off-site and avoid whatever effort had gone into making Bradford the guilty party.

That made Bradford the target, and the dead woman a placeholder, and herself a bystander, helpless without facts.

Munroe drew the last of a line within a web of circles and set the pad on the counter, staring at the unknowns while the question that would answer all questions fed on them like a parasitic tumor.

Why?

Day 2   5:00 A.M.

In the dark, before dawn, Munroe left for
ALTEQ-Bio, detouring to approach from
the facility's blind side, and parked the
Ninja far down the road and out of sight.

She walked, scanning buildings and alleys,
and found her observation point on the
landing of an outside stairwell across the
street, three floors up. The sun rose. Cars
pulled into the lot at an increasing trickle.
Employees, converging on foot from the
nearest train stations and bus stops, entered
in straggling numbers. She searched for the
killer among them, the liar, the thief, who'd
reached a fist into the heart of happiness
and ripped it, beating, from her chest.

Tai Okada pulled into the parking lot
before eight.

Munroe gave him time, waited until the
workday was fully under way, and then left
her perch and crossed the road for the front.

At the guard desk she gave the uniform

her name, asked for Okada, and stood aside, breathing in the ambience: the smell of paper, ink, cleaning chemicals, and Bradford's absence. Through the eyes of a killer she traced the lines of the lobby, confirming cameras, gauging security, measuring the activity that passed through the area.

Even she, chameleon and strategist, would have never chanced bringing a dead woman into this building. The risk of being seen, or of being caught for a second at an odd camera angle that might be missed when deleting evidence, was too high. Whoever had murdered the woman had done the killing inside.

Okada arrived in wrinkled clothes, as if he'd slept in them or at least had tried. He nodded curtly, his expression unreadable and laced with lack of sleep, and without a word, signed for Munroe's badge, taking responsibility for her.

She followed him away from the desk, and when they were out of earshot, Okada said, "Why are you here?"

"This is the only place I can come for answers."

Okada remained rigid, which spoke of fear or anger, and he led her in silence across the wide entry to one of the halls and from there turned into a smaller hall. He opened the first door and motioned her into the tiny waiting area with its two chairs, forlorn coffee table, and a dusty fake ficus tree.

He closed the door behind them but didn't offer her a seat.

"There's nothing I can do to help," he said. Layered beneath the words was an undercurrent pleading to be left alone. "You shouldn't have come."

Munroe waved a hand toward the door. "The person who did this is out roaming free, Tai, in your building, under your nose, while you let your friend stand accused for a crime he didn't commit."

Eyes on the floor, in more whisper than voice, Okada said, "You'll cost me my job." His words were an explanation of the plea, because in this society employment was never just a job but the core of life and security and identity, and to lose his place was to lose face, and future, and hope.

"I need to see his office," she said.

Okada avoided eye contact. He shifted from foot to foot and then, as if he'd made a decision and had to move quickly for fear he'd change his mind, he reached into one of the folders he carried, pulled out a thumb drive nearly identical to the one he'd given her last night, and thrust it toward her.

Munroe took it from him cautiously.

"What's on it?" she said.

"Phone conversations," Okada said. "Noboru Kobayashi, my boss, head of all security, believes Miles Bradford was here working for the American military, to steal the same trade information that he was hired to protect."

"What does this have to do with the murder?"

"Maybe nothing. Maybe everything. Maybe this was a motive."

Munroe tucked the thumb drive into a pocket. Bradford would no more have discussed the company's trade secrets within a building wired to record every word and every movement than he would have provided the evidence to convict himself for murder.

"You knew I would come?" she said.

Okada whispered, "He told me you would."

The words wrapped around her chest, threatening to stop her heart. "You've spoken to him since his arrest?"

"In the days before," Okada said. He glanced up and met her gaze. "If something unexpected happened to him, eventually you would ask for me and I should do all I could to help you."

"I need to see his office," she said again.

"The police have already been there."

Munroe stayed silent, expectant. Okada relented. "If I do this, then you won't return again."

She didn't respond. He watched her, waiting, and when after a moment she still hadn't given him an answer, he opened the door, peered out, then motioned her through.

He led a doglegged roundabout route, and Munroe followed, mapping inside her head, searching out cameras until Okada stopped.

He waited, so she opened the door and faced an empty room — no desk or chairs, nothing but bare carpet and empty walls, as if the mere idea that Bradford had once been here was so offensive that it required obliterating all evidence that he'd existed.

"The police did this?" she said

"They took computers and papers."

"Where did everything else go?"

Okada shook his head: didn't know or couldn't tell.

Munroe stepped into the office, her eyes scanning the corner seams and tracking up the walls, her memory searching through e-mail conversations she and Bradford had shared, an effort to predict what might haunt them when the investigators combed through Bradford's correspondence.

116

Anything could be twisted and made to appear to be something other than what it was. How long, then, before she was hauled in for questioning? Maybe she was already implicated in whatever this was and the authorities simply hadn't found her yet to arrest her.

Munroe followed the edge of the room, checking the floor and finally the window frame. If Bradford had told Okada she would come looking, then there were things Bradford expected she'd find, but he wouldn't have stored them in the one location guaranteed to be searched.

The hair on her neck rose in animal awareness of being watched, that sixth sense of intuition that kept her alive and that she'd learned to trust without question a long, long time ago. She turned to Okada, who was staring at her from the doorway, and he averted his gaze.

Munroe walked to him and stood just a little too close.

Okada took a step into the hallway to maintain personal space and kept his focus just to her right.

"When he wasn't here," she said, "when he wasn't out wandering and talking to people and doing interviews, where did he spend the most time?"

"We did a lot of paperwork review in one of the conference rooms."

"I need to see it," she said.

He led her down the hall and around a corner to another room, slightly bigger. A conference table occupied most of the space, with six wide-back rolling chairs around it. A whiteboard filled the far wall. Narrow windows opened onto a view of the rear parking lot. As she'd done in Bradford's office, Munroe followed the walls, searching for anomalies and inconsistencies.

Finding nothing, she tugged the chairs away from the table.

Okada stepped into the room and shut the door.

Munroe crawled beneath the table and flipped onto her back. Flush against the decorative edge was a thin drawer. She closed her eyes and sighed, then ran her fingers around the edges, feeling for a crease or line or lock, found a small metal circle.

To Okada she said, "Did Miles leave you a key?"

Okada's feet moved from the door to the table, but he never knelt.

"He left me nothing," he said.

Munroe knocked one of the chairs over,

pulled off a caster, and hammered the pin into the drawer. Okada said something, but the noise drowned him out, and she pounded metal against wood until a corner loosened enough for her to get a finger wedged into place. She yanked hard. Wood split and bought her an inch.

She wiggled another two fingers into the space, wincing against a splinter, and pulled hard against tongue, groove, and glue. She caught the pieces before they hit her head, flipped onto her stomach, and dumped the contents on the floor: manila envelope, external storage drive, and a number of calendar sheets.

Munroe scooped everything back into what was left of the drawer and pushed it ahead of her, out the opposite side. She stood and then slid into one of the chairs. Okada glanced at her, then at the splintered drawer, and said, "I'll be back in a few minutes."

The door opened and closed.

Munroe shoved the drive into a pocket and opened the manila envelope. Inside was an English version of Bradford's work contract. She flipped it open to a marker on the sixth page and to a clause underlined and highlighted.

Munroe read, and then reread, legalese

that clearly stated that Bradford, as a security contractor, had the right to hire subcontractors of his own choosing — which explained, possibly, the security badge with Munroe's name and face clipped to the pages and the official-looking paperwork folded behind it.

Munroe leaned back and, without really seeing, stared at the wall.

Bradford could have hired her at any point in time, had even had a badge made and paperwork processed, and had never given her either. He'd seen this coming. *This.* He'd put this here for her to find. *This.* This fucking box with its fucking trove of access that said *Sorry I wouldn't let you work when you wanted it, but thanks for coming in to clean up my shit, I hope you can help me out.*

Munroe read the clause once more, and then the conditions under which the corporate heads could terminate any subcontracted arrangements, and then picked up the badge and angled it toward the light. The picture wasn't recent — it had been taken from Capstone Security files.

Everything was presented in her male persona.

Munroe drew in a deep breath and let out the anger.

Maybe he thought he'd be dead at this

point, not arrested, and had meant this as a way to provide answers when she came looking for them.

She flipped through the calendar pages, single sheets, printed off the Internet or from a calendar program, just blank dated squares into which he'd jotted occasional notes. She worked backward from the day of his arrest and hiccupped over a night, a few weeks back, one of several in which he'd said he'd had to stay late at work and had ended up sleeping at the office.

Sure.

If office meant *hostess club* with an address somewhere in Kitashinchi, Osaka's high-end nightlife area.

Munroe flipped to the next page, thoughts growing more vehement, searching for other nights he'd said he'd slept at the office and, according to these calendar entries, hadn't.

Hours that he could have spent with her — and hadn't.

Truths he could have told — and hadn't.

Munroe stacked the loose pages and shoved them, together with the security pass and the contract, back into the envelope.

He'd locked her out of a job that he'd clearly needed help with, had refused her help and used her anyway, had lied about staying at work overnight, had lied about

God only knew what else.

She kicked the chair beside her and it toppled over.

Okada opened the door and, seeing her face, stood for a long second, half in the room, half out, and then came inside and shut them in.

He put a bottle of tea on the table.

"If you're thirsty," he said.

DAY 2　　11:15 A.M.

Far down the street from the facility, in a slice of paid parking beside a *konbini,* where customers came and went and life rushed on with the steady pulse of city movement, Munroe pulled the helmet on, straddled the bike, and then just sat.

The contents of the drawer rested against her chest, zipped up in her jacket, bulky and uncomfortable, urging her toward action, toward answers, while inside, deep inside, where air should have been, and knowledge and assurance, was darkness so real it coated her lungs and bled out into her veins, tangible and physical.

She needed speed, movement, to cleanse her head of the fog. Needed the soothing of violence and pain to shove feeling into the background.

She closed her eyes.

Motion and aggression would only provide the illusion of doing something, anything, under the guise of controlling a situation that was chaos.

There was nothing here to control.

Air seeped into her lungs and she held the breath, allowing darkness to rise.

Despair.

This was the same pit that had swallowed her when those she loved had been tortured to control her, when she'd been forced to stand aside as they suffered, unable to save them. Despair. Because the man who had saved her life, who'd had her back, had turned around and stabbed her in it.

One moment to the next, reality, gone.

Munroe brought the bike to life. The machine called her to fly into the arms of fate and once more roll the dice of mortality. She crawled onto the street, staying beneath the speed limit, and followed the most direct route back to the apartment.

There were still no police, no investigators.

Munroe opened the door to an empty home that had once felt vibrant and alive in its emptiness and now screamed of abandonment. She carried Okada's newest thumb drive and the items from the broken drawer into the living room, dumped them on the coffee table, and glared down at them in a bad dream from which she couldn't wake.

She inserted the drive into the laptop.

There were five files — phone conversations, as Okada had said — text files consisting entirely of time stamps and English transcripts.

Without hearing the actual dialogue she couldn't know if one of the speakers was indeed Bradford, but even accounting for typos and misspellings it was clear that both participants were fluent in English military jargon. But there'd been no exchange of information or promise of such, only banter that referenced prior conversations and events in the veiled language of two people who knew they being were listened to.

Bradford had plenty of friends with military connections; that he was spying for one of them was an idea she would have aggressively rejected two hours ago. His lies and obfuscations forced her to reframe what she'd thought she'd known and now left everything open for debate.

Munroe shut the laptop. Didn't bother with the drive she'd taken from the drawer. None of it really mattered anymore.

She shoved the computer into a backpack and followed it with both of Okada's thumb drives and everything Bradford had left for her at the office. She went into the bedroom.

Pulled a couple of outfits off hangers, grabbed a few days' worth of essentials, and added them to the backpack. She took what she needed from the sink room and turned her back on the rest. Things only slowed her down, became chains to the past or chains to a place, and she wanted none of that.

She went back through the bedroom and home office for Bradford's things; took his watch, and the money stashed beneath the bed. She grabbed his favorite shirts and went through his valuables and papers, dumping anything of importance into a second bag. Didn't matter that he'd speared her in the gut; she wasn't going to leave anything behind that could be used against him.

She paused and stared at the drawer that held her knives.

She picked up the first and flipped the blade open. The handle was warm in her hand, an extension of her body, alive with its own will, as all knives were when they nestled against her skin. Hunting knife, fishing knife, combat blade, switchblade, fixed blade, and balisong, they were all the same: different weights, different needs, different force and movement, but always, the knife was alive.

Munroe flicked the blade closed and dropped both of them into Bradford's bag. She couldn't take them with her, anyway. In the *genkan* she put her boots back on, then stood and smelled the air and breathed in the last of this place that had been home. The memories burned at her, the happiness, the laughter — a fraud, a fake, all of it, none of it real because the man she'd shared it with wasn't real.

DAY 2   2:15 P.M.

In the airport arrivals parking garage, between a concrete pillar and a stairwell, Munroe strapped the helmet and Bradford's backpack to the Ninja's seat and abandoned them there. Eventually the bike would be towed — probably with the backpack and helmet still strapped to it, such was the level of honesty in everyday life here — and she would count the loss of the machine and the money she'd put into it as the price of a hard lesson learned.

She carried her own bag into the departures terminal, where wide de facto corridors were governed by ticket and check-in counters, and lines of passengers and luggage carts snaked between corded, winding pathways. A dozen airline logos lined up on either side like running lights on a bowling lane, and Munroe scanned signage, searching for a carrier that would get her direct to —

She paused and turned a full circle.

Dallas wasn't an option, not like this, with the wounds so fresh and raw; neither was a return to Africa, the continent of her birth, where the comfortable familiarity of living and working in despot-run dens of corruption would only loop her into a repeat of past mistakes.

Beneath the blue and red of Malaysia Airlines, the line had already begun to lengthen, which meant a pending departure. Munroe stepped in behind a luggage cart and followed the wheels, moving brain-numb and rote from ticket counter, to ticket in hand, through security, to the gate for a flight to Kuala Lumpur.

In the departure lounge she sat on the floor by the window, the afternoon sun casting shadows on her arms. Ear buds piped music in from her phone, drowning out the world enough that if she closed her eyes, she wasn't there at all, but still Bradford was inside her head, an innocent man with his calendar pages and notes and, most of all, the lies.

She shut off the madness, disgusted by her own hypocrisy.

His few lies, the little he may have used her, didn't even cover the entry fee into the games of deception and betrayal that she'd played. She'd told thousands and been told thousands — even by those she loved and trusted. Had filled years with manipulating others to achieve her goals, and sometimes been knowingly manipulated in turn so that others could achieve theirs. She'd allowed that. Had gone into the jaws of death as a tool for those she loved, knowing that they used her — and never cared.

And that was the point then, wasn't it? That she cared.

Bradford, in lying to her, in taking choice away from her, had done the one thing that no one else had yet managed.

Across from her a young couple, deep in conversation, leaned into each other over the armrest. Happiness was etched across their faces and oozed out of their pores so thick it created an aura.

Munroe blocked them out.

She'd been there; she'd had that. One minute to the next, it had been ripped away. She would have paid any price to keep it.

Could still pay that price.

In self-righteous fury she readied to throw everything away, to throw him away, to make the pain of love's betrayal stop.

Munroe tapped the boarding pass against her fingertips and weighed the ticket against never knowing what had happened in that facility, weighed killing her soul against abandoning the person she claimed to love most in the world, weighed a chance of having what might have been against allowing him to rot.

She stood. Picked the backpack off the floor, shut off the music, and began the long stroll out of the airport. Victimhood was unbecoming. Bradford's actions didn't control hers. She wasn't finished here until she chose to be finished.

DAY 2   5:28 P.M.

The entrance to the manga café wound up narrow stairs to the second floor of a four-story building, to a single room that took up the entire floor, where the lighting was dim, the ambience subdued, and two clerks in their late teens or early twenties manned the front counter. Beyond the entry, half the room was row upon row of head-height cubicles, the other half shelving that held magazines, books, and DVDs — enough manga and anime to satisfy every cartoon fetish known to man. At the back were smaller rooms with proper walls and doors, snacks and drinks, and showers and laundry facilities.

Munroe paid in advance for a twenty-four-hour stay and one of the clerks showed her to a numbered booth. She left her shoes in the hall, slid the door open to a tatami floor, and stepped inside a cubicle just large enough that she could lie down flat. It had been over thirty-six hours since she'd slept.

Manga cafés, not really cafés, were twenty-four/seven businesses, renting out space in expensive quarter-hour increments, providing solitude away from heat and cold and rain; places where those who'd missed the last train after a night out drinking could catch a few hours' sleep and clean up before the next daily grind, where students who lived at home with three generations of family could luxuriate in an escape from human contact for an hour or two, and where the creepy manga fetishist could get his freak on in private.

Munroe slid the door closed, sat on the futon, leaned her head back, and closed her eyes. Here, without the need to supply an ID, where there were no cameras, no security to speak of, and where she had unlimited access to the Internet without attaching her name to searches and queries, she could rest and figure out the next step. Here, for a time, a tall white foreigner could disappear.

She woke with a start, eyes burning, dazed for a heartbeat before she caught her bearings. She blinked back against the dryness, the reawakened nightmare, and checked the time on her phone: four hours of sleep.

Munroe pulled herself off the floor and angled for the low table, where a computer monitor, TV, DVD player, and game consoles all competed for precious tabletop real estate. She tapped the monitor to life and stumbled through nearly indecipherable clicks and links and succeeded in changing the settings to English. She needed to know, to understand.

She'd caught a glimpse two nights back, when she'd learned that Bradford had been arrested and had killed the battery on her phone waiting for Okada, of what it might mean if a murder charge was the enemy; knew that the investigators could detain Bradford for twenty-three days for each charge — longer if the prosecutor convinced the judge that there was good reason; knew that until formal charges came, Bradford had no right to legal counsel and even his own lawyer, once he had one, wouldn't be allowed access unless the investigators allowed it, and all the while he would be isolated and interrogated, and anything he said under those circumstances would be summarized and opined upon by the investigator whose words, however inaccurate or conflated due to language misunderstandings, would be treated by the court as if Bradford had said them himself.

The culture's shame-sensitive tendency to admit to wrongdoing made confessions an integral part of the process, but there were no laws to protect against coercion, nothing to regulate how long the interrogations could last or the methods used to elicit the confession. Torture and cruel treatment were common enough that human rights organizations decried the violations.

Munroe searched through papers written by foreign sociology professors, and found blogs and forums and firsthand accounts of foreigners who'd been through the Japanese legal system.

If Bradford was formally charged, and if he went to trial, the odds of winning were slight. Japanese prosecutors averaged a ninety-nine percent conviction rate. If it was presented as a capital case, he would face life in prison with relatively little chance of parole. A lesser murder charge might see him out in fifteen years, but Japanese prisons were not like American prisons where a man like Bradford, the Great White among a school of smaller sharks, could easily fend for himself. Incarceration in Japan, especially if attached to hard labor, was but a few rungs up from the prisoner-of-war camps of World War II.

Footsteps and whispers, rustled curtains and sliding doors, marked the passing of time as the day crowd shifted into night, and the voices beyond the thin divider grew drunker. Head pounding, Munroe slid back, away from the table, leaned into the futon, and allowed the thoughts to churn.

If she planned to save Bradford, hope lay with the prosecutor. The prosecutor's office ran on a tight budget and tended to only bring the most obviously guilty to trial. That's what they had now: obvious guilt. But throw the evidence into question, muddy the waters of inevitability, or find new evidence to make a conviction less certain, and perhaps Bradford could escape indictment. If she was to do this, she had twenty-three days to accomplish the impossible task of proving a negative. Twenty-three days to end this nightmare before it pushed forward to a trial and the best of Bradford's years were lost to the echoing halls of the forgotten.

Two days had already come and gone.

Bradford had been cut off from the world, and she needed to see him.

Family members could make visiting arrangements, and possibly a representative from the U.S. embassy. No friends, no acquaintances, certainly no *girlfriend,* but there were things to be said before she could shed the role of pissed-off lover and become his pissed-off avenger.

Day 3   7:46 A.M.

To advance irresistibly, push through their
gaps. To retreat elusively, outspeed them
— MASTER SUN TZU

Nonomi Sato passed through the stiles and
walked, head down, toward the elevator,
listening to the furtive hushed movement
within the company's morning song. Death
— murder — had so quickly deepened the
timbre.

The cowboy had been framed, fingered as
the guilty party, and his threat had been
removed, all of these actions adding instruments to the haunting melody of deception.
But beneath the suspicion and dread — she
could hear it now — flowed running notes
of doubt.

Not everyone believed in the cowboy's
guilt.

The beauty of fear, the beauty of social
control through judgment, was that that

thought would never be voiced. To rise above the collective soul, to raise an opinion that contradicted the accepted sequence of events, was to commit an honorless career suicide. No, the truth had died when the cowboy was led in handcuffs out the front doors.

The police had come, asking questions, bringing intense scrutiny that Sato would have much preferred to avoid, but the deed was done and she couldn't change that. The only thing left to her now was to contain the fallout.

She wasn't concerned. Not yet.

She continued to remain above suspicion, but like the running notes in the air around her, she, too, had her doubts. Doubts that the cowboy's departure was truly the end of the threat. Those who were skilled at the unorthodox, men who were worthy, men like the cowboy, were inexhaustible like great rivers. When they came to an end, they began again, and when they died, they were reborn.

And so it had been.

Another foreigner had shown up in the cowboy's absence, hunting, sniffing, and scouting. He'd arrived at odd hours, conspiring with Tai Okada, the cowboy's former accomplice. Sato hadn't seen this newcomer, but the rumors had reached her by the morning after the murder.

She suspected the man on the motorcycle, the faceless man behind the visor. The rumor said that the newcomer, unlike his predecessor, was not a man of strength or war but was long and thin, likely weak and easily intimidated.

There was no thrill to be found among the weak.

Only time would tell what this strange turn would bring.

Sato reached the elevator and handed the guard her badge.

A new guard, recently hired to replace Haruto Itou, the groper, the stalker, who had written to say he was sick and then skipped the next day and then another. His employer had never looked for him. By now his family would have begun to wonder.

Sato had driven him to the forest and seduced him up a path. Had settled him naked on a blanket, drunk and overdosing on a cocktail of pain medication and muscle relaxants, with pornographic magazines clenched in his hand. She'd stayed long enough to ensure that he'd stopped breathing.

Japanese culture, without a Judeo-Christian morality, held few sexual taboos.

Uncommon fetishes, yes: sex with young girls, sex with animals, sex with inanimate objects, sex with animate objects. Yet, somehow, strangely, homosexual sex was the unacceptable shame.

The Japanese had over a dozen words for suicide.

She'd seen to it that Haruto Itou had experienced one of them.

Sato passed beyond the elevator security for the cubicles. The new guard didn't grope her. With any luck he wouldn't try to follow her home, either.

Day 3   8:40 A.M.

Bradford had been married and divorced twice, though he claimed the second marriage, for only eight months, didn't count. Munroe followed the digital trail of that short-lived marriage through public records. She filled out online forms for a certified copy of his marriage certificate and hunted through searches until she found a specimen of what the real thing would look like, courtesy of an abandoned blog.

She tracked down a custom office-supply business in Thailand, her way to a forged county seal, and, on the chance that she'd be running multiple identities on multiple passports, included a scan of her passport's entry stamp so that she would have the means to create her own. The manga café became her residence for express shipping, her credit cards an unfortunate trail for expedited processing.

Five hours of hyperfocus and untold

broken laws had laid down those first steps, and now with nothing but time and questions, she straightened out body kinks and turned to the external drive Bradford had left in the drawer.

The café's computers had allowed her anonymity; her laptop, disconnected from the Internet, gave her privacy. Munroe rolled up the futon and stretched out on the floor. Head propped up on the cushion, she plugged in the drive and, with the computer balanced on her stomach, began the slow quest of perusing folders: personnel files, financial records — documents that Bradford likely had legitimate access to but didn't want anyone knowing he was scrutinizing, nothing personal or illegal.

Three sets of folders, titled 1one, 2two, and 3three stood out from the rest. Each contained five to twenty subfolders beneath, and each of those bore a name, two of which Munroe recognized from promotional material as C-level employees. The subfolders themselves contained material that had been downloaded and assembled from company files, presumably by Okada.

She sat up and scooted across the tatami for the desk. With her laptop on one side, and the café's computer on the other, she cross-referenced the folders' names with public information. Extrapolating from those that turned up hits, as best as she could tell, one set of the folders was comprised of members of upper-level management, the second most of the members of the security departments, and the third a selection of employees who worked in the lower-level labs.

By the time midnight rolled around and the subdued noises of the café had grown slightly louder, Munroe had found nothing to explain those nights when Bradford's words had said he was at the office and his calendar notes said he wasn't. She lay down and draped an arm over her eyes to block the room's low light.

The lies returned, and the months of conversations and interactions, prodding and searing like hot branding irons, casting doubt on every kiss and every promise. She knocked her head back against the futon in a physical attempt to make the roller coaster stop, yet couldn't sever the personal obsession from cold investigation.

Munroe pulled out the calendar sheets and went over them again, measuring every entry, every day, against the days she'd lived, the experiences they'd shared, the stories he'd told, the touches, the words of affection; judging and questioning, attempting to divine truth from obfuscation and growing angry in the process. Wary and guarded was who she was to the world, but not with him, and she hated him for having stolen from her that one small shred of trust.

DAY 4   8:37 A.M.

With a list of phone numbers in hand, Munroe left her temporary haven for the outside, where the day had already long begun and the remnants of rain that had fallen in the night had thickened into weighted humidity.

Here, the streets were wider than where the apartment stood, and the sidewalks were actual sidewalks. Tucked out of the way of foot traffic, she dialed the first of the numbers that, for the sake of privacy and her desire to be able to speak freely, she couldn't dial from within the café.

An hour of calls and many lies led her to the facility in which Bradford was held, and the confirmation that he was there and he was alive, such a small connection to him, brought both agony and relief.

The marriage certificate was the first package to arrive. Clock ticking on a booth that she kept paying for, Munroe left for the train station and found an electronics store nearby, where three tightly packed floors of cameras, TVs, computers, and gadgets put American big-box retailers to shame in the way a Swiss village cheese shop trumped a Walmart deli counter.

In the camera section a question she posed to the first employee seemed to transfer of its own accord through tiny huddles of conspiracy and finally netted her a phone number for a photography studio. A call provided walking directions and Munroe found the place just down the road, four floors up a narrow stairwell, with a coffee shop, hair salon, and restaurant stacked like LEGO blocks beneath it.

The door led into a single room, the entry separated from the studio by a long, tall glass-topped counter that held a display of urban photography. At the far end of the room, a woman glanced up. In flawless English, she said, "Can I help you?"

Munroe pulled Bradford's marriage certificate from the envelope. "I need a document photographed," she said. "We spoke about thirty minutes ago."

"Oh," the woman said, and then, as if the surprise had escaped her lips before she'd had a chance to censor, she smiled slightly

147

and said, "Your Japanese is very good. I didn't realize you were a foreigner."

"Your English is good, too. California?"

"Oregon. Went for college and married instead."

"You miss it?"

The woman reached for the document and Munroe handed it to her. "Sometimes," she said, "though I don't miss my ex." She tilted the paper against the light so that the watermarks showed. They were what had turned getting a quality digital copy into more than a visit to a scanner.

"This shouldn't be too difficult," the woman said. "I need to set up the equipment — maybe a half hour or so."

Munroe left for the restaurant a few floors down, another little box with a countertop that ran parallel to a windowed wall, the accoutrements of a kitchen behind the counter, and lounge-style seating filling what was left of the space.

She ate without tasting, without enjoyment or appetite, pork cutlet — *tonkatsu* — and rice and cabbage, satisfying a need for protein and a semblance of nourishment because her brain required fuel. When the food was gone and an hour had passed, she collected her prize from the studio upstairs and returned to the manga café.

Altering the digital file would have been easier if the available software had been in English, but eventually, pixel by pixel, Bradford's ex-wife's name became Munroe's. A quality print on heavy-weight paper cut down to letter size created a replica so near to the original that only the absence of watermarks separated fake from original, with nothing to indicate that watermarks had originally been there.

The seal arrived by special delivery in the afternoon and its embossing became the texture of the lie. On such short notice and without connections, the forgery was as close to the real thing as Munroe could get. She ran her fingers over the raised seal, closed her eyes, and breathed in the illusion.

The marriage certificate was a prop, a way to satisfy bureaucratic expectations. Far more important was her ability to play the role ordained by the paper and so become what those with the power to say yes expected to see and no one thought to question the paper's provenance.

She needed one visit, only one. If she failed to acquire that, if the officials insisted on verifying the document before letting her in, then even she, as Bradford's best hope, wouldn't be enough to fix this mess and he was already lost.

DAY 5   10:00 A.M.

The taxi pulled off the street and Munroe, in the backseat, leaned down to see through the window, up the three-story concrete square that housed the precinct police station. The structure was separated from traffic by asphalt and parking on two sides and hedged in by taller, less blocky buildings on the others. There were few windows and no easy unconventional access, and somewhere behind those walls, on one of those floors, was the man she'd schemed to see while the days to his indictment clicked steadily onward.

Without knowledge of the enemy or of what Bradford may have already said, if he'd said anything at all, she could only pretend to predict the consequences of every word and action, so she'd come alone, without the pretense of an interpreter, willing to face whatever questions and accusations might later arise if her fluency was forced to surface.

The taxi stopped just shy of the entrance and Munroe paid the white-gloved driver. The passenger door swung open on automatic hinges and she stepped out, into midmorning heat, onto the doorstep of the belly of the beast.

Munroe pushed through the lobby doors, wedding ring on her finger, the modest dress on her frame, makeup heavy on the feminine, and papers stuffed into an enormous purse that she'd picked up at a boutique in the nearby shopping arcade. The interior was a cool contrast to the stickiness outside, relatively quiet, textured, and fragranced with standard open-floor-office air.

There were no uniformed officers that she could see.

No indifferent desk sergeant, burned out by a never-ending chain of human misery; no rank smells; no coughing, sniffling, dull-eyed bodies filling the few seats that lined the nearest wall; no radio background noise and incessant ringing phones; and no relatives and friends waiting with stress and fear and defeat etched into every movement. Instead, paper- and computer-cluttered desks were sandwiched in on one another end-to-end and corner-to-corner behind a wall-to-wall counter, while nonuniformed clerks went quietly about their work.

One of the women stood when Munroe reached the counter.

Munroe said, "I'm here to see my husband."

The woman smiled the earnest smile of helpful nonunderstanding and slid a laminated sheet onto the counter. She brushed a hand across the page with an encouraging nod, inviting Munroe to point to the problem.

Cartoon drawings illustrated varied emergencies: I'm lost. I've been robbed. I'm hurt. I've been in an accident. Munroe shook her head and raised her wrists together in the universal sign of handcuffs. *"Gaijin,"* she said. She pointed to the ceiling and then to the floor. "He is here." Then she pointed to the gold band on her finger. "I came to see him."

The mental gears clicked and the woman said, "Ehhh." She turned to her deskmate. *She's here to see the foreigner. She is his wife, maybe.*

No visitors for him without approval, the deskmate said. *Call for Mori-san, he should be the one to handle things.*

The woman turned back to Munroe. "Yes," she said in English. "Seat, please." She motioned toward the chairs with a polite smile and courteous bow.

Daichi Mori arrived several minutes later, stepping out from behind a door that had appeared to belong to an office but which, from the force with which he pushed through, had more likely connected to a hallway. He was a man in his early fifties, short and stocky, dressed in impeccably pressed civilian clothes, with thick wild eyebrows and a permanent scowl that hung deep into drooping jowls.

Munroe stood when he approached, stuck out a tremulous hand, and pushing a quiver into her voice, she said, "Detective Mori?"

"Captain Mori," he replied, his English lightly accented. He wore an air of unquestionable authority, but his voice was soft and his demeanor gentle.

He stared at her outstretched hand as if disgusted by the idea of touching it, then shook it gingerly. Munroe drew in a nervous breath and brushed strands of hair away from her tear-rimmed eyes. "My husband is missing," she said, and her voice quivered again. "I'm told that he's been arrested and that I can find him here. I don't know what's happened, but I have to see him, please can you help me?"

Mori held her gaze and Munroe pleaded in silence, desperate and hurting, while he sized her up. She'd come prepared to segue into tears, then hysterics, and if those failed, to quote chapter and verse of local laws to prove that she knew her rights — few as they were — and to dig in her heels with threats of publicity and noise, refusing to leave until she was able to see her husband. But Mori motioned a hand toward the counter and said, "There is some paperwork."

He walked with her, then stood beside her long enough to give a round of instructions to the clerk, and when he turned to go, Munroe held up a plastic bag. "I have clothes and hygiene items," she said. "I was told that these are things he's allowed to have."

"We will have to inspect them first," Mori said. He nodded to the woman again and another set of forms made its way onto the counter.

Munroe filled out papers written in a language she couldn't read, and the red tape and formality consumed an hour — certainly long enough for the station officer to contact the prosecutor's office to inform them of her arrival and allow official objections to put an end to hope. But the opposition never came and in the end the marriage certificate was an afterthought, necessary only because the last name on her passport didn't match Bradford's.

A young officer arrived to take the items in the plastic bag, assuring Munroe that they would get to their intended recipient, and shortly thereafter another led her from the front and down an empty hall to a small room, where she was required to leave all personal belongings before continuing on.

The visitation area was a box of a room with institutional paint, one institutional chair, and a wall interrupted by a single plexiglass window. Munroe took a seat in front of the rectangle where a series of holes were drilled below mouth level. Bare walls and an empty chair faced her on the other side.

The young officer who'd escorted her in stood to the side, a few feet to her left, in no apparent hurry to go anywhere, and she waited in silence for several long minutes, counting the time in her head because there was no way to keep track otherwise. And then a flash of movement and color caught her eye, a reflection of a reflection on the other side of the plexiglass, and a moment later Bradford was in front of her, hair greasy, eyes bloodshot above dark circles, wearing the same clothes she'd last seen him in, now dirty and wrinkled.

He sat across from her, separated by the window, and he smiled a sad, sad smile.

Day 5   11:32 A.M.

Seeing Bradford, seeing him like *this,* hurt, and Munroe hated that she hurt. He leaned forward and, his voice hoarse, full of disbelief and abandoned hope, said, "Thank you for coming."

She matched the smile. "It's a pretty pickle you're in."

Bradford sighed and she could read in his exhaustion the desperation that came from having been cut off from real life with no way to communicate, no way to know if anyone knew where to find him or if they'd even try, and the caution of knowing that anything they said here would be interpreted, possibly reworded, and used against him.

They sat quietly for a long while, as if neither of them really knew where to start. "I didn't," he said finally.

"I know," she said.

Bradford rubbed a hand over his eyes and

then dragged his palm across several days'
worth of stubble. "How bad is it?" he said.

"You need a really good lawyer."

Lips pressed together, he glanced off to
the side.

"I've already called the local U.S. consulate," she said, "as well as the embassy in
Tokyo. I'll contact your office once I get out
of here today — I didn't want to call them
until I had something worth saying. I know
someone who used to work with the David
House Agency and I've put out some lines
to see if this is something that meets their
criteria." She paused. "If you've got any
strings worth pulling, they'd certainly be
useful now."

"Whatever strings I have, the office will
know how to utilize," he said. "What's the
David thing?"

"International crisis resource organization.
They take on cases where geopolitics and
corruption make getting justice a difficult
thing. At the least they might be able to
make sure you don't get screwed over by
your local lawyer — whenever you get one."

Bradford stared at the ceiling and the
silence ticked on, and then he searched her
face in the way of a starving man looking
through to the diners in a restaurant window. "Is it fixable?" he said.

"You lied to me," she mouthed. And then, voice barely loud enough to carry through the drilled holes, "You shut me out when I desperately needed the work and then used me anyway. You knew I'd go looking," she said. "That's what burns me most of all, you and your Easter eggs after the fact when I was there all along. I begged you, Miles, every fucking day, going crazy with boredom while trying to play happy and domestic."

Bradford's eyes closed in a long, slow blink. She wanted him to argue, to contradict, to tell her she was wrong and give her a reason to fight with him and lash out, but he only offered silence. "I waited out these months for you," she said, "for us — for love — out of hope of what better things could be. You knew what it meant, and in return you gave me lies and stole what I would have given you freely."

Bradford put his fingertips to the glass and his mouth opened, though it took a half-second for the words to form. "It wasn't like that, Mike," he said.

"No?" she said. "Then tell me what it *was.*"

"You *know* what it was. Trying to give us a chance, same as it's always been."

Her eyes cut toward the officer. "*This* is giving us a chance?"

160

"I had no idea it would become this."

"Don't play semantics. You knew something was going down."

"Nothing I could lay out logically, nothing I could point to."

"Fuck that," she said. "I was right there, every single goddamned day, right there, begging, enduring, and you knew, Miles, you knew! And then you left a nice little parting gift when it was too late to do a fucking thing about it."

Bradford shook his head, wearing that same sad smile. "That's not what it was, not what it looks like."

"So you keep saying, but you've said a lot of things, haven't you?"

"Dammit, Mike, yes, I knew what it cost you. I wanted to give you what you wanted. That's why I put things in motion, processed the paperwork."

"And then just let it sit there while the world burned down?"

He put his other hand to the glass, both of his palms pressed in toward her as if he would have reached out and held her and buried his face in her neck. He said, "You think that was easy? You think I didn't hurt every damn day I went into that building without you, wondering if this would be the day you'd had enough and got up and walked away again? You think saying no was fun? I'm trying to keep you alive, Mike, I'm trying to keep *us* alive. What kind of hypocrite does that make me if the moment I think my own ass *might* be on the line, I'm suddenly willing to risk yours again? I'd rather die than put you in that position."

"That wasn't your fucking choice," she hissed. "You had no right to control my decisions by withholding the truth. You'd rather die? *This* is death, and I would've given anything to keep it from happening."

"*I* would've done anything to keep it from happening. You think I knew? Things got . . ." Bradford paused. "Things were . . ."

She crossed her arms. "Complicated, you said."

"For God's sake, Mike, I'm not an easy man to take down, you know that. Not after twenty years of staying alive while people around me were blown to hell. I had this. I figured whatever came at me, would be more of the same ol', same ol', not this underhanded bullshit."

"But you sat and waited for them."

"Of course I did. This isn't Afghanistan. Different sandbox, different rules. That was the only way to fight it, and you know it. You would have done the exact same thing."

"No, I would have fucking called you."

"Michael," he said, his voice low, chiding and knowing, full of protective pain. "I call you, you show up — and you know you would have — and that makes you an accomplice and buries you in the same shit I'm in."

Munroe glared.

Bradford stopped. "You're right," he said. "I should have called. But would you have, had the roles been reversed?"

His question ground the conversation to silence. She would have done the same as he — tried to distance him, protect him just as he had her, and he would have been just as angry as she was now. Munroe shifted back into the chair and straightened her legs. Bradford's fingertips remained pressed against the glass.

She felt his hurt inside her chest, as if her own heart had been squeezed and wrung, as if it had been she who'd spent the last four nights unable to sleep, believing quite possibly that what she'd tried to hold on to had abandoned her for good. She wanted to reach for him, to comfort him and make things better, but that just made her mad and so she stayed where she was, arms crossed, glaring at the small ledge beneath the window. Finally she said, "How long have you known? How far back does this go?"

"As far as I know, the day I got there."

He paused, as if he'd left the sentence unfinished. She looked up and met his eyes. He said, "You see atrocity and you think of me, you know it?"

The belt, the murder weapon.

"Yes," she said.

"Maybe two weeks on the Easter egg squares —"

Information left on the calendar sheets.

"It'll flow from there like Chutes and Ladders —"

Follow the trail.

"You have the jewelry box?"

Have you looked at the external drive?

"I tried on the three pendants," she said. "They don't fit."

"That's all I had, all I could afford. You might have to take it back to the store. I left you the receipt."

"Yeah," she said. "I've gone back to look at a few pieces but haven't had a chance to go shopping."

Another beat of silence.

"I didn't know, Mike," he said. "Not like this."

"You should have told me from the beginning."

"In hindsight I see that."

She waited, then said, "Remember what I told you in Argentina? Back when Logan and his friends were using me to get what they wanted — when you begged me to stop because you thought the risk was too high?"

"Choice," Bradford said, and he searched her face. "You chose to let them use you, knowing it might be the end."

"We've come around full circle," she said. "I'm here now because I choose to be, not out of some sense of duty or obligation or even because I love you, but because untangling these types of puzzles is what I fucking live for."

Bradford glanced down and, lips pressed together again, he traced a finger in random patterns on the counter that edged out on his side. Finally he said, "Never mind the big picture. Are *we* fixable? Can I undo what I've done?"

"I don't know," she said.

Pain etched in his facial creases. He sat back and sighed, then nodded and went back to the previous subject. "What about the current situation?"

Munroe jutted her chin toward the glass, the walls. "Have you said anything?"

He shook his head.

"They won't stop."

"There's nothing to confess," he said, but he said more with his eyes and his expression than he did with his words and in everything he left unspoken he told her that he knew how the system worked and that he would hold out against the worst of it.

"Then maybe," she said. "Possibly. I haven't looked at it hard enough yet to know what can be done, but if it is fixable, the fixing won't be free."

Bradford smiled again, that sad, sad smile, and with his focus drifting back down toward the counter, he shook his head again. His pride would never allow him to articulate it, so Munroe answered the question for him.

"Logan used me, but I didn't go to Argentina to save *him,*" she said. "That's what makes this different. I'll do everything I can to save you, Miles, but I won't do it for love. You want me to work? You want out? Pay me."

"I'm kind of between a rock and a hard place here, Mike — it's not exactly like I can say no, no matter how fucked up that is."

"You can say it," she said.

"That's how it is, then? One bad turns deserves another, and either I succumb to blackmail or you leave me here? Abandon me? Will that make us even?"

She crossed her arms and he glared at her and she glared back.

"Look, you can hate me now," she said, "I don't care. There'll be plenty of time later for hurt feelings and licking wounds. I prefer pissed off and angry, anyway."

"Michael," he said. He put his hand to the window again. "I'm genuinely, from the bottom of my heart, sorry. Sorry for thinking I knew what you needed more than you did and not giving you work when you asked for it. Sorry for not telling you there might be storms on the horizon. Sorry for putting you through this." He tipped his head in the direction of the officer who'd remained standing on his side of the wall. "I thought I was doing the right thing, but I was wrong and you deserved better."

"Stop," she said. "I don't want to hear it."

"Tell me what you want to hear and I'll say it."

"I want you to write the goddamn check so I can go to work."

"You're being an asshole."

"I'm very good at that."

"This isn't you, Michael. This isn't who you are. Not to me."

"These past few months?" she said. "The lies, the stolen moments and stolen choices while I tried to change who I was for you — for us — was that *you*?"

Bradford's eyes wandered over her shoulder, toward the officer behind her. Voice distant and hollow, he said, "When you contact the office again, tell Walker the score. She can make sure you're compensated."

"Give me your authorization codes."

"What? You want a blank check?"

"You want to rot in here for the next twenty years? You know what I'm worth."

"I don't have *that* kind of money."

Munroe shrugged. "What's the rest of your life?"

Bradford's expression hardened. He'd run the full gauntlet from sorrow to pain to anger. "Tell Walker I said to put it all on Armageddon."

"I'm not coming back until this is over," Munroe said. "There are no do-overs, no opportunities to clarify things, so you'd better be sure she'll understand exactly what that means."

"I know it's hard given the way things are," he said, "but please, a little trust."

"Okay," she said. She stood to go. Business was done, that's what she'd come for.

Half out of his chair, Bradford pressed both palms to the window. "Michael," he said. "Please, not yet."

Munroe paused, then sat again, and Bradford did, too. He drew a long breath. "There are a million things I wish I could tell you, so much I wish I could undo. It plays in my head over and over, the little choices, the what-ifs, the smallest things that might have made a difference. I miss you," he said. "If I could rewind and do things differently, I would, but I can't. All I can do is hope you're able to figure it out. Maybe at least then you'll understand that my intentions were good and that even in the lies I never meant to hurt you. None of that matters now, but I wish you could know it."

Munroe gritted her teeth. She didn't want him to beg, didn't want him to suffer, and didn't want an apology, either — it was easier to feed the monsters from a place of rage. His earnestness tore at her, shredding resolve.

She placed her hand against the glass, lining her fingers up against his, aching for the touch that had once been, separated by an inch of material that might as well be an ocean and a lifetime.

Given the circumstances, it might truly be a lifetime.

Bradford leaned nearer and she did, too, and his eyes traced over their fingers and then up to her eyes. His expression, tightening as if he had no voice and only the agony of failure, ripped the heart right out of her.

There were no words for good-byes like this.

Bradford whispered, "Always."

Munroe closed her eyes and smiled his sadness.

This might be the last time she saw him. Ever. And the things she said today might be the last words from her he heard and carried. Even the anger and the sting of betrayal, the confusion and disorientation that had stained and sullied the memories of every moment they'd shared to now, wasn't worth the future regret of never having said what she needed him to know.

"Maybe one day you'll understand, too," she said. "I never meant to hurt you." She put two fingers to her lips and then pressed them to the glass. "Always," she whispered back, "I love you." And then she stood, and before he could respond, she walked away.

DAY 5   4:16 P.M.

Munroe left the precinct station on foot and wandered the streets to clear her head and to shed the emotion of the visit until the evening drew on and the sun had set and then she returned to the manga café, where she'd left her things burning money by the quarter hour. The cubicle haven had served its purpose and now it was time to move on.

Far, far down the street, in the parking area where she'd left it, Munroe strapped Bradford's backpack to the Ninja's rear sliver, slipped the straps of the other over her shoulders, and started the engine. She rode the streets away from the café and the apartment, following a zigzag toward AL-TEQ, keeping to the main thoroughfares and doubling back along roads that ran parallel to train stations until she found a business hotel that fit what she wanted.

The building was ten stories, narrow as

most buildings were, and at the grungy higher point of the low-end, with a clean and brightly lit lobby minus security cameras and overattentive desk staff.

Munroe filled out the requisite information card using a false name and false local address, claiming to be a resident. Only foreign visitors were required to show their travel documents and if speaking fluent Japanese didn't convince the clerk she lived there, nothing short of an ID would. Had he argued, insisted on seeing her passport, she would have left and tried again elsewhere. Rules were rules, but polite unwillingness to be confrontational made enforcement hit or miss.

He handed Munroe the key and she carried the helmet and backpacks up to a room that was small, even by hotel standards, with a solid molded-plastic shower and sink to act as bathroom and barely enough space to walk between the desk and the double bed.

Munroe closed the curtains, adjusted the thermostat, set an alarm, and tumbled into oblivion. She woke four hours later and booted up her laptop.

International calls were easy enough with a wi-fi connection and voice-over Internet app, but the extreme time zone difference was an issue. Her darkness was Dallas's daylight and the clock in Osaka was just now heading toward ten at night.

The phone at Capstone Security Consulting rang twice and then a male voice she didn't recognize answered with the baritone smoothness of a Madison Avenue advertising firm, belying the bullets-and-blood outfit Munroe knew the business to be. "This is Michael," she said, "calling from Japan for Sam Walker."

"You're with?" he said.

"She knows who I am. Put me through and tell her it's an emergency."

The line clicked over to Beethoven's Ninth and Munroe pressed her thumb to the bridge of her nose, waiting for a conversation that she really, really, really didn't want to have. There was history here, most of it left unspoken, all of it better left untouched.

The line picked up and Walker said, "Michael?"

Munroe searched for ice in the tone, for bitterness or anger, and didn't find them. "Sorry to barge in on your day," Munroe said. "Have you heard from Miles at all in the past couple of weeks?"

The line filled with a pregnant pause and then Walker said, "I thought he was with you."

Munroe sighed at the nonanswer answer.

For anyone else she would have continued with argument and manipulation, but for the woman who wore scars and a permanent limp because of an explosion that never would have happened if not for her, for the woman whose intermediate lover had picked up and moved across the world to play house with her, Munroe had only the dance of avoidance and the game of guess-who-knows-what. "Miles was arrested for murder a few days ago," she said. "He's being held at a local detention center."

Another long pause filled the line, and in that pause was the answer to the first question: Bradford hadn't called the office to notify them of his pending arrest any more than he'd notified her.

Finally Walker spoke. "Objectively," she said, "how bad is it? What are we looking at?"

"Personally, I think it's a hit job," Munroe said. "It's not good. There's plenty of evidence to convict him. He's going to need a lawyer and he's going to need someone to run interference for him. I've already notified the embassy, and there's an international organization that deals with these types of situations but they have to be retained through legal counsel and I can't take care of that. He said if any of his friends could help pull strings, you'd know who they were and what to do."

There was another pause and Munroe could hear the whispered swearing. Walker already had her hands full managing the gunpowder-and-testosterone-fueled company while Bradford was away, but he would come before the company — he *was* the company — and for Walker, too, this was personal.

Munroe spared her from having to beg for details.

"I don't know anything more than what I'm telling you," she said. "I was able to get in to see him — he's holding up okay — but with everything recorded, there's not much we could discuss. He knows I'm making this call. I need to know who he was talking to at the Pentagon."

Walker said, "He was doing what?"

Munroe listened past the words for the tone; wished it was possible to see Walker's face, to read her body language. Information was only as good as its source and this source had motive aplenty for holding back pertinent details. She said, "The accusations from within are that he was using his position as security contractor to turn around and sell what he learned to the U.S.

military or military intelligence."

"That's absurd. You burn that kind of card in this industry and you never get another client."

"I agree," Munroe said. "And Miles didn't have access to any data worth stealing or selling, but that's beside the point because he *was* talking to someone about *something.* I've read the transcripts."

"Taking your word for it," Walker said. "I'll have to dig through his files and see who I can turn up — gonna have to get back to you on that."

"Add another to your list," Munroe said, "and this I need ASAP. You have access to Miles's e-mail, his phone logs. I need the person on this end who contacted him, the one who set up the approach for the contract."

"Approach was through an intermediary," Walker said, "one of Miles's longtime acquaintances, but the name won't be on file anywhere — standard precaution to protect the sources from blowback."

"You know who it is?"

"If I did, I couldn't tell you. Nondisclosure agreement and all that, but he's vetted."

"Then I need the someone who handled things on this side of the intermediary. There's going to be a record somewhere of conversations before the initial meet — contract negotiation notes, e-mails, whatever."

"Hang on," Walker said, and in the silence, Munroe closed her eyes again and pressed her fist into her forehead, counting long, deep inhales that muted the need for action, for movement. The rustles that came over on the line hinted toward opening drawers, fingers against a keyboard, and shuffling paper. When Walker returned, she said, "I've got a Nakamura-san and Tatsuo Nakamura."

The names were variants for the same person; Munroe recognized him from one of the folders on Bradford's external drive. "Are there any notes?" she said. "Observations? Personal opinions?"

"Nothing that seems worth mentioning. I can scan and e-mail copies if you think it matters."

"It matters," Munroe said. "I'm going to find a way to get him out, Sam, and bring him home — legally if I can, by other means if I can't — but my involvement comes with a two-hundred-thousand-dollar price tag."

"You can't be serious," Walker said, and this time the spite was there.

"I'm very serious," Munroe said, "and that's a discounted rate that doesn't account for expenses. You can hate me later. He said to tell you to put it all on Armageddon."

"Fine," Walker said, and she spit out the word, venom dripping. Munroe didn't begrudge its presence. If anyone had a legitimate reason to hate her, Walker did, and so much more now that this discussion of money and payment had come as a result of her helping Bradford.

Munroe ignored the bite, wouldn't be baited.

Explanations and apologies, if there were to be any, could come later.

"I have contracts in Miles's office," Munroe said. "They shouldn't be difficult to find. The language and terms are standard and nonnegotiable, but you'll have to fill in the blanks for the fee and the contract length, which is three months from tomorrow. If I haven't fixed things by then, extra time won't matter. Wiring instructions are included in the contract. I need you to sign that, e-mail it to me, and I'll get you a countersignature. I start work when the money arrives."

"And if the money never arrives?"

"That's not your decision to make," Munroe said.

"That wasn't my question."

"That's my only answer," Munroe said,

and she disconnected.

In the resultant silence she stared at the laptop screen.

In Bradford's eyes, in Walker's, to the rest of the team at Capstone, her demands were indefensible. Twice Bradford had put his work, his company, his team, on hold to cover her ass when she was falling into the abyss. He was there to pull her out when self-medicating seemed to be the only way to keep the nightmares at bay. He was the one who'd risked everything to save her life and the lives of her loved ones nine months later when death came knocking again. And the same explosion that had nearly killed Walker had taken the life of Bradford's best friend.

Because of Munroe.

They had suffered, all of them had suffered, because of her.

To them, this demand for payment to do what they had done willingly, unquestioningly, out of loyalty and devotion, was nothing more than a mercenary knife in the back, a middle finger in the air as a way to say thanks: the very opposite of leave no man behind. Munroe had no desire to defend herself or to try to make them understand.

She and Bradford were two fucked-up

people who'd had no business playing at love, and yet they had, and that love had been real. In giving in to happiness, she'd let go of the anger and rage that had driven her hard; in accepting what it meant to love, she'd put the predator to rest, and in its place a foreign thing had risen, soft and weak, full of easily hurt feelings and self-righteous indignation. There was either happiness or brutality; love or anger; laughter or the driving need to win. She couldn't play it both ways and be any good at either.

This was the only way that she could help him.

Munroe shut the laptop and breathed through to nothingness, drawing back to what she'd been before Bradford, back to the time and place when being the lone operative had been enough: shut off, focused entirely on work, on the adrenaline of the hunt, on doing what needed to be done.

The moment the money hit her account, the link between love and work would sever. She would have a client, a job, a history of success to defend, and an obsessive passion that would compel her to succeed or die trying. The moment the payment hit her account, the apex predator would rise from hibernation.

To be saved, Bradford needed the predator.

She hadn't demanded payment to purchase Bradford's freedom.

She'd made the demand to sell her own.

Kitashinchi, the high-end nightlife and drinking district at Osaka's heart, was what most people envisioned when they thought of Japan: a maze of narrow, pedestrian-crowded streets with building facades covered in neon signs of every shape and color. This was where the rich and the beautiful and the weird and the exotic collided, and the party raved the long night through in clubs and restaurants and bars and all manner of dens of iniquity, yet always in the best of taste.

Munroe came to the end of a block, glanced at the address she'd written down from Bradford's calendar and the hand-drawn lines she'd copied off online maps, and took a left, down another street within the matrix.

Storefronts and stairwells, bathed in light and cluttered by advertising boards, opened directly to the passersby. Taxis crawled among the pedestrians who, without sidewalks and crosswalks, went where they pleased as they pleased. Scantily dressed women — both hostesses and ladies of the night — competed with transvestites and street hawks for the attention of the salarymen in their suits and ties, many of them incoherently drunk, and the businessmen who came to entertain clients, and others who came for entertainment and thrills.

Munroe paused, and in the middle of the street, jostled by pedestrians on all sides, she turned a slow circle, glancing up and around.

The street was familiar, but not in the way the last ten had been.

This was familiar because she'd been here before.

Munroe swore under her breath and pushed forward until she stood in front of the stairs that led to the restaurant where Bradford had taken her to dinner less than two weeks back.

What's the special occasion? she'd asked.

Do we need one?

Well, apparently fucking so.

Munroe replayed the night in her head: the way he'd lingered over a meal that had kept going with dessert and coffee, and his distractedness.

And the lies. Of course the lies.

All I can do is hope you're able to figure it out, he'd said. *Maybe at least then you'll understand that my intentions were good and that even in the lies, I never meant to hurt you.*

Motherfucker.

Bringing her here was far too abstruse to have been planned out as a hint, like the clues left in the drawer. No, Bradford, the romantic, had used her as cover to case a target and inked the location onto the calendar after the fact.

Munroe glanced up at the window where they'd sat and then turned again, tracking a line of sight up and down the street, gauging what he would have seen from his side of the table. And there they were: hostess club option one and hostess club option two.

Munroe started with the nearest club, almost directly across the street, where a glass box frame embedded in the wall showed off a menu of names in the same way the plastic food replicas were the menu for the restaurant next door.

The stairs led down and Munroe followed two men into a smoky atmosphere, where the ambient music was low and a backlit bar faced the entry. The rest of the room was a single lounge with sectional seating that created faux divisions of space and a sense of privacy. Blue under-counter LEDs and soft-colored drop shades were the extent of the lighting.

The mama-san, a woman in her late fifties, if one was generous, elegantly clothed and wearing enough makeup and perfume to make a cliché of her age, greeted the men with an air of touchy-feely warmth and familiarity that only just bordered on flirting, then she guided them toward a table.

They sat and the mama-san left them, and a moment later two young Japanese women joined the men with smiles and coy girlish flirtation.

Munroe's view of the interchange was cut short by the man who stepped out from behind the bar and headed in her direction. He was in his early thirties, maybe, dressed in a designer suit and tie with shoes at a spit-polish shine, his hair gelled into styled asymmetry. He was the master, the man who handled the girls, the male counterpart to the mama-san who catered to the clients, and he glanced up and down just once, as if trying Munroe on for size.

She'd changed into jeans and a blouse, but her hair and makeup were still heavy on the feminine side in the wake of her visit to

Bradford.

In broken English the man said, "American?"

Munroe nodded, her focus trained over his shoulder, toward the interior, catching glimpses of the routine as the bartender sent a half-full bottle to the newcomers' table and the two young women, full of coquettish giggles, poured drinks and made conversation.

The master shifted, blocking Munroe's view. "You speak Japanese?" he said.

Attention still on the tables and the men, and fighting for an unobtrusive look, Munroe said, "A little."

"Come tomorrow afternoon," the master said. "Busy now. We talk again."

Munroe cut her eyes back to him, her expression blank for a heartbeat, and then she nearly laughed. This had been a job interview. And of course. Why else would a foreign woman have wandered in alone, looking confused and possibly in need of money?

She smiled and said, "I don't need work." She handed him the slip of paper on which she'd written the hostess club's address. "Is this here?"

The master studied the paper and shook his head, and it was difficult to see in his

186

polite manner if, now that she was neither customer nor future employee, the head-shake was of disappointment, relief, or indifference.

He swept a palm toward the door and said, "That way."

Munroe mimicked his motion with one of her own. "Down the street?"

"Yes, yes," he said. "Address that way."

She bowed. "Thank you," she said.

"You look work? Work here is good."

"No work," she said, "only friends." And she glanced over his shoulder again, snagging a final impression of the interaction. Hostess clubs would be different in some ways and the same in others. Master and mama-san here meant master and mama-san there, and mama-san was all about making the male clients happy. Unless Munroe intended to snuggle up to strange men under the watchful eye of her new master, getting access to the target location would require a change in plans.

Day 6   1:13 A.M.

Down the street, trading one hostess club for the next, Munroe studied yet another menu of names, this one handwritten, beautifully scrolled in colorful chalkboard paint, and nestled in folds of lavender satin.

She checked over her shoulder for the second-floor restaurant window in the near distance, at the face so clearly seen beyond the pane standing in for Bradford and providing a perfect line of sight. The menu had no address to compare against the slip of paper, no prices, but the location put the place in the higher-end, about a hundred dollars an hour, and that was before drinks or any talk of sex.

Hostess clubs weren't brothels, not in any technical sense. They were closer to a diluted offshoot of the geisha tradition in which young girls trained for years to become the perfect evening companion. But here, instead of the classically trained, were attractive women who flattered men who paid in minute-based increments for the privilege of being fawned over and lied to.

Hostess clubs were drinking establishments where businessmen came to relax and feel good after work, little niches carved out for the sole purpose of sexual titillation, fully integrated into a culture in which work continued long after business hours ended. The more attractive and more educated the woman, the higher the price paid to acquire her time, and whether the women slept with their clients was a separate issue. Some did. Some didn't. The pressure was always there.

Prostitution in Japan was only illegal as intercourse in exchange for payment. Oral sex, anal sex, any other kind of sex was wide open, as was made clear by the many "soap houses" and "fashion health" spas that operated in high numbers, turning Japan into one of the top destinations for sex-trafficking victims.

Munroe left the window display for the restaurant.

The same foreignness that marked her as a perpetual outsider also turned her seemingly odd behavior into an amusing quirk, and when the table at which she and Bradford had sat was finally free, the proprietress, with demure smiles and a welcoming bow, offered Munroe what she had insisted upon waiting for.

Munroe ordered, and ate, and waited, and ordered again, and waited some more, while the evening deepened and the street began to empty somewhat, and because keeping the table prevented the restaurant from serving other clients, she continued with high-priced flavor-infused drinks that kept the money flowing.

Men came and went into the club and Munroe evaluated them by their ages, their modes of arrival, the length of time they stayed, and the numbers in their groups. The night drew down to closing time and Munroe, having seen as much as she had, paid the bill and left.

She didn't bother with further surveillance.

She'd gotten what she'd come for; she'd found her mark.

Day 6   2:49 A.M.

The challenge had already begun to churn the turbid waters, nudging the hibernating hunter beneath, shoving the nightmare into the background where personal things belonged. The bed called out, offering sleep and dreamless rest. Munroe tugged off her boots and reached for the laptop, logged into her bank, and checked the account.

No money from Walker yet, but it would come.

She showered and slept and woke with the sun, then dressed in yesterday's clothes and accessed the account again. This time the numbers were there. In response the stirring rose, tangible and soothing: inner demons laughing at having been loosed to wreak havoc, setting her free from the encumbrances of fear of loss and love and the emotions that clouded reason and jeopardized clarity.

An e-mail from Walker waited in her inbox: confirmation of the wire transfer, scanned images of the contract, a name and number for the military contact Bradford might have been talking to, and a request for information on everyone Munroe had spoken with about the case.

The language was formal: the type of cover-your-ass legalese that had under-pinned most of Munroe's jobs before she'd met Bradford. This was Walker stating that as long as Munroe planned to be a dick, Walker had no problem being a corporate asshole.

Munroe smiled.

This was familiar ground, comforting in its own strange way.

She typed out a reply: names and numbers that she'd promised to send and a formal assurance that regular reports would be provided as per the terms outlined in the contract. She'd have to find a way to get the paperwork countersigned and returned, but that was a formality. The deed was done.

She hit send, copied out the info on Bradford's military contact, opened a browser window, and hunted for Warren Green. A reverse search of the phone number led to a work line that didn't allow for corroboration, so she scoured profiles and databases and social networking profiles until she found him.

Green was African American, career military it would seem, an athlete and father of three, and she'd have to wait until evening to catch him during his morning.

Munroe placed the items from Bradford's drawer on the bed, gazing over them, allowing her mind to wander freely, attempting to match abstract questions with abstract answers, but there was nothing new.

Whatever else Bradford was, he wasn't stupid. He may not have known who was coming after him, or even how or what or why, but there was no reason to throw his foresight away. She picked up the security pass, tapped the laminate against her fingers, then held the card sideways to get a better look at her face without the distraction of the hologram.

Munroe stood, faced the mirror, and studied the reflection.

She needed into the hostess club, needed into ALTEQ, and wouldn't get respect or access into either looking as she did.

The shopping arcade was a fifteen-minute walk from the hotel, essentially a series of covered pedestrian streets. A department store anchored an intersection and on the floor with beauty supplies Munroe tracked down a set of grooming clippers. Two floors down, where an assortment of stationery supplies filled half the floor with enough miniature office everything to put a hard-core crafter into a cutesy-color coma, she bought pens and paper.

In the hotel room she dumped her trove on the bed and carried the clippers into the bathroom cubicle. Her hair, already overgrown by the time she'd left Djibouti, had lengthened even more over the last few months. Not long enough to be explicitly feminine, but long enough to cause doubt, and doubt was never a good thing in subterfuge.

Munroe leaned over the sink and turned

on the shears.

With well-practiced fingers she ran the blade guard up the back of her head and then the sides, switching out combs as needed, feeling for places she'd missed. Strands of dark brown fell into the basin, and then smaller slivers, and then those smaller still.

She shut off the clippers and stood staring at the image made blemished and blotchy under the fluorescent lights. She was no longer the woman who'd arrived in Japan to visit her lover, but the man who would set him free.

Munroe shoved the television to one side of the long, narrow desk and taped several of the large sheets of paper along the wall in a de facto command center. Working off the notes she'd scribbled while still at the apartment, recounting the details claimed from perusing Bradford's external drive, she compiled the information into a visual representation of the many threads entangled inside her head.

She had no interest in the thief for the sake of uncovering theft; that had been Bradford's job. But espionage and machinations walked hand in hand, and since theft was why Bradford had been hired, theft would lead her to whoever had set him up.

She drew the facility building according to satellite images and sketched the department divisions according to what she remembered from her visits. Onto index cards Munroe wrote the names from Bradford's drive, taping them to the facility map based on where they ranked in the company's hierarchy. This outline was the beginning, the path to the end, and at the moment it was nothing but a big black hole where information should be.

The company employed more than eight hundred people, which provided plenty of wiggle room for murderers and spies. Bradford had, in so many words, told her that the three folders on his drive were the only avenues he'd seen for stolen data to move out of the facility: through upper management, the team down in the lab, or security personnel.

Munroe tossed a pillow from the headboard to the middle of the bed, leaned back, and studied her handiwork, and when thinking reached the point of diminishing returns, she dug through the backpack with Bradford's things and pulled out a shirt and a pair of pants. She dressed in his clothes, though she didn't fill them out the way that he had, and emptied the spare wallet he'd left behind, replacing the contents with her own.

She shoved the wad of leather into her pocket, picked up the helmet.

This was her element: stealing secrets.

Now it was time to steal another.

Munroe swiped the badge over the reader, the arm swung open, and she strode through without a backward glance, heading for Bradford's office.

Above her, cameras tracked her movements. In the security operations center, databases processed the readings off the badge's RFID chip, and she took her time, providing ample notice that she was in the facility, allowing the security team to red-flag the clearance that had gotten her inside and track her down.

Munroe stopped outside of Bradford's office.

She knocked and, receiving no reply, opened the door to a room just as empty as it had been when Okada had shown it to her. She stood in the doorway, arms crossed and waiting, and when after several moments there was still no response from the security team, and six employees had passed with the same eye-avoiding courtesy nod-bow that they would have given to anyone else, she continued up the stairs and into the left-branching hall.

Three doors down and then to the right, she found the personnel department, a wide room filled with desks crammed front to back and side to side, much like the desks in the police precinct station had been.

Folders and binders were stacked here and there and the whispered whir of quiet activity and conversation filled the air against finger strokes on keyboards and the hum of photocopy machines.

A woman carrying a tablet stopped and asked Munroe if she needed help. Munroe unfolded the forms Bradford had left tacked to the contract and in English said, "Who do I see about this?"

The woman glanced over the first page, reading it out loud, talking to herself as much as to Munroe, and then motioned down beyond a row of desks, to another door.

In the end, it took less than twenty minutes to get the paperwork sorted out. Bradford had been thorough on the back end and clever in his arrangements, giving basis to his claim that he'd intended to bring her in long before this nightmare had started.

Her role as a consultant meant payments went directly to his company, not to her, skirting the issue of her having been hired and putting the need for a work visa into a gray area. For now, having presented herself with the proper documents, Munroe was officially on the company roster, though not as an employee.

She commandeered Bradford's office through another round of red tape and bureaucracy, culminating in the guarantee that a desk and chair would be waiting for her when she next returned, each step made as visibly as possible, and by the time she'd finished, there was no possibility that either branch of security was unaware of her presence.

Finished, she left the facility for the landing across the street from which she'd watched the doors waiting for Okada to arrive, killing time, building familiarity with faces and cars and train and bus schedules while the employees began the slow trickle home: far better than sitting in a hotel room, staring at the wall, attempting to conjure something out of nothing.

Evening came. Lights switched on. When only the late stragglers remained, Munroe left her perch and returned to the bike.

■ ■ ■ ■

At nine in the evening Kitashinchi had barely begun to wake. Munroe found an empty doorstep within sight of the hostess club and, with her face and her foreignness somewhat disguised within shadows, she waited in the night and the neon and the numbing boredom of surveillance as the streets filled and the clock pushed on toward midnight and at last her mark arrived.

He was a man with expensive shoes, a portly belly, and a blush-red nose that spoke of having already experienced many hours and many drinks before arriving for the evening's final hit. His visit to the club should have been a group affair, a way to make deals and bring finer points to agreement, ensuring that when they were raised in the boardroom no one risked the loss of face, but he arrived alone, just as he had the night before, chauffeured in a private car rather than by taxi.

Somewhere inside that club a woman counted off bonuses each time he returned for her, because surely that's why he returned, and it was why Munroe had chosen him.

The car pulled to a stop, blocking the narrow street. The driver stepped out and Munroe rose from her perch. She timed her steps to the driver's as he opened the rear door, timed her steps to the portly man's as he heaved himself up from the backseat and the driver returned to the wheel, and collided with her target as his hand reached for the hostess club's door, knocking him off balance.

She caught him when he tripped, straining as his weight bore down on her and the alcohol off his breath clogged her airway. She mimicked the deference that she'd seen from so many men in the everyday hierarchy that encompassed life in Japan, and then like in a scene from a badly acted movie, she brushed off his clothes with humbled apologies while he huffed and muttered in extreme offense until he realized she was a foreigner.

His tone changed to forgiveness midsentence.

He smiled with a mouth of yellowing teeth, launching into a monologue in drunken English that came close to a donkey's bray.

Munroe humored him and begged to buy him a drink, knowing that at best he might infer that tonight was a difficult night for such things. She was a foreigner and foreigners were notoriously oblivious to the subtle ways of saying no, and that would allow her to push harder, but there was no need.

He was drunk and pleased to meet her.

The man with the broken capillaries and crooked teeth pounded her on her back and wrapped a meaty arm around her shoulders, and slurring Japanese just slightly more intelligible than his English, he walked her through the door.

DAY 7   12:11 A.M.

The mama-san lit up when they stepped through, yen signs flashing in her eyes with every bat of her thick fake lashes. She was a beautiful woman, soft and feminine with genuine warmth that said she'd known the mark a long time.

She led them to a table in the far back of a room that, like the hostess club Munroe had visited the night before, was lit with mood and ambience. Here, waist-high walls at intersecting angles were topped with tea lights, adding a touch of the dramatic and providing a greater sense of privacy, and off to the side was a small dance floor, where two couples swayed to piped-in music.

The portly man sat and Munroe took her place opposite him, eyeing the hostesses, a mixture of foreign and local, all of them stunning. The mama-san lingered beside the mark, head dipping in rhythm to words Munroe couldn't hear, body and face saying *Yes* and *I agree* and *Of course.*

One of the foreign women, wearing a gold-sequined dress that hardly reached her thighs, blond and petite and with baby blue eyes recognizably dulled by drugs or alcohol, sauntered over and slid onto the sofa bench beside the portly man, snuggling up as if she'd been waiting for a longtime lover.

The mark reacted to his plaything like a cat to sun or a puppy to fingers behind the ear, and paused just long enough to reach for his wallet. He retrieved a business card, thick and heavy, and presented it to Munroe with a flourish of ceremony. Business cards, treated as reverently by the receiver as one would treat the giver, left Munroe fishing for her pocket.

She presented one of Bradford's cards while an open bottle of Glenfiddich, ice, and glasses arrived from the bar, carried on a silver tray by a young woman in very high heels and a barely there dress.

The blonde reached for the bottle of whisky and the mama-san stood. Full of polite apology, she encouraged Munroe to take a space of her own at a table made available across the room.

"Go, go," the portly man said in English, waving Munroe on magnanimously. Munroe bowed her thanks and followed the mama-san and, in what had to be a prearranged collusion, a tall pale brunette reached the table at nearly the same time.

Munroe slid into the quasi-booth formed by the bank of sofas and low table and smiled at a woman who couldn't have been older than twenty.

She sat beside Munroe and, in Japanese that was fluid in the way practiced lines were fluid, said, "I am Gabi, please allow me to request for you a drink."

"I drink what you drink," Munroe said, and then she repeated the sentence in Russian. The language was a guess, the closest she could offer the foreign accent from within her repertoire, and she'd not been far off. Gabi's eyes widened and her mouth opened just slightly, and she stumbled through placing an order with the bar girl who'd already arrived, perfectly timed, at their table.

When the liquor came and the drinking began, Munroe learned that her hostess was Lithuanian. Her Russian wasn't fluent, but the conversation flowed far better than it would have in Japanese or English, and when the ice had been broken and Gabi had relaxed, Munroe slid a picture of Bradford onto the table. "He's my friend," she said.

"I'm trying to find him, I've heard he's been here."

Gabi leaned forward, picked up the picture, then moved it closer to a nearby candle and examined it more closely. She handed it back with a nod that might as well have said *You'd better put that away.*

Munroe tucked the photo into her wallet.

Gabi traced a finger across Munroe's hand and managed to both flirt and pout in the same breath. "He has been here, but not with me," she said, and she leaned back slow and sultry, each muscle tensed with the perfection of a stage performer fully aware of how every movement was watched by someone, somewhere. Gabi looked down the room toward the front, closer to the door, and kept on looking until Munroe followed her gaze.

"You see the red dress?" Gabi said.

Red dress was an understatement.

Munroe turned back to the drinks and said, "I see the dress," although what she'd seen were long legs that kept on going forever, stopped by clingy red material topped out with a chest that had to have been enhanced. And long blond hair that flowed in coifed waves over bare shoulders, which were attached to elegant arms and hands pouring drinks at a table with three

Japanese men.

"That is Alina," Gabi said. "She was at the table with your friend."

An elegant Filipina approached and Gabi said, "You know how it works?"

Munroe shook her head. "Tell me."

"You want me to stay? You want a new hostess?"

"Stay," Munroe said, "and when the red dress gets free, I want her here."

Gabi smiled, waved the other girl away. "Give me some minutes," she said, "I will make sure you get what you want."

They chatted more, small talk to fill the time, and then Gabi slid out to the floor, only slightly stable on platform shoes, and she wandered out of sight, either to the mama-san or the master, it was hard to know.

Munroe was an hour in and a hundred and fifty dollars lighter when the red dress showed up. Munroe patted the seat and invited her to sit, just a bit too happy, as if she was a little too affected by the booze.

Alina smiled and offered more of the same coy, playful fawning that permeated the air, but no amount of sensuality could hide the bored indifference that punctuated every move.

She was older than Gabi, perhaps twenty-five or twenty-six.

"Twenty-seven," Alina said, and showed no surprise at Munroe having engaged her in her own language.

Presumably, Gabi had spread the word.

Alina answered the next question before Munroe could ask, as if this was a litany she endured with all new customers and pulling off the exchange without descending into condescension or implied snark would take effort. "I've been in Japan for four years," she said. She took the tiniest sip of the drink Munroe had bought her and then added, "I can speak enough Japanese to get by."

"I'm looking for a friend," Munroe said. "I was told you've seen him. I'm hoping you would tell me what you know of him."

"I've seen him," Alina said.

"You don't want to look at the picture?"

"There's no need. Any one of us would recognize him if he came back."

"He came here often?"

"Three times, I think." Alina shrugged. "Do you smoke?"

Munroe shook her head. Three nights accounted for each of Bradford's unexplained absences according to the notes on his calendar.

Alina sighed, dropping the pretense that Munroe had come for any other reason than information. Time was time, and she got paid either way. "Another hour and I go home," she said, and lit the cigarette, leaning back into the sofa and crossing her long legs. She inhaled and then let out the smoke toward the ceiling.

Munroe said, "Tell me about my friend."

Chin raised, cigarette balanced between two fingers, Alina traced her eyes over Munroe's face. Munroe knew the look; she'd seen it on strippers and fortune-tellers and politicians — those who'd so finely perfected the ratio between bullshit and charm that people believed what they heard and willingly opened their wallets for more.

"I tell you about him," she said, "and in exchange you tell me about you: one for one."

Munroe picked up her drink and ran the glass between her palms.

In a few words the woman had said she believed Munroe had something she wanted and she'd hold the information about Bradford hostage to get it.

DAY 7   1:40 A.M.

Munroe set the glass on the table. Alina had left her own untouched, which, because the hostesses were paid for every drink the men bought, meant she was losing money. "Let me buy you another," Munroe said.

Alina's eyes drifted from Munroe's face to the table, where her glass dripped condensation, allowing the obvious to stand in for her reply.

"This place closes soon," Munroe said. "We can waste the rest of the night playing games of avoidance or you can tell me what you want, and I can tell you straight up if it's reasonable."

Alina eyed Munroe again, then turned away and stared across the room at nothing in particular. "I watch people," she said. "I know people."

She'd have to in this line of work. Probably knew each customer better than he knew himself within a minute of his walking through the door.

"I know criminals and soldiers. I know weak men from strong."

She glanced at Munroe for the briefest of seconds. "You are not a weak man," Alina said, and her focus turned to the rear of the room, where the portly mark's red face continued on far too cozy with the tiny blonde.

"You came in with him, but you didn't come with him. You came to ask questions, but you came without asking questions. You are a strong man, and clever, and you have no ties to the owners of this club or you would have come here under other means."

"What is it you think I can give you?"

"Protection."

"From what?"

"From the man who owns this place," Alina said. "The man who keeps my passport. The man who claims he owns me. If I tell you what you want, then you keep me safe in exchange."

Munroe began to speak, but Alina's expression shifted, instant metamorphosis, and her body language switched from indifference to flirtation. She leaned into Munroe as if she were whispering in her ear and stroked her hand. A heartbeat later, a tiny man in a deep gray designer suit passed by their sectional, and when he was gone, the change vanished and Alina shifted back again. "The master," she said. "It's better that he sees me working."

"He's the one you need protection from?"

Alina smiled, a real smile. "He's just an employee."

Munroe set her glass on the table and leaned back, her arm draped over the sofa mirroring the woman's faux indifference.

"Can you protect me?" Alina said.

"I could," Munroe said, "but I can't imagine anything you tell me would be worth the effort."

"I saw things," Alina said, and in her earnestness she leaned in. "I saw your friend kill a man."

Munroe stared hard. Everything in the woman's body, her micro expressions, her posture, held that she told the truth. Brow furrowed, Munroe said, "That's a serious accusation. You'd think for something like this, the police would have been called and he would have been arrested."

"Yes," Alina answered, and as if in her earnestness she'd betrayed too much, her tone went back to indifference. "It's what I saw. The friends of the man carried him away. I only found out much later that he died."

"There was more than one person?"

"Yes, but only two men fighting with your friend."

"Do you know why they were fighting?"

"I do," Alina said, "but that's all I will tell you for free."

Munroe picked up the glass again, set it down, ran a finger along the rim while priorities ordered and reordered. There were very few reasons a woman like Alina would beg for protection from a stranger in a country as safe as Japan, and every one of them was attached to organized crime.

Strategy set itself out in an array of possibilities.

Hating that she'd been boxed into a corner without room for negotiation, Munroe said, "I can keep you safe in exchange."

"Where can I find you after work?"

"Tonight?"

"Tonight or not at all."

Munroe took a napkin and motioned for a pen. Alina sought one out and gave it to her, and Munroe drew a map from the hostess club to the *konbini* not far from where she'd parked the bike — a five-minute walk, maybe ten in Alina's stupid shoes. "You know where it is?"

"I'll be there by three," Alina said.

"If I have to protect myself before I get a

214

chance to protect you, then I'm not waiting for you to get there."

Alina smiled and flicked Munroe's nose. "It will be fine," she said.

Motorcycles were common, foreigners on motorcycles not so much, especially not at this time of night. Munroe waited under the streetlight, ignoring glances and double takes from the few who came and went.

Alina arrived at three just as she'd promised wearing flat shoes, jeans, and a T-shirt, with most of her makeup removed, and her long tresses pulled up into a messy ponytail, speed-walking and looking over her shoulder as if she feared she was being followed. She carried an oversize purse stuffed full, and her steps faltered slightly when she caught sight of Munroe and the bike.

"This?" she said when she'd reached it.

"Unless you'd rather walk."

Alina glanced down the street as if genuinely considering the possibility. Then, expression grim, she said, "Please. Let's go quickly."

Munroe handed Alina her only helmet.

She hadn't had the foresight to bring the spare when leaving the apartment, never imagined that in her decision to fix Bradford's problem she'd wind up with this type of baggage.

Alina fumbled with the straps and Munroe helped her get the helmet on and then waited patiently for her to settle. "You need to go home and get some things?" Munroe said.

The helmet shook: No.

"You sure?"

"Not safe," came the muffled response.

Munroe rotated back, flicked the visor up and found fear in Alina's eyes.

"Do you have a phone?"

Alina glanced down at her purse.

Munroe held out her hand.

Alina dug and pulled out a cell phone. Munroe turned it off, opened the back, and removed the battery. "Carrying this is like carrying a tracking device," she said. "Don't put it back together unless it's an emergency. Got it?"

Alina nodded. Munroe pushed the visor down again. "Don't fight me," she said. "I'm not going to do anything to get us killed, but if you tense up and throw your weight, you're going to cause problems."

"Don't tense," the muffle said.

Munroe nudged the bike toward the curb and Alina tensed.

Munroe sighed. "Hold on," she said, and when Alina grabbed tight with the cushion of the purse pressed uncomfortably between them, Munroe took the bike out into the street. Riding without a helmet was a risk. If she got stopped, she'd lose her license and see the bike impounded, but this wasn't a throwaway jaunt. Instinct told her that Alina was right: *Tonight or not at all.*

Munroe drove in circles, street to street, farther and farther from the drinking district until, certain they hadn't been followed, she wound back to the hotel with its web of diagrams taped up along her room's wall.

She could have gone elsewhere for the night, holed up at one of the many fanciful love hotels where privacy was sacred and rooms that played to want and whimsy could be had by the hour — hotels that, like the manga cafés, offered temporary escape from overcrowded living. Could have but didn't because love hotels were often run by organized crime and, without knowing what territory belonged to whom, they became a greater risk.

Instead she stopped in a small parking lot where owners without better options paid by the quarter hour to keep their vehicles from being towed and stood by while, in the shadows, Alina emptied her purse, item by item.

Munroe took the purse and ripped out the lining in search of tracking devices. She'd not expected to find anything — fear and pain were far more reliable methods for controlling a victim — but she couldn't risk not knowing. Munroe returned the purse without explanation and Alina said nothing as she shoved her things back inside.

At nearly five in the morning, Munroe slid the key card into the room lock and swung the door wide. She stepped inside. Alina remained on the threshold, face white, purse in her hands, staring into the darkened space, as if it only now dawned on her what she'd done, and worse, what she was about to do.

Munroe flipped on the light and motioned around the room. "Nothing here but me," she said.

Alina stayed put.

Munroe opened the desk's bottom drawer and pulled out one of the hotel-provided *jinbei* — pants and jacket — the Japanese version of pajamas or a robe, yet not so intimate that they couldn't be worn out on the streets during the evening hours.

Munroe sat on the bed, held the *jinbei* toward the door, another invitation for Alina to come inside. But still she stood frozen, the fear on her face more pronounced than it had been from behind the visor, and Munroe understood.

Making the plea for help had been easy in the spur of the moment — a daydream practiced often. Even getting on the bike and going where Munroe chose to take her had been doable. But to be locked in a small room with a strange man who might in the end be worse than the man she'd just fled?

Munroe set the loungewear back on the bed, stood, and unbuttoned her shirt. She tossed the outer layer aside and then stripped out of the T-shirt beneath. Concealing her gender had never been particularly difficult. Nature, in making her taller than many men, hadn't been generous with other gifts.

"I want to know what you know," Munroe said, "and now you see that I have no reason to hurt you."

Alina's mouth dropped open slightly, though it was difficult to tell if that was due to discovering that Munroe was a woman or a response to the scarred slivers that crisscrossed Munroe's torso as mementos of the knife attacks that had occurred near-nightly over the space of two years.

Alina stepped inside and shut the door. Eyes never leaving Munroe's torso, she slipped out of her shoes and left them in the entry, then dumped her purse on the desk. Fingers outstretched, she reached to touch the longest, thickest scar that ran from the right side of Munroe's rib cage down to her belly button.

"Who did this?" Alina said.

Munroe snapped a hand around Alina's wrist before skin connected with skin. "It was a long time ago," Munroe said. She let go slowly. "Don't touch me." Then, releasing Alina completely, she added, "Please."

Alina took a step back, just out of Munroe's personal space. Never dropping eye contact, she pulled her own shirt over her head, then unbuttoned and unzipped her jeans and pushed them off. She stood and, arms wide, turned a slow circle, her gaze finally disconnecting when physics forced her head to follow her body.

Angry gashes marred the pale skin along her back, her chest, her buttocks and upper thighs, all body parts that had been hidden by the alluring red dress. Creeping up beyond Alina's panty line was the pink of a still-fresh wound.

Munroe clenched her fists and inhaled a

long, long, deep breath.

She didn't need to ask who'd done it: Alina had told her as much inside the club. Munroe let the air out slowly and with the air the burden.

This woman was not her fight.

"He did this to break me," Alina said. "He needs to be sure that I know I am worthless, that no man will ever find me beautiful once my clothes are off. He says that when he doesn't need my face to make money anymore, then he will take that, too."

"You tried to run away?"

Alina nodded, lips taut, expression grim.

Munroe offered her the *jinbei* again and this time Alina took it, slipping the cotton jacket over her shoulders, wrapping the belt around her waist, and knotting it with experienced hands.

Munroe pulled her T-shirt back on, sat on the bed, and patted the space beside her.

Alina offered a slight smile, then, like a kid, she knelt on the bed and crawled across to the side that backed up to the wall. She pulled the band out of her hair and lay back on the pillow and closed her eyes. Slowly, tears trickled down toward her ears, eventually making water spots on the pillowcase.

Munroe shifted and leaned against the headboard.

Questions about Bradford chased each other in a race against time, but Munroe held them back, allowing the silence to settle, giving Alina a chance to absorb the possibility that her torment might soon be over.

Without opening her eyes, Alina whispered, "You promised to keep me safe. How will you do that?"

"Keep you hidden while we work on getting you a new passport," Munroe said. "When you have that, I'll put you on a plane and send you home."

"I have no money."

"I know," Munroe said. "I consider it a cost of doing business — payment in exchange for the information you have."

Alina looked down at her chest and patted her crotch. "I thought maybe, you know, I should have to buy my way, but not so?"

Munroe smiled, and Alina laughed a snot-wet laugh and dried her eyes.

"I came to Japan legally," she said, "through an agency in my country. They hire girls for the hostess industry, put them on contract for a few years, and then when the contract is finished the girls go home. I had many friends who have done it. The work, it sucks, but the money from two years in Japan goes very far in making a better life in Russia. You know of these things?"

Munroe nodded. Alina continued in fluid fact-based sentences that neither played for pity nor masked frustration and pain. She told of how when she'd arrived, her passport had been taken with the understanding that the travel documents would be returned when the contract expired — how this was an accepted practice to guarantee that the agency recouped its money for transportation and housing, ensuring the girls didn't take off to work on their own once they'd arrived in Japan. But unlike most girls', Alina's passport and the passports of a handful of others who worked in the club were never given back. Without passports, they overstayed their visas, were there illegally, were afraid of the police and afraid of their bosses.

The owner of the agency, also the owner of the club, claimed her for his own, providing her with an apartment and clothes and food while taking from her the money she could have used to provide for herself, always threatening to throw her out into the streets, to strip from her the higher-classed privilege of hostessing and turn her to prostitution, and then to kill her and bury her where no one would ever find her. "I knew from the beginning that the agency is run by the mafia," Alina whispered. "Most hostess agencies are, yes? But I thought that this is Japan, and in Japan they follow the law — not like the mafia in Russia, which owns the law — I thought this was different."

"Not so different."

"It's exactly the same. Business and crime and government all tied in one ugly bow. The other girls think I am lucky. They hate me a little, I think, even though I am here against my will just the same. He promises to return my passport, but he has promised many times and beats me when I ask. They think I have it better — they don't know." She paused and looked at Munroe, her face ten years older than it should have been. "They don't know about the many trips to the hospital and the many trips I don't make because I am too scared to go. You think it's strange I trust a stranger after a few minutes of conversation, that I trust a stranger to protect me and then I leave everything and go into the night?"

Munroe didn't answer.

Alina said, "My youth is fading, and Jiro tires of me. He will kill me soon — or worse, give me to one of his men. There is nowhere for me to go that is safe, nobody I can ask for help. But you're a foreigner, less likely to have connections, and I thought you were a soldier like your friend, I thought maybe you could help me. If not, what did I lose? Either way, I die."

"I am like my friend," Munroe said.

Alina sighed. "We'll see." She rolled over and, lying on her side, she said, "Your friend killed that man in self-defense — he was provoked."

That was the second time Alina had spoken of Bradford killing a man. The notion itself wasn't impossible, only strange and incongruent, an accusation that Munroe had never seen coming considering that Bradford was now sitting in jail for a murder he hadn't committed. What was the point in that when a real one was so readily available?

"Your friend came to the club three times in the past two months," Alina said, "each time with the same group of men."

"Did you know them, or know how I can find them?"

"They weren't regulars, but your friend knew them well — they were all from the same workplace. Maybe that helps?"

"You're sure he knew them from work?"

Alina rolled back over and offered a knowing smile. "There are things you learn when you do this job as long as I have," she said.

"There is a certain feel. This is a country of traditions and ceremony and yes, they were from work. And, like you, your friend made an effort to be like the others, but he didn't drink."

"The same men for each visit?"

"Yes, until the end when the problems started."

"Would you recognize them if you saw them again?"

"In the club, yes. By picture, I don't know."

"What about in person?"

"Maybe."

"Tell me about them," Munroe said.

Alina shifted and stuffed the pillow under her head. "There's nothing to say about them. They were men, and one man is the same as another."

Munroe reached for Alina's face and gently brushed the hair aside. "Not all men are violent," she said.

"Maybe there are some good men," Alina said. "Maybe your friend is a good man. To me, one is the same as the other. I'm only food, a good meal that they can look at but not eat." She turned her head and glanced at Munroe. "The other girls do *dohan,* you know what this is?"

Munroe shook her head.

"*Shimei* is like when you ask for me inside the club. A date, yes? So I get paid for the time we sit and talk. *Dohan* is same thing, but outside the club. In *dohan* is much money and no eyes to watch. *Dohan* means many things, depending on the customer." Alina paused, waiting for the implication to settle. "You understand?" she said.

Munroe nodded.

"Jiro would not let me go for *dohan* — it's easy to get my own money that way, to get sympathy. Anyway," Alina said, rolling back to her side, "that has nothing to say about the men who came with your friend. They were not regular customers, also not so rich like most customers we see. They were Japanese, and they came from work with the same business workclothes like every businessman."

"Did they speak English?"

Alina paused. Half smiling, eager, she pushed up on an elbow. "One. One spoke English. He was the one who talked to your friend. Good English, I think."

"The others?"

"One of Jiro's men, yes."

Munroe glanced at Alina. With the inclusion of Jiro's men, Bradford's story had just taken an epic jump that would have to be roped into the chronology when this thread was finished. She said, "Did my friend talk with you?"

"Mostly with Anna. She's from the Philippines. She's beautiful. Very small. Tiny. She speaks beautiful English."

"Did any of them smoke?" Munroe said.

Alina pressed her palms to her forehead. "I can't remember."

"Wear glasses?"

"Yes, two."

"You said Jiro's men were there. I assume they were part of the problem at the end. Tell me what happened, from the beginning."

"The beginning?" Alina said. "Which night?"

"The last one."

"Your friend came with the people from work, same as the other times before. This night, before the club closed, two new customers came and they were placed at the table next to your friend's. I knew them from Jiro. You could say they are work associates, right, but nobody important — low-level associates. But this night they are dressed in suits and looking like businessmen and given the choice of hostesses and provided drinks. Something is wrong with this, you know? Maybe to everyone else in the room this seems normal, but the mama-san knows, the master knows, you can see it in their faces and it's clear that I am meant to ignore everything.

"Eventually Jiro's men, they start a conversation with your friend. They make a big deal that he is a foreigner, that he is at a hostess club, which is a big part of Japanese culture. Shinji, I think his name is Shinji, he speaks good English, so he is the one to do the talking and soon he is offering drinks to your friend. It's uncomfortable because your friend doesn't want to be there, but he makes a good show of being friendly. Soon Shinji is asking where he is from and makes a big deal about Texas with hats and cattle and guns, and he asks to see the belt of your friend. Shinji is making a lot of noise like he is drunk, but he's not drunk and your friend is more and more uncomfortable. The others around the table, they are laughing and they tease him, all of them, and so to make the peace your friend takes off the belt and gives it to Shinji to look. But then Shinji refuses to give it back."

Munroe closed her eyes. She could see where this was going. "I should stop?" Alina said.

Munroe shook her head. "The more detail, the better."

"At first, your friend seems to play it like

231

a joke. But then after more asking and still Shinji refuses to give back the belt, it turns into an argument and Shinji becomes very not drunk and very angry and the table gets moved and some drinks are spilled. Me and Anna — Anna was hostess for your friend — and Ivana and Yuki, we are trying to make the peace and calm things, and then the mama-san comes and the master and also the man who is like security for the club, and very politely, with many apologies, they say the men are disturbing the guests and to please go outside. So it is six men outside.

"I know that something is wrong and I make an excuse that I need air, and because there is the commotion and the mess and everything needs to keep calm for the other guests, no one cares that I am gone. I reached the street after the fight is already started. The men from your friend's work are on the other side of the street watching the argument. They're very scared, I think. But also drunk and it appears they don't know what to do.

"Your friend is calm at first, and he asks for the belt and then Shinji tries to hit him with something. Not the belt; I don't know what. Maybe a bottle, maybe a brick or a knife — I couldn't see — only after that

232

everything moves very fast, and then Shinji is on the ground and Dai — the other one — he takes a knife and tries to cut your friend. Your friend breaks his arm first. Then slams him to the ground, then everything goes quiet.

"The men from work, they grab your friend and they make him run. Shinji still has the belt and he stands and lifts Dai by the waist and pulls him away and then I couldn't stay longer, so I don't know what happens after this, but I overheard the conversation with Jiro the next week that Dai was dead. All of this for a belt," Alina said. She looked up at Munroe as if Munroe might possibly have the answers. "It makes no sense to me. Why not give it back? Why make so much effort for this small thing? Why did Jiro want it? Was it worth a lot of money?"

"It's not an expensive belt," Munroe said, "but my friend wore it every day. Someone used it to kill a woman."

The room fell silent for a long, long while and Alina turned her head toward the wall above the desk and stared at the diagrams, the cryptic notes, the arrows and fact pieces too far away in the dark to truly see. Finally she said, "You aren't looking for your friend, you already know where he is."

"In jail, awaiting trial for a murder he didn't commit," Munroe said. "I'm trying to find out why."

By the time they'd drifted into sleep, the tiniest touches of light had begun to creep beneath the curtains. Munroe woke a few hours later, and when she was dressed she woke Alina, who startled at her touch.

Seeing Munroe, Alina groaned and dropped back down onto the pillow.

Munroe sat on the bed to lace her boots. "We need to get to the consulate," she said.

Alina rubbed sleep from her face, crawled out of the bed, dragged her purse off the desk, and shut the bathroom door behind her.

Water rushed through the pipes behind the wall.

Munroe leaned into the headboard and closed her eyes.

According to Alina, Jiro had government connections. Munroe assumed that meant within the police force as well, and if she were a possessive, violent man whose woman had walked out on him, she'd be vicious in trying to get her back, if only to kill her. If the woman didn't have a passport, the consulate would be the first place she'd start looking.

In leaving for the consulate first thing this morning they might already be too late.

The Russian Federation embassy in Tokyo was an alternative.

She didn't have the time to spare to make the trip north.

In the hotel garage Alina pulled the helmet over her head and her shaking fingers fumbled, unable to thread the strap through the buckle. Gently, so as to avoid putting Alina more on edge than she already was, Munroe moved her hand and secured the helmet, then gave her a slip of paper and fifty thousand yen.

"My phone number," she said, "and money to pay the fees for the passport."

The helmet nodded. Then Alina shoved the paper and money deep down into a pocket.

Munroe mounted the bike, turned on the ignition, and brought the horses to life. Alina climbed on behind her. Had circumstances been otherwise, Munroe would have dropped the woman off at the consulate with enough money for taxi, hotel, and airfare and that would have been the end of it. History wouldn't allow her that, and she could only hope that today's mission would be simple.

Good deeds had a tendency to get people killed.

The Russian Federation consulate was a two-story, pine-tree-fronted, modern-style, windowless white-and-orange block that stood on a clean and quiet street in a neighborhood of upscale block-shaped apartment buildings. Separating the consulate from street traffic — had there been any street traffic — was an array of plastic cones, a few police officers, and an official van parked on the sidewalk against the white concrete of the compound's security wall.

The street dead-ended into a metal traffic barrier a block or so down.

Munroe passed the building once for orientation, then looped back and stopped on the sidewalk beside the front gate.

Alina slid off, clutching her bag with one hand and attempting to unbuckle the helmet with the other. The nearest police officer approached the bike, irritation written in his expression. Eyes on him, words to Alina,

Munroe took the helmet and shoved it on her own head. "I need two hours," she said. "Call me on the consulate's phone if you think you'll take longer."

"Thank you," Alina said, but her focus, too, was on the officer, as if he was a dangerous thing. She quickstepped for the gate.

Munroe rolled off the sidewalk before the policeman reached her and waited nearby while Alina talked her way past consulate security and beyond the front door, then returned to Bradford's apartment while her mind spun through the fallout that would come if instead of helping Alina she'd just dumped the woman into a trap.

She parked blocks away and walked a circuitous route, as much a caution against having been followed as of stepping into a different kind of trap, and then opened the door to dusty hot air and the apartment exactly as she'd left it.

The calm and order was frustrating. Maddening. Wrong.

Japanese criminal investigators were known for being effectively thorough. Even if they had everything in place for an open-and-shut conviction, if they believed Bradford was guilty, they should have come as a way to cover all the angles and double-down on evidence and motive.

Munroe grabbed the second helmet and stuffed another backpack with several more days' worth of Bradford's work clothes. She checked the windows, the doors, and left them closed. The food in the fridge had started to mold, but she'd have to take care of that another day. She routed to the hotel first, to drop off the clothes, and by the time she put the battery back into her phone, more than two hours had passed and Alina had called twice.

Munroe stopped the bike in front of the consulate gate. The door opened and Alina came bounding for the street. The look on her face and the posture of her stride said that she didn't have a passport.

The policemen watched her from the van.

Munroe pulled the second helmet from the backpack and shoved it onto Alina's head. "We'll fix it later," Munroe said. "Don't talk now, we need to go."

Alina slid up behind Munroe and clenched hard when the bike started up.

Munroe headed away from the consulate, away from the hotel and the airport, and toward Kyoto, where, because of the sheer number of white-skinned tourists, those who searched for Alina would be less likely to find her.

Kyoto station was three levels of glass and steel surrounded by multi-level department stores and restaurants. Munroe led them up from the parking level and out the main entrance, across the street to a Starbucks whose large portico patio and interior were filled with so many foreigners they'd never stand out.

It had been more than a day since she'd eaten, was probably the same or longer for Alina. Munroe ordered enough food from the cold cases to feed four people. They found seats near the back and between bites that curbed the shaking hunger, Munroe said, "How long before they give you a passport?"

Alina looked down at her food. "How did you know?"

"I'm familiar with bureaucracy and red tape. Did you tell them the truth?"

"They would keep me longer to ask questions and would want to make a police report, and Jiro would use that as a map to find me."

"How long?"

Alina reached into her purse and handed Munroe the remaining yen and the receipt for the paperwork. "Two days."

Munroe scanned the receipt and passed it back, with the money. "Keep it," she said. "I'll drop you off at the hotel, I have to work."

Alina's hand, halfway to her mouth, froze. Voice low and desperate, she said, "Please let me go with you."

"Not a good idea."

"Please."

Munroe stared at the table weighing options between bites and swallows. Alina had seen things, knew things. Carting her around, out in the open, carried risks; so did leaving her defenseless in a hotel room. She said, "If you saw the men who were with my friend that night, would you recognize them?"

Alina nodded, far too vigorously.

Munroe sighed, appetite gone, burden heavy. When height and skin flashed attention-grabbing neon at every step, two days was a long time to keep a target hidden from a man who wanted her dead.

They sat on the landing, across the road, not far down from the sheared-off glass face, watching the parking lot and facility entrance, and when Alina had grown comfortable in the shadows, Munroe handed her a small notebook and a pen and then stood to go.

Alina grabbed her wrist. Munroe yanked free.

Without sound, without sobs, as if a secret tap had been turned on, tears started to flow down Alina's cheeks.

Munroe crouched so they were face-to-face. She had felt this fear, had lived the fear, but never the incapacity. "I have to go farther and I can't take you with me," she said.

Alina's mouth opened, but no words came out.

"You've kept the battery out of your phone?"

Alina nodded.

"Nobody knows where you are. Nobody can see you sitting here, tucked away in shadow, and if they can't see you, Jiro can't find you."

Alina nodded again.

Munroe tapped the notebook. "This is why I kept you with me instead of taking you back to the hotel," she said. "If you see anyone familiar, write down everything: clothes, colors, glasses, hairstyle, if he goes to a car or walks to the train — even the smallest detail, okay?" Munroe took off Bradford's watch and placed it on Alina's knee. "If I'm not back in two hours, it means I'm not coming back, *ever,* you understand? If I don't come back, then take a taxi, go to the consulate, and stay there until they give you your passport. But until two hours have passed, you can't panic."

Alina stared at her feet.

"You're not helpless, Alina," Munroe said, and stood. "You have enough money to hide until you get your passport." She paused, pulled a small roll of bills from her boot, and shoved it into Alina's hand. "And you can buy your ticket out."

Alina's fingers wrapped around the roll, but her focus stayed on her feet, so Munroe turned, jogged down the stairs, and continued across the street.

The *why* behind Bradford's setup ate at her.

Behind that was the *why* of his hiring: why a company wholly insular in its drive to protect its secrets, operating in a country equally insular in protecting its labor force, had gone through the effort of bringing in a foreign contractor as a security consultant.

Today was for the food chain: the men who, in part or in whole, had pulled the levers and cranked the gears to bring Bradford to their doorstep.

Munroe pushed through the lobby doors. If she fucked this up, there'd be no one coming behind her to clean up the mess.

At the entry stiles she swiped her badge. There'd been plenty of time for the facility's security to invalidate her access, but the light flashed green and the arm swung open.

C-level offices were on the second floor and Munroe headed up the stairs with a truncated list of Bradford's folders cycling through her head.

She reached the door for Yuzuru Tagawa first: head of operations and Bradford's boss. She stepped into the anteroom without knocking.

A plain woman looked up from the monitor that graced a plain desk. Beside her, several filing cabinets were the extent of decor and furniture, and the walls were just as drab as those in Bradford's office, but without the scuffs.

Hands slack, gaze lowered, Munroe asked for Tagawa.

"He's busy," the woman said.

Munroe stayed at the desk, silent and expectant.

After a moment, the woman looked up again and said, "Tagawa-san is unavailable."

"Yes," Munroe said, and she stayed put, allowing her foreignness to absorb the impact from the breach in etiquette.

After another moment the woman eyed Munroe over the rims of her glasses, and when Munroe still didn't speak or turn to leave, she reached for the phone with an exasperated sigh. A brief conversation later, she stood and opened the door to her boss's office.

Yuzuru Tagawa, shirtsleeves rolled up and tie askew, glanced up from a stack of paper. He was in his early fifties, with a soft midsection and hair combed over to hide a mostly bald pate. He motioned Munroe inside, and when the door was shut, he turned back to his papers, ignoring her.

She waited, military at ease, taking in the room and the man who, due to a diversion in the chain of command for the sake of accountability, had become Bradford's boss and now was hers.

Tagawa's focus continued from papers to computer screen and back, his right hand keeping a running commentary on the keyboard's number pad. Minutes passed and at last he looked up, then stood and stepped around his desk.

Munroe thrust a hand forward, though bowing would have been the culturally appropriate thing.

Tagawa shook it uneasily and greeted her in broken English, clearly uncomfortable with its use and, by proxy, uncomfortable in her presence.

Bradford had always had Okada as an interpreter.

Munroe lifted the security badge high enough and long enough that Tagawa would get a clear look. Switching to Japanese now would only be awkward and make the discomfort worse, so she continued in English.

"I've been hired by Miles Bradford to finish his work," she said.

Tagawa's lips tightened as he studied the badge, as if he tried to construct words and draw grammar from years-old study. At last he bowed and said, "Thank you for come."

He stuck a palm toward the door as if adding *next time make an appointment and bring your interpreter* and said, "Talk security, you help."

The air of the door kissed Munroe's backside in its haste to close.

She nodded at the plain woman in glasses on her way out.

One down, two to go.

Noboru Kobayashi was Tai Okada's boss, the man who would have been Bradford's boss if Bradford's position hadn't been assigned to operations in an attempt to segregate power and accountability. Lies that had become truths granted a quicker, easier access — she had indeed come straight from Yuzuru Tagawa and she did indeed have a message.

Kobayashi was younger than Tagawa. He was perfectly conforming in his salaryman uniform of navy-blue suit and tie, but had an air of hunger about him and wore an edge of rebel in his highlighted and slightly gel-spiked hair.

He spoke fluent English with the accent of one who'd lived or studied abroad years ago, and when Munroe repeated a larger, better-worded version of the introduction she'd made a few offices over, Kobayashi crossed his arms, sat on the edge of his desk, and studied her with a mixture of smirk and challenge.

Then he held out a hand for her badge.

Munroe lifted the lanyard from around her neck, gave it to him, and waited, silent, while Kobayashi glanced at it. Like Tagawa before him, he didn't seem surprised to see her. He handed the badge back and said, "When were you subcontracted?"

"Right before the arrest — it's taken a while to get caught up on all the notes, so this is the first chance I've had to make official introductions."

Kobayashi's head ticked up just a little too quickly. "He left notes? I thought the police cleaned out his office."

"He handed them off to me the day before."

"Well, that was fortunate timing," Kobayashi said, then stood. "It's good that you have something to work with — we won't have to start at the beginning. Have you already arranged for a liaison? Are you working with" — he paused and snapped his fingers, as if trying to remember a name, though the action had a certain falseness. "Who was it?" he said. "Tai Okada, right?"

"I should start fresh," Munroe said. "Mr. Tagawa said to speak with the security department. I'm on my way downstairs to put in a request."

"I'll take care of it," Kobayashi said.

He walked with her the few steps from his office door to the end of the hallway, and she felt his eyes boring holes in her back as she continued on. She turned once, not for confirmation that he watched her, which she didn't need, but to let him know she knew.

She waved, as did he, then he returned to his office and Munroe started up again, head down, eyes to the floor, attempting to sift an accurate sense of what had just happened through a sieve of cultural mores that avoided directness and potential conflict.

There'd been not a question asked about Bradford.

She could excuse the lack of surprise at her arrival — that spoke to the security departments having done their jobs well since she was last on-site and explained why the clearance was still active. But even if touching on the issues of murder and arrest pushed hard against the boundaries of politeness, she would have expected Kobayashi, with his good English and foreign familiarity, to have at least asked about her work history and connections to Bradford, especially when she'd provided him the opening.

Like the office downstairs, it was as if Bradford had never been.

Of the three men Munroe had come to observe, up close and in person, Tatsuo Nakamura, member of the ALTEQ-Bio board and one of the company's seven directors, was the man she most wanted to see, and he was out of the office.

She knew his face from the company website, his résumé as translated into horrendous English by Internet translating software, and his connection to Bradford from the name on the contract that had brought Bradford to Japan.

Without Nakamura, Bradford would never have come.

Munroe made an appointment with his office staff.

Four days forward was his earliest opening.

Munroe left for the ground floor, for Okada's department, and her key card granted her access to the room full of monitors just

251

as Bradford's had.

Okada was missing, which conveniently spared her the necessity of making awkward conversation and spared him the discomfort of playing dumb when he inevitably recognized her. She only stayed long enough to catch glimpses of the toys the men played with, count heads, watch faces, and gauge body language, and then moved on to the next department, where Bradford had had no allies.

The second security door, too, opened to her clearance badge.

Four faces tipped up when she stepped through. Makoto Dillman, at the desk farthest from the door, stood and came toward her, as he had with Bradford when Bradford had brought her in all those weeks ago.

He stopped just outside her personal space and before he could speak Munroe extended a hand. "Michael Munroe," she said, "subcontractor on the Capstone contract, here to pick up where my boss, Miles Bradford, left off. Just swinging by to say hello, let you know that I'm around."

Dillman gripped hard. "Makoto Dillman," he said. "You look familiar. Have we met?"

Munroe tugged her hand free. "Not that I know of," she said, and fought the urge to wipe the sweat off on her pants. "Vanessa was with the boss a few weeks back, you might have met her, we're related, look alike." Then to change the subject: "So, look, I just had a chat with Kobayashi-san upstairs. He said he'd work out a liaison, but if you're short-staffed, take your time with that. I'm not in any rush — most of what I do will be based on people, not files, and I've got a pretty good grasp on the spoken language."

"That so?" Dillman said, and he crossed his arms. "You live in Japan a while?"

"I've studied."

He stayed just at the edge of her personal space, sizing her up with unveiled hostility. He said, "My understanding was that the train wreck of last week shifted the work back over to this department."

"Yeah?" Munroe said, and shrugged. "What do I know? I'm just a trained monkey. Here to do a job, Mac. I've got no plans to piss on your fence."

Dillman's expression clouded, as she knew it would, but unlike Bradford who'd poked the bear, her inflaming served a purpose.

"Makoto or Dillman," Dillman said, "never Mac."

"My bad," she said, and threw as much sincerity into her tone and demeanor as she could muster. "The boss referred to you as Mac, so I thought . . . Anyway," she said, and stuck her hand out again, as if she'd be on her way now that she'd inadvertently insulted him.

"No big deal," Dillman said, and his posture relaxed and he took a step out of her personal space. He motioned to the other men in the room. "Have you met the team?"

"Still new on the job."

Dillman switched effortlessly from English to Japanese, and with the change of language came a change in character: harsher, deeper, more authoritarian. He introduced the other three in order of department hierarchy: Shigeru Hara, Ken Suzuki, and Yuki Abe, and Munroe sized each man up far more subtly than Dillman had done with her.

She'd come to sign a temporary truce with Bradford's antagonist, and having gotten more than she'd asked for, Munroe turned to leave.

The hair on the back of her neck rose in animal awareness, the instinct of the prey that a predator was near. "Hey, Dillman," she said, and spun midstride. "If you need to find me —"

He glanced up, distracted, already focused

on something else. "Bradford's old office,"
he said.

"You know it," she said.

The three other faces watched her go.

Munroe returned to the landing with nineteen minutes to spare. Alina smiled, relief and anxiety washed into one brief flash. Munroe sat beside her and glanced at the notebook, which lay open on her lap.

"Nothing?"

Alina shook her head. "It's been very quiet."

Finding the men who'd been with Bradford the night the belt was taken would have been too easy, too lucky, like this. Munroe stood and said, "Let's go."

They returned to the hotel the hard way, the long way, along random streets and out-of-the-way misdirection, on the small chance Munroe had been followed from the facility to the stairwell to the bike, always mindful of pedestrians, police, and the many instant roadblocks that arose in the form of delivery bikes and delivery trucks.

A summer rainstorm became an extra

delay and an additional precaution, which allowed them a chance to grab something to eat. The sky had started its descent into gray by the time Munroe took the bike into the hotel parking garage.

She was off the bike, helmet beneath her arm, when that same animal instinct of hours earlier, of being watched — hunted — raised the warning along the back of her neck. On the other side of the Ninja, Alina tugged at the chin strap and pulled off her helmet. Munroe put a hand to her arm to get her attention, then her finger to her lips.

With a cut of her eyes and the tip of her head, Munroe motioned Alina over behind a concrete pillar. Alina slipped out of sight and, without turning, Munroe shut her eyes and breathed in the ambience of the garage, feeling for sensory input to tell her what went on behind her back.

The fight had come to seek her out.

They would have been watching when the bike had pulled in, would have likely seen Alina slip away. They'd searched and found, and now they had come to collect and kill, just as Alina had said.

Munroe knelt on one knee beside the bike, buffing scratches and smudges with a sleeve while footsteps reached out from both ends of the garage: a timed pattern that said the bodies coordinated their move in her direction. Seven days of frustration, of stolen life and stolen love, of the need to protect and avenge, stretched out from dark recesses like filthy arms from dungeon bars, crying for release.

Hope, in the coming attack, opened the floodgates of rage.

Time slowed and sound compressed into water condensation echoing a musical drip off concrete walls and floors; into the drizzle-spray of tires on the pavement as a car drove by outside; into children's laughter in the distance.

And footsteps, three sets of footsteps, moving in cautiously behind her back. Munroe waited, focused on the reflection in the bike's red fairing. Behind her head, shadows of brandished pipes stood tall like baseball bats readied for the pitcher's windup, elongating and warping as the men neared.

Munroe counted heartbeats and felt the rhythm, and then she rolled.

The metal bars came down hard into the empty space where she'd been a half-heartbeat before. She came up swinging, helmet chin-guard in hand, all her weight, her full momentum thrown into that backward strike. The man on the right flinched.

He ducked too slowly, moved too late.

The swing smashed helmet into head. He collapsed.

Time blurred and lost meaning.

The past layered on top of the present, blow against blow; speed, the ability to react and defend, resurrected from those many nights in the dark where, ruthless and savage, she'd survived through absolute refusal to die.

But this was wrong, all wrong.

In every swing she felt it, every dodge and parry.

These men weren't the past, weren't even the present.

They had arrogance but not skill; they weren't fighters.

She waited for them to come at her again.

Instead, they looked at one another: nervous, off-script: foot soldiers who'd brought the fight to her but weren't the fight she wanted.

The pounding inside her chest groaned in understanding.

The drive for release, for pain, pushed her at them.

She pointed the metal bar toward one, letting him know that she'd marked him for attack. He took several steps toward the garage exit.

A shadow moved in her peripheral vision: his partner flanking and closing in. Munroe pivoted, swung, and connected the metal bar to his shoulder: small pain, a half second of diversion. He retaliated and opened himself up like a fool. She dodged and dropped, then drove the metal bar across his shin: crippling pain, unbearable pain, she knew.

She wrenched the bar from his grasp and cracked it hard against his rib cage. His mouth opened in a soundless yell and he dropped to his knees. She hit him again, then rotated toward his companion, who, in those same seconds, had backed away another few steps. His eyes darted from her to his partners and then he turned and ran.

The crippled one dragged himself away, full of surrender, and Munroe stood in place, rocklike and solid, eyes tracking him, breathing past the urges that drove her to move in for the kill and finish what he'd started. Then he, too, was gone.

Somewhere on the edge of awareness her shoulder throbbed.

With one bar in each hand she walked toward the unconscious man. She kicked him, placing anger and frustration where it was least effective, and then stood over him. Boot to torso, she shoved him onto his back.

He was in his very early twenties, maybe five foot seven, all bone and sinew and stylish hair. In the echo of the garage footsteps shuffled and clothing rustled: movements small and cautious. Munroe knelt and placed the pipes beside the body, then, without turning, said, "You can come out now."

Slowly Alina came and stood beside her.

Munroe said, "You recognize him?"

Alina shook her head, knelt beside her, and with trembling fingers unbuttoned the man's shirt and tore it open. She glanced up at Munroe, surprise etched deep in her expression. In a near whisper, she said, "No tattoos."

Munroe said, "Fanfuckingtastic."

Then, "We're leaving. Get your stuff."

Alina walked past the motorcycle and picked the second helmet up off the ground. Munroe felt for a pulse, then put her ear to the man's chest, where his heart thumped out strong and steady. She opened his eyelids and checked his pupils. He'd have the mother of all headaches when he woke, but at least she hadn't killed him.

Munroe searched his pockets for a phone, a wallet, some form of identification, and came up empty. She checked his teeth for damage, but they were clean, and his arms and hands for needle tracks. She didn't find them, though that didn't eliminate addiction as the motive that had made him stupid enough to start a fight on someone else's behalf — money had the same effect.

She stared at his skin, clean and blemish free.

No tattoos, but that didn't mean anything in and of itself.

For the same reason that members of organized crime embraced tattoos, many also shunned them. *Irezumi,* ink inserted under the skin needle point by needle point, was painful, time-consuming, and expensive: a badge of honor and manliness, and a mark of the outlaw so culturally taboo that public bathhouses, fitness centers, and hot springs — places where bare skin would be seen — barred those with tattoos from entry, and politicians on witch hunts rallied an already tattoophobic public to fire tattooed employees.

The lack of tattoos wasn't what marked these attackers as something other than Jiro's men, their softness did. Boys like these, full of bravado and without a lot of skill, had no business coming after her and she couldn't begin to guess at who'd sent them.

Munroe stared out toward the exit where

the other two had gone. They were a piece of the puzzle that didn't fit — raised questions and possibilities that she hadn't even begun to ask — not the least of which was how they'd come to be there, lying in wait, well in advance of her arrival.

Munroe rode the streets at random, slow, to compensate for the lack of focus that the adrenaline dump brought. Each time they passed a hotel, Alina tapped her on the shoulder, and when at last Munroe found one that felt right, she took the bike another several blocks away and left it there.

The front desk was on the second floor, and against Alina's protests, Munroe left her downstairs. She secured the key, then returned to the ground floor for Alina and used the elevator to bypass the lobby and prying eyes who might remember the blonde. The room was slightly bigger and slightly older than the little cube that had been their prior hideaway.

Munroe turned to leave again.

Alina, eyes wide, voice hoarse, said, "Where are you going?"

"To collect the things we've left behind."

Alina stood, reached for her shoes, grabbed her purse, and held it to her chest. Munroe, patience worn thin, tolerance for babysitting used up, said, "I don't mind another fight, you want one, too?"

Alina dropped to the bed, drew her legs up, wrapped her arms around them, and tucked her chin into her knees, small and childlike. She stared up at Munroe, eyes red and face full of hurt. Munroe stomped into the hallway for the stairs, door thud echoing in her wake.

Their original hotel room was undisturbed, everything as they'd left it, which meant the boys with pipes had never gone beyond the garage. Munroe untaped the diagrams from the wall, folding each page as neatly as possible. Together with the laptop and whatever else she could fit, she stuffed two backpacks.

To take it all, she'd have to make another trip.

Frustration burned her. These things were part of the costume of becoming, items she could have shed if she'd had money to spare and time to waste. She'd return for the rest when Alina was no longer her problem.

Alina glanced up when Munroe stepped through the door. Munroe dropped the backpacks on the floor. "Take a shower and try to get some sleep," she said. "We're starting early in the morning."

Like a petulant child, Alina shut off the

television and carried her stuffed purse into the *ofuro*. A few minutes later the water kicked on and Munroe pulled out the laptop, connected to wi-fi, opened the phone application, and dialed the number Samantha Walker had sent for Warren Green, the military contact on the other side of Bradford's phone transcripts. It had taken this long to make the go-go-go of real-time work with the time-zones differences and follow the thread.

When the line connected, Munroe said, "Miles Bradford calling from Japan. Please let Warren know it's urgent."

"Mr. Green is in a meeting," a pleasant voice said. "I'd be happy to take a message."

"When's he expected back?"

"After eleven."

"I'll try again later. Just let him know I called."

The line went dead. Munroe shut the lid, then blew out exhaustion and irritation. Confirming the truth behind Bradford's conversation — if she could even get to the truth — wouldn't help Bradford in the moment, but it would be one less land mine to step on in sorting out the mess of lies.

Munroe stood and shoved the television to the far end of the desk. She unfolded the diagram, straightened the pages, and taped the web of connections back up as they'd been before. The questions were the same, relentless in their press for answers, and the attack inside the garage only raised more of them.

In a big bold scrawl, Munroe added the young men with pipes to an index card, stuck it randomly among the others, and sat in the desk chair tipped back with her hands behind her head, contemplating a puzzle whose pieces had just gotten dumped out and switched around.

She drew down, down, away from the clutter, into the mind of an entrenched spy-thief. She became the conductor in this orchestra of obfuscation, became the thief. Thoughts that had nagged her, incongruences she'd shoved to the background during the last two days of constant movement, came bubbling to the surface.

Munroe opened her eyes, stared at the web, and then stood.

She could make sense of Bradford's setup. If he'd gotten close, been on the verge of discovery, or had already discovered something without realizing what he had, he would have had to be removed. Murder, too, would have made sense — if it had been *Bradford* who'd gotten dead.

But setting Bradford up through the

murder of a third party, in the same facility where the spy had been entrenched — no, that was wrong.

That was very much a case of shitting where you ate.

If, indeed, a corporate spy had embedded within the organization, if technology theft was a true issue and not merely a pretense used to bring Bradford in as a scapegoat for something else, then the thing that spy would want more than anything other than the technology itself was invisibility.

An investigation conducted by law enforcement on company property looking for accomplices was not conducive to invisibility. Gnawing suspicion among fellow workmates was not conducive to invisibility. And yet, in spite of this, a woman *had* been murdered inside the company — a Chinese woman — so Bradford could take the fall.

Munroe replayed his words: *Company executives seem pretty convinced that the theft is coming from China's direction.* Bradford had used the plural, as if many in upper management were in agreement.

I figure someone's watching for something I don't know anything about, he'd said, *that they're using my presence like a stick in the bush to flush game, a wedge to split the log, a straw man, a distraction.* He'd evaded when she'd asked him if he'd had any idea who or what, but had left behind an external drive with three lists of suspects. The Chinese woman hadn't been on any of them.

In the dark, before dawn, Munroe stood beside the bed, staring down as Alina slept on, an arm thrown over her head, blond hair tangled between sheet and pillow. She debated a run for freedom; she could write a note, leave the woman on her own for the day. In the end, her promise of protection wouldn't let her.

The streets were still sleepy and sluggish when they reached the landing across from the facility. Munroe waited until Alina was settled, then left her there with the notebook and a bag full of food and drinks that they'd purchased from a *konbini* along the way.

She walked into the wide glass doors at seven, ahead of all but the most dedicated of employees, and took the stairs up, winding through the hallways toward the back half of the building, to the research and development lab that didn't require high-level clearance.

Munroe waited outside the hall that branched to the department, spent fifty minutes nodding and greeting employees as they arrived, until her target appeared: white blouse and bland gray skirt, same as every other woman in the building, short black hair pulled into a clip just as it had been on the day Bradford had pointed her out. Two Chinese women had lunched and left together that day she'd visited with Bradford, and one of them was still alive.

The woman shied away when Munroe approached, cringing, like she'd been backed against a wall by an attacking dog. Munroe presented the security badge and the woman blanched, then whispered in protest.

"The police have already spoken with me," she said. Her Japanese was fluent with only the slightest hint of an accent. "I've already answered the other security men's questions."

Munroe touched the woman's elbow, using her body as a tool to crowd her. "We'll be very quick," she said, guiding her back into the main hall.

Other employees passed by, staring blatantly. The woman glanced right and left, as if seeking help or assurance, but she didn't resist the pressure encouraging her forward.

Munroe walked her down the stairs to the

conference room that Okada had taken her to when she'd surprised him on the day after Bradford's arrest. He knew the layout of the building's listening devices better than most and if the room had been good enough for him, then it would suffice for her.

Munroe opened the door and the woman, eyes wide and jaw clenched, went to sit in the chair farthest away, clutching her bag up tight to her chest.

Munroe pulled the second seat from the wall and positioned it so that she was at an angle, blocking the view to the door, yet close enough that their knees almost touched, though not so close that they crossed the boundaries of propriety. Leaning in, Munroe said, "Don't be scared, you're not in trouble. I'm new with the company. You've been here a lot longer than me, so maybe I should be scared of you."

The woman cracked the tiniest of smiles, then swallowed. "I'm not scared," she said. Tension in her body and her shallow breathing said otherwise.

Voice soothing and friendly, Munroe said, "You must be so tired of the same questions over and over. I have just a few more — they're new to me, but if in my confusion they're already old to you, will you tell me? So I can save you time?"

The woman nodded again and her grip on the bag eased just a bit.

Munroe said, "Tell me your name, please, just so I can be sure everything is accurate."

"Xiao Wei," the woman said.

Munroe smiled and said, "See? This is so easy."

That earned another slightest blush of a smile.

Munroe said, "The police and the security men have asked you about Meilin's work habits, her friends, and her personal life, but it seems they didn't ask you about her boyfriend."

A victim had been killed inside the facility and found in an emergency exit stairwell, yet there'd been no cries for help and no evidence of a struggle — not even the smallest skin sample beneath her nails to keep Bradford out of the situation he was in now. On its face, the woman had died at the hands of someone she trusted enough to rendezvous with in an-out-of-the-way place.

The victim hadn't been married, so a boyfriend had been a place to start, and this was cold reading, starting from a logical assumption and using this woman's answers and body language to guide the conversation. Being right didn't matter; making her comfortable did, so that she'd clarify what was wrong between the facts.

The woman in the chair whispered, "Yes, they asked."

Munroe said, "But you told them that you didn't know anything, correct?"

The woman nodded.

Munroe said, "You and Meilin were good friends. She may not have told you who her boyfriend was, but there are things you do know about him that you haven't mentioned."

The woman's grip on her bag tightened and when her eyes jumped back up, there was fear.

Munroe placed a gentle hand on her shoulder and said, "It's not your fault that you weren't asked the best questions." She waited a beat. "Meilin's boyfriend works here, too, doesn't he? Perhaps he was someone important and they needed to keep their relationship a secret."

The woman nodded and whispered, "Yes."

"Do you know why it had to be a secret?"

"Only what you said, that he worked here and he was important and they couldn't be seen together."

"Because of his wife?"

"I don't know."

"Meilin was happy with this type of relationship?"

"Sometimes."

"It can be difficult to keep a relationship a secret — she must have also been sad at times."

Xiao Wei nodded again.

Munroe waited several heartbeats, then said, "Was her boyfriend good to her at least? Did he treat her well?"

The woman stiffened slightly. She said, "Sometimes."

Munroe followed the resistance. "Meilin had bruises."

"She fell."

"You didn't believe that."

The woman's eyes stayed toward the floor. "She wouldn't talk to me about it."

"You couldn't help her then," Munroe said, "but there were chances to make things right after she was killed. The police asked about her relationships. That would have been a way to tell them about the boyfriend and the bruises."

"They only wanted to know about the foreign security man, they asked if he was her boyfriend, they asked if he showed anger and jealousy. I told them that I didn't know anything about the foreign man, that Meilin's boyfriend was Japanese but that I didn't know his name or anything about him."

"They asked if he worked here?"

"They seemed only interested in the foreign man."

"What about the security men?"

"They never asked."

Munroe leaned forward again, so close that she could smell the fear on the woman's skin. "Let me ask you this," she said, "and there is no wrong answer, no right answer. If you had told the police who you thought might have killed Meilin, do you think they would have believed you?"

The woman's eyes remained downcast and she didn't move, didn't speak for the longest time. Finally she whispered, "I'm a foreigner, and Meilin was a foreigner." She glanced up and this time her eye contact was intense, almost pleading. "We are outsiders, but worse, we're Chinese. If I tell them her boyfriend is an important company man, why would they listen?"

Why, indeed? Across borders and culture, race and neighborhood lines, problems and blame always lay with the *other;* individuals so quick to rationalize sins and motivations in their own kind were blind to the torches and pitchforks taken up against the same in the *other.*

There was always an *other* to marginalize and dehumanize. Always.

And in this country, where nearly ninety-nine percent of the population belonged to the same collective culture and identity, outsiders of any kind made an easy *other*.

The victim was an other.

Bradford was an other.

Munroe rested her hand on the woman's shoulder again. She said, "If it matters at all, I believe you. I can see how you might fear losing your job — maybe even your life, just like Meilin."

The woman offered a weak smile.

Munroe said, "You're very brave."

The woman blushed and went back to staring at the floor.

"I don't have any more questions," Munroe said. "We can make a deal. Your coworkers know that you've spoken with me, and that means eventually everyone will know, and soon the gossip will start. Tell them I wanted to know about the man with the cowboy hat because I suspected he had a relationship with Meilin. If anyone asks me, I'll say the same."

The woman's breathing slowed and her shoulders relaxed, as if the world might be put right again. Munroe said. "If anyone questions you, it's because they're afraid of what you might have said to me." She handed the woman Bradford's card with his number scratched out and her own written in. "If you feel scared, you find a way to let me know. I'll protect your secrets."

DAY 8   4:30 P.M.

Munroe sat with Alina on the stairwell landing, sweat-drenched and waiting out the
remainder of the day, where Alina might, if
they were lucky, catch a glimpse of whoever
had been with Bradford the night the belt
had been taken.

Two men walked out of the facility entrance. Alina straightened, said "Oh!" then
sighed and said, "No."

Another false positive.

After the first three, Munroe had ignored
the rest.

Another half hour of nothing and Munroe
said, "I have to work late tonight — into the
morning. It's the type of thing that would
be better if you stayed at the hotel."

Alina's lips pressed together. She wrapped
her arms around her knees and said, "I will
come with you."

"You'll be safer in the room."

Several minutes of silence passed. As if

279

picking up where they'd left off, Alina said, "I will come with you."

Munroe glanced at her. "At the hotel, you're in one place, behind a locked door. If you come with me, I can't promise that you won't get hurt. If things go badly, I can't promise that I won't leave you behind."

Alina nodded, contemplating. She said, "Jiro will find me at the hotel and there I am, alone, behind a locked door, with no one to see him come or go."

"There's no trail for him to follow to find you."

"Someone already found you without a trail."

"That's different," Munroe said, and she turned back to watching the facility entrance.

"He is very well connected," Alina said. "Government. Police. Business. Like a small army to do what he says. He has to make an example of me. We don't see him, but his people are looking and I don't want to be in the hotel alone when his men come."

The facility doors opened again. Alina glanced up, but still nothing.

They stayed on the landing until the workday ended, and then Munroe retrieved the Ninja and parked it at the side of the building, down a pedestrian path, near a dozen bicycles and a single scooter. The evening came, the sky darkened, and shortly after nine, Okada left the building with a group of several men.

Munroe nudged Alina and they jogged down the stairs for the bike, sudden action after so much waiting. Okada and his workmates drove in two cars, and Munroe followed, keeping a long line of vehicles between them.

Twelve-hour days at the office weren't enough. Now came the afterwork in snack bars, which were hostess club lite, or karaoke clubs, hostess clubs, or *izakaya,* which were drinking establishments.

Several kilometers took them to a strip of pavement just wide enough to get off the road. The two cars parked. Beside the parking strip was a single structure, old and worn, with wooden walls and a clay tile roof. Neon at the door and window clashed with the serenity of the paper lanterns that hung off wide, curved eaves. Munroe continued past.

Finding a break in traffic, she looped a U-turn, pulled off the road, and squeezed the Ninja backward into a narrow alley between buildings just up the road. Bradford hadn't been joking when he'd said she'd be grateful for the Mira's smaller size, but even the car needed conventional parking.

Munroe tugged off the helmet and Alina did likewise, asking no questions, making no conversation, but remaining a pebble in Munroe's boot all the same.

Okada left the bar shortly after eleven while the rest of his coworkers remained. He wasn't falling down drunk, but clearly not sober. He put key to ignition and Munroe smiled. In a culture where conformity meant everything, Okada was a rule breaker — or at the least, a rule bender.

Society cast no shame on public drunkenness, rarely required ID for alcohol purchases, turned a blind eye to minors drinking, and viewed inebriation as a pressure valve: a socially acceptable excuse for inexcusable behavior.

But there was zero tolerance for driving under any influence.

High-end restaurants and *izakayas* often refused to serve alcohol to drivers. Police checkpoints for breath analysis were common. Okada, simply by getting behind the wheel, risked the loss of his license, fines, and years in prison. Munroe followed him east, toward the mountains, in the same direction they'd gone on the night Bradford had been arrested.

They were in the hills when he turned off, into a neighborhood of square and modern houses, neat and tidy, squished tightly in long stretches of single-lane alley-width streets.

Munroe increased the distance, following the reflection of Okada's taillights against the road to guide her in a delayed turn-by-turn. She stopped before the entrance to his street, left Alina with the bike, and walked ahead to watch as he maneuvered his car backward into a space between light pole and house, parking so narrow it would have been reserved for motorcycles back in Dallas. He went from the car up the plant-hedged walkway to the front door, and lights turned on upstairs.

Munroe returned to Alina and crawled the bike away.

The upstairs light had been Okada's wife, waking to welcome her husband home, to prepare his food and heat his *ofuro,* to do laundry as he ate, and then to clean up his mess when he was finished. If she was traditional, she would also rise again in five hours to prepare the bento he'd take to work and lay out his clothes.

Things were changing, but many still adhered to the old ways: some out of habit;

some out of cultural expectations; some because tradition bound wives to their husband and his family and a myriad of time-consuming rules and societal roles; and some because marriage — no matter her education, talent, aspirations, or value — was a death knell to her career that would soon find her fired, leaving her no other option. But the light in Okada's window only said that a wife who'd already fed and bathed the children, put them to bed and gone to bed herself, had risen when he'd come home.

Several streets over, Munroe found a park and playground and waited there, utilizing a bench as a bed, ignoring Alina, studying the stars, allowing memory and strategy to take her to the random places memory often did. When the night had deepened enough, Munroe rose, left Alina with the Ninja, and followed the streetlights to Okada's little blue Nissan.

DAY 9   12:19 A.M.

Munroe inched beyond Okada's car, into the carport and the semi-cluttered space between the side of his house and the iron bars of the neighbor's vine-covered fence. She scooped several stones out of the gravel and dropped them to the ground.

No dog barked. No lights turned on. No windows opened.

She tossed a few more against the concrete steps leading up to the sliding door and then others through the gaps in the siding around the pier-and-beam foundation. The house remained quiet.

She tried the screen on the side door, whose glass had been left open for air circulation. The screen slid open. As with so many other home owners in Japan, the Okadas hadn't bothered locking doors or windows.

Boots off and carried in one hand, Munroe stepped up into a single room divided by a dining table, with a spotless kitchen on one side and an open living area on the other. Baskets of children's toys and game controllers took up almost as much space as the low-slung table and couch. She paused long enough to confirm that the downstairs was empty, then slipped into a tiny hall, past the *genkan,* and rounded up tightly curved stairs, pausing on each step, testing for sound.

Munroe found the wife and two small children in one room — futons filling the floor space and the sleepers tangled up in sheets and light blankets like campers in an oversize tent. Okada was in the room two doors down, with only one futon on the floor, snoring away. That was common, too — wives and husbands sleeping in separate rooms after the children came along.

Munroe knelt on the tatami beside his sleeping form and placed her free hand over his mouth. He kept sleeping, so she nudged him and his eyes snapped open, first dully, and then in terror.

"Shhh," she said.

He nodded frantically.

She removed her hand and said, "Get some clothes on, we need to talk."

It took him a moment to draw the connections, but then they clicked. "What are you doing here?" he hissed, and then shock gave way to anger and he propped himself on an elbow and glared at her. "You're in my house. My house!"

"Shhh," she said again. "I'll wait."

Munroe turned her back to him and no movement happened, so she glanced over her shoulder and said, "I'm in your house, Tai. Your wife and children are down the hall. Shouldn't you be motivated to get *me* out? Put some clothes on, let's go."

Okada mumbled and grumbled, then pulled pants on and then a shirt and shoved his glasses onto his face. Munroe followed him down the stairs. He grabbed slippers from the *genkan* and shuffled into them when he stepped out the side door. He glared when Munroe sat in the door frame, stuffing her feet back into her boots, and then walked sullenly beside her until they were several houses down the street and he challenged her again.

"You were in my house."

"Yes," she said, "and now I'm out of your house. You should be happy."

She continued to the far end of the park, away from the Ninja and Alina, whose shadow Munroe could just make out. She motioned toward a bench, but Okada stayed standing.

"I apologize for coming into your home," she said. "I would have preferred something else, but this is the only way to talk privately. I need your help and I don't want to make you my enemy."

Okada's expression remained unreadable.

Munroe pulled out the security pass and held it toward him. "Did you know about this?" she said.

Okada reached for the pass. Angled the plastic to catch light from the nearest street lamp and then handed it back. "I didn't realize it would be you."

"Do you know why he wanted it made?"

Okada shook his head.

"You've been tracking my movements these past few days?"

"Of course," Okada said. "That's my job."

"When were you planning to confront me?"

"What have you done to yourself, you look like a man?"

"When did Miles have the badge made?"

"I don't remember the exact day, maybe four or five weeks ago."

Munroe ran the calendar pages in her head.

That pushed back to somewhere around the second time Bradford had gone to the hostess club, definitely before the fight, definitely before he'd brought her in to take a look around and talk about the Chinese women over lunch, which gave credence to what he'd said about having processed the paperwork with the intention of giving her what she wanted. And pointed to why he hadn't.

She said, "Miles asked you to help me because he trusted you."

"I don't want that honor," Okada said. "Never asked, never offered to help him, or you, or anyone. I've already done all that I can."

"You did offer," she said. "You might not have realized it, but you did."

He leaned forward ever so slightly, as if his body begged her to explain.

"The nail that sticks out gets hammered down," she said. "You know the proverb?"

"Everyone knows the proverb."

"You're that nail, Tai. You may not stick out to the people around you, but you do to people like Miles and me. He could see it, I can see it, and by being different from everyone else Miles worked with, you invited him to trust you."

Munroe paused, waiting for Okada to interject, and when he didn't, she said, "I've already set up my position in the facility. I've had things that have kept me from being at work full-time, but tomorrow I intend to take over Miles's responsibilities. I'll be there, each and every day, long days, until they throw me out."

"This has nothing to do with me," Okada said.

"I'm going to need a liaison," she said. "I need to know what you know, Tai, give me that and I'll find someone else to work with. If you were in my position, who would you avoid? Who would you be afraid of? Who are you afraid of now?"

Okada shuffled to the bench and sat beside her, staring out into the overgrown grass.

Munroe reverted to easier questions. "Let's start with the woman who died," she said. "What did Miles have on her?"

"Nothing," Okada said. "She was quiet and kept to herself. Did her job every day. Went home. After this whole thing happened, I pulled her records again and couldn't find anything worth flagging."

"What about a reason to kill her? Was she sleeping with anyone in the company — one of the bosses, maybe? Did she have access to anything that would have allowed her to accidentally stumble on damaging information?"

"The police will have looked," he said. "I

have looked also, trying to find connections. There's nothing unusual in her hiring, no special favors or courtesy involvement. She was a biochemist, part of the research and development, but not down in the lower lab, which you already know. Everything was routine, done through the proper department, all her paperwork in order, and nothing unusual regarding payments or schedule. No disciplinary problems. No suspicious activity."

"Did anybody try to stop you from looking into her history after she died? Redirect attention elsewhere? Focus on other things?"

"The opposite, actually, I was encouraged to keep digging."

"By whom?"

"Kobayashi-san. He's head of security, my boss."

"You found nothing in her personal life?"

Okada shrugged, as if to say that was beyond the scope of his department.

"What about the other security team, they looked into her, too?"

"Both departments coordinated. Kobayashi-san led the investigation."

"All of the people involved in this investigation believe Miles is guilty?"

"He was arrested. If he wasn't guilty, the

291

police would have let him go."

Munroe ran a palm over her hair and counted ten long seconds before responding. She could have written off Okada's stance as a quaint by-product of a rule-revering, order- and authority-deferring society, except it mirrored a common American belief that prosecutors only pursued the guilty and everyone who claimed innocence was lying. Shit like this only reinforced her misanthropy.

She whispered, "That doesn't answer the question."

Okada leaned forward. He laced his fingers and stared at them while seconds ticked on. Finally he said, "This came as a surprise, even for those who didn't like Miles and weren't happy he was hired. But who would want to believe he didn't do it? That would make the police wrong, and if this is true, the murderer could be any one of us."

"It's easier to believe the foreigner did it," Munroe said. Easier for everyone from law enforcement to company executives to the casual observer to simply accept the first story at face value and eliminate the need for hard questions and hard choices.

Okada said, "Kobayashi-san is the one I am afraid of, because he is my boss. But he's not your boss. For you it is Tagawa-san, head of operations, do you know him?"

"We've met, but that's not the kind of fear I'm talking about. Who hated Miles most?"

"Dillman," Okada said. He pronounced it Dee-ru-ma-nu. *"Hafu.* You've met him, I think."

"Hafu?" she said.

"His mother is Japanese. Father is American."

"Ah," she said, "half. Miles suspected him for theft?"

"Not a suspect, an annoyance. Miles found ways to make Dillman show his anger and lose face. Dillman hated him most."

"Enough to murder someone to get even?"

"I don't know who killed the woman," Okada said.

"Miles went to Kitashinchi a few times with others from work. Did you know anything about that?"

"This type of after-work drinking, socializing, is very normal," he said.

"Yes, mostly. Did you know he'd gone?"

"I think so," Okada said.

"He never mentioned anything unusual?"

Okada shook his head and then paused, as if he wasn't entirely sure, and she allowed him time to think back and count the days.

"Maybe yes, but not with words," Okada said. "He behaved differently."

293

"Explain differently."

"It's not possible to explain," he said. "The difference was air, something felt but not touchable."

"When did that start?" she said, but she knew the answer before Okada spoke it. The last time they'd discussed this, in the *takoyaki* seating area the night Bradford had been arrested, Okada had said Bradford had changed, had become more private, after she'd come into the office. But her day in the office had also been the final night Bradford had gone to the hostess club. He hadn't changed because he'd learned something from her, he'd changed because the belt had been stolen.

Confirming this, Okada said, "The last time."

"Do you know the men he went with?"

"If it's important, then it may be possible to learn."

"Without bringing trouble on your own head?"

Okada smiled slyly, as if she'd pleased him by acknowledging his predicament, and he gave a curt nod.

"That would help," she said, and then in a long-shot reach, "For certain you have no idea who Miles suspected?"

Okada's hands tensed, as if he committed

some discomforting betrayal. "We spoke of many things, insignificant things, but he never mentioned suspects."

"It must have been hard, being taken away from your department."

Okada shifted, as though her concern embarrassed him. "I received honor in learning from someone with such experience."

"And to spy on him? Report his movements to your own boss?"

Okada didn't respond.

Munroe stood and took a step away from the bench. "I like you, Tai," she said. "Miles liked you. You know more than you think you know, so watch your back, okay?"

Munroe leaned into a moss-covered wall at a corner near the street's dead end, insides itching at the stillness and the passing time. Across the road, a bird screeched, chasing a rival from a favored perch. Somewhere in the distance a dog barked. And far down the block, in the shade of trees overhanging the consulate wall, two police officers conversed with the casual indifference of men who'd not yet experienced the urgency of danger and, at their current post, didn't expect to.

Only the passport stood in the way of freedom — hers and Alina's both.

It had been thirty minutes since she'd dropped Alina off at the consulate gate. In the wait Munroe had taped over the Ninja's license plates, a precaution she'd undo outside the neighborhood if they got that far without incident.

She was close, so close to cutting the

woman loose.

In a preempt against further delays, predictable and corruptible, she'd sent Alina inside with air ticket in hand — providing proof of today's departure and a sense of desperation — and enough money to ensure they wouldn't be coming back for another round.

Munroe checked the time. Alina would call; should have called by now. And although the gesture was pointless, she checked for missed calls, too, then stiffened at movement far, far down the street.

Two black European-made cars turned the corner.

The neighborhood was a matrix of roads hosting any number of houses and apartments. The vehicles could have come for other reasons, but it didn't take a life spent living on the edge to know that they hadn't.

Inside her chest the first drumbeats tapped out faint and quiet.

The cars crawled in the consulate's direction, the lead car stopping when it reached the police van. The window rolled down. Conversation ensued and Munroe measured body language between law enforcement and occupants.

One of the officers motioned down the road, in Munroe's direction.

Her hands tingled and she clenched them tight.

The cars reversed and then parked just far enough beyond the van that they weren't directly in front of the consulate's property, and anyone passing to or from the consulate would be forced to slow and run the gauntlet.

The phone in Munroe's hand vibrated.

The arrangement had been a call from the consulate's phone, just a few rings to signal that Alina was ready for pickup. Munroe answered instead.

Alina said, "Oh."

Munroe said, "Are you in a place where you can talk?"

The smile in Alina's voice faded. "Yes," she whispered.

"There are issues outside. We can still catch that flight, but only if you do exactly as I say."

Alina, voice choked, said, "Jiro."

"Do you have your passport?"

"Yes."

"Check your purse. Make sure your money and ticket are there. Tuck them inside your passport and secure it all together inside a zipper where nothing can fall out. Tell me when you've done it."

There was a pause and Alina's heavy

breathing, then Alina said, "Everything is secure in the purse."

Down the street, the doors to the rear car opened.

"You're going to have to move quickly," Munroe said.

Four men stepped out. Two waited beside the hood, while the others walked toward the lead car, to the rear passenger side, where the window rolled down again. Munroe said, "You'll need to convince someone that you have to go out the staff exit, to the parking-lot gate, and you'll have to convince them to walk with you. Can you do it?"

"Yes," Alina said.

"Call me when you're ready."

Munroe straddled the Ninja, shoved off the kickstand, and thumbed the ignition. With the bike rumbling beneath her, she waited, counting off time in her head. Move too soon and Jiro's men would come after her and she'd have to fight her way through them to reach Alina; move too slowly and they'd reach Alina before she did.

The phone vibrated. Alina said, "I am ready."

Munroe said, "Do you trust me?"

Alina whispered, "Yes."

"Make sure your purse strap is over your head, not just your shoulder. I'll reach the gate when you do. Get through. Grab the helmet. Get on the bike. We'll be rolling before you have a chance to sit fully."

Alina responded with the heavy breathing of panic and then hung up.

Munroe shoved the phone into her pocket and the helmet on her head.

There had to be someone on the inside, someone who'd known Alina was soon to finish and called them to come and collect their package, and who hopefully wasn't the one walking her out the door.

Munroe eased slowly into the street, a big black and red mark on what had otherwise been empty pavement.

The four men standing outside the cars straightened and faced her.

The doors of the lead car opened and two more men stepped out.

Munroe guided the bike in their direction, riding an imaginary line down the middle of the road. She stopped as close to them as strategy would allow.

Boots to the pavement, she balanced the machine while four of the men strode toward her and beat by beat the inner count continued.

The taps of adrenaline turned another rotation. Closer they came, and her focus shifted between them and the gate and then them again.

Timing meant everything.

On they walked, four in a line, past the police van, past the consulate's pedestrian gate, past the metal gate that closed off access to consulate staff parking, past the neighbor's property line.

Munroe gripped the throttle, measuring movement.

The two men beside the car whipped their focus toward the consulate. The parking gate began the slow slide open.

Munroe punched forward. The four men froze, a heartbeat of hesitation and indecision. Munroe cut left, around them, for the gate. Cut too close. Clipped the nearest man in the line of four but heard nothing, felt nothing, her focus entirely on the opening, on the need to get to it and to reorient the bike's nose to the street before Alina stepped fully through.

The four men spun and ran back, past the neighbor's property line, toward her and the opening gate. The two men at the car came at her from the opposite direction, both sides closing in.

The policemen had disappeared into the van.

Alina grabbed the helmet from its straps, took its place, and shoved it in her lap.

All six men pounded forward.

Out of time, they were out of time.

Munroe peeled around, tires spinning, leaving black against the pavement. Alina clutched Munroe, throwing the bike's balance.

Hands reached out, grabbing for Munroe, grabbing for the handlebars, grabbing empty air; hands reached for Alina to pull her off.

The engine screamed; Alina screamed. Munroe fought to keep the bike upright and lurched forward against hips and legs and arms, and then the front broke through, over a torso, past a blur of bodies. In the mirror three men were on the ground. To the right, from behind the window on the lead black car's passenger side, eyes stared out. Jiro's eyes: angry eyes on an indifferent expression, on a good-looking face, a young face.

The bike careened down the opening between the vehicles.

In the mirror, the lead car pulled out after them, scraping a wall in making the tight turn, pausing to let running men into the passenger doors.

One tight corner to the next, Munroe sped out of the neighborhood, toward the airport. Jiro would follow. He didn't need to see her to know where she was going, the passport told him that. It didn't matter that he followed, only that she got Alina inside the terminal where there were cameras everywhere and security was jumpy, and Jiro and his men knew better than to enter on a mission of kidnap or kill.

Munroe diverted down side streets, taking random turns at will. She stopped long enough to unclamp Alina's frozen hands from off her shirt, pull the spare helmet from between them, and stick it on Alina's head so they wouldn't get pulled over along the way.

She stayed off the freeway for safety and to avoid attention, though the slower roads cost her time, and followed lane changes to the airport until she was forced to enter the bridge and ride out in the open.

On the departures ramp black flashed in her mirror.

She sped up and cut off a small van in a dash for the sidewalk. She braked hard and elbowed Alina.

Alina slid off the bike and attempted to unbuckle the helmet.

The black car stopped beside Munroe, blocking her in.

Munroe pushed Alina toward the sidewalk. "Take it," she said. "Run!" The woman glanced up and, seeing the car, bolted.

Behind the dark window were Jiro's eyes. He jabbed a finger at the glass and smiled a knowing smile, a mocking smile.

The black car's doors opened. Feet hit pavement and gave chase. Alina slipped beyond the terminal's sliding glass entry. Having lost her, the men turned back for Munroe while the car with Jiro's laughing face blocked her from the side and vehicles front and back kept her from pulling free.

Munroe took the bike up onto the sidewalk, guiding the front wheel around carts and bodies: people too preoccupied with their own departure and belongings to look up and notice the danger until she was already upon them.

The black car followed her progress alongside. The men on foot gave chase from behind. The crowded sidewalk was a course of moving obstacles and she could do this for an hour and never pick up enough speed to lose the men behind or get free of Jiro. Munroe swerved and bumped down to the road between the luggage of two cars unloading at the curb. Her tires hit the pavement just behind Jiro's vehicle and she followed the pedestrian crosswalk against the light. Horns blared and car brakes squealed. She wound into the parking garage, down a level, and out the entrance against the traffic, to the nearest junction, where she braked, reoriented, and slipped into the airport's outward flow.

The black car was nowhere in sight. No police lights yet, either, though that could change. Adrenaline charged through her system, narrowing her focus to the point of danger. Munroe followed the traffic and turned off the road, down a side street where bicycles and mail carts and vending machines mixed with pedestrians walking where they would in the absence of sidewalks.

Munroe pulled tight against a corner and shut off the engine, waiting, breathing, allowing her heart rate to settle.

Alina was free, promise fulfilled, burden gone.

The last of this thread waited in the hotel room, things left abandoned after the fight with the boys with pipes. She needed to collect them and close out the bill before she was truly able to return to the facility and focus on Bradford.

Munroe ripped the tape off the plates and waited longer still, then finally started up again, turning for downtown, where she could stash her ride for a few hours. She could run this final errand while killing time measuring the response, if any, to the airport drama. She found parking at Osaka station, placed her belongings in a locker, and continued to the hotel empty-handed and on foot.

Lobby air-conditioning was a balm against the heat and the clerk's smile a warning that sent the inner timpani back to pounding war drums. The tell of threat came within the shadows of discomfort in his pleasant welcome.

Prudence said to turn around, to abandon what remained, but the heady rush of need and want pushed her forward.

This was the fight she'd been denied in defending Alina from Jiro's chase.

Munroe took the stairs at a run and dumped into the hall in time to hear the muted ring of a phone. Footfalls soft against the carpet, she approached her room and knelt, ear to the door. A male voice spoke words of acknowledgment and then came a minute of conversation between two men.

The desk clerk had notified them that she was on her way.

Now they waited.

Munroe scooted out of the fish-eye's range. Patient in the drawing silence, she invited the men inside to make the first move. Her absence would create agitation, then anxiety, and the desire to see for themselves.

Vibration came toward the door. Whoever was behind it turned to speak to his companion, close enough that Munroe could make out the conversation as they mocked the desk clerk and dickered back and forth. They'd waited through the night. They were hungry and tired and ready to finish business.

Want built tight inside her chest, her skin tingling, itching for the pain to follow and for the violence that would scratch the itch. She had no fear of fists, or blade, or blood. Nothing could be done to her now that she hadn't already survived. The only caution, muted against the want, was Bradford not yet set free.

The door handle moved. Her heart fluttered in ecstasy.

The door opened. A foot stepped through.

A head leaned forward to peer into the hallway.

Munroe lunged upward, the full brunt of her momentum connecting beneath the jaw. The force of the impact set her ears ringing, bones transferring the crack of violence as his head snapped back. His legs buckled. She grabbed his collar and shoved him inward, using his body as a shield.

Six steps forward, against the window, the second man pulled a knife.

Knife as weapon of choice meant no gun.

Instant assessment, instant strategy change. Firearms laws, a gift to the predator, created of her speed and lack of fear a god among mortals.

Munroe plowed into the tight space between bathroom cube and wall, and heaved the body into the knife man.

He pushed the deadweight aside, buying her a microsecond lead.

The unconscious man hit the desk and bounced backward. In that same heartbeat Munroe went around his legs, up on the bed, and threw herself feetfirst into the knife man's knees, twisting in midflight, her hands clamped onto the cutting arm before her boots fully connected.

Her opponent was shorter than she, but stockier, heavier. He had muscles and street-fighting smarts, his arms and legs writhing and struggling to gain the upper hand.

They tumbled to the floor, between chair legs and bed legs and desk legs.

He folded in half, scissor-locked around Munroe's hips.

She forced pressure points on his wrist, his elbow, and yanked the arm with the knife hard out of place. He screamed, and in that scream of anger and rage he punched with his free hand, blows to her rib cage, her back, her head.

She found relief in the pain and laughed, crazy and blind, forcing more pressure onto his arm. He yelled and hit harder, faster, and she stole his knife, eliminating his bulk and strength, because a knife didn't need power, only contact, and he would bleed the same as every other man.

Munroe twisted and plugged the blade beneath her, low into his side. He kept swinging and she drove hard again, and when he kept punching, she stabbed his legs and with the cutting forced a break in his hold.

She kneed his groin and still he didn't let go or stop punching.

Behind the grunts and yells came shuffling: the man with the broken jaw rising up to continue the fight. Munroe kneed again and shoved hard, throwing her weight forward at the same time her opponent pulled. She slammed a leg backward, boot to the knee of the broken-jawed man.

The force of her thrust popped the knife man's arm out of joint, and she stabbed the knife into his unwounded shoulder, yanked hard through cartilage and back again as she pulled the knife out and then pressed the blade tip up under his chin in that sweet soft spot, with just enough force for the point to cut skin. And with that movement, he froze.

Panting, Munroe reached an arm up off the floor, yanked the ceramic flower vase off the desk, and slammed it into his head. The knife man went limp and she turned to the broken jaw, who'd already started crab-crawling for the door. She stomped on his chest and boosted over him. With her back to the door, she turned to face him, knife ready to work again.

He stared up at her, eyes glassed over, and for the first time she was able to see — truly see — him and his companion. She smashed an elbow down into his head and he slumped over. Knifepoint to his shirt, she sliced the material open. Tattoos covered his shoulder and his chest. She kicked him in the ribs, for herself, for Alina, for the stupidity of them having waited out last night in the wrong place, for their crappy boss and his attempted ambush, and the time all of this had stolen from her freeing Bradford.

She kicked him again, letting frustration loose, and then stopped and glared. She took a breath and glanced around, taking stock of yet another mess.

Her backpack was on the bed, its items strewn.

Munroe stepped over the broken jaw for the bathroom.

She washed the knife in the sink, rinsed blood spatter out of her hair, tore off her shirt, and replaced it with one from the backpack.

She went over the room with a washcloth, wiping down every surface, including — especially — the vase on the floor by the knife man's head.

With the washcloth wrapped around the knife hilt, Munroe dipped the blade into knife man's blood and smeared the blood across the shirt of the broken-jawed man. She would have flicked spatter patterns, too, if it wouldn't have complicated her own exit. She placed the knife into broken jaw's hand, wrapped his fingers around the hilt, and clenched his fist in her fist for a good

312

set of prints. She left the blade out of reach beneath the desk, stuffed the washcloth and the bloodied shirt into her backpack, then packed up the last of her belongings and stepped out into the hall and shut the door.

The hotel had no security cameras — nothing but the desk clerk's word to document that she'd been present. By leaving these men alive, she could flip the burden, could be spared living on the run as a murder suspect while trying to solve Bradford's problem, and worst case — if everything that could possibly go wrong went wrong and then worse — they could claim she'd struck first and they'd retaliated in self-defense. But these were criminals in *her* hotel room.

Someone on the hotel staff had given the bleeding tattoos upstairs a key. Calling the police to deal with that mess would most certainly raise questions the hotel would rather avoid. Immigration had her thumbprints on file and the front desk knew her face. But all foreigners looked alike, and she'd provided false information upon check-in. If law enforcement did come after her, if they were able to connect her activity hotspots, and if she'd been sloppy enough to leave anything in the room that they could use to find her, then she deserved whatever followed.

The flight, the fight, the adrenaline dump, and the need to destroy and shower off evidence brought Munroe in for her first day of work later than she'd intended. The desk and the chair were in her office, as she'd been promised. She ignored them. The furniture and the workspace had been a bid for legitimacy. The building entry would be her office: crossroads between the three arms of the facility, where every employee, from executive to the janitor, was guaranteed to pass at least twice each day.

Munroe parked herself at the edge of a hall and, for no seeming purpose other than to introduce herself and waste time with useless conversation, she stopped everyone who went by. An hour in, Dillman showed up carrying a thin folder and wearing an expression of blatant unhappiness.

Munroe said, "Hello, Makoto or Dillman, never Mac. What can I do you for?"

Dillman's lips pinched, as if he couldn't quite tell if her words had been a welcome or an insult. He said, "I've been assigned as your liaison."

Munroe looked him up and down. "Well, that won't be much fun for either of us, will it?"

"Not my decision," he said. "Kobayashi-san's orders."

Munroe nodded, the only thing she could do, and parsed this curious turn, trying to slot it within the puzzle.

If Dillman was only meant to keep tabs on her and report back to his boss, then it made sense. But the position required reading and translating documents, interpreting conversations and navigating corporate culture. Dillman, as much foreign as he was local, was an odd choice for the job. "How's your written Japanese?" she said.

"Good enough."

Munroe leaned back into the wall. Good enough was subjective. If she actually needed to rely on him, *good enough* had the potential to create all manner of complications. But she didn't, and so she opted for manipulation instead.

"That couldn't have been easy if you didn't grow up here."

"Making up for lost time sucks," he said.

In that moment, in spite of herself, in spite of Bradford's distaste for him or that Dillman topped her list of suspects in Bradford's downfall, Munroe liked this *hafu.* "The pitfalls of being a third-culture kid," she said.

"Yeah?" he said. "You know that term?"

"Parents were missionaries."

"Dad was military," he said, "then private contractor."

"Your accent is awfully Australian for an American military brat."

"Five years in Sydney. Parents divorced when I was fifteen and I moved back here with my mom."

Munroe winced and said, "Ouch. All the unspoken rules and lack of tolerance for nonconformity? Props to you for pulling that off."

"Yeah," Dillman said, "kind of made everything else easy by comparison." Then changing the subject, he held up the folder. "Personnel roster. Tai says he was working on these before — before, you know."

Munroe motioned for the pages. Dillman handed them over.

She flipped through the names, all of which had been on the lists on Bradford's drive. Munroe handed the documents back. "Let's take a break," she said, and nodded down the hall, "do a little strategy, a little planning."

They walked in uncomfortable silence to Bradford's office and Munroe swung the door wide to the room's single chair and lonely desk.

Dillman looked at her first, then at the chair.

"Go on, take it," she said. "I'll stand."

He tossed the folder onto the desk, and with arms crossed he swung the chair around and sat. "Okay, Mr. Michael," he said, just slightly taunting, but without any of the hostility that he'd shown Bradford, "let's do your thing."

Munroe sat on the desk edge and picked up the roster. "In addition to these, Miles had others," she said. "I'd like you to start with the others."

"Can do those, can do these," Dillman said. "Can do whatever you want, but it's a waste of time."

The talk of Bradford's work had been a throwaway to test his reaction. He'd given it nothing but genuine dismissal.

"That so?" she said.

"Whatever you're looking for, whatever he was looking for, you're not going to find it in these." Behind the tone, seeping into his posture, was a subtle taunt that disguised wholesale irritation, with her, with Bradford, and with the waste of company resources and time that had come from bringing in the outsiders. "Every person in this facility has been vetted," he said, "first by the hiring department when checking references, then by a battery of interviews and psychological tests, and finally by the security team — multiple times. Every file in the personnel records scoured. Part of the annual review process involves pulling each record, updating and reconfirming the information." Dillman sighed and tapped the folder on the desk. "And, of course, anything Miles questioned, Tai would have gone over one more time. The personnel records are a dead end."

Munroe waited until the silence drew long enough for Dillman's smug assurance to offer surface cracks.

"How long have you been at this?" she said.

"Since I started with the company. Three years."

"Did you, personally, look into these backgrounds?"

"A fair number of them."

"I'm not calling your intelligence, integrity, or ability into question," she said. "Not calling anyone's work into question. But here's the thing: if — and that's an assumption — there's someone in this company who's been stealing technology, then they've also been at it for a long time."

She inched her shoulders down toward his. "You have to look at it this way. We only have two possibilities: Either everyone who works here is who they say they are or they aren't. If they aren't, then this person or persons knew what they were getting into. They knew everything about their life would be scrutinized — especially someone with a high security clearance. The last thing they would have done would be to offer a map."

"What are you saying?"

This time an undercurrent of ice ran through his words.

"Sometimes what you're looking for doesn't look like what you're looking for."

Dillman stared at her and Munroe stared back.

"You're going to start from the beginning," she said. "Every piece of family history, medical history, education, travel, anything you've got. You'll need to corroborate each detail without relying on a single piece of information in your files."

Dillman's stare turned blank.

"If you're looking at a school, track down a number that's not officially listed, talk to someone who didn't know your employee. If you're investigating a family, turn to neighbors or former teachers or coaches to see what they can verify. You get the idea."

"That's a lot of work," Dillman said.

"Yes," Munroe said. Investigative immersion that would leave him no time for breathing down her neck like an oafish wolf, frightening the field animals away as she walked the halls.

"It's wasted work," Dillman said. Hostility flickered beneath the ice. "Whoever the thief is could be exactly who they claim to be with not one data point of inconsistency. This is stupid. Not to mention we're dealing with Miles's work and anything he touched should be rejected out of hand."

"Why?" Munroe said.

Dillman hesitated. Munroe crossed her arms and smiled a fake smile. Dillman, as foreign as he was Japanese, wasn't averse to conflict. "Go ahead and say it," she said.

"Look at what he did. Look at who he is. Everything he handled is toxic."

Munroe leaned toward him and said, "You vetted Miles's background before he was contracted, right?"

"Of course."

"You personally?"

"Yes. What does that matter?"

"Did you find anything troublesome? Anything indicating he was mentally unstable? Lacked professional judgment? Wouldn't be capable of handling the project he'd been hired for?" She paused and changed inflection for emphasis, "That he might be a murderer?"

"That has nothing to do with anything. Murderers don't walk around wearing a sign. Capable people are capable of atrocious things."

Munroe slapped her leg and sat up straight. "Agreed. Let's start with that. We both agree that Miles is a capable man — capable of killing, yes — but a professional nonetheless."

Dillman nodded, slow and guarded, as if aware of having set himself up for a verbal trap, but not yet quite sure how.

Munroe said, "To get this contract, he wasn't just capable, he was extremely capable. So you have to ask yourself if a man like Miles, a man perfectly able to kill an opponent and make it look like an accident, would have been *stupid* enough to murder a woman and leave both body and murder weapon behind for someone to discover, then just hang around waiting for the police to arrest him?"

Without missing a beat, Dillman said,

"Absolutely. If the price was right, if there was some reason, like buying time to get stolen material on its way to the buyer. We'd see it as stupid, sure, but for him, a decade in prison might be worth it if the money was still waiting when he got out."

Munroe shook her head in mock chiding and, continuing with faux sadness, said, "Wouldn't he at least have removed his belt? Only the worst kind of idiot would have left that behind."

Dillman didn't answer.

"Think about it." She put a hand on his shoulder, using proximity to imply camaraderie: us against them. "The files he had are a place to start," she said. "If I'm wrong, then we'll have eliminated them and can begin fresh. If I'm right, then we save time and you get to be the company hero."

Dillman's glance darted up and his expression, holding back, still revealed far more than it should have. Munroe pressed the issue, just like cold reading.

"I'm here for a job," she said. "I do the work, my company gets paid. I'm in, out, and gone. You're here for the long haul. Six months after I leave, who's going to be remembered as the one to have fixed this mess? Me or you?"

Dillman's lips twitched at the corners, but

he remained silent.

"Blame falls on me if I'm wrong," she said, "and you can always claim that you'd been forced to follow my lead. If you have a problem with that, if you can't do the work, let's get things sorted out now. I'll ask Kobayashi-san to assign me someone else."

Dillman, arms still crossed, said, "I can do it."

Munroe motioned for a piece of paper and scribbled down ten names that Bradford had left behind. They would keep Dillman busy for a while, and if she needed more, she'd get them off the drive and bring them in by hand, because here she'd use no e-mail, make no calls, and provide no digital footprint for the security department to spy upon. Anything that leaked out of her investigation would come by word of mouth from Dillman or his superiors, and that would eventually stop if she tweaked him just right.

Munroe handed Dillman the paper and he scanned the names.

She'd given him the emotionally easy ones. No bosses, no workmates, only employees in the security-level lab. But those files, with the extensive background checks that had already been performed, held the most detail and would require the greatest amount of time to scour and verify.

"I want to see the route you take to whatever information you gather," she said. "I want a trail of names, numbers, and notes for all conversations. Take your time and be prepared to redo the work through other routes if the ones you took don't work for me."

Dillman sighed, then stood. "Is that all?"

Munroe nodded and waited until he was halfway out the door. "Just out of curiosity," she said, "do you keep tabs on the after-work activity that goes on here?"

Dillman stopped and turned. "What do you mean?"

"Do you track who from this facility goes to the *izakayas* and clubs and karaoke bars with whom?"

"Sometimes those details show up extraneously. We've got several hundred employees and that means a lot of afterwork activity." Dillman paused, just a little too fake to be innocently sincere, and said, "Why do you ask?"

Munroe shrugged, humoring him and his lies with lies of her own. "Maybe we're looking for more than one person," she said. "If that's the case, the only reasonable place to conspire would be away from the watchful eyes of you and your men."

"We're not the police," Dillman said. "Our job is to keep proprietary information from leaving the facility, not watch the movements of our employees after hours."

"Okay," she said, but there was no way that a company that screened its employees and spied on them so consistently from within the building simply lost all interest once they stepped out the front door. "Then I'll take whatever you can turn up over the past sixty days."

Dillman held up the paper with the ten names she'd written and with obvious sarcastic deference said, "Where should I place your new request in order of priority?"

"Head of the line," she said. "I want it tomorrow."

Munroe stood in Bradford's hallway, breathing in the unmistakable stench of garbage left rotting in a hot enclosure for too long. From the *genkan* to the *ofuro,* from the bedroom to the kitchen, nothing in the apartment had been disturbed.

Munroe opened the windows. Tied up the trash and hauled it to the front, then collected perishables from the fridge and dumped them into another bag and tossed that out, too. She rifled through the bedroom armoire and pulled out the rest of Bradford's clothes while irritation over law enforcement's reckless indifference to searching for the truth burned her from the inside out.

She stared into the closet and the puzzle wound back again to the murder and why it had been the Chinese woman to die, and Bradford's belt, always the belt.

He'd made three trips from work to the

same hostess club.

The first two would have been intended to acclimate him to the environment so he'd be more pliant when the trap was finally sprung. Enter the thugs who worked for a club owner tied to organized crime and by implication — through fee, favor, friend, or fiat — to someone within the ALTEQ facility.

The only reason any of that effort made sense was because of the belt's uniqueness. It pointed to Bradford like a fingerprint.

But the belt was the only thing linking Bradford to the Chinese woman's murder. Everything else was circumstantial, and if the investigators weren't going to be thorough enough to search for corroborating evidence or eliminate the possibility that someone else had used an identical belt to frame him, then all was fair in war, if not love.

Bradford's DNA would have been all over the belt at the crime scene, but if the events at the hostess club had transpired the way Alina had described them, and if the fight in the street had followed in that same way, then it wasn't *just* Bradford's DNA on the belt, and the DNA of Bradford's attackers couldn't have been cleaned off without also cleaning off evidence of Bradford.

Either way, the result was the same.

The dirty laundry in the hamper, still beside the cupboard in the bedroom, had plenty more DNA to turn a new belt into an old one.

The prosecutor could take his prima facie evidence and choke on it.

The boutique in which Munroe had bought the belt had no website. She'd paid cash, so she had no credit-card merchant authorization to work with, and no longer had the receipt. An hour of searching online maps, followed by a few international calls, netted her a phone number.

Munroe ordered a replacement and then dialed Capstone in Dallas.

The same male voice answered and he put Munroe directly through to Walker's line without a wait.

Munroe said, "I need the number for Miles's lawyer."

"Why?"

"I have something I need to hand over."

"What?"

"Come on, Sam, stop breaking my balls. Just give me the number."

"This is my rodeo," Walker said. "You report to me, not the other way around. You have something to give to the lawyer, it goes through me."

Munroe dropped into reptile mode. "That's fine," she said. "Talk to the lawyer about the so-called murder weapon, ask him how much the case hangs upon that detail, because it's not as much of a one-of-a-kind belt as they'd like to believe. I've got another one right here."

Walker was quiet for a moment. She said, "I'll e-mail you the details," and hung up.

Munroe dialed Warren Green again, went through the same exchange with the same faceless voice, and then the line clicked over to elevator music and Munroe closed her eyes, counting up the minutes, past the ones and into the tens.

This was due diligence, a thread she had to either tie off or pursue.

Green finally picked up near the twenty-minute mark.

"My man," he said. "Tried calling you back. What's been going on?"

"Arrest, followed by mayhem and general unhappiness," Munroe said.

Green paused for a beat and said, "Who is this?"

"This is Miles's conscience," she said. "Miles's brain and body are currently unavailable seeing as they are in jail, awaiting trial for a murder that he may or may not have committed — I say not, the prosecutor says otherwise — and there are a few phone conversations on record of you and him chatting it up like good buddies. This is a heads-up that there may eventually be less friendly people throwing questions your way. Rumors say he might have been attempting to procure a technology of interest on your behalf. True?"

There was another pause. This time slowly, Green said, "You want to run all that by me again?"

"Which part?" Munroe said. "The part about Miles getting arrested or the part about him stealing trade secrets for you?"

"The part about his arrest," Green said. "He wasn't working for me, stealing for me, or doing anything for me — that's a rumor that needs to die. What happened, and is he all right?"

Munroe had expected denial — regardless of the truth, denial was the only answer — but sincerity underlined Green's words: no hemming or hawing or ass covering. His concern went straight to Bradford and that pointed toward Green speaking the truth. "He's okay as he can be, given the circumstances," she said, "but the finger-pointing in your direction is real."

"I don't know what to tell you," Green

said. "Miles and me, we go way back. We keep in touch — have done it that way for years. He's told me about work, I know that's some crazy shit they got goin' on down in the lab, and I know he's been twitchy, especially over these past three weeks. Before you ask, no, I don't know the details. If I did, I'd give 'em to you, honest to God. But like I said, Miles and me, we talk, so given the context of this here conversation I'm goin' out on a limb and guessing you must be Michael."

"Yeah," Munroe said, and she waited, offering Green the chance to fill in the blanks, all the while weighing his version of events against the transcripts.

Green said, "There anything I can do to help? God knows he's a magnet for trouble, but good Lord. Arrested? Murder? You think it'll stick?"

"Still sorting through it," she said. "On the surface, it looks bad. Someone went to a lot of effort to make sure he was the only suspect. If you have any connections in Japan who'd be willing to throw their weight around, ask questions, make sure the local officials know that he's got friends in high places, that would be helpful."

"Let me make some calls," Green said. "See if I've got anyone owing me favors who happens to be in the right place at the right time."

"I'd appreciate it," she said. "I'm dropping off the map, so anything you've got, give it to his office."

"That Samantha, she still the one running things there?"

"She's the one."

"Woman's a bulldog. Take off a man's leg if he's not careful."

"She'll do good by whatever you send her way."

"You got it," Green said, and gushed on about Samantha Walker. Munroe listened through the headache until finally Green got the hint in her silence, said good-bye, and hung up.

Munroe shut the computer and leaned back on the bed.

The conversation wound round and round inside her brain. She sat up and opened the laptop again and reread the transcripts.

People saw what they wanted to see, believed what they wanted to believe, and the conversations could be played off as the banter between friends or the scheming of industrial espionage, depending on the point of view.

Gut instinct would have her believe Green, if not Bradford, but in the big picture truth didn't matter much. The phone calls to the United States, whatever the insiders at AL-TEQ believed they meant, were a dead end: a sideshow she'd had to follow through to closure. Munroe stood and pulled Green's name down off her web.

DAY 10   8:43 A.M.

Test them to find out where they are sufficient and where they are lacking.

        — MASTER SUN TZU

At the back of the lunchroom, in the closet where paper goods, cleaning supplies, and assorted restocking items cluttered disorganized shelves, Nonomi Sato pulled a threaded lens out from a hole in the wall.

She stood quite still, both hands gripping the edges of the palm-size viewer, replaying what she'd recorded. She studied facial expressions and body language, and with each replay the anger grew. The new foreigner was *tall and thin,* as she'd been told, but *likely weak and easily intimidated,* no.

No, no, and *no.*

That assessment was wrong to the point of blindness.

This Michael was younger and smaller than the cowboy, yes, but his eyes were ice

335

and his body moved with the control of a warrior. He'd tensed soon after Sato had peered through the eyepiece — not enough that most people would have noticed the way she noticed — but he'd felt her, had known he was being watched, and had refused to give in to the human urge to turn and look.

The cowboy, removed, had been replaced with an enigma.

Sato shoved the microcamera into the case that held the viewer, anger burning higher. How could anyone, with any sense of strategy or understanding of human nature, have missed such simple observations? How?

Those who didn't know the plans of competitors couldn't prepare alliances. She'd thought she'd known, but no.

Blind, ignorant, worthless . . . worthless . . . worthless . . .

Limited time, work hours, and circumstance had compelled her to rely on a weak alliance, to use the observations of another in the same way she'd used him to drill this hole right here after his overconfident, ignorant analysis had lost her the advantage, forcing her to scout for herself.

The victorious warrior took a stand on ground where she couldn't lose, but she, based on his faulty assessment, had chosen the wrong ground when sending hirelings to corner the newcomer in the garage. Even accounting for exaggeration and shame avoidance, even if half the report was true, the newcomer could have easily killed all three, he simply hadn't.

The victorious warrior won first through strategy and then went to war.

Likely weak and easily intimidated . . .

She'd relied on defective thinking and hadn't properly qualified the men to do the intimidating; she'd sent men to intimidate the weak.

Worse, through faulty strategy she'd shown her hand.

Sato took a breath, then smoothed down her skirt. Anger opened the mind to weakness. Emotional excitement spurred carelessness in battle. She waited for the heat to pass.

The newcomer had good instincts.

That was a problem.

That was *absolutely* the problem.

The cowboy had carried a different kind of instinct, manly and survival-based, dripping of pheromones, testosterone, and war. Backstabbing and blindsiding had taken him down because a direct attack would never have worked. This younger one would require a different strategy still.

Sato grabbed a stack of napkins — the pretense that had brought her into the storage area — and mindful of the voices and conversations that came and went on the other side of the lunchroom's paper-thin divide, she strode back in and with a huff refilled the napkin dispenser.

Such trivialities were beneath her job.

When the air had cleared of bad energy, she stepped beyond the two young men, with their early-morning bento and their manga, for the vending machines, for a bottle of jasmine tea that she drained in long swallows.

The sun couldn't be set back on its course or the days undone, but she could shift, formless like water, and launch again when least expected.

She could use the enemy to defeat the enemy.

Sato tossed the garbage, and with the satchel slung across her shoulder, left for the entry. She'd taken a risk, breaking from her pattern to observe the newcomer, but relying on the faulty word of an ally required gaining her own knowledge.

She had what she needed now.

The terrain had been set and the match begun.

To win by avoiding conflict would be the

highest form of victory.

She could fight — she'd never be a victim like that poor woman in the stairwell, Muay Thai in Bangkok's alleys had seen to that — but she was no fighting fuck toy. Asian girls with their big doe eyes and tiny bones, kicking butt through martial arts and throwing weight that would make a sumo proud, were such a sexist cliché. When force became necessary to win the battle, it meant she'd already lost the war.

She preferred stealth, preferred to let others do the dirty work when muscle was needed, and only got her own hands muddy if she must. Brains were by far the better weapon. The human race proved this in seven billion ways: weak and breakable life forms at the top of the food chain, overrunning the planet like yeast on sugar, all due to rich neural networks and dense gray matter.

And she was a most prime yeast specimen.

Sato stood in line for screening outside the elevator.

The line moved forward, and she with it, and discomfort crawled up her skin, as if someone watched her now just as she'd been watching.

Sato handed the guard her badge, refusing to give in to the human urge to turn around and look.

Her instincts, too, were good.

Hands behind her head, Munroe tilted back in the chair and stared at the ceiling. She'd gotten through the night on four hours of sleep and had returned to the facility before six. Dillman had arrived an hour later. He'd made his presence known at eight by knocking on her office door and tossing a stack of pages on the desk.

"The names you wanted," he said. "The connections between who's done after work with whom over the past two months."

"How complete is it?"

He shrugged. "We're not the FBI. This was pulled together overnight by the team on duty using algorithms that scanned e-mails for keywords."

Munroe's mouth said "Thank you," but inwardly she sighed. The list was worthless. Not just because of holes in the methodology, but because without any idea of who'd compiled the data, the data became value-less.

Dillman left and she thumbed through pages of names, grouped by dates and time stamps, searching for Bradford, but didn't find him. That didn't mean that the men who'd invited him to the hostess club weren't listed there, only that she had no way to connect them to him.

She scanned the list again and recognized two names from her interaction in the hallways and none from the folders on Bradford's external drive. Didn't even know if the men who'd set Bradford up by inviting him to the hostess club had made it onto his drive — didn't even know if *they* knew they'd set Bradford up.

Munroe placed the pages back on the desk. These were threads to compare, names to balance against paths to nowhere. She left for the entry.

The employees knew her now and they indulged her as often as they shied away, the women especially, with their hands up over their mouths as they giggled in embarrassment and crowded into one another like starstruck teenagers. The men were more reserved, especially the older ones, who tended to ignore her or turn their backs on her.

Not rude. Just cultural. Like giggling.

Okada found her forty minutes later. He shook her hand and then moved on, and in her hand he'd left a folded slip of paper. Munroe waited long enough to avoid suspicion, then headed for the toilets and once inside a stall read the note and then flushed it.

Okada had made good on their conversation those two nights back, had delivered what he'd said he couldn't. Law enforcement had, as she'd surmised, been pointed in Bradford's direction after the body had been discovered.

Makoto Dillman had been the one to do it.

In the opening of a hall that branched off from the wide entry, with another afternoon fading, two names Munroe hadn't found on Dillman's list of after-work connections found her.

They were exactly as Alina had described Bradford's hostess club companions: *just like any other man.* Average height, average build, same navy-blue shapeless business suits worn with polished black shoes. Give them each a folded-up newspaper and a briefcase and push them onto the subway at rush hour and they would effectively become invisible.

In perfect English that lifted on a British accent, one of the men said, "Hey! You're Michael, right?"

He stuck out a hand, a tad too jovial, a little too friendly, even for a man who might have lived and worked abroad for years. Munroe connected her palm with his just long enough to be polite, withdrew her hand, and said, "That would be me."

"Nobu Hayashi," he said. "The way you hang out here, by now the entire building knows who you are." He leaned in closer, as if letting her in on a secret. "Miles was a good friend." He glanced around. "We hung out a lot. Crazy what happened — no one expected that. Do you know anything about why? Have you talked to him? He's still in Japan, right?"

Expression tight, deliberately uncomfortable, Munroe said, "I'm just his replacement. Nobody tells me anything."

Hayashi got the hint and dropped the subject. "Couple of the guys are heading into Osaka tonight. Doing clubs Japanese style. Have you done that yet?"

"Don't think so," she said.

"Missing out," he said. "Come with us."

Last time Bradford had gone out with good ol' buddy Nobu, it hadn't worked out

344

so well for him. "Maybe I should," she said. "What time?"

"We leave here at eight. We can carpool and get you home after."

So that was how the game was played. So simple. So easy.

Bradford had gone not once but three times. He would have gone for the same reason she would have gone if she, in speaking Japanese, hadn't had a better way to study her suspects, and if she wasn't concerned about the possibility of showing her face at the same place from which she'd stolen Alina; he would have gone as a way to discover where their connections led. English was the bait: a chance to have a conversation about the facility while away from the facility, a way to gain insight under the lubricant of alcohol. They would have given him something — enough — to keep him going back. Bradford hadn't run into trouble through lack of smarts; he simply hadn't had the benefit of twenty-twenty hindsight.

"I wish I could," Munroe said. "Tonight's difficult, another time for sure. You have a card? I can check my schedule, let you know."

"Of course," Hayashi said. He reached for his wallet.

Munroe took the card and watched Hayashi and his silent partner go, and when they'd reached the entry stiles, she called after them and said, "Hey, thanks for the heads-up."

Munroe found Dillman in his office, hunched over the desk with papers spread out from corner to corner, pen in one hand and a telephone beside the other. He glanced up when she walked in, then went back to the pages.

She stood beside him.

He stopped writing and stared up at her.

She handed him Nobu Hayashi's card. "Do you know this guy?"

Dillman took the card and read it, flipped it over to check the reverse side, and then handed it back. "Only that he works in the accounting department. Why?"

"I need everything we have on him," she said. "Not his personnel file, though that wouldn't hurt. I want everything we have on his after-work, but most specifically, his habits and associations within the facility."

Dillman huffed in exaggerated exasperation and tapped his pen. Munroe leaned down and scanned his progress. Nearly one full day and he'd made it a quarter way through file number one. "Nice work," she said.

"Lots of interruptions," he said, and glared.

"Priorities," she said. "I want it by tomorrow afternoon."

Dillman turned back to the paperwork. "You're the boss." The sarcasm was thick and unmistakable.

Munroe crossed her arms and stood there, looking down at him. Dillman stacked pages and pretended not to notice until finally, hands on the desk in a show of frustration, he pushed back and said, "What?"

"Who pulled the list of after-work connections?" she said.

"I don't know, the guys in my department. That was something anyone could do, I didn't stay to micromanage."

Munroe sat on the desk edge and remained silent.

Dillman scooted his chair farther away so he didn't have to tilt up to look at her.

"I know who you are in this company," she said. "Employees take orders from you, not the other way around. Having to run my errands is beneath you, I get that. But as long as you're assigned to work for me, if

I give you something to do, I expect you to be the one to do it. We're searching an ocean to find one fish. The only thing we know is that you're not that fish and I'm not that fish. Anyone else could be."

"Thanks for the vote of confidence," he said, drier but just as sarcastic.

She let him have his moment.

"I trust you, Dillman," she said. "I don't trust your friends in the security departments any more than you trusted Miles Bradford. Even if they're not directly responsible, that doesn't mean they aren't involved in some way." She held the card up, put it between their faces for a second, and then slapped it onto the desk. "This stays between you and me."

Dillman, arms crossed, his face a blank facade, kept silent.

"Word of this gets around, you're the only person it comes back to," Munroe said. She walked to the door and added, "Don't be the fish, Dillman, don't even look like the fish."

"What about you, Michael?" he said. There were dark undertones in the question, hints of accusations, and a not-so-subtle challenge in the way he stretched out her name as if it wasn't really her name. "Are you the fish?"

Hand still on the door, Munroe turned slightly.

Dillman, one arm draped over the back of his chair, posture casual and face full of judgment, slipped a folder out of his stack and held it toward her.

"Since we're discussing files and fishes."

She didn't move, so he waved the folder in her direction as if to say *Go on, have at it.* Munroe took the bait and walked back for the folder. She held it at arm's length, as though she needed reading glasses to see, and read her name off the label out loud for effect. She opened the cover, scanned a few loose sheets, and nodded theatrically.

Dillman had done his due diligence and come up with about half of what would have been publicly available if he'd dug really, really deep.

"This looks about right," she said. "What's the problem?"

"It's empty," he said.

"Almost empty."

"You don't exist," he said. Paused and then added, "Mi-chael."

"Obviously," Munroe said, dropping the folder back on the desk and crossing her arms, "I exist."

Dillman studied her and she studied him, both remaining silent, neither of them

350

conceding territory or breaking. He said, "There is nothing to guarantee you're qualified for this job. No background on your alliances, no work history, no company other than Capstone to vouch for you or your skills. We have no way to know you haven't arrived to continue stealing company secrets right where Miles Bradford left off."

"That it?" she said.

His hand on the folder, his eyes never leaving hers, Dillman nodded.

She waited. He waited.

Belief was belief, and bias was bias, and getting into a pissing match over Bradford's calls with Warren Green wouldn't change that, but if the concern was serious, Dillman would have already gone to Kobayashi and she'd be having this conversation with someone else, somewhere else.

"What is it you want?" Munroe said.

"You can't buy my silence," he said.

Munroe laughed. She couldn't help it, though that only brought red to Dillman's cheeks, and making him angry was counterproductive.

She coughed into seriousness. "There's nothing you have that's worth paying for," she said. "You're doing your job, I get it, and you're good at it, but waving around a background check as if it means more than what it is only insults us both. Come on, Dillman, you and I know that if you were really concerned, I'm the last person you'd be talking to. Tell me what you're after so we can get this over with and go back to chasing bad guys."

"I want to know who you are and why you're here," he said.

"So it's personal?"

"No, it's not personal," he said, and then stopped. "All right, yes, it's personal. I don't want to end up on the wrong side of whatever is going on."

Munroe heard through the unspoken, absorbed what it meant when even the head of the department charged with knowing all things acknowledged vulnerability to what stirred unseen beneath the water.

"You won't," she said.

"What? Just that? 'You won't.' I have to take your word for it?"

"Take your own word for it," she said. "You just made it clear that you're not afraid that I can't do this job but that I might do a job too well. There's a reason you can't find what you're looking for — it's the same reason *we* will find what *we're* looking for. You want to be on the winning team? You're on it, Dillman."

He tapped a finger on the folder. "This

doesn't *look* like winning. I want you to convince me that we're on the same side."

"Can't do that for you," she said. "Not as long as you still hold Miles Bradford as the enemy. I'm sure you can connect the reasoning." She walked to the door again and stopped at the frame. "I can tell you this, though: Your research skills need polishing." She stepped into the hall. "There's more information out there. You just haven't found it yet." She smiled and shut the door.

Munroe killed three hours chatting with the guards, hitting up the security teams for meaningless information, mingling with the employees coming through the stiles, until the clock hands rolled around and she left for the bathrooms to remove some of the hobo shine put on by long hours with little sleep and infrequent showers.

Hand dryer worked as hair dryer, soap as shampoo, splashes of water and the hand dryer again as a way to remove some of the wrinkles in a shirt now on its second day. She straightened the tie and then, having done the best she could, wound her way upstairs to the office of Tatsuo Nakamura, for her appointment with the man without whom Bradford would have never come to Japan.

His assistant ushered Munroe into a small waiting area, where the furniture was less utilitarian and a large unframed oil painting splashed color that felt obscene in contrast to the blandness of the rest of the building. In soft formal language the woman offered Munroe a drink and returned with a tray with sparkling water. She set a doily coaster on the coffee table and then the glass, and then bowed deeply, apologizing for the delay, which lasted less than five minutes.

The door to the inner office opened and Nakamura stood in its frame, svelte, sun-kissed, and in a better-tailored suit than the businesswear draping every salaryman in the building. He was in his early sixties, though he carried himself with the vim of a man who should have had a lot less gray and far fewer wrinkles. "Please come in," he said.

Munroe followed him into the office, observing, calculating.

Nakamura motioned toward the pair of stuffed leather chairs in front of his desk. "Please," he said. Then: "A shame, such a shame, about Miles Bradford. He was a good man, a very good man."

Inside Munroe's head the gears locked up.

Unlike the other company executives, Nakamura had just put Bradford's predicament front and center. More baffling, he had called Bradford a good man, yet when the accusations had fallen, he hadn't raised a word in Bradford's defense. She'd played this meeting out a dozen different ways, but not once had the projections included what had just happened.

Nakamura returned to the captain's chair on the opposite side of the desk. He stood with his hands on the high back for the briefest pause, then sat, and with his fingers laced atop the mirror sheen, he said, "What can I do for you?" His English was even better than that of Noboru Kobayashi, the head of security.

The ease in his interaction spoke of years of dealing with foreign interests and of understanding Western interaction. Munroe chose her words and adjusted her posture accordingly. "I wanted to introduce myself as a way of keeping you aware of progress," she said. "Although Miles won't be able to fulfill the contract personally, he has made contingencies and the work continues uninterrupted."

"I have been notified," Nakamura said. "This is good news, but a large role to assume. Do you have the necessary skills?"

"That's why Miles chose to bring me on-board."

Nakamura nodded, his lips pressed into a forced frown of contemplation that indicated agreement rather than disapproval.

He leaned back in his chair. "There's been much unwanted attention on the company these past few weeks. All very problematic for our image. I'm sure you can imagine that we hope to avoid any form of repetition."

Munroe held eye contact for a moment, parsing the words, and then followed his westernized opening with facetiousness. "Don't allow myself to get framed for murder," she said. "I can assure you that my priorities align with yours."

Nakamura smiled then and wagged a finger at her. He laced his hands across his midsection and leaned back. "Rather puzzling, isn't it? Given Mr. Bradford's expertise, these events don't seem to fit."

Munroe eyed him warily enough that her accusation of backstabbing, her finger-pointing at him for having kept those thoughts private when Bradford had needed them most, wouldn't need words to be understood.

She said, "Your viewpoint on that seems to be in the minority."

"Unfortunately, that can't be helped," Nakamura said. The layer of what was unspoken beneath his words matched hers. "Here, consensus in decision-making is an integral part of business. Caution is needed to avoid statements that might bring shame to others. Unlike the west, we tend to avoid charismatic leaders, and what's the term the Americans use? Lone Rangers?"

"Something like that."

"I don't believe Miles Bradford killed that woman," Nakamura said, "but as the public head of the company, my beliefs, if they disagree with the majority of executives, remain only mine. The decision to bring in an outside contractor was difficult and divided and so, you see, it could be said that these painful results are what we should have expected as a natural result of dissent."

Munroe dropped her eyes and studied Nakamura's reflection on the desk. In a roundabout way he'd given her a motive for Bradford's setup, and he'd explained the shroud of omissions within the facility: Even for those who believed Bradford was innocent, they would go with the status quo, behaving as if he was guilty rather than be the nail that got hammered down.

Searching through the unspoken, Munroe said, "If there was disagreement, why risk upsetting the company hierarchy? Why hire a foreigner in the first place? Why allow me to continue here after all that's already happened?"

"Ah, yes," Nakamura said. "But lack of

agreement on who would best solve this issue doesn't equate to lack of agreement over the fact that we do indeed have an issue."

"For a foreigner to solve? Whose idea was that?"

Nakamura shook his head, chiding again, as if she just wasn't getting it. "We don't claim ideas as our own," he said. "Ideas and proposals come together collectively, over time."

"Over drinks after work," she said.

He half smiled. "Now you understand."

"Ideas still have to originate from somewhere," she said, "even if it's just the suggestion of possibly thinking about looking into a perhaps."

"Very convoluted," Nakamura said, but he glanced down, body rocking subtly as if intending to conjure memory, and then he cut his eyes back at her. "It's been a very long time. Many conversations, many meetings, both in the office and out, but perhaps Yuzuru Tagawa, my operations chief, was first to put specific words to what others had already indirectly broached."

"Would he feel the most shame over this failure?"

Nakamura answered with silence, but in its own way this would explain the brusque send-away she'd gotten when she'd stopped in to see her boss. She said, "I suppose Kobayashi, with both security departments beneath him, would have fought hardest against bringing in an outside perspective."

"We do have solid technology and a very skilled department."

"Why Bradford?" Munroe said. "How did that come about?"

"That," Nakamura said, sighing, "that was my doing. Once the decision had been made, the consensus was that we should go far to the edge of our options instead of — what's your word? Half-assing?"

Munroe nodded.

"No half-assing," Nakamura said. "We would not only bring in an outsider but a foreigner with specialized history in intelligence as a way to guarantee fresh eyes that might see what we don't see. It fell on my shoulders to handle the issue because I had lived abroad for many years and I knew people who knew people. A mutual business relationship connected me to Capstone Security Consulting."

"That makes Bradford's failure your fault?"

"Collective decisions, collective blame."

"And shame?"

"The problems within the company and the scrutiny they have brought us are reflected on me," Nakamura said. "Certainly I carry shame. But this comes from the judgments of others rather than acknowledgment of my own failing — I am still not convinced that Mr. Bradford is responsible for our current predicament. It would bring great relief if in the process of doing your work you also uncover answers and so restore honor and face to the company leadership."

"There are many pieces that don't connect," Munroe said. "You can see them — it's surprising that the others won't even acknowledge they exist. You'd think they'd want to know if there's a murderer wandering their halls, if only to protect themselves. If it was my company, my first concern would be to find out if this predicament, as you say, was the hint of something deeper."

Nakamura smiled just slightly and said, "Would it?"

"You don't find it rather convenient for a thief when the man responsible for tracking down the theft is removed from the facility? You protect yourself from threat by knowing the enemy. Miles Bradford wasn't — isn't — your enemy, but someone is, and by pretending otherwise, everyone involved only makes it possible for the enemy to thrive."

Nakamura's smile faded back into the forced frown of contemplation. He studied Munroe for a moment and then stood. Hands on the back of his chair, he leaned toward her. "The threat of a thief selling trade secrets is a problem. Police coming into the facility and confiscating equipment is a bigger problem. However," he said, turning away to the window that opened to the rear of the building, "the largest problem is questions that lead to unknown places. For the greater good, for long-term stability, some answers are best left alone."

"If that's a trade you want to make, it's your company and your decision," Munroe said. "But every choice comes with consequences, and hiding from the truth to save face now might leave you with no face left to save in the future."

Nakamura turned back to look at her, but stayed by the window.

She said, "If the murder and the theft are connected, I'll likely learn as much as a by-product of doing my job, but accidental discoveries come with bigger surprises, are difficult to contain, and have the potential to do more damage to the company image. If keeping the company out of the public eye is your goal, wouldn't it be prudent to allow me to pursue both avenues quietly and to keep you updated with the progress?"

Nakamura returned to his chair. "You are very convincing," he said. "How many others would know what you are doing?"

"Everyone might assume, but only you would know."

"Do you have suspects?"

"It's too close to the beginning for that," she said. "Miles Bradford was told that the threat of theft came from the Chinese. Is there a basis for this?"

"The Chinese are a threat to everyone."

His answer dodged the question, and although the cultural norm was to avoid directness, he'd already defied that trend several times, which turned this avoidance into something else. Through her silence, Munroe demanded more.

Eventually he said, "We don't know if the threat is the Chinese, the Koreans, the Americans, or someone else —" He stopped and looked pointedly at her. "Considering what I've heard about the phone calls, the threat could very well be the Americans."

Munroe allowed the provocation to pass. Now wasn't the time. "You speak of the threat in terms of nationalities," she said. "Are those corporate interests or government interests?"

"We would have to assume both. Theft is theft and in the end it would be the same for us either way."

"How long have you suspected?"

"About five years."

"Five years?"

"This is why we were finally resigned to bringing in an outside contractor," Nakamura said. "That would never have been our first preference."

The hesitancy to bring in an outsider, yes, but the rest didn't add up.

"It's impossible to prove a negative," she said. "Five years of not proving a suspicion isn't enough to encourage that type of action. There had to be some proof, some definitive reason Miles Bradford was told that the threat came from the Chinese."

"I don't know who told him that," Nakamura said, "but there have been indications. Our company has been at the edge of innovation for over a decade. Some develop-

364

ment lines take longer than others, but twice now in the past five years, competitors have been first to market with products identical to ours, products that we invested heavily in and that we lost by a margin of weeks. This has damaged our reputation as an industry leader and stolen market share, pushing us into a position of second best for products in which we should have been first."

Munroe opened her mouth, then closed it again.

This was suspicion and jealousy, and that only projected lunacy and turned it into a witch hunt among employees. ALTEQ-Bio didn't own the right to ideas or research, and they certainly weren't the only company in the biomedical and biotech fields.

Nakamura said, "Industrial espionage has a long history, and if one refuses to adopt the weapons of his enemy, one will lose the battle."

And so there it was, then: the pot calling the kettle black.

The reason the company executives were convinced that there were spies and thieves within their ranks wasn't only because they'd been beat by identical products, but because they'd stolen from others and had their own spies placed among competitors. How very generous to throw Bradford into the mix.

No wonder none of them openly accused him of murder, no wonder they behaved as if his departure was a mere inconvenience. Their shame wasn't in Bradford's supposed failure; it came from the unwanted attention drawn to the company. So much easier then to sweep it all away, to allow Bradford to take the fall for what he hadn't done while the engines kept running and the internal hunt to protect the company continued unabated — just a little misstep in a long-standing arms race toward profit and market dominance.

Munroe stood. "Thank you for your time," she said.

Nakamura shook her hand. "It's good that you are here," he said. "You do have support among the executives. Please visit with me again, please keep me informed. I'm very interested in following your investigation."

Of course he was.

Day 11   8:00 P.M.

Munroe didn't have the luxury of catching catnaps on the trains to and from work, or stealing sleep on her desk during breaks like most of the facility employees. She arrived earlier, left later, and then spent hours in the hotel room afterward assembling clues and pieces of the puzzle onto the oversize map along the wall, and perhaps that was why, in spite of thinning traffic, she was halfway to the hotel before she spotted the tail.

Munroe made mirror and blind-spot checks, then switched lanes. The tail, forty meters back and separated by three cars, waited until the last minute to cut over. The blue and white signage of a Lawson called out from down the road, so Munroe slowed and pulled off into the *konbini*'s minuscule parking area. She carried the helmet inside, bought food she didn't want, and browsed the magazine rack, watching the street from the window.

She started up again. Several blocks down the lights were back.

Exhaustion tweaked at her nerves, a warning against her own weakness.

She changed directions, routing into the thick of city residential streets. Better to get this over with on her own territory, out of sight of the masses, away from where police would be called and she'd wind up in a worse place than where she was now.

Munroe turned off for Bradford's apartment.

She parked underground, took the stairs up, and violated the sense of cleanliness by wearing her boots inside. Her knives were in the hotel room in Bradford's bag, so the stash in the kitchen drawer became the surrogate, and with the blades clenched tight, she stalked back to the hallway, slid down to the floor, and waited there.

Time ticked on; the adrenaline settled. She startled awake with the first touch of daylight and kept motionless, breathing and listening. Then she stood, walked softly to the door, and took a look through the fisheye, into an empty outside corridor, questioning her own memory, her own judgment.

The car hadn't been a trick of sleep

deprivation or the product of chasing shadows in the dark. She'd been followed. That had been her purpose for detouring to the apartment, but the attack she'd waited for had never come.

She left the building through the emergency stairwell and looped around the block. Eyes darting about the garage interior, she sought out the imagined, hallucinated threat. She continued toward the Ninja, parked exactly where and how she'd left it. She stared at the machine, its flaming-red fairings reflecting slivers of daylight from the entrance.

And then, temper rising, she stomped back up the stairs to the apartment, grabbed a bag of tools off the shelving that lined the home office, and carried the weight back down to the garage. She worked the Allen wrench and screwdrivers, popping pushpins and loosening screws and bolts to detach the right fairing, pulled it off, and shone a flashlight into the belly of the machine.

The first tracking device didn't surprise her. She'd suspected as much on the first night she'd been attacked. The young men with pipes couldn't have been a result of Jiro hunting for Alina, which left a tracker as the only other way an ambush could have been laid out in advance at an address no one knew.

She'd been careful since, keeping the battery out of her phone, making sure that the bike was far away from where she slept, from where she worked.

But the second tracker, that was a surprise.

Munroe wiggled closer, allowing her fingers to confirm the story told by her eyes, then sat back on her heels, processing. Reconfiguring context and motive. Searching for connections in the unrelated, for ways the data touched without touching.

She left the trackers where they were, same as she had when she'd suspected the first. She replaced pins and screws and fasteners, then dropped the tools into the bag and hauled them back upstairs.

In the bedroom she grabbed Bradford's keys off the hook — the same place they'd been since the day she'd dropped him off expecting to pick him up that evening. Munroe returned to the garage, to Bradford's Mira, tossed her backpack on the passenger seat, and plugged the key into the ignition.

With the engine running, her arms draped over the steering wheel and her chin resting on her hands, she stared at the Ninja. She'd been operating on the logic that whoever had killed the Chinese woman had done so to set Bradford up — that he'd been collateral damage.

Still true, but now on a deeper, murkier level.

If Jiro or his men had followed her last night, the goal would have been to kill her, not track her. This turn in events wasn't Jiro any more than the boys with their pipes had been Jiro.

Collateral damage, yes.

There were two sets of players at the facility, different factions playing cat-and-mouse, and now she, like Bradford, was the ball of yarn, tangled up and caught in the middle.

Day 12   9:29 A.M.

With the belt buckle in one hand and the phone in the other, Munroe punched in the number to Bradford's lawyer's office, one deliberate jab at a time. Three days of calls, all left unanswered and unreturned, and now the rings dead-ended into the same nasal voice offering yet another derisive promise to pass on a message.

Munroe shoved a pen between her teeth to force a smile and channeled venom into a sweet cocktail of sugar and blackmail.

"I know he's in the office and he knows who I am," she said. "If he doesn't take this call, I will personally see that he is removed from the case for ineptitude. I guarantee intense publicity and ample shame for the entire firm. Pass that message along, I'll wait."

The hold was less than three minutes.

The lawyer said, "Your demands are inconvenient."

Munroe reinterpreted the lack of directness into what the lawyer had actually meant: *I'm authorized to speak with you, but I don't want to.*

Bradford had a good team in his corner. They would have vetted the lawyer, made sure this was the right man for the job, but in the time drop of his first sentence, Munroe questioned everyone's judgment.

She said, "Of all people, you should want to speak with me most. I've lived with your client over the past few months, I've known him for years, and I was with him in the morning, right before the murder."

"Perhaps in the future," the lawyer said.

His voice dripped with condescension, the type of derision that sat tall on the assumption of guilt, looking self-righteously down from the high horse of disdain at those who were inferior by association.

Munroe pinched the bridge of her nose and set aside pride and indignation for the sake of strategy. Doing this over the phone was the equivalent of gifting plans to whatever digital ears listened in, and that was always the assumption, but she only had one chance. Conspiratorial and inclusive, redundant for the sake of trying to glean facts, she lowered her voice to a near whisper and said, "I have information for you, information you want. How important is the murder weapon to this case?"

"This is a question I shouldn't answer."

I don't want to answer.

"Was the woman dead before the belt was used?"

"The belt was the murder weapon," the lawyer said. "The office is busy, there are appointments. You can call again another time."

Details at last.

"The victim never cried for help," Munroe said. "Are you aware of how difficult it is to get a loop over someone's head when they're struggling and then cinch it tight enough to choke them? This isn't something that happens in a second or even ten seconds, and it's nearly certain to leave traces of evidence as the victim claws for life."

"The victim was intoxicated," he said, but with just enough of a hitch that she knew she had his attention, if for but a moment.

"Drugs? Alcohol?" she said. "Completely incapacitated?"

"The toxicology report is out of the office."

I don't want to answer.

Munroe said, "Have you considered the possibility that someone other than your client drugged and killed that woman?"

"You are wasting my time," the lawyer said, now with an edge of anger. "This is the Japanese system, not the American system. We don't make a joke of our courts with a circus of excuses, staging a show to sway an audience. The judges examine the evidence and weigh its merit, and there is much evidence against my client. This panel is no friend to arrogance. Without accepting responsibility, without remorse, my client will suffer."

Munroe said, "You haven't spoken with your client yet, have you?"

"Until the investigation is complete, I am limited."

No, I haven't seen him, much less spoken with him.

Without anything resembling attorney-client privilege, that was just as well. Munroe said, "If your entire strategy revolves around negotiating for leniency, you might as well convict him yourself."

"My client refuses to speak," the lawyer said. "This has created difficulties at all levels of the investigation. Unless he cooperates, he will experience the full weight of the law, and I cannot do my job in the shadow of such senselessness."

The words were like cleansing air.

There would have been long strings of

interrogations spread between lack of sleep, minimal food, and meaningless offers of mercy if only Bradford would tell them what had happened. But he hadn't. Hadn't even given them material to account in their own words what they claimed he'd said or admitted, and without even an interrogation summary, the prosecution would be forced to rely entirely on evidence.

"I've been patient," the lawyer said, "but this time has not been useful."

She said, "The only thing connecting your client to the victim, other than circumstantial evidence, is the murder weapon, but there's no proof that the belt was his. I have his belt in my possession."

There was a pregnant pause. "You have what?"

"I have his belt. And why would a non-addict willingly get high that early in the morning, much less while at work in a company that treats its employees as potential criminals? Did the investigators ever search for evidence that your client purchased or had access to the intoxicant in her system?"

"His DNA and fingerprints are all over the murder weapon."

"Not *just* his," she said. "Also others'."

"How do you know this?"

"He didn't wear the belt into the office that morning," she said. "You haven't looked at the security footage, have you?"

The lawyer's voice was less arrogant now. "Without a confession, the facts surrounding the murder weapon bear more weight."

"I'm offering you another way to look at the evidence," Munroe said. "You want to win? You should accept my help."

A duplicate belt wasn't enough to set Bradford free, and the footage of him going without the belt for those weeks prior to the murder wouldn't do much, either. These were doubts, insidious doubts, to taint the certainty of evidence. Getting the lawyer to question his own bias was a start. Getting the investigator and the prosecutor to do the same would be a whole other challenge.

Munroe searched the wall, with its web of interwoven connections and lies, seeking not to eliminate but to include, hunting for the larger picture hidden in the abstract. Hiring an outsider had created a rift in company leadership. On which side, she wondered, did the person who'd murdered that woman fall? Perhaps neither, though it continued to defy reason that a professional thief, undercover and entrenched, would have willingly brought such a level of scrutiny into the workplace as part of removing Bradford.

That was an inconsistency that just wouldn't let go.

Munroe left the hotel for the facility. She was late to work but erratic hours and unpredictability were good for the opponent's soul. She was altruistic in that way.

Noboru Kobayashi's assistant nodded politely when Munroe entered the anteroom, and she ushered Munroe to a small sofa to wait. Of all the evils on the map of possibilities inside her head, coming to the head of corporate security was the least of them.

The wait dragged on past twenty minutes. When the door opened, two young men from the NSA side of things stepped out. Seeing her, their expressions darkened with accusation and mistrust and they walked quickly through.

Voice soft and bow low, the assistant motioned Munroe inward.

Kobayashi stood, offering more of that same overstretched welcome that he'd proffered the first time. "Have a seat," he said. "I'm afraid I'm between appointments and only have a few minutes."

"I'll be quick," Munroe said. "I need an additional liaison for three days. I'd like Tai Okada, if you can spare him."

Kobayashi remained standing and his face

379

drifted into a scowl of contemplation. "My departments are already short-staffed," he said. "This would deprive me of another man we already don't have."

Munroe stood, as if his objection had settled things and now she would go, and offered the closest thing she had to a threat. "I understand completely," she said. "Knowing how management feels about outsiders, I wanted to bring the issue to you first. If you haven't got the manpower, I'll subcontract out."

Kobayashi's scowl softened. "Please sit," he said, and when Munroe returned to her chair, he returned to his. "I appreciate you coming to me first," he said. The rest of him said that she'd backed him against a wall and he was none too pleased. "With the way my departments have been separated from the work you do, focus has been divided. The liaison allows us to pull together and coordinate. We can find a way. Three days?" he said.

"Hopefully not more."

"Additional personnel, I can manage," he said. "Another department head is more complicated. You originally said you preferred to work with someone other than Okada."

"I had thought starting fresh would be the

better option," she said. "That was a judgment error."

"I see," Kobayashi said, though clearly, more than anything, he was trying to see what true meaning lay behind the request and how he might sidestep unforeseen complications.

"Things have been going well in your integration?" he said.

"Very much so."

"You're making progress in the work?"

Now he was just fishing.

"Yes," she said, and stood. "When should I expect Okada?"

Kobayashi eyed her, steely. "If I can make that arrangement," he said, "he should be available tomorrow."

He walked with her to the hall and stayed in the doorway, watching her go, just as he'd done on her first visit, and the pieces on the mental diagram shifted slightly to the right, making space for new data.

Munroe took the stairs to the mezzanine and found Dillman waiting at the base, arms crossed, eyes tracking her progress as if he'd come there knowing exactly where and when to find her.

Munroe flashed her badge, RFID chip included. "Are you tracking me?"

Dillman handed her a large, thick envelope. "Perks of the job," he said. "Saves time. How's Kobayashi-san?"

"He sends his regards and says don't fuck anything up. What's this?"

"The after-work stuff you wanted, redone by me."

Munroe stopped, cocked her head, and smirked. "Really?"

"I'm not even a fish," he said, and handed her another envelope, this one thinner. "Everything I could pull on your accountant friend, Nobu Hayashi."

Munroe glanced down at the envelopes. Hayashi, by inviting her out to a hostess club, had made himself the prime suspect as the English speaker who'd been with Bradford the night the belt was stolen. That, in turn, made every one of his connections within the facility potential accomplices.

"Anyone else know you're looking at this?" she said.

"Sent the night shift out for a break at two this morning," he said, "Cleaned the queries out of the log files when I was finished."

Munroe sniffed and wiped away fake tears. "You make me proud."

"Don't get used to it," Dillman said, and turned to go. Over his shoulder he added, "And find someplace else to look through those because I'm still using your office."

This early in the day, the break room was quiet. Several faces glanced up when Munroe entered and then went back to whatever they were reading or eating. Two men, foreheads on the table, eyes buried on their arms, missed her arrival entirely.

She took a chair at the back, pulled the pages out of the thicker envelope, and looked them over. Nothing jumped out as incongruent. The value in the new data would be as a control against the originals, a way to spot anything that might have been withheld the first time around, and the originals were at the hotel.

Munroe emptied the thinner envelope, although *thinner* was relative.

Dillman had been thorough, or perhaps passive-aggressive, giving her fifty-eight pages of tiny text and columns, sixty days of dates and time stamps and data tables, phone logs, the to–from of e-mail headers, browser history, and the goldmine of RFID matches on every employee that clocked the same location as Nobu Hayashi for more than thirty seconds a hit.

Pen in hand, Munroe started at the beginning, marking and notating, flipping forward and then back again, redacting first what she knew to be unimportant and then what she assumed to be of little consequence, searching for whatever patterns might be buried within the extraneous. An hour in, she stopped and drew a circle around Yuzuru Tagawa's name.

Yuzuru Tagawa, her boss, as the head of operations, had legitimate reasons for interacting with a senior accountant, but the consistency and timing stuck out as anomalous. Tagawa had been on Bradford's drive as one of the company executives, had been on her short list due to his link in the chain of Bradford's hiring, and here in Hayashi's connections Tagawa showed up again within three days on either side of each of Bradford's visits to the hostess club.

Wary of falling prey to the same bias she despised in those who would imprison Bradford, Munroe set down the pen and stared at the spread-out pages. Twenty-twenty hindsight was a beautiful thing but not a divining rod and she didn't believe in her own ego enough to condemn a life simply because the hunch felt right and the circumstances fit.

Her thumbs tapped out thought and analysis in irregular beats against the table. Time passed, people came and went, and four times employees she'd previously bantered with in the hallways stopped to say hello, one more inconsistency. She held the same position that Bradford had, yet except for the men in Dillman's department, they interacted with her without the fear and suspicion they'd displayed toward him.

The room filled with the lunch crowd. Okada entered without food and, pulling out the chair beside her, kept a healthy distance from both Munroe and the table. He sat, shaggy hair hanging over his thick glasses, posture saying he would have preferred anything other than to be there right now, eyes staring large from behind his lenses as if wanting an explanation.

Tone flat, he said, "Kobayashi-san told me to talk with you."

Munroe turned slightly to see him better. "Did he tell you why?"

Pleading, as if in having requested him she'd demoted him in a way that working with Bradford never could have, he said, "Michael, you already have the help you need."

She said, "There are some things that only you can do."

DAY 12   11:12 P.M.

The night air, polluted with light, carried the rumble of evening trains and, with the thinning traffic, less of the city's sense-dulling fragrance. Munroe left the facility for the far end of the lot, where she'd parked Bradford's car, and pulled out to the street, watching for patterns in the rear-view.

Things being what they were, trackers would have been placed on the Mira long before they'd been put on the Ninja, and things being what they were, she expected another tail.

Bradford had known about the trackers. At the least, he had to have suspected. In retrospect, the signs were all there. He'd left his phone behind that night he'd used her as cover to case the hostess club in Kita-shinchi, a gesture that had been sweet in the moment, a way of ensuring that work wouldn't encroach on what little time they

386

had. And they'd gone on foot, supposedly to avoid the hassles of finding parking — lies behind the mask, now just more details rearranged in the maddening clarity of hindsight.

Headlights filled Munroe's rearview mirror. A different set of lights than those of the night before, and a much different driving pattern.

She changed lanes and so did the lights.

She meandered and the car followed, much closer than the sparse traffic warranted, much closer than anyone following a tracker had any right to be.

The mental map changed shape again; mind adding, including, connecting through the abstract from hostess club to Bradford to Jiro to the facility.

She caught two shadows in the front seat, possibly a third in the back.

Munroe flipped the blinker and, taking her time, took a corner.

The car kept tight behind through each random turn and double back. The driver made no attempt to hide that he was there or any effort to communicate. He simply was, like a headache that wouldn't go away, and so Munroe burned time and distance, routing toward high population areas where multiple stop-starts burned fuel faster. The guys behind her with their bigger car would inevitably run out first.

Lights in the mirror flashed brighter, flooding the Mira's interior. The hood behind drew close enough that with a touch of speed, or a hint of her brakes, its grille would plow into her.

Munroe nudged the accelerator.

The headlights closed the distance and then the Mira jerked, as if it had been hit with a battering ram.

Munroe toed the gas and the little engine took up speed reluctantly.

The lights in the rearview trailed behind and then moved in closer.

The next bump came harder.

Munroe gripped the wheel, scanning options, running the odds.

The driver behind her didn't let off the gas the way he would have if he wanted her out of the car, checking for damage. And he didn't try to nudge in beside her to push her off the road, into lampposts, barriers, or buildings.

He wanted her to go faster.

Making the point, the grille slammed hard into the rear and the Mira juddered. Her options were limited. Brake, and the car behind would plow into her and the Mira would accordion and crush directly into an intersection; speed up, race through these narrow streets that had no stoplights or stop signs, and she invited vehicular homicide or its local equivalent, if a wreck didn't kill her first.

The next slam sent Munroe's chest hard into the seat belt and her neck snapped back. Ahead the roads were empty. No pedestrians, no bikes. She stomped on the accelerator and raced through the intersection blind, bracing for a crunch of metal and death.

She cleared through, the lights right up behind her.

Strategy arrived by way of a neon arrow and a parking garage ahead, promising room to maneuver just across the next junction.

The grille bumped her again.

Munroe punched the gas and peeled into the intersection. She slammed a foot onto each pedal and pulled the wheel hard. The Mira spun out, little tires crying against the pavement, chassis shuddering under tension it had never been built to handle. The car lurched to a stop, body angled nose to wall, but off the street.

Munroe threw off the seat belt and dumped out the passenger door.

The grille with the headlights and shadows

sped by. She stared after the car, legs shaking, data sorting, questions tumbling, adrenaline racing.

The vehicle peeled a corner and the engine noise faded into the distance. The night went quiet and all that remained was her, the Mira, bright vending machines, a group of pedestrians far, far down the street, and the buildings standing in mute witness on either side.

Munroe opened the driver's door and stood, eyes on the seat, seeing without really seeing. The boys in the garage with their pipes had been a warning, meant to wound and intimidate. Jiro's men in her room, with their knives, had been revenge. This had been a setup for an accident, for criminal charges, to remove her from the facility in the same way Bradford had been removed.

Whatever she'd just escaped tonight would inevitably come back in another guise. This was just the warm-up.

Day 13   7:08 A.M.

Munroe reached the facility just after seven and found Dillman in her office, hunched over the desk with papers spread out, pen in hand, marking notations. He glanced up when she entered and, with a bare huff of acknowledgment, returned to what he'd been doing.

"You spend the night here?" she said.

He nodded.

"No after-work activities?"

"Would have been nice," he said. "Could use a drink."

"How about some sleep?"

"That, too."

A second chair had shown up in the office a few days ago. Munroe spun it toward her and, straddling it backward, sat just off the end of Dillman's elbow, waiting for him to finish his notes, searching for hints of discomfort that might point out his involvement in the car that had chased her down.

She rested her chin on the chair and shut her eyes in a long, tired blink. If the enemy's goal was to wear her down, they were succeeding. Exhaustion was cumulative. She'd managed a few hours stretched out on her hotel floor, waiting for another followup attack that had never come.

Dillman swung his chair around and handed her several pages.

Munroe took the documents and scanned them. This was the second dossier he'd completed since she'd given him the fact-checking project. He was working on the third, and at the rate he was going, it'd be a year before he finished everything on the external drive.

"Are you busy after work tonight?" he said.

Munroe glanced up. She hadn't expected another invitation to trouble quite this soon. Stress lined Dillman's eyes just beneath the lack of sleep, but he smiled, cocky and disarming. She said, "You're not going soft, are you? Trying to build team spirit with me and all that?"

"Nah," he said. "Just stuff I'd like to discuss about these files."

"I can make time now."

"Better not," he said. That made it clear that either he wanted to talk to her away from the listening ears and prying eyes or he was part of the plan to get rid of her. The only way to find out was to go.

"After work, then," she said, and to set boundaries and test for a motive, added, "Something nearby. I'm short on time."

Dillman didn't hesitate. "I leave at eight."

"I'll meet you out at the front," she said. "You can follow me."

He nodded and went back to his papers. Munroe looked over the dossier and, satisfied that he'd been thorough — at least for a first pass — placed the documents on the desk, patted his shoulder, and left him there.

She found Okada in his car in the parking lot, as agreed. He'd not asked where they were going or why they were working offsite. He said nothing when Munroe slipped into the passenger seat and continued to say nothing on the five-minute drive to the station.

When they walked from the car to the ticket machines, Munroe handed him a handwritten address and a small transit map on which she'd highlighted a stop.

Okada studied both and said, "Where is this? What is this?"

"We'll miss the train," she said. "I'll tell you on the way."

She waited until they'd boarded and had

pushed to the back of the car. "The murdered woman's parents," she said.

Okada looked at her as if he didn't quite get it, so she took him through her first official day at the office, the interview, the victim's friend, and the two details no one seemed bothered enough to follow through on: that the woman had had a boyfriend at the facility — presumably someone in upper management — and that she'd never cried for help.

"The police investigators may have looked into it," Okada said.

They should have, if they'd been thorough, but with Bradford in custody as an easy culprit, Munroe had her doubts. Okada was her avenue toward answers because here, her foreignness was a repellent to forthrightness, and kanji, the complicated written language that comprised thousands of logograms, was a code that locked out her natural ability to find pattern in sound.

Circumstances forced her to trust a partner.

She'd searched Okada hard for signs of betrayal and had found nothing. If, indeed, he was part of Bradford's downfall, then he was brilliant beyond her level of skill, and any attempt to thwart him would be fruitless, anyway.

Okada was a mitigated risk.

Munroe slid the backpack off her shoulders, pulled out a stack of page-size headshots culled from personnel files, and handed them to him.

Suspicion that the boyfriend had been the one to murder the woman and, by implication, set Bradford up, didn't make it true, but based on statistics and Occam's razor, the boyfriend was a damn good possibility.

Okada flipped through the pictures.

With each new face his fingers gripped harder and his lips pressed tighter, until his expression hardened into a facade of nothing. She'd handed him the top executives from Bradford's list, mixed with mostly random employees as a way to limit bias, and if a picture told a thousand words, Okada held a novella accusing one among his bosses of murder.

In a near equivalent to turning his back on her, Okada pushed the pictures into her hand and stared out the nearest window.

The train rocked on in a fit of stops and starts, ever closer to the station where they'd change lines, where Okada could, if he wanted, leave her to sort out this mess on her own. He said, "If I involve myself, will I be in danger? Is my family in danger?"

He'd seen what had happened to Bradford. By asking, he told her that he knew there was more and that she owed him the truth.

"I've been threatened a few times," she said.

The train stopped. They got off to make the connection and Okada held up a hand for her to wait. He pulled out his phone and dialed, and Munroe listened in on half a conversation full of misdirection and side-stepped conflict that concluded with Okada's wife agreeing to take the children to visit the grandparents for a week.

He faced Munroe with uncharacteristic directness. "If your assumptions are wrong," he said, "please keep me away from the repercussions."

"If I'm wrong," she said, "and you never speak of what we do or where we go, then you've only ever been an assistant. I'm just a dumb *gaijin,* after all."

"If that's the best that you can do," he said. "Tell me, please, who do you suspect in all of this?"

Munroe shook her head. "I honestly don't know."

Okada nodded. They walked again and Munroe studied the back of his head. He hadn't asked for her thoughts as a way of learning her mind; he'd asked because he had his own suspect and wanted to compare notes without showing his hand.

From the station they found a stationery store. Okada purchased a funeral money envelope and Munroe slid several bills inside, the best they could do for a gift without knowing the family's beliefs and customs.

They took a tram south into Nishinari, one of Osaka's twenty-four wards, and walked dirty streets, where drunks slept in the shadows of unkempt buildings. Hand-painted signs in front of stores, restaurants, and *doya* — inns that rented matchbox rooms and shared showers — catered to the area's poverty with rock-bottom prices. They passed by cardboard and clapboard and Okada winced for the fifth time in as many minutes.

Munroe said, "First time here?"

He nodded.

Nishinari was different from the rest of the city, from the rest of the country really:

home to Japan's largest red-light district, and to the closest thing the city had to a slum. Nishinari was where the homeless congregated and where most of the day laborers and immigrants lived.

They found the parents on the third floor of a five-story walkup, sandwiched so tightly between adjacent buildings that laundry drying on the narrow balconies touched the opposite walls. Rust stains marked pitted concrete and from open windows exotic fragrances, spices and herbs and incense, spoke of homes far away.

At the apartment door Munroe kept against the wall. She wasn't hiding, per se, merely providing room for conversation to progress without the distraction of a foreign face with its added reason to refuse to talk.

Okada knocked. Footsteps reverberated through shoddy construction.

The mother answered and Okada bowed deeply, offering the funeral envelope with sincere condolences.

The mother let out the slightest gasp of choked-back tears, and when Okada's hands were free again, he showed her the stack of pictures and asked her if she would look.

The woman stood in the doorway a long moment, as if trying to decide whether to invite him in or send him away. When she spoke, her Japanese was coarse with accent and suppressed tears.

"I have friends coming," she said. "I don't have any time."

Okada bowed again and Munroe nudged his foot before he had a chance to apologize and lose their opportunity forever.

"Only one question, please," Okada said. "If you would, help me understand about your daughter's boyfriend before this horrible event."

"Boyfriend," the woman said, and she spat the word. "He was no *boyfriend*. An older man, a married man, too good to meet the family, too good for Meilin."

"Did you know him?"

"Know him?" the woman said. "Boyfriend!" She spat harder, as if the word was an insult. "We didn't *know* him. We followed her to get a look at this man. Wasted youth. Wasted beauty, and now she's dead."

Then the tears began to flow.

Munroe nudged Okada's foot again.

He hung his head in solemn sympathy, and when the woman's crying subsided, Okada offered her the first of the pages in his hand and said, "Was this the bastard who stole your daughter's youth?"

Munroe leaned her shoulder into the wall and smiled. Okada had promise. He was learning, reading his quarry, adapting on his feet.

The woman handed the picture back, and one by one, Okada gave her the others. Time went on forever as the papers shuffled and the woman sniffled and smells from inside the home roiled out stronger with the hint that something might soon start burning.

"This man," the woman said, and she shoved a picture back. "This man, this man." She sniffed. "I have no time right now." And she started crying again, soft heaving sobs, and she shut the door in Okada's face.

Okada stood blinking and, without turning, thrust the page toward Munroe. She took it and glanced down at the face of Yuzuru Tagawa, head of operations, Bradford's boss.

The noodle shop was a counter and seven stools behind a wooden sliding door capped with hand-painted paper lanterns. The grill behind the counter, with its wok and boiling pots, made the room hotter than the already hot outdoors. A fan in the corner transferred the heated air from one spot to the next.

Munroe waited until food had been ordered, the steaming bowls attacked with chopsticks and the meal half consumed, before scratching at the pall of silence that had settled in in the aftermath of their visit.

The mother's tearful identification of her daughter's suitor was a far leap from fingering a murderer, but the implication was there.

Munroe offered Okada an out: a chance to walk away without the burden of knowing. "The mother could have been wrong," she said. "Mistaken identity and eyewitness confusion has sent many an innocent man to prison."

Okada slurped fat noodles. He chewed and swallowed and then shook his head. With his face still to the food, he said, "The mother followed because she wanted to know and she wouldn't have stopped until she'd seen him clearly. That's different from being confused in the middle of a crime. She didn't hesitate, she knew immediately."

"You thought she'd pick someone else."

"Kobayashi," Okada said, and he drank from his bowl. Broth finished, he put the dish down.

Munroe angled the chopsticks and lost the noodles. All along, Okada had suspected his own boss. It meant something that he confided as much to her. She glanced at him and Okada offered a hint of a bashful smile.

"Kobayashi hated Miles from the day of his arrival," he said. "He spread rumors and lies and ensured that we tracked every movement, every paper he looked over, every person he spoke with. The understanding was that we were looking for reasons to eject him."

Complicated, Bradford had said.

"I thought perhaps the murder was Kobayashi taking matters into his own hands to rid the company of a problem that wouldn't go away."

"You never said anything. Not to the police — not to your superiors."

"I had only suspicions," Okada said. "In the end, they were wrong." He stared down at the counter and shook his head. "This whole thing, nothing but a way for Tagawa to murder his lover."

"It wasn't," Munroe said. She took another bite and chewed long and slow. Okada's posture and expression pressed her for more.

"Meilin was convenient," Munroe said. "She was emotionally involved and their relationship was such a secret that she made an easy victim. At a stretch, killing her might have solved two problems at once, but Tagawa's primary motive would have been to

403

discredit Miles and remove him from the facility."

"How is that possible? Tagawa was in support of a contractor."

"Yes," Munroe said. "Bringing in an outsider was his idea."

Okada pushed his glasses up on his nose, flicked the hair out of his face, and then stared at her. His silence stated the obvious: It made no sense for an executive to create disagreement and conflict, pushing to hire someone, only to turn around and frame that person for murder as a way to get rid of him.

Munroe toyed with her food. It also made no sense for an entrenched professional to invite this level of scrutiny. Not even if there were two factions playing cat-and-mouse, fucking with each other, and the woman's murder and Bradford's setup had been a way to threaten or retaliate against Tagawa for bringing an outsider in.

"Someone else could have murdered the woman," Munroe said. "Without a motive, we only have conjecture, conspiracy, and circumstances."

The proprietor took away Okada's dish and Munroe motioned for him to take hers as well. Okada said, "At the very beginning, you asked me about the belt. If it didn't come from Miles, where did it come from?"

"Someone stole it from him."

"Do you know who?"

"Not yet."

"But not Tagawa?"

"Not directly," she said. The belt that had killed the woman had been taken from Bradford at the hostess club. Someone from the facility had brought him there three times. The accountant who had invited her out had fit Alina's description of the men who had accompanied Bradford. The accountant was indirectly linked to Tagawa through RFID interactions before and after each of Bradford's visits to the club, and Tagawa was the murdered woman's lover. Munroe tapped fingers against the table, rhythm to thought, questioning what she'd missed because even with these connected pieces, the puzzle was still missing its frame. "If things were that obvious," she said, "I would have never asked for your help."

"You were right from the beginning," Okada said. "Whoever did this took a lot of risk. If the person who killed Meilin only wanted her dead, they could have made her disappear quietly." Okada studied her face, searching for something, magic maybe. "Do you think Tagawa did it?"

"There are always answers, Tai. The trick

is figuring out how to ask the right questions of the right people. Your wife is out of town, right?"

"She said she would go."

"So we leave tonight."

"We leave?"

Munroe pulled out Tagawa's file and placed it on the countertop between them. Dillman, smart as he was, had protested against useless busywork with a valid argument: *Whoever the thief is could be exactly who they claim to be with not one data point of inconsistency.* And her response in attempting to placate him had been just as true: *Sometimes what you're looking for doesn't look like what you're looking for.*

She needed to know Tagawa.

Needed to know what she was looking at.

Munroe ran a finger down the text and stopped at the biographical data that showed his family address. "His mother is still alive," Munroe said. "That would be a good place to start."

Day 13   1:08 P.M.

Munroe called Dillman from Shin-Osaka, the station from where she and Okada would catch the *shinkansen,* the high-speed rail that connected the major cities. "Not going to be able to make the after-work thing tonight," she said. "Can we postpone?"

"First thing tomorrow? I'll be here early," Dillman said. "Let's go for coffee."

There was no way she'd be back that soon.

She hated lying to the guy, but he was in the office and the calls were recorded and the last thing she needed was an alert to a change in her routine, so she opted for obfuscation. "Soon as I make it in," she said. "I'll get there as soon as I can."

They left for Hiroshima on a train that pulled to the platform to the second of its arrival time and moved out again within a minute: a smooth rush of hundred-mile-an-hour-plus speeds that took them from city to city, through tunnels, along the occasional glimpse of countryside, and let them off less than two hours later in a city where everything was opposite to Osaka's crowded, wire-strung, tiny streets. Here straight, wide avenues were bordered by air and space and relatively modern buildings, the type of municipal planning found in newer cities — those that weren't forced to build around centuries of history — but in this case was the result of annihilation.

They found a business hotel ten minutes away by streetcar, far enough off the city's center, shopping arcade, and memorial sites to avoid the tourists. Munroe paid cash for two rooms, gave a key to Okada, and left him for the relief of solitude, much-needed sleep, and the pressing awareness of time.

Less than ten days to preempt Bradford's indictment.

She couldn't afford this detour and yet couldn't afford not to make it.

They reconvened with the sun, took a streetcar south toward the coast in an hour of stop and start to the ferry docks, and reached Miyajima, the Island of Gods, before the day had fully come alive. On Miyajima the deer roamed free, and shrines and temples drew the faithful and the curious by tens of thousands each year, and a gauntlet of awning-covered stores funneled them to the great *torii,* massive, vermilion, adorner of postcards worldwide, balanced under its own weight on the seabed.

They bypassed the tourist route, taking side roads, skirting deer droppings, following Internet directions up steep hills toward the far edge of the city. Beyond a copse of maple trees, along an unpaved path, they found the house that matched the online map, and an old wooden door with an overhead so low that Munroe's head would have hit it if she'd stood straight.

Okada knocked and called out a hello. Water babbled somewhere nearby and a birdcall answered the knock. At last the door slid open and a woman in her seventies, barely five feet tall, if that, stood blinking out at them.

She was bent slightly at the waist, her hair pulled up tight beneath a wide-brimmed straw hat, and one gloved hand carried the glove of the hand that was bare. The woman smiled a smile of proper politeness and bowed.

Okada bowed low in return and Munroe followed his lead. The woman bowed again and Okada again and Munroe again because she had no choice, until at last the ritual of who was humblest had ended and Okada, in the story that they'd agreed on during the trip down, presented himself as an archivist and Munroe as a foreign student.

"We were told that your family has lived for generations on the island," he said. "Please would you honor us with your knowledge of recent history?"

Whatever the woman's day might have already held, she set it aside as though she had all the time in the world. She welcomed them into a home that smelled of dust and earth and sweet musty straw, and opened *shoji* to a sitting room with a small floor table that looked out over the garden. She brought tea and sweet bean cakes, and when the rituals of serving and receiving had been observed and the woman had grown comfortable with Munroe's ability to converse, Munroe guided the exchange to the woman's knowledge of island history, to her life, and from there to her husband and children.

Munroe had needed to know Tagawa.

Needed to know what she was looking at.

The woman brought pictures. She traced her family tree, and those of the neighboring families, and spoke of her husband who had passed away ten years prior. Munroe sipped tea while her legs fell asleep below the knees and the story she'd come for

410

surfaced in the folds and seams of a mother's pride, waxing strong in fragmented details of her only living son and the honor he'd restored to the family after the older brother had been held responsible for theft in the company he worked for. Suicide was there in the background, and other details deviating only subtly from Tagawa's work file, deviations that wouldn't have been worth investigating on any other day.

When Munroe had heard enough to know that she'd not wasted time in coming, she thanked the woman for her generosity and Okada excused them both on account of ferry and train schedules. They returned to Osaka, an identical trip in reverse made mostly in silence and small talk, dancing around the edges of questions and answers.

Thirty minutes from Shin-Osaka station Tai Okada said, "I know you learned something important from the mother. I'd like to understand."

Munroe glanced at him, at his shaggy hair and the clothes that on their second day of wear didn't seem all that different from his daily sloppiness. In this, he gave off an air of carelessness, of something less than smart and easy to dismiss, but his disguise was better than the one she wore. Okada knew; he was simply second-guessing his judgment after having wrongly suspected his boss of murder.

"What if it had been your brother?" she said. "Wouldn't you try to regain honor for your family, take revenge, ruin the one who did this?"

Okada didn't answer.

"How long has Tagawa been with the company?"

"Longer than me."

"Just over five years," she said. "How long has the lab downstairs been working on this secret project?"

"Quite some time."

His caginess was irritating. Okada had made progress but was still influenced by having been born in a culture of shaming, afraid of making mistakes and the humiliation of being wrong. "Come on, Tai," she said. "There are no incorrect answers, and I know you see it."

"Nearly six years," he said.

"Which is?"

"Close to the same time the brother committed suicide."

"Yes," she said. "Motivation."

"It doesn't work," he said. "If a man sets out to destroy a company, to steal from a company, maybe even to recover the same technology that resulted in his brother's firing, why be the one to push for an outsider to come when that outsider's specific purpose is to discover his plans?"

"Pushing to find the thief makes him look innocent."

"But we never suspected — nobody could have suspected Tagawa as the source of the theft — he is perfect in every way. Bringing in the outsider ruined everything."

"True," Munroe said, and she waited for the first half of the equation to fully sink in. In a way, it wasn't fair to Okada; she had far more pieces of the puzzle than he did, but she wasn't toying with him. He'd see the picture easier if it was laid out piece by piece than dumped in one big pile.

She said, "What if he'd been getting away with it for years and was certain he wouldn't be discovered? What if someone else in the company was stealing the same secrets and undercutting his plans and payments, and what if Tagawa couldn't figure out who they were but felt confident enough in his own invisibility to take the risk of hiring someone to find the competing thief?"

Okada's eyes widened. Possibilities danced behind them. "Do you think?" he said. "Is it possible that Miles suspected the wrong person? The right person? You know what I mean."

Bradford had certainly suspected something, but if he'd known who or what, he wouldn't be sitting in jail right now. Munroe studied the seatback in front of her. "He didn't know," she said.

"Then why? Why would someone like Tagawa, if it is Tagawa, take all this risk?"

"It's possible Miles was close without knowing what he knew. Maybe Tagawa felt a trap closing in."

They both fell silent and Munroe's thoughts kept churning.

Bradford hadn't known; she didn't know: didn't know which of the players had set Bradford up or why; had no plausible alternative scenario to offer the prosecution in exchange for a murder weapon and easy answers; had nothing solid enough to grind the wheels of injustice to a halt while the countdown to Bradford's formal charges kept ticking steadily on.

Day 14   3:32 P.M.

On the street outside the facility, four police cars were parked up against the curb. Two more vans idled in the parking lot. Okada slowed the car, squeezing between oncoming traffic, and stopped before they reached the gate.

Munroe studied the entrance, the sidewalks, the half-empty lot that should have been filled to capacity: no movement outside, not even the stray employee coming or going, giving high odds that the facility had been locked down and employees held for questioning.

Hands on the wheel, eyes straight ahead, Okada said, "Do we go to work today?"

"This look familiar to you?"

He nodded.

"Same number of police cars as last time?"

"There are more now."

Munroe turned back and faced front. She had no doubt that whatever had happened in their absence would point to her in the same way the belt had pointed to Bradford. "I don't have a choice," she said.

The irony of innocence was that reacting to fear looked the same as reacting to guilt. *Of course I sat and waited. You would have done the exact same thing.* "You do what your instinct tells you," she said, "but if you don't go, they're going to suspect you of something."

Okada sighed and, with the heaviness of a convict approaching a firing squad, put the car back into gear.

"They're allowed to lie and they'll try to trick you if they think you're hiding something," she said. "Don't offer any information you aren't asked for and don't try to be smarter than they are."

Far too many innocent people, cooperating because they had nothing to hide, had lost years of their lives on the mistaken belief that the truth would set them free. If this had been a country where they'd had a right to a lawyer and a right to remain silent, she would have simply told him not to speak at all.

The entrance was empty, the facility quiet, and the uniforms at the desk stopped them on their way to the stiles. Gruff to the point of disrespect, they ordered Okada away from Munroe and then stood between them to enforce the separation while radios crackled with coded talk and barely concealed excitement.

An officer arrived within a minute. Okada didn't look at Munroe as he was led away. He'd be okay. She was the one they wanted.

Two additional officers arrived less than a minute later. They hustled Munroe to a conference room without so much as an attempt at broken English and left her there with an underling standing guard at the door.

Time ticked on and in the silence Munroe rested her head on the table and fell asleep. She woke to the door opening. The clock had moved forward twelve minutes.

The newcomer took a seat across the table.

Munroe laced her fingers atop the veneer and gave him a nod.

He was in his mid-thirties, with a bull neck, close-cut hair, manicured hands, and a tyrant's air of authority. She assumed he was rank — possibly detective.

He ignored the acknowledgment and dismissed her with a glance at the paper he'd carried in. "Your name?" he said.

His English was functional, his accent thick.

So much for pleasantries.

"Munroe," she said. "Michael."

He ran his finger down a column of small print, as much a show of theatrics as her finger-lacing nod had been.

He demanded her ID and work permit and she gave him a Spanish passport and a copy of her company paperwork.

"I'm not an employee," she said. "I don't work here, only advise."

He thumbed through her passport, glanced at the photo page, then set it on the table.

"Your relationship to Makoto Dillman?" he said.

With that, Munroe's stomach roiled and it took a conscious effort to keep shock from escaping onto her face. Strategy shifted; synapses raced for connections, reorienting in rapid-fire sequence. She'd expected that whatever had happened would point back to her, but Dillman? She said, "Coworkers."

"The last time you saw him?"

"Around eight yesterday morning."

"Last time you spoke to him?"

"On the phone, about one yesterday afternoon."

"One ten in the afternoon," the detective

corrected.

Munroe nodded, conceding a point that merely confirmed these were but control questions on a polygraph of human behavior. He was testing for lies. Not here for answers but to confirm what he already knew.

"Where were you this morning?" he said.

"I was several places this morning. What time specifically?"

Tone dry, sarcastic, as if he deigned to humor her just once but wouldn't tolerate insubordination, he said, "Seven-twenty-eight, specifically."

Munroe's stomach clenched again, data reordered again, yesterday's phone call to Dillman replayed in her head:

I'll be here early, he'd said. *Let's go for coffee.*

I'll get there as soon as I can.

He'd believed she'd be there.

Someone else had believed she'd be there, too.

"I was in Hiroshima at seven-twenty-eight this morning," she said.

The detective glanced up, his face such a betrayal of thought, that the words when they came were merely déjà vu. "Your access badge shows you in the facility at seven-twenty-eight," he said.

"I have tickets, receipts, and a traveling companion."

"Why were you in Hiroshima?"

"Research as a consultant."

"No one in the company could confirm your location. Why were you in Hiroshima?"

"Research as a consultant," she repeated.

The detective glanced up.

Munroe made direct eye contact and reached for her wallet. She placed one of the *shinkansen* ticket stubs on the table.

In her head she said, *I wasn't here when Makoto Dillman was murdered.*

In her head he said, *No one said anything about a murder.*

And in her head she'd just admitted to having knowledge of the crime and increased her chances of arrest.

Out of her mouth she said, "I was in Hiroshima this morning."

She knew the risks of talking and had rolled the dice.

The detective picked up the ticket stub, looked it over, jotted notes on his paper, took her passport, and stood. "Don't leave the facility without authorization," he said, and then he and her passport and a portion of her alibi walked out the door.

Munroe sat in a chair in a commandeered conference room, hands behind her head and face toward the ceiling, thoughts unspooling, rage simmering.

Her passport and paperwork had been returned shortly before nine.

Effort and manipulation thereafter had gotten her furtive snippets from a security team who'd been afraid to speak. This much she knew: Dillman had been found in her office with his throat slit and burn marks on both arms.

She blew a long exhale of manufactured calm and gained another minute tethered to rational control. Dillman, for all his faults and quirks, hadn't deserved to die any more than Bradford deserved to be sitting in jail.

The investigators had finally left at nine-thirty, and by then most of the employees, released individually after questioning, had been sent home.

There'd been no arrests.

One murder, with an easy scapegoat, had been easy to solve. By a fortunate circumstance she'd had a rock-solid alibi and so deprived them of another. Without her as the guilty party, this second murder changed everything, creating suspects out of any number of employees and turning the facility's atmosphere, already thick with guardedness, into witch-hunt paranoia and suspicion.

A knock on the door interrupted the brooding.

The handle moved, then Okada's head peered in. He slipped inside and shut the door. Munroe cut her eyes toward him. "The investigator," she said. "Tadashi Ito. Was he the same one running things last time?"

"Yes," Okada said.

Munroe went back to staring at the ceiling. Okada took a seat one over and they both sat in silence for a long, long time.

"It's also the same as before," Okada said. "The footage has been altered. There's no evidence of what happened."

Munroe closed her eyes. "Whose security pass was that done under?"

Okada whispered, "Yours."

Anything less would have been too easy.

Munroe motioned for paper and a pen and Okada handed her both. She scribbled a note and a list of names and slid the page over.

Two trackers. Two sets of players. She'd given Dillman busywork to keep him out of her way. He'd wanted to discuss the files he was working on — names she'd culled from Bradford's list of suspects — and died before he could.

Possibilities chased their tails in circles:

Dillman had been the intended target and she the patsy.

Or Dillman's murder, mirroring the Chinese woman and Bradford, and like the incident of the car's grille with its headlights pushing her toward manslaughter, was an attempt to remove her from the facility.

Or, perhaps two for the price of one, covering both options.

Munroe wanted the contents of Dillman's files, suspected they'd been with him when he died — were possibly the reason he'd died — and needed new copies.

"It's not a problem," Okada said.

"Remember your concerns on the train yesterday?" she said. "The reason you made that phone call?"

"Yes," he whispered.

"That's the problem."

"I understand," Okada said. "I will find a way."

She offered him another out. "I can get someone else to do it."

"No," he said. He stood and walked to the door and then remained there, hand on the hardware, unmoving. He turned back and made eye contact while seconds dragged on in silence. "The databases and log files have also been edited," he said. "We don't know who was here when that happened."

In what was unspoken he'd told her he had her back, trusted no one but her, and expected her to guard his in kind. When he'd gone, Munroe closed her eyes again.

"Dillman," she whispered. "Dillman, Dillman."

She breathed the anger in and shut all emotion down.

Personal feelings had no place here.

This death was merely new data, meant to be sorted with the same clinical manipulation as everything else, but she had no cornerstone for it: that single piece of certainty upon which she could build. Every fact, every name on her web of connections had more than one fit, and Dillman's death didn't correspond to any of them.

This felt like a larger planet wobbling in

the gravitational pull of a smaller neighbor.

Something she hadn't seen yet, hadn't found.

Frustration poked finger holes into the dike of logic and control, wiggled in and buried inside her brain, taunting her with the only facts she knew without doubt: Bradford was still behind bars, the prosecutor could formally charge him at any time, and she'd not yet found the lever for release.

She was running out of time, wasting resources, expending energy she didn't have to stay free of the traps and machinations set against her by players she couldn't see, all of whom knew who she was and where she was, while she was left groping in the dark.

Munroe stood. One foot in front of the other, she paced the few steps across the room, back and forth, animal in a cage. And then she stopped and slammed her forehead into the wall. The pain was instant and calming: partial relief to the addict's need, methadone in place of heroin, pathway to clarity.

The hotel room, with its wall of facts and its bed and the promise of sleep, called to her, but Munroe diverted first to Bradford's apartment to return the Mira and collect the bike with its easy to find and remove trackers.

She turned down into the garage to discover that trouble, in the form of four men, had already come for her. They were a mixture of young and middle-aged in buttoned-up dress shirts and loose slacks like the clothes worn by the men outside the bars in the drinking district.

They loitered by the Ninja, haloed in cigarette smoke, but with only a few butts at their feet, they couldn't have been waiting long. Seeing them, Munroe's pulse quickened, the inner war drum signaling impending battle.

The rawness of Dillman's death burned beneath the surface. The desire for pain rolled through her, a craving to inflict and feel it, and to fight to win, because in seeking blood she had control.

They straightened when the car rolled in, all of them attuned to the Mira's approach, and although they didn't go so far as to form a line between her and the Ninja, the impression of a line was there.

Munroe backed the Mira into its space and they stood watching.

She left the engine running and the lights on, and they squinted to see beyond the glare. The oldest dropped a cigarette to the pavement and ground it with his foot. Beneath his rolled-up sleeves the bare edges of a tattoo crept out.

Strategy flowed into battle formation and instant assessment.

Logic, like a parent, soothed against what instinct, a toddler in full meltdown, screamed for: She was weaponless, and they wouldn't have come unarmed. Not after what she'd done in the hotel room.

But the adrenaline uptick had already begun. The fight called to her, compelling her toward the rush where time separated from reality and hurt ceased to exist because all that mattered from one heartbeat to the next was whatever it took to stay alive.

Munroe gripped the wheel tight against

the tingle in her hands.

Jiro's men tracing her to an apartment in the middle of the city, waiting in the right place at the right time, spoke of deliberation and knowledge.

Two sets of players; two trackers.

These were Jiro's men, but Jiro hadn't installed the trackers.

Just like Jiro hadn't invited Bradford to the hostess club.

The men in the headlights stepped away from the Ninja.

In slow motion she watched them, two heading for the garage exit to block her way out and block residents from entering. The others strode toward her.

She felt their bodies inside her head, the way they would rotate and heave and bend. The chemical flood coursed through her veins.

Munroe revved the engine.

The men in the headlights twitched, giving away strength and strategy in that instinctive reaction. This group of four had arrived with a single semiautomatic. Gun out and now exposed, the man holding it changed tactics.

He aimed at the Mira's windshield and headed for the driver's side. His unarmed partner took the left.

In a country where handguns were nearly impossible to obtain and police pursued violators so relentlessly that even criminals lived in fear of gun laws, firing the weapon would be enough for him to face life in prison.

The weapon was for threat, pulling the trigger a last resort.

By their footfalls she timed them, focus burned on the man with the gun and the finger that rested outside the guard, watching his eyes, not his hands, watching his posture and the tension that ran in the lines along his neck.

Footfall to footfall she waited, hand brake released, vehicle in gear, breathing out long with a predator's patience, footfall to footfall, weapon coming ever closer and then.

Munroe lurched forward, gas and wheel and brake working in microbursts, speed and calculation, car spinning, tires screeching.

The Mira's rear curved toward the man with the gun.

He fired in response, the weapon's report a cavernous boom in the underground.

The back passenger window shattered.

Skin and bone thumped and thudded off the side of the hood.

Munroe reversed and hit soft flesh.

She yanked the emergency brake and was out the driver's door, legs in motion before her feet hit the pavement.

Half seconds mattered. Quarter seconds mattered.

In the gap between shock and reality, the time it took for the brain to register what had just happened, she had already reached the front of the car.

The man without a weapon turned a fraction before she hit him.

She twisted midstride. Kicked his knees out beneath him and charged into him. He landed hard on the pavement with her on top, and she grabbed his hair and slammed his head against the concrete, again and again, while he struggled and then struggled less.

The gun was on the ground, three meters behind her, thrown when she'd reversed into its owner. Beneath the car she saw hands and knees crawling for it.

In the garage exit, the other two men were missing.

The handgun had discharged. They would run as far and as fast as possible to prevent being looped in as accomplices and spending equal time in prison.

Munroe pounded her knee hard into the man's chest: leverage to get to her feet. She

431

grabbed his collar and pulled him.

"Stand up," she said. "If you want to escape this, stand up."

Dazed, he blinked and struggled to his feet.

"The police are coming," she said, and she pushed him toward the car. Without letting go she swung backward into the open driver's door, scooted over the console, legs twisting and tangled, and dragged him in after her.

He didn't fight; he understood.

She reached over him, yanked the door shut. "Drive," she said.

He was aware now, not as alert as he should have been, but enough that he reached for the seat belt. She ignored hers; she needed her hands.

She released the hand brake. "Drive!" she said again, and in the vanity mirror the man behind the car got to his feet, weapon aimed toward her again.

What difference did another discharge make now?

The garage echoed loud with the clap of thunder.

The bullet punched through the rear door and spit-popped into the backseat. The driver hit the gas and the car fishtailed. Munroe leaned over and with both hands on the wheel she pulled.

The hood straightened in relation to the exit.

Then came another deafening roar and another shattered window.

The Mira careened up the ramp and Munroe leaned hard against the wheel in the opposite direction. The car wailed into the street, between a moss-covered stone wall and parked cars, then sped through an intersection.

"Slow down," she yelled.

The streets were mostly empty and that saved them, but still they plunged on, through another intersection, the driver's foot solid on the gas while the blank look of shock filled his face.

Munroe took one hand off the wheel, shoved it beneath his thigh, and tugged hard. The lead foot slipped off the pedal and the car slowed.

His eyes widened as if in the sixty seconds that had passed between her pulling him into the car and the third intersection, he was only just now starting to make sense of things.

She hadn't realized she'd hit him that hard.

She slapped his cheek — not enough to hurt, but enough to get his attention. "Focus," she said.

He nodded and she let go of the wheel and the drive smoothed out.

He glanced at her once, the same way he would have had he discovered himself in an enclosed space with a wild boar. He was a tough guy, tattooed and scarred, but weaponless, alone with the enemy, and still shell-shocked and dazed.

"Just drive," she said.

Putting him behind the wheel had been the lesser of evils. With his hands busy, his eyes busy, he'd find it harder to attack her. Exactly the opposite of what would have happened if she'd put him unrestrained in the backseat and attempted to take him with her.

He stopped at the light, waiting for the turn signal, his coordination seemingly impaired to the equivalent of three beers.

"Turn left," she said.

He'd been the oldest of the four and that was to her advantage. Life experience would have already taught him that he wasn't invincible; made him less likely to see fighting as the only way out; would make him more prone to listen to reason.

Munroe glanced back.

Two shattered windows were going to draw a lot of unwanted attention and having the police discover bullet holes in the car would be as bad as if she'd simply stayed in the garage and gotten shot.

The car was registered to ALTEQ. She'd not been in the driver's seat for any part of this, which would help when law enforcement analyzed traffic camera data. She'd report it stolen in the morning.

They drove in silence, Munroe scanning the streets for police while Mr. Mafia kept a death grip on the wheel, his eyes never leaving the windshield. He followed her turn-by-turn directions and the car wound outside the city along the same route she'd followed the night Bradford had vanished and Okada had led her to a place where they could talk.

Population density thinned and the road signs pointed to smaller cities. In the passing signage Munroe recognized the kanji and said, "Is that for a train station?"

Mr. Mafia nodded.

"Find parking at the station."

He did as she instructed, and when at last he'd pulled to a stop, Munroe reached over and removed the key from the ignition.

Eyes still fixed ahead, hands still gripping the wheel, he breathed irregular and jagged.

"I only want to talk," she said. "Give me your wallet and phone."

His eyes flickered toward the door handle.

"If you try to run, I'll be forced to stop you," she said.

He went back to staring out the windshield.

"I can take your things by force if I have to," she said.

Still staring forward, he reached a hand for his pocket.

His name was Hideki Kimura and Munroe knew this, not from his license, which she couldn't read, or from his phone, which would take time to learn to navigate, but because, still disoriented from the blows to his head, he wasn't sober enough to engage in mental battle.

She emptied his wallet and he watched wordlessly as she searched through each piece of paper, business card, and bank card, looking for something to connect him to the person at the facility who had sent him.

"Do you know who I am?" she said.

He nodded.

"Tell me."

"You're the man who stole women from the club to ruin business."

"One woman," Munroe corrected. "She was there illegally and against her will. Do you know my day job? The company I work for?"

"I don't know anything," he said.

"You do this often? Go out hunting and hurting people?"

Kimura didn't answer, didn't shrug.

"I kill people for a living," she said.

He glanced at her then, he couldn't help it, and she flashed him a predator's taunting hungry smile. "Have you ever been to America?"

He shook his head.

That was good. It meant he'd have no way to disprove her lies.

"You like American movies?"

A subtle nod.

"Then you know how it is," she said. "You've seen our assassins and our gunfights and our car chases. I don't carry a gun because I don't need one to kill you." That part, at least, was true. "Will Jiro kill you?"

Kimura offered no reaction to her naming his boss — he had to have still been too addled to catch the significance because he didn't deny the connection, either.

"Why were you waiting for me tonight?"

"Jiro sent us to take you to him," he said.

"How did Jiro know I would be there?"

"I don't know."

Without a hint toward a change in demeanor, she took the car key and stabbed it into Kimura's thigh. Not nearly as good as a knife, the key barely broke skin, but

438

Kimura yelped and swung at her.

She blocked his arm and drove fingers into his throat.

He choked for air.

"You're wasting my time," she said. "How did Jiro know I'd be there?"

"I don't know," he said. There was a plea behind the words.

"You do know," she said. "You hadn't been waiting long. You knew where to go and when and what to look for. How?"

"A phone call," he said, "a phone call."

"Jiro got a phone call?"

Kimura nodded.

Munroe opened her door and stepped out into the night.

Kimura was a flunky, he had nothing more to give; she read it in his body and smelled it in the fear on his breath. She grabbed her backpack from the rear seat, and with his wallet and his phone, she left him with the car and its bullet holes.

Munroe reached the facility just after seven. A night intended for focus and clarity had detoured into chaos and culminated with three hours of sleep grabbed on station benches while waiting for the first morning train. She'd cleaned up in the bathroom and then spent the morning in the security room at Okada's workstation, glued to camera footage, first searching for clues to Dillman's murder that might have been missed when the data was scrubbed, then tracking and eliminating possible suspects through time stamps and footage.

Whoever had tampered with the data had been thorough, though she learned that Dillman's body had only been discovered as early as it had been because the door to the office had been left open.

The open door had been deliberate. The killer had wanted the body discovered.

Another morning burned and still no

closer to setting Bradford free, Munroe left the facility with ten files zipped up inside her jacket, duplicates of what Dillman had been working on before he'd died.

She returned to the apartment long enough to grab tools out of the bag on the home-office shelf and transfer the folders from her jacket to a backpack. In the garage she removed the Ninja's fairings, pulled out the tracking devices, and examined the magnetic cases.

The beacons had served their purpose; playtime was over now.

With the trackers in her backpack along with the files and the tools, she headed to the airport for the short-term parking, where friends and family had gone to see loved ones off at the security gates, and left both devices up under the still-warm chassis of a gloss-black Porsche.

The tedious drudgery of riding through thick traffic was made worse by hot humid air and lack of sleep, but Munroe made it to Umeda station with fifteen minutes to spare. She found parking and took the elevator up to a multilevel shopping bonanza of sound and color, of boutique stores, chain brands, and restaurants, where she could blend in to the extent that blending in was possible as a tall white foreigner and, if necessary, vanish within the multiple corridors and constant crowds. She perused clothes and window displays from the wrong side of the glass until a familiar face entered the coffee shop across the way. She knew him from his online bio; he knew her because she walked up and said hello.

The translator was in his early thirties, out of place among the fashion conscious.

A phone call and an offer he couldn't refuse had guaranteed his short-notice availability.

"Let's sit," Munroe said, and that was the extent of the pleasantries. They took a table and she laid out for him all ten files that Dillman had been working on.

Language, always her strength, the poisonous gift that allowed her to see and be and do what others assumed she couldn't, had limitations. Without being able to pronounce what she read, she had no mechanism to turn writing into sound, and without sound, no ability to understand.

The translator retrieved a laptop and dictionaries from an over-the-shoulder satchel, and they sat side by side, hour by hour, over coffee and sandwiches, and then coffee again, as page by page he turned kanji into English.

These were details Okada could have

handled, or any other liaison from the facility if, after Dillman's death, she could have convinced someone to work with her and if she wasn't worried about inviting another murder, further complications, and more wasted time.

They finished minutes before the shop's closing time, all the other chairs already up on the tables in preparation for cleaning. The translator stood and twisted, popping his spine. He said, "I can have everything typed within twenty-four hours."

Munroe shook her head. She wasn't about to let the files out of her sight — not even for a moment. "The handwriting's fine."

She paid him and watched him leave, then paid the staff to compensate for business lost by the occupied table and wound her way back to where she'd parked the bike.

The hotel room, when she reached it, was quiet and inviting, with its web of clues up on the wall and a bed that sung sweet enticements of sleep and rest and solitude. Munroe stood on the bed and snapped pictures of the diagrams, so that she carried the full array of connections with her, then collected all the notes and papers brought from work over the last week and slipped them together with her laptop into the backpack, and, leaving behind the clothes and personal items she hadn't touched in days, was gone again.

At the front desk she paid for the room and reserved another week, left the bike, without its trackers, in hotel parking, and walked to the nearest station.

She took the subway two stops down and followed memory for several blocks to the manga café she'd seen in passing, and there, eyes burning, head hurting, she settled in for the hunt.

The online work came first: tedious searches, tracking down and verifying the details on the translated pages, hunting through back doors and alternate routes in the same way she'd instructed Dillman. The collection of notes grew and filled the margins until at last she had enough to get started, and she slept until her alarm roused her for the beginning of business hours.

Phone calls followed the Internet searches, hunting for the proverbial needle, not even sure if she had the right haystack, and when she'd exhausted those leads, she started the pattern over again. At 1:03 A.M. on day 17, more than thirty-six hours after she'd walked out of the facility with the duplicate files, names taken from Bradford's list of suspects as a way to keep Dillman occupied,

Munroe uncovered the first inconsistency.

Nonomi Sato, biotech, female, Japanese citizen, age thirty-four.

A picture from a defunct alumni website culled from Internet archives didn't match what was in Sato's personnel file or what showed on current websites.

Two more hours of hunt and peck, copying and pasting kanji into search engines, finally netted Munroe another, and this was all she had: two pictures of the same person who bore the same credentials and family history as Nonomi Sato, but wasn't her.

Munroe woke to an alarm, showered in the manga café's facilities, and redressed in the clothes she'd washed and dried throughout the night. Shortness of time pressed down on her, crushing in its weight. She didn't have enough days to follow the leads on her own. Had no local connections to grant her access to databases and police records. Had no time to establish subterfuge and false storylines to gain access to reluctant sources already disinclined to trust an outsider: She had no option but to rely on shortcuts.

The shortcut came in the form of Ichiro Yamada, a private investigator with a résumé that included seven years of corporate and private research and eight working for prosecutorial departments. Munroe was still weighing that last fact when he showed up, on time to the minute, in clothes casual enough to say that he didn't fit the corporate mold and shoes priced somewhere between very-good-at-his-job and extortionist shark.

They met at the Umeda station Starbucks, one level down from the translator's coffee shop, where, in an exchange that took less than five minutes, Munroe went over a list of names and instructions for the details she wanted on each and handed over an envelope of cash.

In the hotel room Munroe set an alarm and stared at the wall, sending her mind free to fly between thunderclouds and hailstorms until the lack of sleep pulled her into oblivion. She woke in the late afternoon and worked the diagram, shifting the connections between patterns. Dillman's death wouldn't fit. She placed his card in the circle of unknowns: the gravity wobble, that tiny planet she'd not yet found and named.

Only a few of the upper windows were still lit when Munroe returned to the facility, though the front was ablaze, as always, and the handful of cars that spotted the parking lot would likely still be there in the morning.

The night guards glanced up from their reading when Munroe entered and returned to it, heads down, when her badge cleared her through. She strode the halls for Okada's security department and swiped her pass through the lock.

The door clicked open and the lone member of the security team stood when she pushed through. He was third, fourth, or fifth in the pecking order — somewhere down the food chain. She said, "I need to go through old footage."

"How far back?" he said.

"How far back does it go?"

"We keep records for six months."

Munroe asked for a date two weeks prior to Bradford's arrival.

"Every camera?" he said.

Munroe searched his expression for clues to his mind-set, to whatever instructions he might have been given regarding any requests from her. "Entry, break room, and elevator cameras," she said.

He clicked through a digitized directory, a series of screens and menus that for her might as well have been written in hieroglyphics, selecting, until rows of thumbnail files began to cascade across the screen. He stood and offered her the chair, and when she said, "Thank you," he bowed and turned back to whatever he'd been doing.

She checked her watch and began the sorting.

She had eight hours before the facility

would start humming with the first of the day's employees, eight hours to find what she needed, because she wasn't coming back for round two — not on this one.

The process moved slowly at first, time wasted in learning and observing, but it grew easier with each passing hour. On the screen, in fast forward and then slow motion, Nonomi Sato came and went, her patterns predictable, each movement perfect, invisible in its normalcy and consistency from the days leading up to Bradford's arrival, to those after he'd been taken away: an artist in motion, perfection worthy of admiration, worthy of envy.

There were no hiccups, no disruptions, no giveaways, and watching her, Munroe smiled in the way a connoisseur might smile when at last she'd found flawlessness among samples of average. In so much time, with so much room for error, Sato had only twice deviated from routine. The first was three weeks into Bradford's tenure. Sato had approached for a brief conversation, formal and blushingly proper — likely an attempt at proximity as a way to size up the potential for threat.

The second deviation had come after Bradford's arrest. Had come four days after Munroe had first announced her presence as his replacement, three days after the boys in the garage had come after her with pipes.

Munroe knew who they were now; knew who had sent them.

Two trackers.

Two players.

Yuzuru Tagawa. Nonomi Sato.

Munroe keyed forward, then backward, watching the same sequence for the fourth time as Sato, with her bag, arrived late and diverted directly for the lunchroom; she tabbed through thumbnail after thumbnail for the entry cameras coordinating to the same time stamps and found herself, there, on the other side of the break-room wall. She sat back and smiled again.

She'd known she'd been watched and had never found the source.

The observer had been good, professional, she'd known that then, too, and now she knew she'd found the thief — thief, yes, but no answer to what she needed most. Nothing in Bradford's arrest would have benefited this woman. Nonomi Sato was safe from him and she had to have known it.

Sato hadn't killed the Chinese woman. And it made no sense that she would have killed Dillman — not in the way he'd died — not there on company property, creating scrutiny and risk.

There was that wobble again.

A prickle of heat ran up Munroe's neck and she turned to find Okada's security guy watching her. "Did you locate what you needed?" he said.

"There's nothing."

"That has also been our frustration," he said. "We hoped you would see something different."

Munroe sighed. Rubbed her eyes. "I'm so tired that right now I wouldn't see it even if I saw it." She closed the last of the thumbnails. "I've got to catch some sleep," she said. "No more for tonight. What time do you get off?"

"Another hour," he said. "After Hara-san comes to relieve me."

Before Dillman's death, Shigeru Hara had been the number two in the security operations center and had since been promoted to department head in the interim. "I thought he handled the other side," she said.

The young man lowered his eyes. "After the tragedy, Kobayashi-san instructed that Okada-san and Hara-san should spend time in both departments, for cross-cooperation."

So now the two department heads were meant to spy on each other's work. Way to go for engendering trust and camaraderie. "Hara will probably want to know what I

451

was looking at," she said. "Do you need a list of the file numbers? I'm sorry I shut them down already."

Okada's security man shifted, ever so slightly, in response to her admission of being aware of how closely she was monitored and his role in the reporting. His eyes cast down toward the floor and then toward the door, but he didn't answer the question.

Day 17   7:15 P.M.

Even if the opponent is deeply
entrenched in a defensive position, he will
be unable to avoid fighting if you attack
where he will surely go to the rescue.

— MASTER SUN TZU

Nonomi Sato left the facility as early as the
unspoken demands of company loyalty
would permit. She paused beside her car
just long enough to sniff for suspicion, and
when she felt no menace, no interest, she
slid into the driver's seat, turned the ignition, and headed out of the city, to where
the traffic was thinner and she could more
easily spot if someone followed.

She drove for an hour, watching mirrors
and counting cars while ice inside her head
turned her thoughts cold, chilling the fever
that had taken hold these last days as her
carefully constructed encampment had
come under attack again, and then again.

Battle terrain was changing.

The landscape was fogging over and turning marshy.

Sato turned off the two-lane highway, pulled to the side, waited ten minutes, and then started the car again. Drove again, waited again, and when she was certain she'd left work alone, she continued to the nearest station, went inside to the phones, and found them just beyond the ticket machines.

Battle on the marsh should be avoided at all costs.

If the ground had indeed turned bad, if entrenchment was no longer possible, then the only way to avoid loss was to hurry away.

But to know the terrain, she first had to clear the fog.

Sato used coins, dialed, and caressed the cold calm of detachment.

It had been six months since she'd last spoken with the parents, longer still since she'd returned for a visit, but the e-mail from this morning, with its one simple sentence, had the potential to change everything: *Daughter, we have missed you.*

At last the line connected and a soft voice said, *"Hai, moshi moshi."*

Sato became air and innocence and said, "Mother, how is your health, and how have

454

you been?"

"We have been well, my child," the woman said, "very well, although it has been lonely without you. A friend of yours called asking for you. I told him you were away. When will you return to visit? The garden is beautiful now."

Sato bit down hard on her tongue and drew blood.

"Work has been difficult, but I will visit for Obon," she said. "Thank you for news of my friend, did he leave his name or a message?"

"Let me see," the soft voice said, and then, as if reading from a paper, "Kiyoshi is his name. He said that you were close at university."

Sato shut her eyes, squeezing past the doubts of lives past.

Kiyoshi had indeed been a friend at school. The call could have been genuine, possibly, possibly, possibly. Sato said, "He gave you his number?"

"He said you already knew how to reach him and to please call."

"Thank you," Sato said, because that was appropriate, and because staying on the phone brought her nothing, she added, "Please be well," and replaced the receiver with a gentle drop. And then, with shoulders straight, with a demure emptiness pulled over her face shielding the turmoil beneath, she walked back to the car.

She didn't have Kiyoshi's number, had no way to discover if the call had been genuine or if, instead, this had been an enemy using lies and family as a way to reach her. Sato put the key in the ignition and turned out of the parking lot, reconfiguring the positions of her imaginary army.

Throughout three years at the facility, through monthly security checks, random security sweeps, and regular background checks, she'd remained above suspicion, above reproach, yet every day brought with the sun a renewed possibility of being discovered.

That was the problem with long-term commitment, it was why she preferred the quick jobs, in and out, over and done, vanish and start again.

Six months had turned into a year, and that had turned into three, always following more research, further trials, the end of the road ever one more turn around the bend, the promise of ultimate reward taunting from just beyond reach.

The danger was in staying and she'd stayed too long.

Sato put on the blinkers, changed lanes,

and rerouted.

At another station and another phone bank, in thinning invisibility amid the waning evening crowd, Sato dialed, using the information from a prepaid card. She turned her back to the station cameras and after the first ring dipped her finger into the receiver well and hung up.

The only safe way forward was to assume the call from Kiyoshi had been a pretext; the only safe conclusion, that this had come from the newcomer.

In return, the only strategy for the newcomer was deception and ambush.

Doing so wouldn't clear the fog or allow a better view of the terrain, wouldn't solve the issue of the marshy ground or fortify her encampments, but by ridding herself of the need to battle on more than one front, she could turn her forces to the other.

Sato dialed again, hung up again, and then repeated the process a third time. On this last she stayed on the phone a minute longer, holding a pretend conversation with dead air, for the sake of appearance. Then, having in this deception summoned he who would be the foot soldier used for ambush, she left for Suita, for a three-bedroom house, not far from Osaka University.

In the evening dark, off a well-trafficked

road, Sato climbed the stairs at the edge of a wall up to a barren front door and the tiny patches of pebbles where some form of greenery should have gone, had she been the growing kind.

This was what home was for now, three stories sandwiched between an apartment building and a grocery store with two residences above, and parking just a divot off the road between a retaining wall and the neighbor's tiered garden of river stones and bent manicured pines.

Hardly visible within corners and shadows of her doorway, concealed to blend, were the security cameras.

Sato unlocked the door and stepped into an empty *genkan* and hall, to the fragrance of mold spores, humidity, and decaying wood. She left shoes and purse on the *genkan* tiles and walked the wood floors barefoot for the kitchen, pulling the pins out of her bun as she went, running fingers through her hair, massaging her scalp to soothe the itch.

She poured a glass of cold barley tea, distinctly Japanese and an acquired taste that she'd acquired because, no matter where the family had been stationed, Mother had brought the tea. Sato drank it down, staring out over the room, devoid of furniture but for one lone desk and a small folding table on the floor.

The house was a wasted, expensive luxury, so much space for one in a city where every square meter mattered and three bedrooms should house three generations. But she required a residence on its own foundation, within reasonable driving distance from the facility, in a neighborhood where people came and went often enough that her presence as a single woman living alone wouldn't draw the gossip of the neighborhood *obachan* brigade. That hadn't left her with many options.

As her people were so fond of saying, *gaman.*

Polite and fatalistic. *Suck it up:* a national motto.

Sato rinsed out the glass and set it to dry: it was one of the two glasses she owned, in a kitchen as sparsely furnished as the house.

She'd never bought more; she'd never intended to stay.

For her, Japan had always been stifling. Still was. Tight and constricted, spatially and socially: hundreds of unspoken rules that dictated what she could say, to whom, and how; where she could work, in what field, for how long; how she could live, and love, and exist. Made it difficult to understand Mother's melancholy homesickness and the obsessive way she'd taught Sato to read and write, as if Sato would one day become like her.

She'd only returned to Japan because of the job.

Sato picked up the glass again, pulled a handful of ice from the freezer drawer and dumped it in. Poured a shot of whisky.

Gaman.

When the money was good, anything could be endured.

Munroe arrived at the coffee shop eight minutes late and spotted Ichiro Yamada beyond the glass wall, seated on a barstool against the counter. The pricy PI caught her eye and then glanced away, though his focus unobtrusively tracked her to the door and into the venue, just as he'd tracked her approach.

Yamada shifted to face her. His movement showed no hurry, but neither did it have enough indifference to disguise the guardedness that told her he'd been successful. Munroe nodded toward the back, toward empty tables that were less obvious to all who passed by. "Shall we?" she said.

"Are you hiding from someone?"

"Not yet," she said. "Would like to keep it that way."

Yamada's lips turned up with a trace of conspiracy, and he gathered his coffee mug and satchel and walked with her toward the tables at the rear.

He sat and Munroe shifted her chair to the side, so that its back was to the wall instead of the door. Across from him, she placed the second half of her payment on the table.

Yamada thumbed through the bills, put the envelope back where she'd placed it, and pulled two much larger envelopes from his satchel. He slid one across the table, moved the other to his right, and rested his hand on top of it.

Munroe picked up the thicker envelope, flipped through the pages, stuffed them back inside, and nodded to the other. "What about that one?"

Yamada leaned forward, hand firmly on the envelope. He said, "There are times when finding answers can be more trouble than what they're worth."

Munroe reached for the edge of the envelope and left her fingers there, not far from his hand. "Thank you for the warning," she said, and she waited for him to move, but he didn't.

"You've paid for the information," he said, "therefore it belongs to you." Yamada scooted closer and, by proxy, his face moved nearer to hers. "At the risk of overdirectness," he said, "and I apologize, as I don't wish to create offense. Can you assure me that there's been no mistake in asking after this man? Perhaps this is a misidentification or an innocent curiosity that, in the end, wouldn't be worth satisfying."

"There's no mistake," she said.

Lips pressed together, Yamada looked down at his hand. "Sometimes," he said, "merely knowing something can create risks. Having knowledge that someone might not want you to have is dangerous in itself, but once one has the knowledge, there is also the issue of what should be done with it, and occasionally the desire to act upon it."

Munroe waited before replying; waited until the silence became thick and Yamada's eyes drifted up off the table and focused in on hers. "I'm familiar with these types of risks," she said. "As I'm sure you can understand, being unable to read the language presents a unique challenge. Under other circumstances, this is information I would have acquired for myself."

Yamada nodded then and pushed the envelope toward her. He leaned back in his seat. "Be careful," he said.

Munroe rested her own hand on top of the envelope. "Did you stop before you were finished?"

"You have enough," he said. "More than what you paid for. If you want anything beyond what's been provided, then the price goes up."

Munroe dragged the envelope closer and stacked it on the first one, contemplating the charm with which he'd just told her that he wouldn't dig deeper no matter how much she paid.

Yamada handed her his business card even though she already had one. "You might need me again for other things," he said, and then he stood, sparing her the necessity of small talk.

When he'd gone, Munroe followed him out. If there were problems with the information, there would be problems with the source, and the only way to mitigate against that kind of failure was to plan for it. She waited near the bike racks not far from the underground exit, caught the PI's plates when he pulled out, and with that just-in-case in hand, she headed on foot for a manga café, a five-minute walk from the station.

In the quiet of a booth, away from prying eyes, Munroe sorted through the pages in the thick envelope, accompanied by Yamada's meticulous notes, which included time stamps on every action he'd taken, as well as his own opinions and impressions. First was Nonomi Sato, the woman in the alum photos. She was real, her résumé perfect, her family history genuine, but the woman who worked in the security lab downstairs wasn't Nonomi Sato.

The real Nonomi had been dead for a little over three years.

The parents, working-class and elderly, without a history of mental illness, insisted their daughter was alive. Lifestyle and purchases pointed to quarterly windfalls.

If Munroe could have found a way to make Dillman's death fit the narrative, then he would have died to prevent this knowledge from being discovered.

Dillman had done his inquiries from within the facility. Someone had been watching, listening. Someone within those walls knew what Dillman knew, knew or suspected that Dillman had found anomalies, and knew that he'd be talking to her about them.

But Dillman's murder didn't fit any more than the Chinese woman's had.

The value in espionage came from burrowing into an assignment and maintaining the subterfuge. Hiding out in the open could only come with familiarity and normalcy, and the disruption brought on by Bradford's arrest had quintupled in the wake of Dillman's murder.

If Bradford or Dillman had been credible threats, a woman of Sato's skill and professionalism would rather poison them in their sleep, or frame a suicide, than bring an investigation to her doorstep, much less two.

Nonomi Sato hadn't killed Dillman, but neither had Yuzuru Tagawa. Munroe had matched his presence to camera time stamps throughout the morning of Dillman's murder and he'd been nowhere near that office.

There was that wobble again, the gravitational pull of the thing she'd not yet placed.

Munroe took the pages, stacked them, shoved them back into the envelope. There were other names she'd asked for, other connections, but those would wait. She moved on to the thinner envelope. Jiro Sasaki: human trafficker and abusive boyfriend; millionaire, racketeer, venture capitalist, and commander of a small army of thugs.

Most of the dossier consisted of translated printouts of news articles, some that didn't even pertain to Jiro but upon which Yamada had underlined key phrases. Here the investigator's notes were sparse and cryptic, making it plain that he'd been reluctant even before he'd begun assembling the material.

News articles laid the framework, describing a country where mafia families operated in the open, without any attempt to hide affiliation; where many syndicate members maintained offices and carried business cards embossed with gang inscriptions, and CEOs and elected officials openly attended yakuza weddings and funerals, and where local crime bosses held press conferences to air grievances; and explained how a culture built upon rule following and integrity, strengthened by honor and shame avoidance, painted an illusion of legitimacy over a long unbroken history between politicians and the criminal element.

Munroe reached the end of the report and went back again, and then again, always to the same article. The story told nothing of Jiro specifically, but Yamada had highlighted it well. Hidden within was the answer to Bradford's arrest.

Japan's crime families, responding to a cash crunch brought on by two decades of a dormant economy, had used threats and muscle to diversify into legitimate enterprises and were now heavily vested in banking, real estate, and technology.

The dots were there. She had only to connect them now.

Perhaps for Bradford the truth *could* set him free.

Day 18   7:23 P.M.

Munroe stood in the doorway of the hotel room, half in, half out, and then slowly closed the door behind her and took a deep inhale, searching for the fragrance, the scent that had set her on edge.

She'd breathed in a human smell, but not natural and not housecleaning; a smell of body products, or hair gel, or laundry detergent, lingering in the air in the way smells did in rooms without air circulation and climate control — rooms like hers, where a key card in the connector was necessary to keep the air conditioner running.

Munroe pressed a palm to the toilet door and tipped her head inside, then did the same with the *ofuro,* and, assured she was alone, walked to the bed and closed her eyes, breathing deeply again, finding the fragrance there, faint and subtle, mixed in with the heat and not fully dissipated.

Whoever had been there had only left recently.

She turned a slow circle, searching for hints of disturbance and theft.

Everything in the room and on the wall and within her map of diagrams was how she'd left it: the desk with an undisturbed patina of dust due to the many days of Do Not Disturb signs and lack of housekeeping, the TV slightly off angle, her backpacks stacked in a line beneath the window and Bradford's dress shirts still on hangers off the wall hook, as she'd left them.

Munroe turned back to the bed, to the bedspread just slightly askew, and knelt and angled to see the bed top at eye level. The tight hospital corners weren't quite as tight; the bedspread was wrinkled in places where it had been disturbed and smoothed out again, as if someone had climbed onto it, left indentations, and had flattened out the traces in a hurry.

This wasn't Jiro; not his modus operandi.

She stood, glanced at the wall and then at the bed, and then at the wall again and swore in a low grumble. She, too, had stood on the bed, several days back, to take pictures of the wall, documenting her documentation.

Munroe's chest beat heavy, an inner fist

pounding against her ribs, primal and child-ish and full of wounded rage. She stood on the chair and tore the map down. Folded it along the seams, one forceful shove after the next, and then stuffed it into her back-pack. Coded notes aside, she hadn't been back recently enough to have added any-thing of value, but she wanted nothing more than to throw the whole fucking thing at Nonomi Sato and tell her to enjoy herself.

Munroe took the stairs down to the lobby, paused in the stairwell to pull an air of casual indifference into her posture, and then strode to the front desk.

The night clerks were both women in their late twenties or early thirties, one of them she'd not seen before. Munroe smiled. Waited a beat for effect.

"Room 201," she said. "Have I had any visitors while I've been away?"

The women glanced first at each other and then at Munroe; they searched through a message pad for notes, came up without answers, and in near unison, nodded bows of apology. No tell of guile showed in either expression, no betrayal of secrets in pose or posture, so Munroe thanked them and took the stairs back up, counting minutes in her head.

At her door, she ran a finger beneath the

lock, feeling for the data port.

If the person or persons who'd been inside hadn't gotten a key from the desk clerk, they would have had to hack in, though that wasn't particularly difficult to do. The devices to mimic the portable programmers were easy to replicate, if you knew what you were doing, which most people didn't.

Munroe let herself back in, turned the door lock, and ran the chain.

She'd never brought the Ninja, with its trackers, to the hotel.

Never put the battery in her phone.

Finding her here would have meant surveillance, or triangulating off the bike's many parking locations, or pounding the pavement from door to door asking for her, and all of these options would have come with a hefty price tag in time, money, or both. Munroe shut her eyes and drew in the opponent, became the opponent.

No way would Sato have gone through the effort and expense of tracking her down just to take pictures of a wall map she didn't know existed. Nonomi Sato dealt in treachery and sleight-of-hand; there would have been another reason for coming. Pictures of the notes were a little bonus.

Munroe started with the bathroom, searching every place a thing could be hidden, removing the shower rod and the drain plug and checking behind electrical outlets. She cleaned behind each step with a washcloth that she wet, and rinsed, and wet again, wiping off prints and residue and anything that might come back to haunt her. She checked drawers and inside the desk frame and beneath the bed. She pulled the faceplate off the air conditioner and the casing off the back of the TV, and by the time she'd finished, she'd recovered four small bags of white powder.

Unlike Bradford's arrest, unlike Dillman's death, this made sense.

This fit the narrative. This was devious, this was ambush; this was Sato at work removing a perceived threat in a subtle way that the Chinese woman's and Dillman's deaths would never be, in the same way that Sato had sent the boys with the pipes as a warning.

Fucking Nonomi Sato.

Munroe emptied the contents into the toilet and flushed them, one by one. She turned the bags inside out, rinsing them in the sink, washing away the traces, and then cleaned the toilet and the sink once more when that was finished.

Sato would have known when she'd left work. Would have allowed enough time for errands and detours, but the police would be alerted soon, and Munroe had no desire to explain the unexplainable on the chance that she'd missed something along the way.

She packed what she needed most into one of the backpacks, took everything else she could manage to carry on the bike, and left the rest, saying not a word to the desk clerks when she squared the bill on her way out.

She wandered the block to make sure she wasn't followed, eventually looping back to the building next door, and took the stairs up a level to a landing where narrow windows opened to the street below. She waited less than half an hour before flashing lights filled the street. From her angled view she caught glimpses as the police rushed in and again when they came out less than two hours later.

They'd come. They'd searched. They'd left empty-handed, and their posture and demeanor, facial expression and interaction, said they were none too happy about the false alarm.

Soon enough Sato would get the news.

Soon enough she'd move in for another round.

But the mind-fuck could work both ways.

DAY 19   6:52 A.M.

Much strategy prevails over little strategy,
so those with no strategy cannot help but
be defeated. Therefore it is said that
victorious warriors win first and then go to
war, while defeated warriors go to war
first and then seek to win.
> — ZHANGYU, COMMENTING ON
> *THE ART OF WAR*

The train doors opened and Nonomi Sato,
one among thousands, stepped from the
women-only car to the platform, carried
forward by the outward rush. The segre-
gated cars, meant to provide women with a
place free from chronic groping and sexual
harassment, were handy when the com-
muter throng was packed so tightly that station attendants shoved passengers inward
so the doors could close.

She continued up another level, through
crowds running to make connections be-

tween train lines, patterns that disbursed and recongealed in new arrays like bacteria in humanity's petri dish.

She followed another set of stairs, and exit signs, and finally came up top to fresher air, and there, walking around to the other side of the rail, she leaned against the stairway wall and pulled a book from her purse.

He stood beside her a minute later, clean-cut in his white shirt and thin tie, as if dressed for a day in the bowels of insurance paper-pushing hell. He asked for a cigarette and she said she didn't smoke.

He asked if what she read was any good. Sato handed him the book.

"Take a look," she said. "You might find it to your liking."

He was the man she'd dialed to set deception and ambush in motion, and he cracked the pages open to the envelope she'd left to mark her place. He traded her envelope with one of his own, then handed the book back. "It looks good," he said. "I should get a copy."

"You should," she said, and by the time she'd placed the book inside her purse, he was gone.

Sato went back the way she'd come, down the same stairs, and returned to the same platform, waiting for the next train, where she would once more be shoved in tightly among other bodies.

She reached work early, even with the detour and having taken public transport instead of driving. Perfunctory and part of the scenery, she went through the procedure to access the lab.

Sato performed for the cameras, performed for her workmates, perfect in the routine as always in spite of today's lack of focus. Patience was a cultivated skill, but with the envelope waiting inside the book, the weeds of wanting grew wild. She was careful, cautious in compensating for her own weakness, cautious due to the additional scrutiny that had fallen upon the facility.

So much suspicion, so many accusations, and the police investigators who'd made several trips back to interview anyone who'd been on-site during either of the murders. She was lucky in that so far she'd remained off radar, though there was no telling how long that luck would hold.

The danger was in staying, and she'd stayed too long, but the promise of success was around the corner, just around the corner.

Late, late in the evening Nonomi Sato

climbed the stairs at the edge of the wall, unlocked the front door, and stepped inside. She pulled the book from her purse, left the purse in the *genkan,* and headed directly up the stairs for the second floor and her bedroom and the laptop tucked in the drawer beneath her sweaters.

She sat on the low platform bed and flipped the laptop open, waiting for the boot-up and the password control and then the thumb scan. She slipped the envelope from between the book's pages while the system ran through the start-up and dumped the micro card into her palm, feeling what it meant to succeed.

If all had gone well, the threat of the newcomer had been neutralized.

Sato slid the card into its slot and counted seconds as the data loaded, pictures of the newcomer's hotel room, taken by the same hireling who would have left the drugs.

Deception and ambush.

One hundred and fifteen pictures waited.

Sato started at the beginning.

The camera lens took her through the newcomer's room, everything exactly as it had been laid out and left behind: pictures in place of eyes. Pictures to show her what the long hours required by company loyalty wouldn't allow her to see for herself. She needed this, needed to know the enemy.

The newcomer was orderly, but not fastidious. Clean, but not to the point of obsession. He had very few items and few articles of clothing — a man used to traveling light and picking up again on short notice.

The next photo took in a wide angle. Sato paused and zoomed, studying the lack of personal touches — no mementos or touchstones, making the room emotionally barren.

She and the newcomer were not so different.

Twenty-seven pictures in, Sato's breath caught.

She expanded the image to fill the full screen, put the laptop on the mattress, flipped over onto her stomach, and stared.

Now this was a gift. A truly generous gift.

The series of photo arrays started with the whole wall and then, quadrant by quadrant, zoomed in closer and then again closer still so that one picture made the entire diagram. Then four. Then eight. And at last the photographs were so detailed that she could see the depth of the pen strokes against the index cards.

These were the facts as the newcomer understood them, an attempt to untangle the mess that had locked away the cowboy.

The writing was in English, but not exactly. Perhaps a blend of languages? Or perhaps words that meant something to the writer, but without understanding the intent they would mean nothing to anyone else? Sato searched for her own name and didn't find it, searched for various known quantities and didn't find them, either.

So this was a riddle, a challenge.

To know these words and the way that each part tied in to the whole was to have scouts behind the enemy lines.

Sato smiled, then stood and carried the laptop down to the kitchen.

She pulled prepackaged food from the refrigerator. Stripped a small tray from cardboard and plastic and placed it into the toaster oven. Days that turned into nights, and nights into days, turned meals into something no self-respecting human should have to endure. The price of doing business.

Gaman.

Sato poured two fingers of whisky and brought the glass to the small table at which she rarely ate. She sipped and sent eight images to the printer. She taped them together and laid the sheet on the floor. With the whisky in one hand, pulling pins from her bun with the other, she sat beside the printout, mulling over the notes until the timer dinged.

Sato transferred food from toaster to plate, then folding table on the floor. She went for sticky notes on the desk at the long end of the room, and there, in the soft light of the lamp, she stood, staring.

The can of pens, always to her right, was on the left side. The stack of colorful notes, always to her left, was on the right.

Sato took a step back. Everything else was the same.

She ran for the kitchen table, nearly tripping over her feet in the process. She shrugged out of the tight skirt, flicked the laptop screen to life, and scrolled for access to the footage from the bank of security cameras that watched her house.

With hands shaking, it took two tries before she was able to key the password in properly, and when finally granted access she flipped through one black square after the next, the last eight hours blank.

She tore through the door for the laundry room and tugged down a clean *jinbei.* Shoved her legs into the pants, grabbed a folding ladder, and hauled it into the *genkan.* She checked the cameras, up in the corners, inside and out.

The feeds had been cut.

Sato stumbled down the ladder, heart pounding, mind refusing to accept, unable to believe, terrified to know. She dragged the ladder back enough to get the front door shut and ran for the downstairs bedroom while inside her head the beat pounded *no, no, no . . .*

Down the street from the hostess club, bathed in neon on the corner of sex and sin, Munroe joked and jostled among a group of twentysomethings, utilizing the crowd and drunken conversation as a cloak of invisibility while she waited for the night to end and the club to empty.

In her gut, she knew, through circumstantial evidence and connecting the dots, she knew, but knowledge wasn't enough to set Bradford free. She needed a catalyst, and if she was wrong, if confirmation bias had created a false reality, she would lose.

Bradford would lose.

There would be no second try, no do-over.

So she'd returned to the beginning, to where they'd been before the nightmares and unknowns had ripped away happiness, and amid the disguise of laughter and broken English, Munroe watched the door.

Eventually, the group she used for cover

moved on to other parties, in other venues. Munroe retreated to the shadows, waiting, while up and down the block the restaurants closed and the die-hard clientele emptied into the streets and the night wound into morning. The hostess girls left, too, some of them picked up by boyfriends, others walking away in groups of two and three, and others still collecting bicycles from nearby racks. A few would be transported by Jiro's men. Alina had been one of those.

Gabi was one of the last to leave the club, and like Alina on the night she'd fled, she was nearly unrecognizable without the makeup and dressed in jeans and a summer sweater. At the end of the block she split from a group and walked alone toward the train station. Munroe followed from afar until they reached a place where the light was good and the area clean. She called Gabi's name and closed the distance.

The woman turned, young and angel-faced, innocent beneath the light. She stood, puzzled for a moment, and then, recognizing Munroe, she blanched, turned, and walked at a faster pace.

Munroe jogged to catch up and then kept beside her.

"You shouldn't be here," Gabi said. "You shouldn't be anywhere near me."

"I just need you to answer a question and I'll go."

Gabi stopped and spun, shoulders hunched, face full of accusation. "Where is Alina?" she said. "What did you do to her?"

"I put her on a plane. She's in Russia."

"Russia?" Gabi said. Her hands relaxed and the anger radiating from her melted into a softer mixture of sadness, pain, and relief. "This is true?"

"Yes. True. Promise," Munroe said, and pulled out the pack of pictures she and Okada had taken to the Chinese woman's mother in Nishinari. "Do you know any of these men?"

Gabi ignored the pictures. "There's been stress for all the girls in the club because of you," she said.

"I'm sorry," Munroe said. She took Gabi's hand, pressed the pages between her thumb and finger, and raised them closer to Gabi's face. "Have you seen any of these men?" she said.

Gabi looked down and then turned the pictures toward the light. She stopped at Nobu Hayashi, the accountant. "He was in the club those nights with your friend," she said. She continued flipping and stopped at Tagawa's face. "I've seen him, too," she said. She handed the pictures back and

485

started walking again.

Munroe kept pace beside her and held Tagawa's picture in front of Gabi's face, forcing Gabi to stop walking or risk tripping. "Where did you see him?" Munroe said. "In the club?"

Gabi pushed the picture away. "Outside the club." She started up again. Munroe, still beside her, said, "Was he watching the door? Waiting to meet someone?"

"He was with Jiro in Jiro's car. They were arguing, maybe. Most men who talk with Jiro are unhappy."

They passed beneath a rail bridge and turned a corner. Gabi pointed up at a building that nearly backed into the train tracks. "That's where I live," she said, "so good night." She paused, then cast her gaze down toward the ground and then up into Munroe's face. "Take me with you, please," she said. "Take me like you took Alina."

Munroe breathed in the night and exhaled the frustration.

"I can't help you the way I helped her. I can get you to the station, I can put you on a train to Tokyo, so you can get to the embassy, but I can't protect you."

"There have been stories," Gabi said.

"What kind of stories?"

"The girls in the club talk about a *gaijin*

486

who beat Jiro's men," Gabi said. She twirled a finger through her curls, managing both threat and plea in that one simple action. "Jiro is still looking for him."

"I'm sure he would be," Munroe said. "I can't help you, Gabi."

"Anything you want, I give it to you," Gabi said.

Munroe held up Tagawa's picture again. "How do you know that this was the man you saw?"

"It was him."

Munroe turned to walk away.

Gabi grabbed her arm and Munroe smacked her. "Don't touch me," she said.

Gabi blinked, took a step back, and said, "It was him. He stepped out of the car as I was walking to the club. We nearly collided. He yelled at me, up in my face, very close, angry yelling. It was him."

"I want to help you," Munroe said. "I can't."

Gabi's eyes drifted toward the ground, her face growing redder with suppressed tears while she picked at her cuticles.

"Give me your bag," Munroe said.

Hand tight around the shoulder strap, Gabi pulled back.

"You want me to help you? Give me the bag."

Gabi held on, so Munroe let go and walked away.

"Wait," Gabi said, and ran after Munroe, her bag outstretched. "Take it."

Munroe kept walking. Gabi caught up and half turned, tripping backward, held the bag toward Munroe. "Please," she said. "Please. I want to go home."

Munroe grabbed the oversize purse, then Gabi's wrist, and pushed the woman against the retaining wall. Munroe dumped the contents on the ground and sorted through them, tossing makeup, perfume, paper, and a spare change of clothing back in. She rifled through the wallet, found three thousand dollars in yen, shoved the money back in, and tossed the wallet into the purse. Found Gabi's passport.

Munroe pulled the battery from Gabi's phone, and threw it hard down the street. "You don't need my help," she said. "You have the money to get to Tokyo. Go. Get out."

"I have the money, but not the safety."

Munroe pressed her thumb to the bridge of her nose and glanced up toward the light-polluted sky. Gabi was a witness to the connection between Jiro and Tagawa, she could be useful if that card needed to be played, but Alina, with the information she'd provided, had been a burden, and this one was that much worse.

"I can't keep you safe," she said.

"If I run to Tokyo, Jiro will find me even there. He will catch me and kill me to make an example to the other girls."

Munroe stepped toward Gabi, into the young woman's personal space. Gabi smiled sheepishly: manipulation mixed with flirtation.

Munroe stared hard for a moment, then put her hands on Gabi's shoulders. She shook her hard, then shoved her back. Gabi half tripped, caught her footing, then stood and glared at Munroe.

"Live in fear or die free," Munroe said.

She turned and started walking. Gabi called out after her, "I'll tell Jiro you were here. I know what you look like, I'll help him find you."

Munroe waved her off and continued on.

DAY 20   2:00 A.M.

If you know the place and time of battle,
you can join the fight from a thousand
miles away.
— MASTER SUN TZU

Sato slid the *shoji* open and stared an arm's
length in, at the door behind the door. The
cameras between them had been pushed up
to face the ceiling, an announcement that
whoever had been in the house had been
here, too, and wanted her to know.

But the steel door to the vault on the other
side was still secure.

Sato tested the handle, then keyed in the
code on the numerical pad.

The lock popped and she pulled the door
open to cold air.

The room within the room was sound-
proofed and climate-controlled, and the
lights turned on automatically with the motion of the door.

490

This was the reason she'd needed a house, not an apartment.

This was the reason for everything.

Sato stepped inside and sealed herself in, then scanned the waist-high shelves that lined opposite walls.

She shouldn't be here, not still wearing her work blouse, not without showering and gowning for decontamination, but she had to see, had to know that the work hadn't been disturbed.

She walked the shelf, looking over the 3-D printer, the computer, and the wires between, confirming that all was connected as it should be. She knelt to check the refrigerator and the glassed-in temperature box where the cell cultures incubated. This was a small-scale replica of the lab inside the facility, minus the operating theater and the test animals, although maybe one day she would add those, too.

As long as she had this lab, no amount of security at the facility could keep her from walking out with each day's knowledge, and duplicating behind these walls what had worked there. She had no need to risk secreting the data out when she could create the successes fresh and skip the days of mistakes, sending the filtered knowledge on for a hefty fee.

The danger was in the staying, and she'd stayed too long because it had taken her six months just to catch up with the work already in progress while faking an education she hadn't had. But she was good at her job. Both of them.

She knew the research, knew the competition.

Anyone with a 3-D printer, a little know-how, and the right cellular soup could biofabricate organs. The trick wasn't in printing them, nor even in choosing the correct cell structures to lay down the network of veins and build multiple cell types; the trick was in controlling temperature, was in keeping the cells oxygenated and viable and providing them with a way to grow and function like native tissue. The fabricated cell lattice needed to incubate within a host.

They were close now, and in this Akio Tanaka in his genius was years ahead of the rest. They'd done two transplants, a culmination of the six years he'd spent perfecting the inherited technology. In the most technical sense, the transplants had been failures, but Sato knew them for the successes they were. They'd come so far, and they had learned, and they would move on to the next phase.

Sato wiped condensation off the incubator glass, then stood and left the room within the room and sealed the door, shutting the *shoji* to hide the room. She'd harvested her own cells, grown her own cellular soup, and stolen from other labs what she couldn't create herself.

The day Tanaka successfully printed a heart she would print one of her own, and when the first human transplant trials started, she would arrange a trip to Thailand and, honoring Mother as a daughter should, become Mother's own donor. The danger was in staying, and she'd stayed too long. Pride had kept her here, and now this sacred life-giving place had been violated.

Sato glanced up at the cameras, pointed toward the ceiling.

This wasn't the address on her paperwork at the facility. This wasn't the address to which her vehicle was registered. There wasn't a way, in any meaningful sense, for someone to have found her and followed her here without her knowing about it, and yet they had.

Whoever had done this, knew what they were doing.

Whoever had done this had left a message.

Sato dragged a chair from the kitchen and stood on it to readjust the camera angle, then stalked over to her computer and went back through the footage.

Only one camera still functioned, on the third floor, leading to the unused bedroom. Sato ran up the stairs for the futon closet, to the false floor that hid the money box. She pulled hard, pried the board up, and stared into an empty hole.

If she could have screamed, she would have shattered glass.

She'd only had a month's pay in that safe, but that wasn't the point.

Someone had known where to look, had taken what was hers, had taken just enough to cause her pain and wanted her to know they'd done it.

Sato clenched her hands and gritted her teeth, then spun around.

She slogged down the stairs, into the empty dining room, and stared at the floor and the sheet of paper she'd laid down. Her food was cold, but what did that matter, she had no appetite. She grabbed the whisky glass, still half full, and tossed the smooth liquid into the sink. Then she sat, and with the fever burning, she stared some more.

Good warriors sought effectiveness in battle through momentum, not from individual people. The ambush had failed, but this map was momentum.

Munroe found temporary refuge and a few hours' sleep on a futon in a manga café cubicle and was on her way again before the workday began. She took the train to the city center and walked the awakening streets, following directions she'd mapped out a week earlier when threats to Bradford's lawyer had seemed appropriate and reasonable.

She stopped at the western entrance of an eighteen-story building that filled an entire corner, shadowing sidewalks and portions of the wide multilane intersection from the morning sun. She dialed, glancing up, and waited through the tones.

When the line connected, there were no receptionist lies.

Soon the lawyer answered, and Munroe said, "Has your client been indicted?"

"Not yet," he said.

With those two words, the reality of the

present washed in, bringing weakness, bringing loss and longing with the dread she'd not allowed herself to feel. Munroe pushed it all away. This was a lapse, a momentary lapse.

She had a client, she had a goal.

Until the contract was fulfilled, there was only that and nothing more.

She said, "Has he confessed?"

"I've not received notification of such. There has also been pressure from important people on my client's behalf — my client has many friends."

This was good. Perhaps Warren Green had pulled rank. Or someone Sam Walker had drawn in from among those who owed Bradford favors. Regardless of who or where the influence was coming from, it would minimize Bradford's suffering. Abuse of power had a way of dissipating when those in power realized that the seemingly helpless had powerful friends.

"Have you seen him?" she said.

"Briefly, together with a representative from the U.S. embassy."

"I promised to get you what you need to help your client," Munroe said. "I have material for you."

"I have an appointment in thirty minutes."

"I'm outside your office," she said. "Give

me those thirty minutes."

Munroe took the elevator up to the sixteenth floor. An assistant greeted her at the door and walked her through a narrow tiled hallway to a corner office, where a bookshelf lined one wall and the floor space was barely enough to squeeze in a desk and chairs, but the view was nice.

The lawyer was a small man, quick on his feet, oozing the type of energy that came packaged in cans and bottles. He stood when she entered, sizing her up from top to bottom in a blink. He motioned to a chair. "We only have a little time."

Munroe sat, pulled a box from her pack, and placed it on the desk.

"The murder weapon," she said. She'd scuffed the belt and for what it was worth rubbed the buckle with Bradford's dirty laundry, then wiped the leather down to remove prints as a plausible explanation for why Bradford's weren't on it. The lawyer looked into the box, harrumphed, and then capped it again.

Munroe followed with a piece of paper that she laid out flat.

The lawyer took his chair. Munroe picked up a pen.

Convincing him wasn't the same as convincing a judge, but in a system where informal negotiations outside the courtroom were what guided the process forward, she would give him a way to adjust the timbre.

Human nature begged for simplicity, for easy answers within already established beliefs. The more complex the truth, the further a scenario strayed from what was commonly accepted to be true, the easier it became to reject the truth. Belief mattered more than fact.

Belief was effortless, like belts and foreign killers.

She said, "I'm going to throw a lot of information at you — motives and connections — I'll do it in as few words as possible, but it's messy."

"Is it provable?"

Munroe met his eyes and held his gaze.

"Yes," she said, "but not with the money you're being paid. I'll give you the facts, you figure out what you can do with them."

She drew a circle in the middle of the page.

"ALTEQ-Bio Gaisha," she said. "A cutting-edge leader in the biotech field. The executives believe someone on the inside has been stealing trade secrets and selling them to a competitor."

She blocked out a square on the bottom left of the page.

"Yuzuru Tagawa, head of operations for ALTEQ," she said. "Six years ago a security flaw at Kinjo Ichi Gaisha, which was ALTEQ's chief rival at the time, resulted in data theft on a valuable, tightly controlled project. Two months later ALTEQ announced a breakthrough with the same technology. Tagawa's brother, responsible for maintaining Kinjo Ichi's security, was fired. He committed suicide. A year later Yuzuru Tagawa began working at ALTEQ."

Munroe blocked a square in the top left corner.

"Jiro Sasaki," she said. "I'm pretty sure you know who he is. One of his legitimate businesses is also in the biotech field, and starting a year after Yuzuru Tagawa began work at ALTEQ, his company has twice beat ALTEQ to the market with identical products."

She drew a line connecting the two boxes and drew an *X* in the middle.

"If you look hard enough and ask questions of the right people, you'll be able to connect Sasaki and Tagawa through clandestine meetings."

The lawyer, protest and objection written on his face, opened his mouth.

Munroe held up a hand. "I'm just getting started," she said. "Wait until I'm finished."

She drew a square in the bottom right corner.

"Miles Bradford," she said. "Hired on by ALTEQ to uncover the thief." She traced a line from Tagawa's box to Bradford's and drew an *X* in the middle. "Meilin, the murder victim. If you talk to her family, you'll discover that she was Yuzuru Tagawa's clandestine lover. This lead, a plausible motive and a potential suspect, was dismissed and then abandoned by Tadashi Ito, the lead investigator."

She drew a second *X* between Tagawa and Bradford. "The belt, the murder weapon," she said, and drew arrows to both Tagawa and Jiro. "Again, if you ask the right questions of the right people, you'll learn that Miles Bradford had been invited by ALTEQ employees to a hostess club in Kitashinchi, also owned by Jiro Sasaki. Two weeks before the murder there was a fight at the club in which Jiro's men took the belt from Miles Bradford.

"Lastly," she said, and she drew a fourth box on the page and placed a question mark within it. She drew a line between Jiro's box and the question mark and scratched another *X* between them. On the *X* she wrote in Tadashi Ito.

"The man who investigated the murder

your client is said to have committed, the same man who dismissed the fact that the murder victim had a lover at the facility, who never looked beyond the crime scene at the facility or put resources to anything other than establishing your client as the guilty party. Look hard," she said, "and you'll find a link between him and Jiro Sasaki. I got my information from a private investigator, so it shouldn't be difficult for you to do the same. I have met Tadashi Ito and I believe he has a circumstantial detail that points away from your client as the murderer. In the United States we call that exculpatory evidence, and the prosecution, if honest, will turn that over to the defense."

"What is this circumstantial detail?" the lawyer said.

"There's been a second murder at the facility."

The lawyer glanced up, his expression washed in surprise. "When did this take place?" he said.

"Six days ago."

"You only tell me now?"

"I've been busy trying to not get killed," she said. "Technically, I shouldn't have had to tell you at all."

"It's different here," he said. He glanced down at the page and pointed to the empty box in the upper right corner. "What about the question mark?"

"Yuzuru Tagawa has been stealing and selling company technology, but so has someone else. He initiated hiring your client as a way to eliminate his competition within the company. Presumably your client uncovered damaging information and the murder was a way to remove your client from the facility."

"You're saying Yuzuru Tagawa killed the woman?"

"Yes."

"And that he acquired the murder weapon from Jiro Sasaki?"

"Yes."

"And the question mark?"

"I only know that it exists," Munroe said.

The lawyer crossed his arms and leaned back in the chair, leveling accusation and suspicion in that one movement.

"The second murder," he said. "Who did it?"

"That's for the investigator to determine," she said. "But it wasn't your client."

"You evade."

"My concern is your client."

The lawyer continued studying her and then leaned in toward the paper again. The silence was filled with the beat of a metronome on the wall and soft voices from down the hall, while he examined what she'd drawn. At last he nudged the page in her direction. "This presents a very clear theory," he said, "but even if every detail is accurate, without a way to prove the connections we remain in the same position."

"What do you need?" she said. "What would be enough to convince the prosecutor that your client isn't their man?"

The lawyer blew out a long exhale and stared out the window.

He wouldn't say it, but she knew the sigh.

If those investigating the case were in bed with special interests, they couldn't predict who else in the justice food chain might be as well.

"Use the information as best as you can," she said, and stood. "I'm going to get you a confession."

"From my client?"

"From the killer."

"How?" he said.

"Don't know," she said. "But there's a good chance I'll get arrested in the process, and if that happens, you'll get a call. You'd better come find me."

Nakamura's anteroom was filled with the hush of vacancy and the repetitive clicks of the keyboard. His assistant looked up when Munroe entered, and seeing her, the woman stood. Hands placed on her thighs, she bowed and then with a gentle sweep of one hand she invited Munroe to the sitting space as if Munroe was a person most welcome.

"Nakamura-san is in a meeting now," the assistant said. "Please wait if you can."

"Will he be long?" Munroe said.

The woman's bow dipped lower and her head bobbed in time with the apology. "I'm unsure," she said. "I'm sorry, there are many appointments today."

Munroe sat and the woman brought the tray with water and the doily, and the clock ticked around, burning off minutes as though they mattered not. Munroe drank in measured sips and the assistant replaced the empty glass with a full one. Munroe was on the third when Nakamura finally returned, wearing the harried look of a man running late.

He paused midstep when he saw her, then diverted to the seating area.

Munroe stood, shook his hand.

"Sadly, I'm on my way to another meeting," he said.

"Ten minutes," Munroe said. "It'll be worth your time."

Nakamura glanced at his watch and then, with a nod, invited her into his office. She sat without waiting for an offer. Her eyes focused on the desk in front of her while her ears tracked his movements about the room: jacket to coat rack, briefcase to receptacle, and then finally water poured into a glass that he carried to his desk.

"Tell me then," he said, "what do you have for me?"

Munroe placed a file on the desk containing printouts and maps and copies of translated documents culled from her own material — together nearly an inch thick. She folded her hands atop it and said, "You told me once that industrial espionage has a long history and that if one refuses to adopt the weapons of his enemy, one will lose the battle."

Nakamura took a long draw of water and set the glass on the desk.

She said, "The battle has come back around to you."

He leaned into his chair, body angled away, and ran his finger around the rim of his glass. "Is that meant to be taken as metaphor or literally?" he said.

"You've pointed me toward foreigners and foreign interests," she said, "but it appears the culprit is one of your own — within the executive ranks."

Nakamura winced as if she'd nicked him. He swiveled around to face her and stared at her long and hard. "This is a serious accusation," he said.

"Yes, very serious."

"When suspicion is cast, it is cast forever," he said, "left to grow like weeds in a garden that put down deep roots. Knowing a thing, whether it's true or not, gives that thing its own life. Before you divide from within my company, tell me, do you have evidence for what you will say?"

Munroe reconstructed his question into a promise of outright denial and rejection if he didn't like what she'd brought. She said, "I'm confident enough that I consider my job finished here. Unless you have a reason to keep me on longer, I'll need a day or two to tie up loose ends and then I'll turn in my security badge."

Nakamura glanced at his watch and then turned back to her and nodded at the documents beneath her hands.

"Will you leave those papers with me?"

"They won't mean anything to you. The explanations are in here," she said, and tapped her head.

As if the folder contradicted her words, he said, "Only in your head?"

She'd offered him the lie as an opportunity to silence her before she could share the information with others: a preemptive move against the possibility that Tagawa had merely been the most obvious player in a conspiracy of several.

"No one else in the facility is privy to this information," she said, "if that's what you mean."

Nakamura took another sip of water and said, "Not exactly, but that certainly helps in damage containment."

"I've already kept you past your meeting," she said. "If you wish, I can return when it's more convenient."

Nakamura tilted his wrist to check the time again, but his focus was on the papers beneath her hands. "May I see them?" he said.

"Yes," she said. "But if you want them to mean anything, it would be better if I explain them as you do."

He stood and loosened his tie, then walked from his side of the desk to hers. Her body tensed, ready to shift if he moved too close, and she tracked his hands and feet as he crossed the room.

Nakamura stepped out and shut the door.

Voices, muted and hushed, filtered in through the door; not whispers, but guarded speech that could have easily been spoken in her presence or on the phone if he'd not been concerned about her listening in.

The door opened. Nakamura's footsteps carried him back to his desk and, once again in his seat, he said, "We won't be disturbed, so take your time and tell me everything you've learned."

Munroe opened the folder, and fingertips resting lightly on top of the documents as both tease and promise, she said, "Please withhold judgment until I've had a chance to lay out the facts as I know them."

Nakamura folded his hands, matching the way hers had been, and he leaned forward to see better. She spun the first page around and pushed it toward him. His focus settled on the picture just long enough to register the face and then, eyes wide, his head jerked up and he pushed himself ever so slightly backward.

Munroe waited a beat and then began with the facts, much as she had with Bradford's lawyer, adding details she'd neglected in the law office, but leaving out the hostess club, the trackers, the truth behind the attack in the garage that had led to Bradford's car being reported stolen, and the issue of Nonomi Sato.

Nakamura asked questions. He stood. He sat. And stood again, arms crossed, pacing, as she led him along the trail, dot to dot and point to point, and when she was finished, she took the pages back, stacked them, and stuffed them inside the folder. Then she said, "What will you do?"

Nakamura turned from her, a smaller man than he'd been an hour ago, and stared at the wall as if the world pressed down on his shoulders and threatened to squash him. "It's not my decision alone," he said.

"There's an innocent man sitting in jail right now."

He stared out the window. "My responsibility is to the company."

The unspoken was so loud he might as well have screamed. Going to the police about Tagawa's theft wouldn't happen because calling on the law would reveal his own company's practices and open a whole other can of disgrace, loss of face, and legal action.

As far as Nakamura was concerned, Bradford was fucked.

That answered the issue of what she'd do about Nonomi Sato.

Munroe pushed back from the desk and stood. Picked up the folder and tucked it under her arm. "I understand your position," she said.

Nakamura turned from the window. "Please leave the documents."

Munroe returned the folder to the desk, let herself out, and left for the wall of monitors in the security room, where she and Okada could watch in real time as the puppets played to the pull of the strings.

Munroe and Okada stood side by side, watching wordless as the story unfolded in grainy silence, and Nakamura, footsteps heavy, left his office.

In the hour since Munroe had walked out, the activity in the executive wing had picked up, the company bosses leaving one by one for the boardroom, and they were all there now, waiting for Nakamura, all but Yuzuru Tagawa.

Okada's phone beeped. He checked the screen, answered a text, and to Munroe said, "Maybe twenty minutes."

Those were the first words spoken since she'd entered the room, silence their best precaution against electronic ears. They'd soon have company as the evening techs, sent off on errands by Okada, finished the busywork designed to keep them away. On the monitor, Nakamura entered the board-room.

By design there were neither cameras nor recording devices beyond those walls, but she had no doubt that in the security operations center on the other side of the building, there were ears listening in.

Tagawa, too, had gotten wind that something was afoot.

In her days at the facility, Munroe had observed him; first as a part of Bradford's initial list, then as a suspect as the data continued pointing toward him. Tagawa was well-kept, fastidious with his appearance, a man of routine and long hours, never arriving later than seven or leaving before eight, but in the days following Dillman's murder he'd grown disheveled and had begun displaying the jumpy nervousness of a man with demons at his back. Now, at just after seven in the evening, breaking routine and a history of patterns, he was in the hallway, headed for the stairs, head hung low as if in a trance or deep in thought, on his way out of the facility.

Okada pointed toward the screen.

Munroe was already on her way for the door.

Wars were won through exploiting the enemy's weakness.

Shame was Tagawa's weakness, honor was his weakness, and in using Nakamura to force a catalyst, she'd manipulated both.

Tagawa would lose his job, but that was the least of his worries.

Munroe raced down the stairs and reached the entry in time to catch a glimpse of Tagawa through the glass, rounding the corner for the parking lot.

Losing his job would mean losing access to ALTEQ's trade secrets, but selling those to Jiro had been an undermining operation in the short term for which Tagawa had been well compensated, revenge for which ALTEQ had no proof, thus no way to retaliate legally or otherwise.

The technology in the lower lab had been Tagawa's ultimate goal, the theft for which his brother had been held responsible and over which the brother had taken his life. Tagawa's failure to steal it back would be a bigger shame but not the end of everything. No, the reason for his slow coming-apart, the reason he'd left the facility dazed and weighted like a man on the way to his own funeral, was the murder. Tagawa knew what the authorities didn't, knew that if his role as thief had been uncovered, his connection to Jiro would soon follow, and then accusations, possibly arrest, for murder wouldn't be far behind.

In this shame-based society, where judgment was the social control, where a man maintained his value not by choosing right over wrong but by living according to the expectations placed upon him, Tagawa had exceeded his brother's dishonor. He would bring his family greater shame.

Munroe gave him time to reach his car and then tagged after him to the Ninja, which was closer. She followed him because suicide, embedded as a noble tradition within the culture's history, and still often viewed as a moral responsibility, meant that many a man, facing financial pressure and much less disgrace than Tagawa did now, had turned to death by his own hand as the means of preserving honor. *Inseki-jisatsu,* responsibility-driven suicide.

Munroe wanted Tagawa dead.

To save Bradford, she needed him alive.

He drove a wandering route, erratic and unpredictable as he braked, then sped up, and made lane changes at the last second or too far ahead of time, driving like a drunk or a man so distracted that he was no longer mentally present. He received calls and made calls, then rerouted back toward Osaka proper, and in a sudden about-face, turned in for a train station and abandoned his car in a no-parking area. Munroe swore, looped around, and lost sight of him in the process.

She hastily parked, left the helmet with the bike, and rushed for the entrance, searching for her target and for traps so easily missed in the hurry to find him.

The station had four tracks, two to a platform. She slipped the transit pass into the ticket stile, pushed through, and took the first set of stairs.

There was no way to hide if he waited for her at the bottom.

Speakers chimed. A woman's voice announced a train arrival.

Munroe stopped halfway down for a glimpse along the front end of the platform, then leaned over the rail and scanned the parallel platform. Tagawa was there, two tracks over, in line at the door mark, hands limp and head down, oblivious to the lights of the approaching train.

Munroe raced up, ran down the concourse. The train hissed to a stop below. She pushed against the crowd of bodies starting up. Her feet hit the platform as the doors began to close and she rushed the nearest car, shoving an arm between rubber stoppers. She pulled the doors apart enough to slip between.

All eyes in the crowded car were on her when she squeezed inside.

The train lurched and Munroe grabbed a handhold ring, caught her breath, and then started the slow walk, car to car, in Tagawa's direction. She stayed with him for several stops, followed him through a line change, and when at last he stepped off onto the white tiles of Kitashinchi station, Munroe slipped along the stairwell's edge, realizing what he'd done.

This was Jiro's territory.

The flow of passengers headed up the stairs, but Tagawa crossed to the other side, just shy of the yellow safety line, and stood there even after a train had come and gone. Munroe inched closer and watched him: every step, every muscle; the way he held his head; the way he breathed; tense and ready to call upon speed and reflex and intervene if necessary.

A *human accident,* the polite term for railway suicide.

She expected him to jump, eventually, but not there. Not yet.

He hadn't seen her following him, but someone in the facility had; someone had called him. And then Tagawa had made calls and he'd changed paths and abandoned the car. He'd brought her to Jiro, laying the trap and gifting the gift, and waited for Jiro's men to take her first: revenge for what she'd done to him, honor before an honorable death. Two wins for the price of one.

The taste of underground, of metal and heat and oil, filled the air inside Munroe's head, where on a chessboard of strategy knight played against rook and pawn against king. Shoes and boots thudded down the stairs, echoing a tell of a cluster greater than regular foot traffic. There were six of them, conspicuous in the way they didn't belong, conspicuous enough that transiting passengers averted their eyes deliberately so as not to see as Jiro's men fanned out among the crowd, searching for white skin in a sea of beige.

Munroe looped around the back of the stairwell in Tagawa's direction.

She stood behind him at the edge of the platform, on the danger side of the caution line. He felt her presence and turned; seeing her, his eyes narrowed.

Munroe drew nearer to him.

Jaw clenched, he said, "You heap shame upon me."

"You brought it on yourself."

A shout not far away overrode whatever next escaped his lips.

The station's speakers chimed. The voice announced an arriving train.

Jiro's men came striding for her.

Waiting passengers moved out of their way.

Familiar eyes bored into her from a familiar face distorted in rage: the man with the gun, the man she'd hit with Bradford's car. He moved in close and took a swing.

Munroe braced for impact.

He hit her back and punched her side.

Munroe gritted her teeth and smiled while his fellow thugs crowded in, sandwiching her and Tagawa in the press. She grabbed a fist full of Tagawa's shirt and belt while blows rained down, and she panted past the need to strike, counting seconds, feeling the rolling thunder through her feet, and then she jerked — away from the fists and kicks, backward, off the platform, dragging Tagawa with her, into the path of the oncoming train.

Somewhere beyond the screech and squeal of locking brakes were screams and yells and a blur of motion on the platform above as time slowed and divided and divided again, and Munroe rolled and shoved.

The same man who had been dazed and listless just five minutes earlier now fought for his life, driving fists into Munroe's shoulders and against her head. Hand to his trachea, she squeezed and choked him, thrusting him over the rails, rolling him flat against the far wall.

The rush of hot air and burning metal brushed by her head and the train came to a stop. Voices rose on the other side, yelling and commanding. Beyond the view of witnesses, free from cameras and observation, Munroe leveraged her full height and weight against Tagawa.

He fought and scratched and bit, drawing blood.

She detached from the pain, blinded by the need to survive and win.

She pushed her thumbs hard into Tagawa's carotids, pressing down until the man passed out. And then, having subdued him without leaving bruises, having endured the fight without throwing one blow, she lay beside him fighting back the consuming fire inside her head.

Munroe pulled her phone from her pocket and texted Okada.

Call the lawyer.

Tagawa woke. Flashlight beams and shouts reached out from beneath the wheels at both ends of the train. Tagawa struggled to his feet and Munroe didn't fight him. He called for help and rescuers arrived and with them were the police. He threw accusations at Munroe, which she denied, and she in turn accused Tagawa of assaulting her.

The bite marks and scratches, the bruises rising in response to the punches Jiro's men had thrown, gave testament to her claims, and in the end they were both arrested and taken away.

Munroe lay on the floor in a room small enough that she could touch the walls without fully stretching out. Beside her was a narrow mat, a joke of a futon, and she eschewed it for the concrete's greater discomfort.

The guards had yelled at her once, ordering her to sit and face the door, and she'd ignored them. If they wanted to come in and beat her for the transgression, they were welcome to do so, but she expected they wouldn't bother.

Cameras had recorded her arrival at Kitashinchi station. They'd documented the way she'd approached Tagawa, and the attack by Jiro's men, and then the shove that had, for all intents, pushed them backward off the platform.

She'd been arrested because Tagawa accused her of assault. She would have been released already if that was all that there was.

She'd been kept because people in power had questions.

Munroe drifted in the twilight of memory and interrupted sleep where time blurred and mattered less. She slept and woke and woke again when officers stood on the other side of the door, barking for her to stand.

She got to her feet slowly enough that she obeyed on her own terms. The door opened. Like a swimmer taking a breath in anticipation of plunging into the depths, she pushed down hard against the instinct that would arise should the officers touch her.

They ordered her out, yelling when no yelling was needed, commanding for no reason other than to degrade her. She breathed in the calm and avoided eye contact and they led her down bare halls to a door, then ordered her inside a room barely twice the size of the cell and locked the door behind her.

Munroe ignored the table and chairs and lay out on the floor again. They'd come for her when they were ready and she wouldn't lose sleep over wondering when that might be. Arms draped across her abdomen, she allowed the time to take her back under.

Sound and movement pulled her up again.

The door swung open, an investigating officer stepped into the room, dropped a few sheets of paper on the table, and took a chair.

He was maybe in his early thirties, dressed in shirtsleeves and slacks and with shoes polished to a high-spit shine. "Please sit," he said. His English was heavily accented.

Munroe stood and slid into the chair beside the school-desk-size table.

He looked down at the papers in front of him. "You were fighting," he said.

"I was assaulted," she said. "I am the victim. I want my lawyer."

"We would like to hear your version of what happened."

"I was assaulted," she said. "I am the victim. I want my lawyer."

"I understand," he said. "You will speak with your lawyer when finished. A statement is necessary to release you, please explain the fight."

"I was assaulted," she said. "I am the victim."

"Yes." He scratched his cheek. He tapped pen to paper. He looked at her then, and very slowly, speaking as he wrote, glancing up between words, he said, "Was assaulted. Is victim."

He turned the page around so she could see it.

"Now," he said. "Please tell the rest."

Munroe dropped her eyes to her hands and remained silent. Without evidence that her statement was witnessed or recorded, with no guarantee her words wouldn't be misinterpreted and paraphrased, she had nothing to say.

"We cannot release you until you speak," the officer said. "You will be held indefinitely, you will spend years cut off from your friends and family, cold and hungry. Why do this? Tell me about the fight and you can go."

Munroe nodded to acknowledge his threat and kept silent.

Not only was he a liar, he was a bad liar.

They could deport her, certainly, and could hold her for twenty-three days for each charge though she had no idea how many charges they'd laid against her, if any, and they were under no obligation to tell her. But not indefinitely. Not years.

He stood, and his words grew stronger and the volume louder.

She closed her eyes.

He smacked her on the head with the rolled-up papers.

Munroe glanced up just long enough to smile and exhale.

Outside these walls he would be a dead man.

The badgering continued and Munroe blocked the investigator out, descending deep, deep into twilight, where the world was dark and quiet and his spittle and venom were but whispers in the background.

Somewhere out there he struck her with the rolled-up paper again.

She grabbed hold of the rising demons and yanked them back.

And then the door opened and he was gone, and Munroe left the chair for the floor and the cold that seeped into her skin to mute the fire raging beneath.

The door opened again. Two men entered, one older, one younger.

Munroe sat in the chair again, went through the same routine again. They knew there was more; they were hunting.

The younger one said, "You associate with criminals. You are in Japan for criminal activity and you bring shame on your country."

"I was assaulted," Munroe said. "I am the victim. I am willing to answer any question but only with my lawyer to act as a witness."

For something as basic as a fight in which she was clearly not the aggressor, a lecture followed by her formal apology for her involvement should have seen her on her way.

The two men conferred, speaking in front of her, oblivious to the weapon of language and how in their assumptions their words were used against them.

They picked up again with offers to release her if only she would provide an account, and when that failed, they continued with threats of long detention: They were lions without teeth.

Munroe waited them out.

Eventually they left, and she lay down to

sleep again, and when at last the first officer returned, Bradford's lawyer was with him.

He scanned her face and her lips, his eyes lingering on the places where her skin was tender and sore. The officer motioned to the table and the lawyer sat next to Munroe. He placed a digital recorder on the table.

Munroe coughed and said, "Thank you for coming."

The status light on the voice activation lit up.

"You have your lawyer," the officer said. "Tell us about the fight."

Eyes to the table, Munroe began. She spoke slowly. Enunciated clearly. Darted an occasional glance at the recorder to be sure it continued functioning as it should, and she walked them through the day, from the beginning.

Law enforcement in Japan was a single force without jurisdictional issues and territorial grabs, and even two districts over from where Bradford was being held these officers would have no problem connecting the cases.

She explained why ALTEQ-Bio had brought in consultants and used that as the basis for why she'd trailed Tagawa, laying down in simple sentences all that connected him to the murdered woman, and to organized crime, and to the theft from within. Additional questions followed and with each answer Munroe wound back to Tagawa, always Tagawa, and the murder, the mafia, and the theft.

Her cuts and bruises and her accusations of assault were enough to guarantee that they'd hold him for at least twenty-four hours. Now that he was in custody and she'd connected the dots for them, it was only a matter of time before they started asking better questions. Tagawa, the paranoid man with guilt on his soul and blood on his hands, the same man who'd watched his carefully constructed world crumble at his own doing, would do what he was expected to do: confess. Tagawa would break.

She hadn't had the time to conjure proof, but she'd conjured a crisis.

The officers left the room and Munroe and the lawyer sat in silence.

On a pad of paper he asked if there was more that he should know.

She scribbled that they should have coffee when this was over.

The officers returned and the clock ticked on. The lawyer left. Procedure and bureaucracy took over, and by the time Munroe was dumped out onto the front steps of the detention center, the night was over.

The lawyer, in his car, met her at the train station.

She sat in the passenger seat and he offered her a steaming Styrofoam cup. He left the engine idling. At her feet was the backpack she'd left with Okada when she'd torn after Yuzuru Tagawa. She sipped the coffee and said, "Are the investigators taking the accusations seriously?"

"My impression is that they are proceeding cautiously," he said. "Any lack of follow-through will become problematic for careers now that there are criminal elements threaded through the story, even if some are paid not to look."

"If they pursue it, the confession will come."

"You're certain?" he said.

Munroe smiled and reached for her backpack. "Thank you for the coffee," she said, and stepped out of the car.

Day 21   7:45 A.M.

Munroe stood just inside the facility entrance, watching and waiting, as she'd done for the last hour, while the trickle of employees passing through the stiles grew to a rapid flow. Spotting Munroe, they averted their eyes.

News had traveled fast: another scandal tied to another foreigner.

Facts never really mattered.

Arms crossed, Munroe kept her focus beyond the glass to where Mother Nature, sighing her own breath of fresh air, provided an overcast sky and early-morning rain in a temporary welcome relief to the muggy heat.

A flash of gray caught her attention: the reflection of Nonomi Sato's car pulling into the lot. Munroe counted off the beats and then moved to the door, allowing the woman time to gather her things and begin the long walk in.

They met a quarter of the way down the sidewalk.

Munroe stopped in front of Sato, who, in a perfectly timed bow, said, "I'm sorry," and continued on around her.

Artistry filled her walk, her demeanor, and the lies and pretenses tightly controlled behind a veneer that never cracked. Munroe let her go a pace or two and then said, "I know who you are and what you're doing."

Sato kept walking as if Munroe had spoken to someone else.

"If you enter the facility today, you'll be arrested."

This time the woman stopped. She turned just slightly and looked over her shoulder. "You are speak at me?" she said.

Perfectly timed, perfectly performed.

"I am," Munroe said.

"I help some things?"

"Let's take a walk."

Sato blushed, as if Munroe had uttered an alien language. She waved a hand in front of her face as if fanning away a bad smell, the Japanese gesture for *embarrassment* and *no* and *go away* and *discomfort* and *refuse to engage*. Mixing *l*s and *r*s perfectly, she said, "I am not understand English."

"I'm sure you do."

Sato blushed deeper and waved her hand

faster, and she turned and walked away, continuing the charade, perfect as it was, far past its useful point.

"Nonomi," Munroe called out, singsong and lilting, "don't make this harder than it needs to be. Go in there and I will permanently blow your cover. Come walk with me and you'll have a chance to continue things as they are."

Sato stopped again, turned again. She bowed in apology, still blushing, face scrunched with confusion and in a tone that offered not even a fine-line crack in the veneer, she said, "Am not understand English."

The beauty in the performance was real to the point of creating doubt.

Like a pilot disoriented in the fog, unable to tell up or down, Munroe trusted the instruments. She'd done her homework, she knew the facts, and she knew the performance in the way she knew herself. Facing Sato, with her perfect masquerade, was like facing a mirror.

Munroe motioned the woman nearer. "Come with me, I'll teach you."

Sato responded to Munroe's sign language with measured cautious steps and an expression full of skepticism and shy doubt.

Every inch closer was a reconfirmation of

the illusion, the guise.

When the woman was close, Munroe stuck out her hand and said, "I'm a great admirer of your work."

With a face full of innocence and uncertainty, Sato shook Munroe's hand limply, as if handshakes were a foreign thing, as if she wasn't in that same heartbeat calculating how best to eliminate this threat.

Day 21   8:00 A.M.

The coffee shop only had three tables with their accompanying chairs, but it was a block away from the facility and two floors up; it got them off the street and away from prying eyes and listening ears.

Sato sat poised and model still, hands in her lap, and face down toward the table while the drinks were made and served. The artistry that had been enchanting at the beginning was wearing in its endurance.

The espresso came. Munroe prolonged the quiet with the rituals of adding sugar and sipping cautiously, and then returning cup to saucer, she said, "This long into silence and the average person becomes uncomfortable. They start with questions, tell a nervous joke or two, and then offer a few reasons why I've made a mistake and they shouldn't be here right now. If they become desperate or scared enough, they move into demanding to know what I want."

"Not all people behave that way," Sato said. "Not all Japanese people."

Her eyes never left the table and her voice, just above a whisper, was soft and childlike, but it had none of the stilted broken English of fifteen minutes prior.

"Wouldn't you like to know how I know?" Munroe said.

"You spoke with my parents."

"That wasn't me," Munroe said, and she took another sip of the rich dark daylight. "But if you're aware of that connection, then there's no reason to continue pretending. If I wanted to ruin you, I would have done it a while ago."

Sato glanced up and her facial expression shifted, almost as if she'd turned into someone not quite her. "Why haven't you?" she said.

"I don't care who owns the technology."

"You were hired to find me, to out me."

"Correction," Munroe said. "Miles Bradford was hired to find you and out you. My only interest was in figuring out who set him up and why. Now I'm done, so I'm leaving."

"You're certain your discovery was accurate?"

"As certain as you are," Munroe said. "I wouldn't be surprised if you've got proof that ties Tagawa to the murder — video footage, maybe — stashed away on the chance he ever managed to get close to you."

Sato smiled and picked up the bone-white cup, took a sip, then, her eyes never leaving Munroe's, she set the espresso down. "Tagawa was a plaything," she said, "easy to manipulate, fun to watch dance. He was never much of a concern."

"Until he brought Miles Bradford in to find you."

"I do admit, that was enjoyably clever, watching Tagawa set his barn on fire to burn out the mice. I wasn't worried. What do you want from me?"

"Your partner."

"What makes you think I have a partner?"

Munroe leaned back, smiled, and shook her head. "You know what I am and you know that I know."

"I only presume to know. You're not an easy person to learn."

"You know enough."

"I know that every word out of your mouth, lie or truth, is a way for you to measure and read and learn more than you know."

"All I want is your partner."

"Why?"

"Makoto Dillman."

"I'd much rather Makoto Dillman was alive right now," Sato said. "I didn't kill him."

"But your partner did."

"Partner," Sato said, and she snorted. She took another sip of coffee, crossed her legs, and stared out the window. "To be frank, I can't tell you what you want. Assuming you're right, assuming such a partner does exist, I don't know who he is and I have no control over what he does, just as he wouldn't know who I am or what I do. I would assume that the same people who wire money to my accounts would wire to his, but I had nothing to do with him being brought into this and I've never communicated with him directly."

That explained the wobble, the part that didn't fit. Explained how Dillman had gotten dead against Sato's best interests.

Munroe leaned as far forward as the small couch and knee-crunching coffee table would allow and said, "He's in one of the security departments."

"I can't help you with what you want."

"Oh, I'm quite certain you can." Someone had destroyed footage, changed records, listened in on conversations; someone had known what Dillman was doing, and only those in security had that kind of access, a dangerous kind of access. "There's no way you'd trust your safety, your security, or your mission to an unknown quantity, so who is he?"

Sato sighed. "This is tedious."

"I can find him on my own, but I'm done here. I want to move on, I want the shortcut. Think of it as an exchange of favors."

Sato smiled then, an evil dangerous smile. Munroe's heart fluttered in response, drowning in the joy of affinity, the same surge of bliss that made lovers ache. She cared not a whit that Sato read this and played her now, just as Munroe played her in turn. They sat, staring at each other as equals and opponents, knowing and measuring, and finally Sato put down her cup and said, "What I don't get is why you'd pursue this because of Makoto Dillman. You don't impress me as the righteous avenger type."

"There's nothing righteous about it."

"The technology is worth a lot of money. Removing the one who watches my back would allow you to cash in on that prize."

"Like candy left out in an open jar," Munroe said.

"Why tempt me?"

"Measure you," Sato said.

"I could have stolen the data from your house."

"You stole my money."

"I'm short on cash. Dillman was scouring your background when he was murdered, you know? I take the blame for that. I pushed him down the path to discovery and then your idiot partner made the mistake of trying to take out two for the price of one."

"You're certain it wasn't me who did it?"

Munroe smiled the same vicious smile. "Not because of your denials. If you wanted Dillman gone, you would have done to him like you did to me."

"No hard feelings, I hope."

"Not if you give me your partner."

"I give him to you and you walk away?"

"I am you, Nonomi," Munroe said. "I've had my share, I've done my time. Staying one step ahead of the world comes with a price and I'm tired of paying it. I'd found a way around it until Tagawa fucked things up, so I can assure you that there's nothing you have that I want badly enough to chase."

Sato's shoulders relaxed and the facade that had slowly come undone throughout the conversation shed completely and she was a different person in the same way Munroe would shed her character when an assignment had ended. Sato ran her spoon along the inside of the espresso cup and, timed to the tinkling musical notes, said, "If today is for confessions and blame, then I'm to Meilin's death what you were to Dillman's. It was from me that the rumor of Chinese infiltration came, and then, as you say, that fool Tagawa made the mistake of trying to take out two for the price of one."

"Why the Chinese?"

Sato shrugged. "Everyone hates them. Everyone suspects them. It made good entertainment watching Tagawa destroy himself trying to find them."

"And your partner?"

"Technically, my partner doesn't exist," Sato said. "When my contacts pass intel my way, they go to great lengths to make it appear as though it has come from multiple sources. And my requests, in the few times I've made them, have produced results without any direct evidence as to how. Deniability. It protects their assets from contamination. It would seem they believe I'm smart enough to get this job done but not quite smart enough to understand the way they play the game."

"Regardless, he knows who you are." Dillman would still be alive if he didn't.

Sato's lips widened and the smile, so full

of darkness, came back in an impish grin. "There is always a long-term strategy and sometimes one must sacrifice infantry to capture the castle. Why don't you turn me in?" she said. "What makes you stop short of glory?"

"I gave them their thief. They'll pay for the job completion, and that's enough."

"That doesn't answer the question."

"They'd allow an innocent man to rot rather than risk investors and customers discovering they'd stolen the technology to begin with. If they're not smart enough to figure out who you are, I see no reason to help them."

"Shigeru Hara is the man you want," Sato said. "He was Dillman's number two, promoted to number one after the murder."

Munroe set the small cup down and said, "Thank you."

Bradford's lists had been drawn from three directions: company executives, security, and lab. She thought he'd suspected one from among them; in reality there'd been one from each. She said, "If you warn Hara before I get to him, *then* you'll have created something that I want badly enough to chase."

"Don't tempt me," Sato said. "It's been a long time since I've had an enjoyable challenge and you'd be an exquisite thrill."

"Perhaps, but costly nonetheless."

Sato waved a hand, as if to brush Munroe's concerns away. "Hara's been playing both sides, working as Tagawa's inside man, cleaning up Tagawa's evidence, watching Tagawa's back, while at the same time getting paid by my employers to clean up after me and watch mine, all very entertaining until he killed Dillman. Hara's an idiot, a dangerous damaging idiot, and I want him gone. You'll save me the trouble. Tell me, Michael, who are you really?"

"Does it matter?" Munroe said. "Yesterday's truth is today's lie, and tomorrow we'll both be someone else."

"Indulge me," Sato said. "Two tigers meet by chance in a forest, seeing for the first time in all dimensions the same supple power that has, until then, only met them in the flat reflection at the water's edge. For that, it matters."

Munroe smiled and drained the last of her coffee. "A woman with your talents should have no trouble finding what you want."

Sato sighed an exaggerated sigh. "You torment me," she said.

Day 21   9:20 P.M.

The building was a modern three-story walkup, with a glass front and a pebbled wall of buzzers and speaker beside the entry awning. A pricy little pad just beyond the budget of what one would expect for a man of Shigeru Hara's means.

Munroe punched doorbells at random until the lock whirred and she pushed inside to a tiled foyer and ambient light. Short halls branched right and left, three doors to a side. A head appeared from one of the upstairs levels and an older voice called out, "Who's there?"

"I'm so sorry," Munroe said. "I pushed the wrong number."

A door above shut. Munroe took the stairs to the second floor and paused outside of Hara's apartment, attuned to the entrance below while she scrubbed the lock, working with skills gone rusty through lack of use.

But, even rusty, locks were easy.

542

Locks were an illusion that helped mostly honest people stay honest.

Munroe slipped inside to the chemical fragrance of leather and new upholstery. The front half of the apartment blended kitchen, living, and dining area into one. The walls were bare and the furniture sparse; nothing to indicate permanence or home. Directly ahead, an overhead light in the stubby nook of a hallway illuminated the frames of three doors, and Munroe stepped out of the *genkan* in their direction, shoes still on, moving slowly, testing the wooden floors for squeaky boards.

The hallway doors led to *ofuro,* toilet, and the single bedroom, where a sword was mounted on the wall above the unmade western-style bed and the desk had nothing on it, not even dust. In the stand-alone closet, Hara's clothes, expensive as they were, were few.

The kitchen fridge contained a small assortment of food and the cupboards only a handful of dishes. The drawers were similarly limited in knives, silverware, and cookware, leaving the impression that there might be other homes, other places where Hara spent his time, or that this situation was temporary and he'd soon be moving on to better things.

Munroe crossed the living area for the far wall. Tagawa was still being detained and there'd been no further news on Bradford's case, so Munroe slid into the chair that backed into the corner and sat in the dark, waiting with predatorial patience for the man who'd killed Dillman, the man who had, in aiding Tagawa, facilitated Bradford's setup and arrest.

She had nothing but time.

Shortly after midnight, a key turned in the lock.

Hara stepped in, haloed by the hallway light. The door shut behind him. He dropped a satchel by the umbrella receptacle, stepped out of his shoes, and, oblivious to Munroe's presence, continued on to his bedroom.

Munroe sidestepped across the room and turned the deadbolt.

She had her hand on the satchel when Hara stepped back out, bare-chested and barefoot with a *jinbei* bottom tied loosely around his waist. He stopped cold when he saw her, froze for a half second, and then darted back into the bedroom.

Munroe unplugged the phone jack, carried the satchel around the kitchen counter, and stood on the other side, where the knives were within easy reach. She rustled through his bag, removed the cell phone he'd stupidly left behind, and pulled the battery.

A bump against the wall, and then another, was notice that Hara was moving about. Munroe pulled a dish towel, thin and light, from off the counter and ripped a strip of cloth from it. She took a narrow canister off a six-piece spice rack and wrapped it tightly into her palm, clenching into a fist.

Hara stepped out into the hallway, sword lifted, body tensed for attack.

Underestimating an enemy was a fast way to get dead. Hara had been clever enough, strong enough, to kill Dillman, but his movements and mannerisms only spoke to the sword having ever been an ornament. Refusing to dignify him, Munroe studied her hand and said, "Put that down before you hurt yourself."

She pulled papers out of his satchel and spread them on the counter, scanning language she couldn't read, looking for pictures and hyperlinks and anything familiar, while he stood there, sword raised, postured in rage and menace. She stacked the pages and looked back at him. "Tagawa wanted me dead," she said. "Here I am, saving you the effort of figuring out how to do it."

Hara's face went red, his jaw clenched, and his eyes darted from the front door, to the phone on the two-seat dining table, and then back to her.

She shoved the papers into his bag.

Continuing the psych warfare, she opened drawers, letting them bang as they came out on their rails. She pulled out the three kitchen knives and placed them on the counter.

"Come on then," she said. "Now that you know that I know, you can't let me live. Let's get it over with."

Hara took a step in her direction.

Munroe ignored him, making a show of testing the knife blades for sharpness. She palmed them for heft and balance. In her peripheral vision, Hara took another step; he was nearly within striking distance.

"I won't go easy the way Dillman did," she said.

The accusation caught him off guard and he stopped.

Munroe picked up her knife of choice. Her fingers closed around the handle. Soothing comfort leached up her arm and into her chest, like chamomile tea and honey in front of a warm fire.

She looked at Hara and smiled a genuine smile.

Hara lunged at her then, all the tension in his arms throwing the sword in a curving arc toward her body, curving in slow motion the way the hands on a clock held still between ticks. Munroe went up, over the counter between kitchen and living area, into the space between hallway and front door.

The sword crashed down into the spot where she'd been, and Hara went forward with the swing, thrown off balance by the lack of connection.

Tile cracked, and so did the replica sword, and Hara was now in the kitchen, boxed in the way Munroe had been seconds before.

He grabbed a knife off the counter where she'd left them and held it up — perhaps as a threat, perhaps for his own self-confidence — and she beckoned him to her, chest full of want, mind full of need. "I'll wait," she said.

Hara went over the counter in the same way she had, lithe and nimble, providing sensory detail that she used to measure the strength of his threat: He was more comfortable with a knife than a sword, more comfortable now that time had passed and he'd found his element, now that shock and surprise had given way to the edge of adrenaline.

In the room where space was limited and the walls close enough that three long strides would have carried them from one to the next, Hara faced off against her, circling for an opening. He was shorter than she by two inches, his body defined but not built, light on his feet, his reflexes good. His movements were smooth and she waited for him to attack.

He could try, and then he would learn the difference between years of practice in a dojo and the speed that came from fighting for life out on the streets and in the nightmare the jungle had been.

Hara charged. Munroe ducked and spun.

His fingertips grazed her neck.

The knife in her hand, alive and warm, breathing and bleeding, cried out to be put to use. She felt for the rhythm of his heart; her mind inside his mind, her chest inside his chest, anticipating, waiting, while the adrenaline surged and heightened her senses, slowing and elongating time.

He struck again, she dodged again, searching and seeking.

She found weakness and came in close and threw her left hand, weighted with the metal tube, into his throat.

Hara gagged and she jabbed again, into his head, hit and hit and hit, before he had time to react or brace for the impact.

Speed was life and speed was death.

Speed was his undoing, and his attack turned into defense.

The knife, an extension of her body, pleaded for release and came to life against her will, cutting a long jagged slice across his torso. In horror at what she'd done, Munroe tossed the knife. Threw it to the floor as if she'd been scalded, threw it before the instinct, built and cemented in the struggle to stay alive, overtook her and caused her to slit his throat.

In that moment of hesitation, Hara punched her and threw her aside. He grappled and knocked her down. She fought back and then she was on top of him, striking him with the weighted fist in a blind frenzy again and again.

How long until she realized he no longer struggled?

Munroe shoved off him, crab-crawling backward, while repulsion mixed with the thirsty need to finish what was started.

Munroe picked up the knife again and grabbed Hara's ankle. She dragged him down the hall into his bedroom. She tore the sheet off the bed and pulled the frame away from the wall. She cut strips and secured his hands and feet and shoved him up, securing the ties that bound him to the legs of the bed.

And then she sat on the floor, her back to the wall, adrenaline dumping, exhaustion consuming, while inside her head the clouds roiled dark and thunderous, and self-loathing rode the lightning flashes.

She hadn't meant to cut him; she'd lost control.

Not because of Dillman.

More than a breach of suppressed emotion over Bradford.

This was rage over everything that men like Tagawa and Hara and Jiro represented, men like the mercenary who'd made her what she was; rage over the lives they took in selfish interest, the pain they caused, and the destruction they left behind.

Hara moaned and Munroe stood, pushing hard against the storm until the emotion was tight and small and she could lock it away.

He moaned again and then came to gradually. Realizing he was bound, Hara yanked at the cloth and strained his head upward. Seeing Munroe, he sighed and dropped his head. "Why didn't you kill me?"

"I can," she said. "If that's what you want."

He closed his eyes. "What do you want?"

550

"To know who you work for."

"Are you mad? Blind? You come into my house, attack me, to find out where I work, but you've seen me at work every day for the last month."

Munroe sighed. Pretenses and lies in the face of the obvious could be so damn exhausting. She sat on the bed and leaned over him so he couldn't avoid her. "Drag this out if you want to," she said. "The one thing I don't have to worry about is time."

"They'll miss me at work. My family will get worried."

"Your family hasn't heard from you in a year. I'll call in sick for you before morning, and I'm about to quit your job. It's a shame, too, because once you quit, you'll lose value to everyone who pays you and then what will you matter?"

Hara gritted his teeth and yanked hard against the cloth, and when he opened his mouth to scream, Munroe stuffed the last strip of sheet between his lips.

She patted his face. "Get some rest," she said. "It's going to be a long, long night."

Munroe left Hara for the kitchen, and with the bedroom door open so she could hear him and he could hear her, she pulled together ingredients from his meager food supply and made a meal. She left the dishes in his sink unwashed, set an alarm, and slept a few hours on his couch with the subtle groan of his yanks and tugs playing in the background.

When she returned to the bedroom just after dawn, he was still awake.

She checked his wrists, red from the struggle. She pulled the cloth out of his mouth and he gulped greedy breaths. "I don't want a lot," she said, "just the contact information for your employer."

He choked back a crazy laugh. "I don't have anything to give you."

She stuffed the cloth back into his mouth. "Maybe not today, maybe not tomorrow," she said, "but eventually." She turned and left him there.

When business hours rolled around, she left the apartment long enough to call Bradford's lawyer and held her breath when he picked up. "The charges will be dropped," he said. "My client will be released."

"When?"

"There is paperwork, there are formalities. It may be another day or two."

"Did the investigators get a confession from the killer?"

"It's not possible for a man in my position to know. Regardless, circumstances have changed."

Munroe's hands shook and she tried to calm the rapid breaths that were fast turning to hyperventilation. "Information has a way of doing that," she said. "Does his office in the United States know?"

"The news came only fifteen minutes ago, I've not yet made any calls."

"I'll take care of it," she said, and he rang off.

Commercial flying time out of Dallas was a minimum of sixteen hours — longer, depending on the connections — and if Walker caught the first flight available, she might possibly make it to Osaka before Bradford was released.

The fourteen-hour time difference put Walker in the early evening, and without time to waste collecting a computer or hunting down prepaid cards, Munroe put the battery back into her phone and dialed directly from her cell to Samantha Walker's, waiting impatiently through the long rings, hoping that an international number on display would be enough for Walker to take the call.

When Walker answered, her voice was tinged with the kind of rushed distraction that came from juggling several things at once. Munroe said, "Miles is going to be released. I don't know when, the lawyer will have that information. Get a flight booked and be ready to pick him up."

"Wait," Walker said, and Munroe could hear the mental brakes lock up. Everything else on the other end came to a standstill. "When did you get the news — how did you get it?"

"Five minutes ago from the lawyer. I don't have any details. If you want them, you'll have to call him."

"You're not going to be there when he's released?"

"Can't promise to make it," Munroe said. "Better to be sure that someone is."

"I'll be on the first flight out," Walker said,

and the line went dead.

Munroe turned her face to the sky and the moment swept in, dry and thirsty, waiting for rain. Repressed emotions came rushing hard, uncontrollable, like a wall of water off the ocean. She let them come, and when the surge receded, the wash took with it the detritus and left a barren landscape in its place.

This wasn't over yet. Not for her.

Using Hara's keys, she let herself back inside the building and into the apartment with its new furniture smell, stale air, and the muffled yells of captivity from the bedroom.

Thirst was a weapon, as was hunger, and fear of the unknown, and fear of the knife. Hara broke long before a better man would have — the price paid for being soft and pliable, for living out an infiltrator's fantasy within a civilian mind, for being a fool.

She only cut him twice and that more theatrics than damage, more drama than pain. When he caved, she dripped water down his throat in exchange for information. By the time he was finished, she had phone numbers, e-mail accounts, and a name that might or might not mean something; she had geolocation tags and copies of correspondence, and Hara offered up his secrets, giving her access to his own understanding of the workings of the facility.

Knowing that Dillman was working on Sato's file, that he'd discovered something worth discussing with Munroe outside the facility, Hara had reported as much to his handlers. They'd given him leeway in fixing the problem. Killing Dillman had been his idea, and he'd carved out his own promotion in the process. Munroe could have admired his cleverness, justified his actions in a perverse way, might have excused him if there'd been any long-term strategy to what he'd done. But he'd reacted without artistry or intuitiveness, just short-term thinking and blind ambition, ignorant of far-reaching consequences and oblivious that his actions were a greater threat to Sato's entrenchment than Dillman had originally been.

Hara was a thug, a minion: dull and incapable of seeing beyond immediate gratification, unable to make sacrifices for long-term gain. She despised him for that weakness, and having made him bleed and stolen from him what he valued most, she wouldn't squander life energy killing him.

Dillman's murder investigation was still open, and there were always anonymous tips. The proof was there if anyone was willing to look. She'd make sure they did.

Hara would claim she'd kidnapped and tortured him.

He had no way to prove it.

Munroe worked through the apartment, wiping down the few things she'd touched, cleaning blood streaks off the floor, washing away the few traces of evidence she'd left behind. In Hara's bathroom she found a handful of pill bottles, brought them to him, and had him read the labels.

The best she could do was a combination of pain medication and antihistamines, and she stuffed enough pills down his throat to push the limits between oblivion and overdose.

She wouldn't cry if she'd guessed wrong.

"I'm going to let you live," she said. "You talk about me and you'll be dead in a week. Understand?"

Hara nodded and eventually drifted off into a medicated fog.

She unbound him and gathered the sheets and stray threads and bagged them together with the dish towel she'd shredded, then wiped down his room to catch blood drops, stray hairs, and footprints. She'd spent thirty-two hours in that apartment, with his cries muffled and his torment heightened by tricks of the mind: long enough for Walker to get from Dallas to Osaka; long enough for the bureaucracy to move its slow way through the release process.

Munroe stood in the doorway, staring at Hara's unconscious body, then left the apartment and the building, carrying the bag of evidence far across town, to mix with wet garbage behind a grocery store. She then turned for the precinct where Bradford was housed and the hope that she might watch him walk out into the light, a free man.

Day 23 4:21 P.M.

Munroe took a cab to within a block of the detention facility and continued on foot to the bus stop with its unobstructed view of the building's front doors. Ear buds blaring to block sound and voices and unwanted emotions, Munroe leaned into a beam that supported the small overhang and there she waited.

She'd returned Bradford's things to the apartment, had tucked his passport and valuables back where they'd once been and rehung what clothes were still clean. She'd cleared out everything of hers that mattered and thrown away what didn't. Walker would return with Bradford to collect what was his and turn over the keys. They wouldn't stay long. They'd be eager to get out of the country lest fate tempt good fortune and find freedom taken away once more, but there'd been no reason to leave remnants of her presence as a form of torment — for

Bradford, for Walker.

Munroe's stay would be longer, if not by much.

She'd told Sato the truth when she'd said there was nothing the woman had that she was inclined to chase and had lied by omission. Nothing Sato had, true, because why steal from a thief when for far less risk she could draw payment for silence from those who employed the thief?

She'd gone after Hara to learn who pulled his strings, and he'd handed over the entire puppet show. She'd have to disappear, build a subterfuge, and then disappear again. She'd need time and distance, but the challenge was seductive.

At just after five, the lawyer's car pulled into the lot.

Samantha Walker rode shotgun.

The car parked. Driver and passenger stepped out.

Jet-lagged and exhausted as she must be, Walker oozed charm and sensuality, as had always been her way. Physically, she was everything Munroe wasn't: petite, voluptuous, and exotic. This was the first that Munroe had seen her since those first months following the explosion, when Walker's days had been counted in terms of nurse cycles and visitation hours and then gradually segued into assisted living and physical therapy. Now the visible scars were few, the limp less noticeable, and her thick black hair as luscious as it had been before.

The biggest damage had been on the inside.

The lawyer and Walker strode together for the building's front doors and in their interaction it was clear, even from a distance, who called the shots. For Walker, the leash and the way she maneuvered men on her lead was merely a way of facilitating business. The lawyer, like Warren Green, like most who came in contact with her, was oblivious to the reality that nothing he fantasized or projected would ever materialize.

They entered through the front and time came and went, marked by the progression of music tracks and buses and passengers and traffic signals: a process that was repeated again and again and again, until movement across the street flashed color beyond the doors and then Walker and the lawyer and Bradford stepped into the lowering sun.

Bradford was haggard and his eyes were dark from lack of sleep, but he tipped his face up to the sky and breathed deeply, then he smiled.

Munroe's heart beat hard and her insides churned, urging her to rise and walk, to reach for him, to hold and touch and kiss.

The hurt welled up, like a fire devouring everything in its path, and although she stepped away from the bus stop and stood alone on the edge of the curb, she never attempted to cross the street.

Seeing him, she could breathe again, she could hope again, and the emptiness and the solid walls she'd relied on to block out emotion began to bleed from her, melting in thick fat drops from her fingertips to the pavement, only it wasn't her body that shed but her eyes, and not blood but tears.

Walker, who'd had her arm looped with Bradford's, who'd smiled at him with that smile that men couldn't resist, let go and climbed into the backseat of the lawyer's car. Bradford stood for a moment, his hand on the car's roof.

His eyes scanned the area, because he knew.

In spite of all evidence to the contrary, in spite of what Munroe had said and done, he knew, and his gaze at last fell on her and their eyes connected.

He stayed frozen that way, as she remained across the street, and time ground to a halt while traffic continued on between them.

Bradford put his fingers to his lips and turned them toward her, and she raised a hand with the universal sign for love. They stayed like that for a moment, an hour, a day, until a bus pulled between them and Munroe boarded it. From the window she watched Bradford's face when the barrier between them passed and he understood that she was gone, watched him stay rooted to the spot with one hand on the roof and his eyes on where she'd stood, until she was out of sight.

He knew that she would come, just as he knew she'd return.

And she would return to him again, when she'd finished what she'd set out to do, and then perhaps, when they'd both healed and mended, they could slowly begin anew in the understanding that what they'd shared had never been lost, merely delayed.

The call came just after midnight, a blinding vibration that lit the room and set Munroe's phone dancing on the nightstand. On seeing the number, time stood still and, for a brief moment, Munroe refused to move.

So many ramifications, so many possibilities, so much burden.

Munroe picked up, gritted her teeth, and braced for the news.

"Michael," Tai Okada said, "they are with me in my house." He choked. "They have my family, my children."

Then, on the other end, rustling and tapping marked the phone being passed from one hand to the next. Another voice filled the void, smooth and velvet soft, the type of voice that used whispers as weapons. "You took something of mine," it said, "and now I have something of yours."

"What do you want?" she said.

"Yourself. Alone. Tonight."

Munroe didn't answer.

"You will come to me," he said. "You will not call for help, you will not report to the police. There are precautions made against your reputation. Follow these instructions and perhaps a child across the city will not die, and perhaps the evidence will not point to you."

"Let the family go," she said. "They've done nothing to you. Face me honorably and I will meet you man to man."

"You will come to me as I have said or by first light they will die."

The line went dead. Munroe shut off her phone.

She reached for the backpack and retrieved the knives, the blades she'd taken from Bradford's apartment three weeks ago and whose use she'd managed to avoid. On the edge of the bed, she sat, staring at empty space in the dark while she hefted the weight, feeling the metal, one in each hand. The sweet warmth of rapture seeped through her palms, up her arms and into her brain, releasing the promise of reward and redemption.

Jiro took hostages as if she needed threats to compel her to him, as if she hadn't already begun building the trail to track him down, as if he hadn't just saved her the time. But the burden of innocent life weighed on her.

In the silence, she sat, flicking the blades, while the past three weeks, and the blows she'd taken, and the lives she'd spared for the sake of a greater objective, rose fully formed into the present.

Pain and loss, and love and hope, chased shadows around the room.

Munroe stood. Set the knives on the desk and booted up the laptop.

She was already packed, the room wiped clean. And on the chance that law enforcement had figured out the connection between the Ninja and the facility, the bullet holes in the Mira and the body count around the city, she'd already made preparations to leave the country by sea rather than air.

But there were things to be said to Bradford before she was free to die.

Munroe wrote and sent her heart unedited, then pulled on her jacket and strapped on the knives. She unlaced her boots. Pulled a roll of thick tape out of the bag of office supplies and wrapped tape around her socks, creating sleeves on each foot, wrapped around and around, loosely enough to prevent constricting blood flow, layer after layer to create a barrier. When she was finished, she put the boots back on, now nearly too tight to fit. She grabbed several pairs of socks and two black shirts from her backpack and shoved them into pockets, then picked up the helmet and strode down the stairs and into the city lights.

Tonight, one way or the other, through Jiro's death or hers, the story had to end. Jiro had called for her, and she was coming.

Day 24   12:22 a.m.

Munroe brought the Ninja to life and rolled into the street, descending into the calm of focus, of hyperawareness, while the metal strapped to her shins sang a lullaby of death. She left her phone outside a *konbini,* ensuring that she couldn't be contacted again, no way for Jiro to know when she'd come, or if she'd come, and reached the edges of Okada's neighborhood at just after one.

Control was only control when the opponent played the game.

The unknown would make him anxious.

She stopped where the road branched off the main road, turning up into the tidy array of small homes and postage-stamp yards. Out here, away from the city, light pollution was limited to streetlamps and sporadic traffic signals, to the train station in the distance, and what few cars passed by and it was possible to see a few stars; out here, crickets still had voices and there were trees through which the wind could rustle, and this single entry point was the only vehicle access in or out of the neighborhood.

You will come to me, he'd said.

Okada had said they were with him, in his house.

Presumably it was there that the ambush had been set. Presumably the family hadn't since been moved. But this road was a choke point and Jiro's men would lie in wait. The only unknown was where.

Riding gloves and jacket on, Munroe left the helmet with the Ninja invisible in the shadow of a weed-lined retaining wall at the base of the hill. She walked on, head down, ears attuned to what secrets the night would offer, keeping tight to the stone face separating the road from the earth it had been carved from.

The incline was steep and Munroe climbed slowly, guarded against a quickening heartbeat and starving lungs that would drown out the pillow talk whispered by the dark.

Jiro had strength in numbers; her strength lay with the night. She felt before she heard and stopped in the shadows of the switchback, where moonlight danced in illusion and disguised her skin. She heard before she saw, pauses and movements of uncertainty.

Like cold reading, she played off what the enemy couldn't know.

Voice softened in a mimic of the high girlish way many Japanese women spoke, she said, "Is someone there?"

The response came as a quiet groan and then tones of disagreement between two men whose words were lifted away elsewhere. A body dropped down off the upper end of the wall, ahead of where the curve in the road evened out and the fall was less than a meter.

His full-sleeve tattoos were visible in the moonlight.

Munroe let out a gasp, loud enough that he would hear. She retreated deeper into the shadows and said, "Please go away, please leave me alone."

The pleading emboldened him and he stepped toward her.

His companion dropped down off the wall behind him, and they sauntered forward, thumbs hooked in pockets. "Why are you out so late?" the first one said. "Where are you going?"

The darkness gave her knowledge: the thud of their footfalls and the timbre of their voices and the way their bulk sliced down the road without respect to the dangers that lurked because they were used to being the danger.

She knelt and released the knives.

"Please don't hurt me," she said.

"Where are you going?" the first man said again.

"To visit a lover," the second man said, and he sniggered. "See the way she sneaks around? We would do her a favor to punish her."

"Home," she said, voice shaking. "I live here, just up there."

Each sentence brought them closer, nearly to striking distance, but they stopped just beyond her reach.

"Come into the light," the second man said.

Munroe stayed quiet, kept motionless while instinct calculated the distance between them and the fragmented seconds it would take to move from one kill to the next. Cut by cut, the fight played inside her head.

"I said come!" the man said.

Munroe didn't move, didn't speak.

He lunged toward her kneeling shadow, as if to grab her by the hair. "Foolish girl," he said. "We will teach you."

Munroe cried out for the benefit of the

man behind him and met the movement with a knife to the throat, through the trachea, so he couldn't yell.

She squealed again, said, "No, stop," and pulled him close, shoved hard, up at the base of the ribs, into his liver, and between the ribs, into the lungs, faster than he had time to register.

Cleaner and quicker would have been the carotids, but then his blood would have painted her, contaminating crime scenes yet to come.

Munroe let go and his body dropped.

The shadows were a disguise, not a cloak of invisibility.

The second man, still half moving toward her with gravity's pull, turned and bolted up the hill. Munroe chased him, caught him in the shoulder with a blade, and yanked him back. He gasped and fell, and she put a boot to his throat. "Scream and you die," she said.

His eyes stared wide.

Then her foot to his chest, she leaned into him, one knife to his throat, the other to his groin. "Does Jiro have other men on the road?"

His eyes stayed on her, no subtle search for rescue, no hints to give away the secret hope he might be saved. His head shook: No.

"At the house up the road?"

"Yes," he whispered.

"Is Jiro there?"

"Yes."

"How many others?"

He didn't speak.

She poked the knife between his legs. He yelped.

"How many?"

"Five, six," he said.

"Which is it? Five or six?"

Headlights turned in at the base of the hill. Her eyes flicked up and his hand grabbed for his jacket; she stabbed his hand and he screamed.

Against her will, the second blade plunged into his throat, cutting off the noise. She followed the cut through and stabbed into his chest: a mercy kill. He stopped moving, stopped breathing, and she kicked him in misplaced anger.

Munroe dragged his body off the road and waited for the vehicle to pass. She nudged his jacket aside and, with two gloved fingers, pulled the handgun out.

She released the magazine, counted it full, removed two of the bullets, reloaded, and racked the slide. She pressed the gun into his palm, muzzle pointed toward the gutter. She laid his hand down gently, wrapped his fist around the butt, and then cautiously, millimeter by millimeter, slipped his forefinger behind the trigger guard.

In two or three hours, rigor mortis would begin; it would start at his head and work its way down, and eventually his hands would clench. If she was lucky, she'd already be dead or gone when it happened. Either way, the weapon report would summon the cavalry.

Day 24   1:32 A.M.

The matrix of alley-width roads was clean and quiet, the houses perfect like miniature models on a sculpted platform. Streetlights kept the neighborhood flooded just enough that there were no true spots of darkness. Munroe skirted from shadow to shadow, searching for signs that Jiro had sent roaming patrols, and turned before she reached Okada's lane.

She crept the length of the street, continued toward the row of homes opposite Okada's front door, and waited in the shadow of a small knotted pine while one minute dragged into two and then five and then ten. There was no movement at the Okada house, no extra cars parked nearby, no men visible standing watch, and nothing to indicate that the neighbors were wise to the death that had entered their enclave.

Munroe rounded into the lane behind and slunk in a slow stop-start from tree to doorstep, until she reached the house that backed up to Okada's. A bush-lined ornamental fence separated the lick of front yard from the street. Munroe boosted over and knelt, waiting for a reaction.

The neighborhood continued on in its undisturbed slumber.

She crept to the side of the house, to a narrow sliver with barely enough room to maneuver to the semblance of a backyard, where every bit of space was taken up with a short pebbled walkway, a miniature koi pond, and a two-person iron-and-glass mosaic table.

The fence lines delineating neighbors were more politeness than privacy, in the same way the living room windows of one house opened to face the kitchen of another. From there she could see into Okada's equally small backyard.

Her eyes scanned the space, separating shadow from shadow, until one of Jiro's men emerged in outline, seated on the wooden deck, knees bent, with his back to the house. Time bled away as she watched the balcony that ran along the side of Okada's second floor and eventually an arm stretched out to lean against the railing.

How many men are at the house?

Five or six.

576

In her head she became the enemy.

Two men on the road, for ambush.

Two men outside the house as sentries.

She would keep her captives on the second floor: harder to reach. She would place one man in the *genkan,* the most logical entry point, and another on the stairway, the only inside access to the second floor. She would put the third with the captives to keep them scared and quiet, and she as the last man would be free to roam and move about.

Munroe retreated down the sliver between house and fence. At its mouth she knelt and removed her boots. She pulled the extra pairs of socks on over the sleeves of tape. Not as good for protection as rubber soles, but flexible and silent against pebbles and garden detritus that would otherwise crunch underfoot and enough to keep her from wincing barefoot at every step.

She tied the shirts around her head as bandannas that covered face and neck: a poor man's war paint — camouflage used in years past when making it to dawn was far less certain than the next sunrise was now.

Munroe pressed her palms to the gravel, drew in the texture, and breathed her way to the past, to the musk and mud of the rain forest undergrowth. She drew forth the animal, hunting and hungry, and absorbed the night, the humidity, the heat, and returned to the jungle from whence she'd come.

And then she rose, soft and silent, and slipped through the shadows, one house north, and from that house over the fence to Okada's neighbor, and from the neighbor over the decorative iron into the tightly covered carport that she'd entered the night she'd followed Okada home.

She rolled into the crawlspace beneath the pier-and-beam home, beyond the scope of the sentry above. Earth, dank and damp, filled her nostrils. Creatures of the dark wiggled beneath her hands, her legs. Munroe pulled herself forward, elbow by elbow, toward the center of the house. She rolled onto her back and closed her eyes, fingertips touching the floor, feeling for vibration, attempting to place bodies in the rooms above her. The floor creaked, right about where the hallway between *genkan* and stairway would have been.

Munroe flipped to her stomach and pulled toward the rear of the house, toward the cigarette fragrance that guided her to the kill. The law of the jungle was at home in this perfect polite neighborhood full of polite people in a polite country that laid a veneer over the brutality and bloodshed flowing through their history's veins; politeness that made it possible for men of force and violence to thrive.

Elbow to elbow she slipped behind him and inched out into the open corner to where the air was fresh. She edged up against the wall, eyes closed, attuned to the nuance in his movement, waiting until clothing rustles and a soft inhale said he'd raised cigarette to mouth, waited until the hand he'd use for balance was nowhere near the ground.

She rushed the corner and snatched his throat, crushing his windpipe with one hand, pushing fingers into his eye sockets and pulling his head to the ground with the other. Seated, he had no leverage. By waiting until his hand was busy, she'd bought the advantage.

His head hit the gravel, her knee pounded into his head. She pinned him down and squeezed his windpipe. His hands fought and tried to break her grip. His legs bucked, trying to push his body up.

She pressed a knife to his throat.

He kept clawing, fighting to get leverage, to get out from beneath the weight of her body pressing down on the side of his head.

She drove the knife hilt into his solar

plexus and when he clenched in a shock for air, she slipped off him and pounded his temple even harder. His body trembled. She ground down on his head again. His hands went back to clawing at her thigh, but they weren't as coordinated. She slipped off the side of his face and slammed him harder with the knife hilt. He went limp.

"How many are in the house?"

Words came out of his mouth, but they were slurred.

She hit him again and he went out. She put her hands to his shoulders and scooted back, pulling him around the corner. With her feet she shoved him under the house and then crawled under and pulled him fully in.

She searched his pockets and found his phone. Her gloved hands fumbled in the dark to pull out the battery. She found his wallet and left it open on his chest. Pushed his arm up and plunged a knife inward.

Blood pooled quickly, a sign that she'd hit his axillary.

This was killer semantics: she hadn't murdered an unconscious man outright, but even if he came to before he bled out, he'd still likely die all the same.

Munroe pulled out from beneath the house, kept low, and tested the sunroom's sliding door. The Okadas hadn't been much for locks; she could thank herself, or Jiro, for this one. She slipped back under the house and crawled to the carport and skirted beneath the balcony for the front, where only a door stood between her and the thugs inside. Beside the entryway neatly groomed tree branches reached toward the second floor.

Less than four months ago, her mornings had begun in the dark, pulling herself four stories up, handgrip and toehold from wall to balcony, balcony to rooftop edge, and over, where she could sit in solitude under the sky's cathedral and wait for the sun to rise. But back then there hadn't been parents and children waiting to be slaughtered if she failed.

Munroe tested a tree branch for strength.

Her internal clock said she'd passed 2:00 A.M.

Inside the house footsteps pounded down the stairs.

Day 24   2:04 a.m.

Munroe shimmied as far as the tree branch would take her. High enough that her toes could find purchase on an upper window ledge and her elbows reach the lowest part of the rooftop's gentle slope. She dragged upward, until she rested on clay tiles, and moved slowly up the incline, body weight distributed through forearms and shins.

The moon laughed in its arc across the sky, stealing time.

She didn't have long before Jiro grew anxious and began calling his lieutenants. He would need to be gone before the neighborhood began to wake. Alina's still fresh scars had spoken to the pleasure Jiro took in combining psychological pain with the physical; they spoke to the sincerity of his threats and to the possibility that he might not wait until first light for the killing to start.

Munroe crested the roof, slow in the

descent, shoulders and arms pushing back to keep from sliding headfirst over the side. She reached the edge and tipped her face over, marking the man who kept watch on the balcony.

He was near the middle, far more alert than he'd been the last time she'd seen him, making a slow pace back and forth, seeking and searching for something in the dark. She inched to where the balcony had no doors or windows.

She closed her eyes, measuring time by his footsteps.

She rolled in a controlled fall off the edge, grip releasing last of all. She dropped behind him. Hand around his mouth, she yanked him into her, into the blade that sought his organs and finally, as he dropped, his throat.

She shoved him up against the house, where he couldn't be seen from either room that opened to the balcony. Felt through his pockets and found his phone, same as she had with the others. She pulled the battery and placed the pieces beside him, then searched for more and found nothing.

Munroe hugged the wall, inched toward the front of the house, and nudged the sliding door. The glass was open, the screen locked. Voices, softly spoken from down the hall, filtered toward her, and she placed that man in the hall below. Footsteps creaked up the stairs. She pressed palms to her eyes, creating a deeper darkness. When her eyes had adjusted, she lay on her side, floor level, less likely to be seen should someone in the room be looking out, and pressed her upper face to the screen.

This was Okada's wife's room, where she and the children had slept. The futons were spread across the floor like so many camping mattresses, the blankets and sheets disturbed, indicating that the occupants had been roused and pulled out of bed. Munroe slipped the tip of the blade into the screen and, one small nick at a time to limit the noise, poked up the frame until the hole was wide enough that she could peel it back and slip inside.

Her torso was on the tatami, legs still outside, when the footsteps entered the room. She pulled hard, made it fully through but was not off the floor before rough hands grabbed her hair and a muzzle pressed in on her cheek.

Munroe dropped the knife and lifted her hands.

The fingers in her hair yanked her face upward, toward a grinning mouth with crooked teeth and eyes laughing in triumph.

He ordered her up, impeding the process with his manhandling. Muzzle to her head, he turned to yell into the hall, to tell the others what he'd found, and that one microburst of distraction was his last mistake: blade of her hand into his elbow joint, the fingers of her other hand stiff into his throat; knee to groin, palm heel-up under his nose: four movements, swift and fluid in less time than it took to inhale.

Mute, gagging, bleeding, he dropped to one knee. Knife to palm, she took him down at the base of his skull, then knelt beside his bleeding head, fingers racing through his pockets. She nudged the weapon out of his grasp and disassembled his phone, wasting precious seconds in the contemplation between metal and metal.

She'd never be faster than a bullet, but in close contact she was faster than the hand that drew the gun. Knives, personal and silent, were her weapon of choice, but she wasn't a knife fighter; she was a survivor, fast, brutal, and effective with a blade for whom self-preserving pragmatism would always win in the end. Munroe picked up the knife she'd dropped, sheathed it, then hefted the 9 mm and crept toward the door, map to the interior shifting inside her head.

One room cleared; three men still inside,

at least one downstairs; hostages on the upper floor. She stuck her head beyond the door frame and back: empty hall. Two upstairs bedroom doors closed.

Then Jiro's voice broke through in angry whispered yells. Muted thuds with the timing of punches reached out from the room down the hall, followed by muffled cries as Jiro threatened. No phone calls were getting through, his men were missing, *the* man responsible hadn't come, and that made the hostages useless. The children were pawns, the parents less than that.

The cries and thuds reacted to every sentence, begging for mercy, swearing to innocence. Time was up and first the children would die.

Munroe grabbed a porcelain figurine from off a narrow shelf, stepped through the room, and threw it hard toward the floor just at the edge of the stairwell.

The figure shattered. The door flew open. Footsteps thundered up the stairs. Munroe stepped into the hallway and fired. First round to the chest of the man on the stairs and he fell backward and tumbled down. Second round into Jiro's thigh. The third spit wood as Jiro drew his own weapon and fired back.

Munroe charged the hall, firing as she ran,

rapid pulls that forced Jiro to rush for cover; rapid pulls that bought her time and got her to the end of the hall and to the door where he'd retreated; rapid pulls that emptied the magazine and made her gunpowder deaf.

She threw herself along the floor toward Jiro's feet, while his bloodied arm and shaking hand sought a target higher up and the reports from his weapon thundered over her head. She pulled him down before he had a chance to grab a child as collateral and bargaining chip and, before the muzzle could find her, plunged the blade into his wrist, severing tendons to the hand that held the gun.

She knocked the weapon away, counting seconds, counting life, counting time to flee. The neighborhood had come alive, even with her eardrums ringing she could hear the noise, the calls, the yelling.

Soon the sirens would come.

Jiro's free hand darted to his leg and came back stabbing.

Visions of Alina and the still fresh scars burned hot beneath the motion. Munroe rolled. Jiro's knife connected with her thigh.

Pain was out there, somewhere, in the night, in the jungle, inflicted by the man who had taught her to hate. They grappled on the floor, hand to wrist and wrist to hand, struggling for dominance. Jiro broke free of her defensive grasp and in microsecond slivers she felt the knife plunging for her side. She threw her head forward, into Jiro's face, smashing cartilage and shifting the center of gravity.

Blood gushed forth beneath her, Jiro's knife hit high, slicing through the leather of her jacket, grazing skin, adding a wound that would add to the scars. She stabbed his arm, stabbed his gut, fighting to survive, to kill, to win, fighting mad and fighting blind because reason had fled and the past returned and the only thing that mattered was keeping the animal alive. She stabbed until Jiro's movements settled into whimpers, and only then did she glance up to assess what she'd taken in through the fog of war.

Okada and his wife were to the side of the room, tied together back to back, Okada's face bloody and his wife's mottled from a recent beating. The children were huddled, terrified, in the corner, eyes squeezed tight, arms wrapped around each other.

Downstairs the front door opened and rapid footsteps faded into the distance. Munroe stretched for the firearm lying on the floor. She grabbed Jiro's foot and stood, then limping, dragged him into the hallway. She closed the bedroom door to hide him from the children, from the parents, to shut away her own atavistic animal and remain separate from the human Okada had known.

Red dripped from Jiro's lips. Gurgling sounds came from his throat as he drowned in his own blood. Munroe stood over him and he stared up at her, eye to eye, killer to killer, and he mocked her even now.

She pulled the two bullets taken from the weapon down the hill and put one in Jiro's hand. "A gift from me," she said, and clenched his useless hand around it. She racked the other into the 9 mm and put the muzzle to his head. "A gift from Alina," she said, and staring him in the eyes, she fired.

In the far distance, sirens wailed.

Like a preying beast startled by noise in the forest's calm, Munroe's head ticked up. She dropped the gun and ran the hall, pushed through the mother's room and out the ripped screen. She went over the balcony and dropped to the roof of the carport, then went over its side and crouched in the small backyard while lights and yelling and dogs and confusion responded to the chaos inside the Okadas' home.

Adrenaline pumping, pain far off beyond awareness, she skirted open windows, went over the fence, grabbed her boots, and hustled on. Far down the hill another weapon report rang out.

The sirens were closer now: the cavalry had arrived.

She'd be on the ocean by the time anyone put sense to the massacre inside the house. Strength came in many forms, not least of which were speed and cunning and the ability to think fast on her feet; she was the predator reborn, fully formed and ready for flight.

AUTHOR'S NOTE

If you're a new reader to this series, I'm so glad you've discovered Vanessa Michael Munroe and were willing to take a chance on her most recent adventure. I truly hope you've enjoyed it and I would love to hear from you if you have. If you're a fan, or a former reader back for another round, I can't tell you how happy I am to be able to share this world with you again. Thank you for keeping Munroe riding.

Now that this series has grown to five and a quarter books, I've begun to receive more frequent inquiries on the chronology, as well as questions asking if it's necessary to read the series in order.

The short answer is no. I do my best to keep each story self-contained, providing just enough backstory that it's possible to fall into any book in the series and pick up from there, but not so much as to annoy those who've started at the beginning and

591

heard it all before. When it comes to plot, each book is a stand-alone and one could read a single volume, or all of them, in order or out of order, and each story will work well in isolation.

There is, however, an arc that flows from the beginning, where the characters — just like real people — are affected and changed by prior events. For readers who read primarily for plot and thrills, the chronology won't matter. For those who read as much for character as for plot, there will probably be a richer reading experience by at least including the first book, *The Informationist,* at some point.

In order, the books are:

The Informationist
The Innocent
The Doll
The Vessel (a novella that ties up loose ends from *The Doll* and leads into *The Catch*)
The Catch
The Mask

In addition to the Vanessa Michael Munroe stories, on my website I also share extensively about the publishing industry, the mechanics of storytelling, behind-the-book research that has gone into each volume, and my path from growing up as uneducated child labor in the communes of the apocalyptic cult into which I was born, to bestselling novelist.

If you'd like a more personal connection, or would like to go beyond the book, I welcome you to join me on this journey. You can find me at: www.taylorstevensbooks .com/connect.php and I look forward to hearing from you.

ACKNOWLEDGMENTS

At author engagements and book events, I'm often asked about the cadence and vocabulary in my writing, and how, seeing as I grew up deprived of an education, I'm able to do what I do. The best answer I can give, really, is a story that also does quite nicely in acknowledging the many hands that have touched this book.

Shortly after *The Informationist* was published, on the third stop of my very first book tour, I found myself doing a Q&A for a cozy little group. After the interviewer had finished her questions, we opened the floor to the participants, and it was then that an elderly gentleman, mid-seventies if we're generous, leaned forward and pointed a thin, shaking finger in my direction.

"You claim to only have a sixth-grade education," he said. "But I've read your book, and I don't believe you."

"Well," I said, "you would if you'd read

the first drafts."

Much like those invisible early years where teaching myself how to write came into play, what we have in this beautiful, finished package belies the hundreds of raw, rough pages that wouldn't have been fit for reading without the unseen effort of so many along the way.

To everyone at Crown Publishers — those in publicity, marketing, sales, foreign rights, production, audio, design, and more — everyone who's put in so much effort on behalf of this series, I thank you. Through structural changes and personnel changes, you have been a constant, and I appreciate your support more than you know. To Lindsay Sagnette and Nora Evans-Reitz, thank you for making the production and publication process run smoothly.

A very special thanks to my editor, Christine Kopprasch, for being the bestest, smartest, hardest, fastest, and amazingest; for "getting" me, my stories and characters, and for knowing just how to bring out the best in me; for being collaborative and a perfect teammate. It's been a joy and privilege working with you.

Love and appreciation also go to my agent, Anne Hawkins, for her knowledge, experience, and instinct. I wake up every day grateful that she has my back. Anne, you got me into this game and you've been my rock since day one: thank you for being you.

When a larger-than-life character like Munroe fills a story, it's the political, cultural, and geographical accuracy that grounds the adventure in realism. Google works fine for laying a foundation, but you can't smell the streets, feel the texture of the air, or get a reliable sense of humanity over the Internet. For that, and so much more, I make every effort to acquire first-hand experience in the environments I write about. But even with having traveled to Japan to get that boots-on-the-ground vibe as I did, authenticating the level of detail that threads through these pages wouldn't have been possible without the help of two friends who, between them, share roughly four decades of living and working as *gaikokujin* (foreigners) in Japan. To Dawn McDonald, thank you for answering my questions, for not getting tired when I kept coming back for ever more clarification; thank you for the things you investigated and the details you confirmed, and for so generously sharing your time with me. Erinn L. in Kansai, without you, and the places we visited, the stories you told, the experiences you shared, the knowledge you imparted, the interpreting you did, and the way you humored my sometimes odd requests, this story would have been something else entirely — something far, far less — if it could have been told at all. Thank you for making this one possible.

To my friends, family, and children, who are always there even when I'm often not, thank you for your patience and endurance. To the muse, thank you for the laughter, insight, and always stretching my thinking in new directions. And to my readers and fans — especially all the "cool kids" who interact with me through e-mail — you bolster me daily with love, support, and encouragement, keep this series alive, and are responsible for the days I go without washing my hair or getting out of my pajamas. Thank you for that.

ABOUT THE AUTHOR

Taylor Stevens is the award-winning *New York Times* bestselling author of *The Informationist, The Innocent, The Doll, The Catch,* and the novella *The Vessel.* Featuring Vanessa Michael Munroe, the series has received critical acclaim and the books are published in twenty languages. *The Informationist* has been optioned for film by James Cameron's production company, Lightstorm Entertainment. Born in New York State into the Children of God, raised in communes across the globe, and denied an education beyond the sixth grade, Stevens was in her twenties when she broke free to follow hope and a vague idea of what possibilities lay beyond. She now lives in Texas.